Revenge of the PAK

A Story from the Realm of the Blind

William Wilkin

Bell Street Publishing, LLC

Bell Street Publishing, LLC

Published by Bell Street Publishing, LLC,
7360 Middlebrook Cir
Nashville, TN 37221-6545

Copyright © 2019 by Bell Street Publishing, LLC

ISBN: 978-0-9600387-2-5

First Published in the United States, 2019

Cover Art:
Digital Painting: James W. Wilkin
Graphic Design: Matthew A. Stone

Contents

Preface...1

Heathrow..3

Hogwarts Redux..24

Chess..30

The Old Boy's Club...37

The Father...40

The Board..49

Tourney...65

Gold..68

Paris in the Springtime..81

Foreign Aid...84

Tournament..101

The Best Laid Plans...111

The PAK Are Back...120

Heathrow Again...139

Tales From Mars..159

The PAK Leave A Calling Card...173

The End of English literature...186

Gold Pays Galleons..189

Beirut is a Great Place to Visit, but I'd Hate to Die There....................198

Heathrow III..218

The Return of Jasmine..225

Return to Space..245

The PAK in the Flesh..277

There Are Only Two Answers: Yes and No...302

You Can Go Home Again 321

Ginny's Story...344

Epilogue...362

Foreward

I owe an immense debt of gratitude to several people who have contributed substantially to this book's artistic integrity.

There are my two sons, James and Matthew Stone.

James contributed the digital painting on the cover which captures as I never could my vision of the sense of the book. He also made a number of graphic design suggestions that are incorporated in the cover design and interior of the book.

Matthew Stone made manTy suggestions for the layout and design of the interior as well as completing the cover layout.

My wife, Lou, contributed in both obvious and subtle ways to the completion of the book. She is a Spanish teacher and has extensive experience editing and correcting texts—both student and professional. Any remaining grammatical and spelling errors must not be accounted to her. They proceed from my eccentric ideas about the value of deviating from standards occasionally to accurately portray a state of mind or emotional content. A subtle way that she supported the completion of this book was her endless patience with those eccentric ideas.

In addition, she was willing to endure the many, many times that I worked into the early morning hours pursued by my characters who insisted on telling their stories at the most inconvenient hours.

She has always been emotionally constant in the shifting winds of our lives throughout the long thankless years of the struggle to bring these stories to print. Bravo Lou!

Preface

For those who are not familiar with Hogwarts School of Witchcraft and Wizardry, I provide a brief resume of the recent history of the venerable school that precedes this tale and the most important *dramatis personae*.

Following the tumultuous events surrounding the death of Tom Riddle, the most powerful dark wizard of the age and possibly of all times, the world was attacked by an interstellar traveling race of parasites (known to themselves as "Souls" and to humans as "Ghosts") that could infest and control intelligent and semi-intelligent species. This invasion was thwarted by the combined efforts of wizards and Muggles.

Hardly had the world recovered from this invasion, than an even more mystifying series of events happen. A small group of AWOL US soldiers assembled and launched a Faster-Than-Light interstellar ship. James Wendt, leading a team of wizards and Muggles, pursued this group to attempt to learn their purpose and stop it. Their failure to do so was fortunate as future developments (not yet documented in a story) show.

The Ghosts returned to beg the help of humans in solving a mysterious series of widespread deaths on some of their colony planets. The solution uncovered a different race that was determined to completely annihilate the Ghosts because the Ghosts are a pestilence on all intelligent races. Wendt assembled a team and prevented the destruction of the Ghosts' home world.

In this story, we discover that the Ghosts problems have not ended.

The main characters whom you would have encountered in previous stories are:

James Wendt is an English literature instructor at Hogwarts. He has been married to the Headmistress of Hogwarts, Minerva McGonagall. However, she died trying to save the Ghosts. Wendt was the victim of an experimental polyjuice potion, which altered his DNA to match that of a witch at Hogwarts. He became a witch who none-the-less retained all Wendt's mem-

1

ories. The result was that he had all of the genetic inclinations of a witch. This resulted in the formation of a new personality that was female. This new person decided that she did not want to be turned back into the male Muggle, James Wendt. She fled and went into hiding. She named herself Jaimie Sinistra, which honored both of the people who went into her creation. She applied for and got James Wendt's teaching post. She met and married a widower who had a daughter at Hogwarts. Then the Ghosts showed up begging. The Ghosts pressured the Ministry of Magic to find James Wendt to help them. Jaimie decided to return her body to James Wendt.

Dudley Dursley was the cousin of Harry Potter. Everyone thought he was a Muggle until shortly after the defeat of Riddle. He applied for and got the post of apprentice to the janitor of Hogwarts, Argus Filch. Filch is of the old school who thinks that Hogwarts ought to go back to the old punishments—like hanging upside-down.

Aurora Brahms (nee Sinistra) was almost the first person Wendt met. They had a lengthy and sometimes troubled relations. Her marriage to Nicholas Brahms largely put an end to the troubling part of that relationship.

Nicholas Brahms, the husband of Aurora Brahms, has the nickname, the Boy Genius (aka B. G.). He runs a computer security consultancy from the Srieking Shack.

The Headmaster of Hogwarts is Professor Horace Slughorn who took over after the death of Headmistress McGonagall. He is now both the Headmaster and the potions instructor.

The Minister of Magic has been for a number of years, Pamela Moertl. She became Minister of Magic shortly before the invasion of the Ghosts.

Ginny Weasley entered the auror academy shortly after her graduation from Hogwarts. She distinguished herself in the fight against the occupation by the Ghosts. She has advanced in her career, and at the beginning of this story, she is a Chief Inspector, who is frequently consulted by the Minister of Magic on issues involving Muggles.

For a more thorough history of James Wendt, read the first subchapter of the chapter of this book titled, *Heathrow Again.*

Heathrow

Haley and I had come through customs at Heathrow. I tried to think of the last time that I'd gone through customs at an airport without a witch in tow. I realized that it had been the defeat of Riddle.

This time had been easy. The only thing that I had that had the slightest whiff of magic about it was my old purse. It was in my pocket and the customs agent didn't even ask me to empty my pockets. Of course, he didn't ask about magical artifacts either.

We walked away from customs with the satisfying feeling that we were home at last. That feeling lasted for about five seconds. At the end of that eye-blink, a figure separated itself from the people waiting for those leaving the secured part of the terminal. She approached us.

There was no mistaking the fiery red hair and face of Ginny Weasley. She walked directly to us and threw her arms around me, planting a quick kiss on the cheek facing away from Haley. She backed off and hugged Haley as well. Then she said, "Well, lucky you. I've come to disapparate you both home."

Haley immediately said somewhat stridently, "We can find our own way home, thank you very much."

Ginny just shook her head and said, "No. No. This will be quicker and easier all around. I'll just take both your arms, and we're off." And with no concern about who might be watching, she put an arm around each of our shoulders and we disappeared into the ether.

We materialized just outside Haley's apartment building. Haley took a second to realize where we were. When she did, she said, "Well, thanks. We can handle it from here."

Ginny said, "No. No. Let me help you up to your apartment." She picked up Haley's carry-on and marched off for the entrance to the building at a pace that would have done Minerva credit. Haley and I could only follow. Haley unlocked the door to the building and we all entered the building and proceeded to the elevator. When we entered it, Ginny managed to shoe-horn herself between Haley and me.

We got to Haley's apartment. She unlocked the door and entered. Then Ginny took one of my hands and announced, "Well, on to your destination, Wendt." With that we disapparated. I hadn't mentioned to her what my destination was.

Ginny had chosen a destination for me. It was in the middle of the country-side somewhere. We were standing in front of a building that would have been described as a cottage if it were not that it was several stories high. Ginny had opened the door and I realized where we were—at the Weasley home.

She motioned me in. What else could I do but enter? She called out, "Mom, Dad, guess who's here?"

Mrs. Weasley appeared first. She stared at me for a second. I suppose my appearance out of context had made it a little difficult to recognize me. She finally did and strode forward to hug me. She said, "What a pleasant surprise. Won't you join us for breakfast?"

I opened my mouth but didn't really have a ready answer. It didn't matter because she released me from her hug only to take an arm and pull me forward toward the kitchen. She provided the answer for me, "Of course, you will." Then she shouted up the stairs, "Hurry down, Arthur. You'll never guess who's joining us for breakfast."

There were three place settings for breakfast around the table. Molly quickly added a fourth as Mr. Weasley arrived. We shook hands, and he said, "It's good to see you. I see that Molly's set a place for you. Ginny and I have to get off to work shortly. So, let's not waste any time tucking in."

I nodded agreement.

After grace, there were a couple of minutes spent simply assuaging hunger. Then Mr. Weasley asked, "Now, remind me, what have you been doing since the death of Minerva?"

Ginny immediately began an answer for me, "Oh, he's been busy with settling various affairs." She reddened a little and said, "I happen to know a little about that because of my position in the Aurors." She hesitated and then said, "But I can't really say anything about that. You understand, Dad. It's sort of hush-hush."

He nodded. Molly asked, "But why are you here this early in the morning?"

It appeared that I'd not get to answer a single question. Ginny gave an answer to that one, too. "Oh, he just flew in from the States. He was there for a visit with his family. I took the initiative to offer him a 'lift' from the

4

airport." She hesitated and said, "I thought he might prefer a home-cooked breakfast to something in the airport."

Molly approved heartily. "You are so right, dear." She turned to me and said, "It surprises me that you have any appetite after flying at hundreds of miles per hour so far up in the air. It takes me ever so long to settle my stomach after a simple broom ride."

I could have said something about settling your stomach after disapparating, but I thought it would not be grateful to complain about the way that Ginny had got me here.

Mr. Weasley filled the conversational gap. "It's too bad that I have to leave for work. I've had ever so many Muggle acquisitions since you were last here. I'm dying to show you. By the way, when was the last time you visited?"

I had to think about that. I said, "I think the last time was when we took a little excursion to collect a few 'Muggle artifacts' for me. I guess that was the year of the Tri-Wizard Tournament."

He nodded. "Right you are, sir!" He then turned to Molly and asked her, "What do you think about inviting Wendt to stay a couple of days with us? I could give him a tour of my collection tonight. I'm sure that he needs some time to recover from the harrowing experience of crossing the Atlantic in the air."

Ginny nodded and said, "Oh yes, mum. With all the boys out on their own, there's ever so much room for Wendt to knock about in."

Molly nodded slowly and said, "Yes, a capital idea. Lad, did you have any plans that you couldn't change for the next few days?"

I shrugged. "I was just planning to go to Hogwarts. Headmaster Slughorn has generously offered to let me use my old office for accomodations whenever I wanted."

Molly smiled broadly. "It's settled. Hogwarts will be like a ghost town with the term just ending. What am I saying? Hogwarts IS a ghost town without the students. The only people there are the staff and maybe Slughorn. I don't think many teachers stay."

I tried to demur. "But surely you have family plans for Christmas. The family will be in and out constantly. I'd just be under foot."

Ginny smiled slyly and said, "Rubbish. You are as welcome as any of them."

Mr. Weasley said, "If you're not comfortable intruding, you could go to Hogwarts Christmas eve. Nobody will show up before that night. And really, you'd be welcome even on Christmas Day. We always have the odd family friend or two in for Christmas. Why don't you just stay until the beginning of the Hogwarts term? I know that you've resigned, but I've heard that Slughorn would love to have you back as a professor. With all the students there, you might feel differently."

Ginny interrupted with a reminder that Mr. Weasley and she had to leave for work. She looked over at me and said, "Look forward to seeing you at dinner." That statement was accompanied by a stocking toe massaging my calf.

We all stood. Mr. Weasley led the way to the hearth. He stepped in, took a handful of floo powder and was gone. Ginny took a handful, turned back, smiled at me, and was gone as well. I said, "Mrs. Weasley, the least that I can do is to help you cleanup breakfast."

"Oh, piffle! You must be exhausted from crossing the big pond. You march right up and get a good nap." Then she reconsidered and asked, "Which room would you like?" She didn't allow me to answer. She immediately said, "Of course, you don't know our bedrooms. Follow me with your bags."

We ascended the stairs. At the first floor she commented. "This is Arthur and my room. Ginny's is across from it." She kept ascending. At the next floor she pointed to a room and said, "Bill and Percy shared this room. We'll go in."

The interior of the room was neat and clean. The walls were decorated with Quidditch posters. We then went across to a room that was Fred and George's. It too had Quidditch poster but also had a couple of rock band posters. It somehow was still not neat. Mrs. Weasley explained. "The boys were still living here when . . ." I realized the event she was talking about. After a pause, she went on. "I just couldn't bear to change anything after Fred died." She thought a minute and said, "Really, I'd prefer you didn't stay here."

"Absolutely. Fred was one of my. . . " I too paused to consider what I would say. I ended up saying, "Most interesting students. You know that we collaborated on a project or two when Riddle took over the Ministry?"

She sniffed and nodded. "Yes." Then she pointed up and said, "The next floor has Ron's room. I wouldn't wish that on a banshee."

I quickly stepped in and said, "Bill's room would be perfect. Thanks."

She added proudly, "Did you know that our house has a ghoul. If you wanted, we could go up and maybe get a glimpse of him?"

I suppressed a sour face and said, "Maybe another time. I am pretty fagged out."

"Oh, of course, dear. Just go ahead and make yourself at home in Bill and Percy's room." I did.

I got a good nap that lasted until early afternoon. I got up, shaved, show-ered, and went down to the living room. Mrs. Weasley had heard me stirring and came in to offer some lunch. I said, "No, thank you. It's a little too close to dinner time for me. Is there anything I can do to help out around here?"

"Oh, no. Just make yourself at home. If there's anywhere you need to go, I'd be glad to give you a 'lift'. Is that what you Yanks call it?"

"Yes, it is."

She had an idea. "Have you finished your Christmas shopping yet? I could take you down to Diagon Alley."

"No, I haven't, but I'd appreciate that. It would probably be better to-morrow so that I can have the whole day to shop and so forth."

She smiled. "Just let me know when you want to go. I don't have any-thing on tomorrow."

I thanked her and asked if I could read their copy of the *Prophet*. I was sure they didn't have a copy of the *Times*. They actually had a couple of back copies. I decided to at least have a glance at them as well in order to catch up on recent events in the wizarding world.

That kept me busy for a while. After I'd read the paper, I thought about getting in touch with Haley. I knew that she'd be at work during the day, so I didn't want to do a voice call. Instead, I decided to do a text message. It ended up being kind of bizarre. "I've been invited to a former student's house for Christmas. Little or no cell service. I'll be in touch when I can." I then went out for a walk to try to find some cell service. I walked for about a half hour. The most bars I had during that time was one. I had to back track to find it. When I did, I sent the message. I waited a while for an answer. None came. I returned to the house.

When I arrived, I found Mrs. Weasley and Ginny in the kitchen working on dinner. I said, "A little early to be back from the Aurors isn't it?"

Ginny turned, smiled, and said, "Oh, it's a special day. We don't always have guests for dinner. Why don't you help? You could work on a salad."

Despite Mrs. Weasley's objections, I did make a salad. Ginny managed to work next to me and occasionally kicked one of my shins gently. Before long, Mr. Weasley arrived. He caught a glimpse of us working on dinner. He said, "What a charming family tableau! Where is Norman Rockwell?"

Molly said, "Why don't you set the table. We're close to being ready to eat."

We shortly had dinner. During the meal, Mr. Weasley reminded me that I'd agreed to see his Muggle collection. It was a way for both of us to get out of cleanup. Ginny tried to join us. She said, "I've not seen the collection in a long time. I'll join you."

Mr. Weasley said, "I didn't know you were interested in . . ." He didn't complete the idea because Mrs. Weasley interrupted, saying, "Miss Ginny, you stay here and help with the dishes." She whined a little but stayed with Mrs. Weasley.

Mr. Weasley and I went out to the shed to see his collection. He moved well in and took a quick look around. He walked over and picked up a flash drive. He said, "This is a cute little doodad. I don't have the least idea what it does. Do you?"

He handed it to me. He was right. It was an interesting design. I said, "Well, it's called a flash drive."

Weasley didn't let me complete what I was saying. He asked, "Flash drive? Does that mean that it lets you drive your car very fast?"

I couldn't help saying, "Well. . . it's more like something for storing information. That one would probably contain all the *Prophet*s for as long as they have been published."

Weasley scratched his chin and said, "Oh, I've got it. It's got sort of like an extensible charm on it so that you could get all those papers in there?"

I was about to answer when a voice behind me said, "No, I think it's more like a place where you could keep the text itself from all those papers.'

I recognized the voice, but turned to be sure. It was Ginny, but I realized that she sounded a lot like her mum. Come to think of it, she had a temperament much like her mum, too. She was looking over my shoulder and I found myself almost nose to nose with her. She raised her eyebrows as sort of a challenge for me to say that she was wrong. I just smiled and said, "You've got it." She punched my shoulder.

Mr. Weasley said, "Well, well." Then he turned back to his collection to find another treasure. Ginny used that as an opportunity to tickle me. I just gritted my teeth and resisted laughing. Meanwhile she engaged Mr. Weasley about his collection: Had he ever figured out what a rubber duck was for? How about the PEZ dispenser? What was a PEZ?

Weasley said, "Well, I found out about those long ago when Wendt visited us the first time. Why don't you ask him?"

Ginny moved closer still and asked me, "Well, what about that Wendt? Just what does a PEZ dispenser dispense?" I gritted my teeth and tried a straight answer to a silly question.

The night ended for me on the way back to the house. Mr. Weasley led the way. He reached the door and opened it. He held it for Ginny and me. Inside, I announced, "I'm going up to my room to end the night by reading a week old *Prophet*."

I started up. At the second floor, I found that I was being followed by Ginny. She said, "I'm going to my room, too." She grabbed my shirt, pulled me within kissing distance and delivered a quick but burning kiss. She let go and said, "What I dispense is better than PEZ."

I only had time to say, "Agreed." before she entered her room. I proceeded to my room and spent the rest of the night trying to forget the kiss while reading the *Prophet*—both impossible tasks.

The next morning, breakfast was not up to Hogwarts standards, but still pretty good. Mr. Weasley asked what I was going to do with myself.

I replied that I was going Christmas shopping. Mrs. Weasley added that she would give me a lift.

Mr. Weasley was the first up to leave for work. Mrs. Weasley joined him, and I could just catch a glimpse of him giving her a goodbye kiss on the edge of the hearth. Ginny leaned over the table and pantomimed a kiss while kicking me under the table. She then leaped up and followed her father.

After she'd left through the floo network, Mrs. Weasley returned to the kitchen and said, "Are you still interested in helping clean up?"

"Sure."

"Good. Let's get that done, so we can go shopping."We worked through that task quickly. I collected and scraped the plates, and Mrs. Weasley washed them in a sink of soapy hot water. I dried. We were soon at the hearth. She asked me what my plan was.

I didn't have a detailed plan. I just said, "Well, I was hoping that you'd drop me off at the Cauldron. Then I'd go into Diagon Alley and buy some gifts for my magical friends. Then I'd leave through the Cauldron to the Muggle world and find an internet cafe to shop for presents for my Muggle friends and relatives in the States. Then, if you were kind enough, you could meet me at the street entrance to the Cauldron around 3 PM to bring me back here. Neat and simple for you."

She seemed to be disappointed. "You mean that you don't need help actually shopping?"

I shrugged. "Well, I've been doing it this way for years. It's seemed to work out all right."

She frowned. "How do you know what to get for people?"

I said, "Oh, I just use my experience with the people that I'm shopping for combined with reason to come up with gifts."

She shook her head. "Well, what about Mr. Weasley for example? What would you get him?"

I thought a minute. "Well, I was thinking of maybe a neat photo frame that I saw last year. It can display a number of photos that it cycles through. I thought he could put it on his desk at work or maybe in the bedroom or . . ."

She nodded. "Not a bad idea. What about me?"

She had me stumped. I admitted as much.

She then asked, "What about Ginny?"

My mouth opened, but nothing came out other than, "Uhhh."

She said, "Well, let me tell you that she's got a little something in mind for you. It would be a good idea to have something for her."

My mouth was still open, but I managed to ask, "Have you got an idea?"

She said, "I saw her admiring a simple jade bracelet at Madame Malkins recently."

My mouth was still a bit open. I asked, "You wouldn't consider that a little too . . . uh . . . personal?"

"Not a bit of it."

"OK. Thanks for the heads-up. Now can we go?"

She still looked at me doubtfully. "You still don't want me to help?"

"Right."

She shrugged. "OK." She stepped in the hearth and held her hand out to me. I took it, and we appeared in the Cauldron. We parted company there.

I went into Diagon Alley after tipping Tom with a drink. I found gifts for my Hogwarts friends fairly easily between Weasley's Wizard Weezes, the bookstore, and Madame Malkin's.

In Wizard Weezes, George noticed me and came over to talk. He offered me a friends and family discount. He said, "Well, I hear you're practically family now. And you're definitely a friend, so you qualify both ways."

I was afraid to ask about being "practically family", but George clarified the situation. "I hear that you're staying in Bill and Percy's old room. Anyone who gets to use that room is definitely on the approved list of the family."

I scoffed. "Well, there's no telling how long I'll stay on that list."

"Oh, I wouldn't underestimate your tenure there. Dad certainly loves anyone who will take a Muggle Mystery Tour of his artifact collection—especially Muggles. Also, I hear that you're on Ginny's approved list."

I mumbled to myself, "That may not last that long."

George heard a little of that and asked, "Are you using the *Muffliato* curse?"

"Oh, I just said that a little bit of me goes a long way."

"Not the way Ginny tells it."

I left before delving any further into that ambiguous remark.

I finished my shopping for my Hogwarts friends with a visit to Madame Malkins. There was only one jade bracelet—a white one. When I bought it, Madame Malkins asked, "Christmas for Aurora?"

I smiled. "No."

She waited for amplification that I didn't provide. However, she did wrap it for me and gave me a shopping bag with a temporary extensible spell. I put my other gifts in it. I then went to the Cauldron for lunch.

It was an early lunch. That gave me lots of time to shop for people in the States. I caught a cab ride to a nearby internet cafe where I browsed the internet looking for gifts. I mostly shopped the JCPenney site. Even at this late date—only a couple of weekdays from Christmas, I could be sure to have them wrapped and delivered on time.

I actually had a little time to spare. I bought a couple of magazines—the *Scientific American* and *Nature*—and a book, *TriPlanetary*. Since my Kindle didn't work at the Weasley's, I needed some reading material.

I had time to walk lazily back to the Cauldron. I reached the street a couple of minutes after 3 PM. As I stood there, a wind seemed to kick up some dust about halfway down the block. Out of that walked Mrs. Weasley. She bustled up to me and held out her hand. I took it and we were outside the Burrow.

I went upstairs to my room to wrap the one gift that I'd not been able to get wrapped. I opened up the *Scientific American* and decided to read an article or two before dinner.

Later Mrs. Weasley invited me down to dinner. The family was all present. After dinner, a snow storm began. The rest of the evening was quiet. Ginny was in her room. I sat in the living room reading and listening to a musical program on the radio.

The next day was very quiet until after dinner. It was a clear, cold night. Ginny asked me, "Let's go outside. With the new moon on the snow, it's a nice view."

I went up to my room to dig around in my duffel bag for my one warm coat. We went outside and walked away from the house. She led the way behind the shed, thus blocking the light from the house. The fresh snow on the ground with the starlight and scant moonlight from the new moon was striking. I said, "This reminds of a night in Columbus, Ohio."

Ginny turned to me and asked, "Columbus, Ohio, really?"

I nodded. "Oh, yes. I was going to school there. One night I was riding a bus to a movie theater. It was a night like this. We drove through a slum. The fresh snow and moonlight covered the tough neighborhood with a beautiful topcoat."

She asked, "Are you saying that our home is like a slum?"

I shook my head. "No. I'm just saying that there is the potential for beauty everywhere. . . Also, the potential for devastation."

She wrapped one of my arms with hers and shivered. I turned to her, and we were kissing. It was a long, wet kiss. When we finished, she said, "You know that you'd be welcome in my room any time."

I chuckled. "I kind of got that idea. I just don't want to do anything under your parents' roof that would estrange us."

She replied cheerily, "You know that Dad loves you, and Mum thinks you're brilliant."

"Maybe. But, I'm not going to do anything to change that on this visit."

She squeezed my arm, which she'd never relinquished, and said, "You know we could freeze to death out here before we stop kissing." With that, she pulled me a little closer and renewed her proof of that possibility. By the time we gave up and returned to the house, we were both pretty chilled.

Inside, Mrs. Weasley declared that she was almost ready to send out an Auror to track us down. She then noticed that we were pretty cold. She declared, "The both of you come in the kitchen and have some hot tea and it's the end of the night for the both of you."

Ginny smiled at me and said, "Hot . . . tea." I nodded.

The next day was much like the previous. We ended up out, enjoying the brilliant, cold stars lighting the snow field—for about two minutes. Then we couldn't admire anything other than the passion of each other. Ginny didn't press the bedroom option.

Christmas was on Thursday. On Tuesday, at dinner, I raised an issue that had been bothering me more and more as the week wore on.

I broke the topic by saying, "Tomorrow is Christmas Eve. I know that you've got family coming in then. I've decided that I'll spend Christmas Eve until Boxing Day at the Cauldron. All I need is a lift there."

The three Weasleys competed to object first and loudest. Finally, Mrs. Weasley won out. "There's absolutely no need for that. You will stay here and LIKE it."

I had to laugh. "Sorry, no offense meant, but I just wondered if you were going to hold me against my will." A glance at Ginny made me wonder if she might be willing to do just that. That thought was punctuated by a kick under the table.

Mr. Weasley said, "Look here, dear boy. Absolutely every one of us and all our relatives would love to have you here. Right?"

Mrs. Weasley nodded and Ginny said, "Absolutely love it."

"None-the-less, I am not moved. Or rather, I will be moved tomorrow."

Ginny had a wicked grin on her face as she asked, "Just how are you going to get there, hmmmm?"

I said, "I'll get there if I have to walk."

Ginny laughed and then realized that I was serious. She said, "All right. If you insist, I'll take you."

That night was a cold night in more ways than one. Ginny didn't suggest our going out to enjoy the cold in a warm embrace. It was probably more like enduring the cold shoulder in a warm living room.

We all went to bed early that night.

On Christmas Eve, I packed for a couple of days with the intention of leaving in time to have lunch at the Cauldron. Mrs. Weasley insisted that I stay for lunch. I'm sure that she wasn't surprised when George showed up for lunch. He arrived almost exactly at noon. He was warmly greeted by everyone, including me.

George pretended to be surprised that I was there. He asked me, "What brings you to the Burrow?"

Before I could answer, Mrs. Weasley called us to lunch. After seating and grace, I answered, "Well, I was invited here."

He looked around at the *dramatis personae*, nodded, and said, "Well, I won't eject you from whatever room you're in. I'm staying in my old room and I'm sure, you're somewhere else."

I answered, "No one will eject me from my room because I've already ejected myself. I'm going to the Cauldron for the next couple of days. I wish you and all the other Weasleys that are coming the heartiest Merry Christmas."

He nodded and said under his breath, "I'll bet that greeting is heartier for some than for others." I didn't dignify the comment with a response.

The lunch was good. When it was over, George volunteered to take me to the Cauldron. I didn't have time to reply because Ginny cut in. "I'm taking Wendt." She said it with such finality that even George just nodded mutely.

While everyone else was cleaning up—yes, including George, I went to the living room where there was a Christmas tree up with some presents underneath. I opened my duffle bag and pulled three presents out. I placed them as inconspicuously as I could. I then moved to the door.

Ginny came through and said, "Over here at the hearth, silly."

13

I smacked my head and said, "Of course."

She held out her hand. I took it. She shifted my hand so that she was holding it more palm to palm. Then we twisted through the ether and arrived at the Cauldron. She continued to hold my hand closely and whispered, "See you later." Then she planted one of those quick, hot kisses on my cheek. Instantly, she dropped my hand and disappeared in the hearth.

I registered for two nights and went up to my room to read a while before dinner. When I did come down, I was expecting a quiet dinner with only a few diners in the Cauldron on Christmas Eve. Instead the place was packed. I had to wait at the bar for at least twenty minutes.

While I was at the bar, I talked with Tom for a while. He welcomed me back. He went on. "I'm glad we'll be seeing you like the old days, right?"

I shrugged. "Sure."

He followed up by asking, "Just what did you do while you were gone?"

I looked down into my glass of Dewars for inspiration and decided to play it lightly. I said, "Oh, I took a cruise ship to the States. Then I went to visit my parents for a while. Then I flew back to England."

Tom smiled. "Good for you. After what you've been through, you deserve to take a good vacation. I hear you meet hungry ladies on those cruise things."

I managed a smile and said, "Well, I did go dancing one night with a crew member."

He slapped me on the shoulder and said, "Atta boy! Was she hot?"

"Oh, she was a little older than I but looked good."

He served another customer and then polished a few glasses and returned to me. "It was nice of that Weasley girl to treat you to dinner that night before you left. Do you think she's interested in you?"

I sighed, "Oh, her family have always been good friends of mine."

He chuckled. "I wish I had a good friend like her."

By this time, a table had opened up for me. I was glad to end the conversation. It just left me depressed to remember the last couple of months.

The next day, it was really quiet at the Cauldron. Breakfast was only a couple of people who had stayed the night and checked out. I knew because Tom complained about having to keep the business open on Christmas day. I reflected that he could probably close if it weren't for me.

In the evening a few people showed up for dinner. Tom made a decision that everyone would sit around one table and eat "family style." That extended to the staff as well. They cycled in and out with there always being someone left to manage the bar. Even the cooks joined us.

I was glad that this would be the last evening that I'd be here. I hoped that Mrs. Weasley would show up early in the morning to pick me up to return to the Burrow.

I hung around at the bar for a while after dinner nursing a whiskey and finally gave up. I went up to my room and went back to the adventures of Rod "the Rock" Kinnison.

I had read a couple of chapters when there was a knock on the door. The only person that I could imagine to have come to visit was Tom, although I hadn't the slightest idea why he would. So, I said, "Come on in. It's not locked."

The door opened and in walked Ginny Weasley carrying a shopping bag. I scratched my ear and asked, "What in the world brings you here?"

She smiled and said, "I'm delivering Christmas." With that she opened the bag and pulled three packages out which she placed on the bed.

I realized that I wasn't a good host, so I got out of the one comfortable chair in the room and invited her to sit while I took the bed.

She thanked me and said, "Before you open any of your gifts, I'd like to tell you how your gifts were received."

"Tell on."

She leaned forward conspiratorially and said, "No one expected any-thing. Your gifts were a complete surprise. Mum really liked the scarf you got her. Dad spent most of the day trying to figure out the Muggle toy you gave him. What is it, by the way?"

I couldn't help smiling. "Oh, it's a pen with a laser pointer and a flash-light."

She nodded. "He figured out the flashlight. He didn't have an idea what the red beam was. But, you say it's also a pen. How does it work?"

"You twist the upper half, and the ballpoint comes out."

"Well, he took it straight out to the shed to figure it out. Mum was really vexed that she had to drag him back in the house to be the host."

"Sorry about that."

Ginny chuckled. "Don't be. Dad loved it, and I think that Mum kind of liked getting to let off some steam. It does get a little cramped with all the family in."

I asked her about her gift from me. She was wearing a sweater with long sleeves. She pulled her left sleeve up a little revealing her wrist and the bracelet. I was happy to see that she was wearing it. "It looks good on your wrist." She smiled, too.

Then she said, "Why don't you open your gifts."

Without taking my eyes from hers, I picked a package off the bed. I started to struggle with the ribbon. Ginny laughed and said, "It's so easy,"

She took hold of the package, covering my hand, and used it to pull an end of the ribbon. The knot easily loosened and the ribbon fell away.

I asked, "Magic?"

"No, silly. Just a good knot." For a moment she kept hold of the package and my hand. She released it, and I ripped the paper off. A box was revealed. Inside there was a little note: "Hope you enjoy this as much as I have—Arthur." The box contained a bullet.

I stared at it for a while. Seeing it reminded me of the fight with the aliens on the Soul starship.

Ginny asked if something were wrong.

Before answering I rubbed my eyes to remove any trace of tears. Then I said, "Your dad has returned a present I gave him the first time that I visited your house. It's a bullet that I could use in my Glock. It made me think of the battle that resulted in Minerva's death."

Ginny shifted onto the bed next to me and took one of my hands in hers. We sat that way for a bit. Then I sighed and said, "What else do we have here?"

Ginny picked up one of the packages and put it in my hand. I pulled the "magic ribbon" and the knot evaporated as easily as the last had. I removed the paper. Inside, I found a monogrammed ski cap. Ginny explained, "Mom didn't have much time. You're actually lucky. Most of the rest of the family get monogrammed sweaters or pajama tops. You might actually wear that."

I laughed as I modeled it on my head. Ginny laughed, too. Then we both reached for the last gift. I guess she was going to hand it to me. We ended up clasping hands over it. I managed to say, "Sorry." She shook her head. Her crimson tresses shimmered, and she said, "Don't be."

We both picked an end of the ribbon and pulled. I said, "Do you want to open it?"

She made a funny face and said, "As a matter of fact, I do." She removed the paper very carefully and flattened it out on the bed on the side opposite me. She then opened the box. Inside was the present, a CD in a jewel case. I took it in my hand and stared at it.

She became impatient for an opinion and asked, "Well?"

I said, "How did you know to get this?"

She asked, "Twelve Nocturnes by Chopin?"

I nodded. She asked, "Do you like it?"

I took her by the shoulders and kissed her. "I love it. How did you know? It's wonderful!"

She shrugged and said, "Well, I asked Dursley what I should get you. He suggested 'Piano music, preferably Chopin.' I asked him how he knew. He said that you two shared your office for a while in my last year at Hog-warts. I didn't realize you two had.

"Anyway, he said that you used to complain that the one terrible thing about Hogwarts is that the only music you could get was scratchy because it came from a hand-cranked Victrola playing vinyl records.

"I went to one of your Muggle music stores. I asked the attendant for advice on Chopin piano music. He gave me this. A right git too. He asked me out."

I smiled. "He was dead right. I once went to a piano recital where the pianist played a couple of the Chopin Nocturnes. I fell in love with them, but since I couldn't play CD's in Hogwarts, I never took the trouble to buy them."

I squeezed her hand and thanked her profusely. She twisted around to face me and kissed me. I put my hands around her waist and placed a hand on her thigh.

She disentangled herself and held a single finger up to stop any protest on my part. She slipped off her sweater and then the bracelet followed by earings. She said, "I don't want anything or anyone to get hurt. Now feel free to work on whatever part of my clothes you like." With that she crossed to the bed and took me in her arms.

After a while, I asked her, "Won't your family be worried if you don't get back soon."

She giggled, "My family knows that I'm a big girl and can take care of myself."

My only comment was, "Well, you certainly can take care of me." Then she shifted around so that I was spooning her. That was perfectly fine with me.

We lazed around in the morning and got down to breakfast late enough that you might have thought it would be an early lunch.

I asked Ginny if she were going in to work today.

"No. Last week I arranged to have Boxing Day off.

I chuckled. "Pretty sure of yourself, weren't you?""

"Yup."

We discussed what to do on Boxing Day. She asked if we could do something Mugglish. I suggested going to see a movie.

"You mean a motion picture?"

"Right."

She agreed. We went out and found a *Times*. Searching through the listings, I found one that excited the curiosity of Ginny. It was "*Good Night and Good Luck*." We saw it and found that it was more serious than we really were hoping for even though it was pretty good.

On the way back to the Cauldron, Ginny asked, "Are they all that serious?"

"No, I'll find a comedy the next time. Speaking of time . . . uh . . . are you going back to the Burrow tonight?"

She smiled mischievously, "Are you?"

"No."

"I should hope not. And, no, I'm not either."

We took a table in the bar area and talked over a drink. I said, "That movie was a dramatization of real life events. You see that Muggle politicians can be just as prejudiced and power-hungry as the wizarding sort."

She thought about that a bit and said, "Yes, but it seems like the Muggle news media can be more honest."

I grimaced. "What you saw in that movie was the best. We have our news organizations that toady to the politicians they like just as much as the *Prophet*."

She laughed, "Oh, that's one thing that you Muggles can't beat us at."

That was a pleasant night. The next morning, Ginny was up early, pulling a change of clothes out of the shopping bag and asking for forgiveness for leaving so early.

All I could do was shrug and admit that I had nothing to complain about.

Just before she left, she took my head between her two hands and asked me, "Has your policy on visiting my room at the Burrow changed any?"

I just shook my head, and she nodded, saying, "I'm not surprised."

Later that day, another Weasley showed up at my room. Mrs. Weasley came to give me a lift back to the Burrow. She asked if I had been bored. I responded that I'd not been. She smiled a sly smile.

That night after dinner, Mr. Weasley spoke. "We need to have a little family conference here."

I got up to leave since I was not part of the family. However, Mr. Weasley prevented that, saying, "That includes you, Wendt."

I resumed my seat.

He said, "OK. Shortly, we're going to start to hear from friends asking what is it with you and Ginny. What do we say?"

I opened my mouth and was rather stuck for something to say. My mouth was still open when Ginny's mischievous self surfaced, "Yeh, Mr. Wendt. What do we say?"

Mrs. Weasley was on my side. She said, "Give him a minute to collect himself. Go right ahead and take your time."

That had given me time for thought. What I said was really obvious, "Well, I'd just returned from the States, and I really didn't have anywhere to stay but Hogwarts during the break between terms. You took pity on me and invited me to spend the Holiday with you. I accepted.

"I chose to be out of the way when all your relatives and close friends visited for Christmas. I stayed at the Cauldron."

Mr. Weasley asked, "What about Boxing Day?"

"Well, Ginny and I had been enjoying each other's company. I offered to show her some Muggle pleasures on Boxing Day. We spent the day together."

Mr. Weasley laughed. "That might be all right for friends, but family knows a bit more. What do we tell them?"

I said, "Just that we wanted to start early in the morning on Boxing Day and go late, so Ginny stayed at the Cauldron both nights."

Mr. Weasley shook his head and said, "OK."

Then Mrs. Weasley turned to Ginny. "Dear, what about Harry?"

Ginny said, "Just have him talk to me."

There was silence for a while. Then Mr. Weasley said, "On to another topic." He hesitated and then said, "I want to make one thing clear. I like you, Wendt. As a matter of fact, I wouldn't mind having you as a son-in-law if you and Ginny were so inclined. Molly and I are agreed on that. I think the rest of the family would agree if the question were posed to them."

"Good."

He went on, "However, I don't want you visiting Ginny's room or vice versa unless you actually become a relative. Understood?"

I nodded. I wanted to take a little more control of this conversation, so I said, "Mr Weasley, Mrs. Weasley. Ginny and I talked about this subject already. We determined that I would not visit Ginny in her room. I guess we didn't talk about her visiting mine, but obviously we would observe that limitation as well."

Ginny observed, "Well, finally. I thought this family conference was never going to end." She turned to me and said, "Let's go out for a little walk."

We did go out and stayed out as long as we could stand the cold. I think Ginny could have warmed us up some with magic, but she didn't in order to test my devotion.

19

With an understanding on the limits of Weasley hospitality settled, the rest of the week went well. When New Year's eve approached, Ginny and I had a little conference.

She insisted that with the new understanding, I should stay for the New Year's Eve party. I had to take a deep breath and prepare for our first real fight.

I began, "I know that you're not really going to like this, but I feel like I've got a duty to Minerva's family on New Year's Eve. "

"Ohhhh?" Her eyes seemed as full of fire as her hair. "You can't even be with the family for one of the two Holidays. You have a lot of nerve." I could see her wand hand twitch—a bad sign.

I stood my ground. "Yes. I used always to spend New Year's Eve and a day or two around it with her sister and other relatives. This is the first year without Minerva. I think I ought to be there for her family at the traditional get-together."

Ginny is not unfeeling. I could see the war going on in her emotions. She finally sighed and seemed to collapse a bit. "I guess I can't really complain about that good-hearted intention. Yes. When do you have to go?"

"I'd like to be there for supper—assuming that they want me to come at all. Would you send my message by owl?"

She did. The response was rapid and definite. I was invited to dinner on New Year's Eve and to stay the night. Ginny helped me send my acceptance along with a request that Ginny would return me to Hogwarts on New Year's Day.

On New Year's Eve, Ginny disapparated me to the McGonagall cottage. Before we went to the door, I took her hands in mine and led her aside. I said, "It just occurs to me that I've not mentioned something important." Here I paused for breath and courage, "I love you with all my heart."

She chuckled. "You are really a twit. I've known that for a very long time."

I harrumphed, "Well, I wanted to be sure—just in case."

Then we went to the door so she could assert her right to take me to Hogwarts on New Year's Day. Maggie was a little surprised to see Ginny along.

I explained that the Weasley's had been very kind to invite me to stay with them for the Holidays and she'd volunteered to take me to Hogwarts.

Maggie was surprised, "Oh, Wendt. You should have asked me. I'd have been happy to have you stay. You are just like family. . . As a matter of fact, you are family."

Ginny answered for me. "When my dad heard that Wendt had returned from the States, he insisted on us giving him a place for the Holidays." She hesitated and added, "And, really, I was very happy to have him join us." She was still holding my hand that she'd not released since we'd arrived and added a nice squeeze.

Magee looked from the one to the other of us and understood. She said, "Well, I'm glad you took some time to be with us. You know that Beryl is going to join us as usual." Then she added, "Miss Ginny, isn't it?"

Ginny nodded agreement.

"Well, Miss Ginny, why don't you join us for dinner? You could make it an even four—like the old days. And, if you would, you could stay and play Back Alley Bridge with us." She nodded encouragement.

Ginny was stumped. She didn't seem to want to be ungrateful, but she had her own family to be with. She said, "I think I can join for supper, but I really don't know about cards."

The idea excited me. "Sure. You'd love it. It's a perfect game with four."

I could see her waver. Finally, she said, "Oh, for a little dinner and maybe a couple of hands. I'm afraid that whoever would be stuck with me as a partner would be in deep trouble."

I smiled happily. "Believe me, I'd love to be stuck with you."

Maggie was happy too. "It's settled then."

Beryl showed up shortly and was pleased that there would be four. However, first we had to clear up a couple of misapprehensions.

Beryl asked, "Who are you young lady?"

Ginny began to answer, "Ginny . . ."

However, Beryl interrupted her to say, "Of course, who could mistake the fiery red hair. You're a Weasley! The Weasley Girl. Right?"

"Yes . . . "

"Are you here selling Young Witch Scout cookies?"

"No. ma'am. I'm . . ."

Maggie said, "Now Beryl, Ginger here is at Hogwarts, must be a sixth or seventh year."

I could see the signs that Ginny wasn't taking this well. Her nostrils flared. I tried to head off trouble by saying, "No. She's actually . . ."

I didn't get to complete the sentence. Ginny burst in and said, "I'll have you know that I'm an Auror."

Maggie said, "I suppose Georgina's a personal assistant to some real Auror, maybe that young Longbottom lad."

I noticed Ginny's wand hand flex a couple of times. I decided that better her wrath fall on me than anyone else. I said as quickly as I could, "I'll have you know that Ginny was very important in repelling the invasion of the alien Souls."

Both ladies took a more careful look at Ginny and said, "Ginny, eh. Short for Virginia, I suppose."

I thought that might be the proverbial straw, but Ginny took it well, "Yes, lots of people think otherwise, but it's Ginevra."

Beryl asked, "Are you Wendt's date for the night?"

Ginny turned a shade of red that would put to shame a radish. Maggie immediately went on, "There's nothing to be ashamed of." She turned to me and asked a question to which she perfectly well knew the answer, "How long has it been since Minerva passed?"

I didn't have a ready answer. That had happened hundreds of light years from earth on a space ship where it's hard to tell the difference between day and night. I made a rough approximation. "It's been about six months."

Beryl said, "It's high time that you were seeing some nice young lady like Miss Ginny, here."

Maggie chimed in, "I always said that Minerva waited far too long to snatch up young Wendt here."

I had my own opinion about who had done the snatching up, but Ginny asked, "Don't you think that Wendt might be a little old for me? After all, you were about to put me in the Young Witch Scouts."

Beryl said, "Oh, piffle. Wendt's younger than Minerva was when they started dating, right my lad?"

I opened my mouth. What eventually came out was, "She always seemed to me the soul of youth."

Maggie shed a tear and said, "Well said, Wendt."

Ginny asked if we were ever going to get around to eating.

We did. I think everyone was anxious for the meal to be over. Beryl wanted to get in a little Back Alley Bridge before Ginny had to leave. I was sure that Ginny wanted to get back to her family. I didn't want to get into hot water with her family for keeping her away on New Year's. Maggie was anxious to get to the gossip that always accompanied card games.

Ginny was a little nervous about playing a completely new game. When I described it, the lines left her face and she declared, "Why that's almost Wizard Whist. You just have to remind me of the differences as we go along. Let's start."

There was the question of how long we would play. I suggested that we begin by dealing one card out and work our way up to the full thirteen, provided that Ginny didn't have to leave. That would be better for learning the intricacies of the game. The small hands would be easier.

We usually drew cards to determine partners, but this time Beryl suggested, "Why not let the young couple be partners. That will give you and me a fighting chance."

We all laughed and agreed.

Between learning the game and playing thirteen hands, I expected Ginny to leave any time after we'd reached the seventh hand. She seemed to really enjoy it, and we were fifteen points ahead at that point. She declared that she'd leave when our partnership fell behind. On the tenth hand, we were a few points behind. I stood to make it easier for Ginny, but Ginny surprised me.

"What! Give up when we're only a few points behind. We'll keep going."

We did reach the thirteenth hand. We were actually tied. I rose again. Ginny stayed seated and looked around at all of us. She asked, "We'd ordinarily work our way down again, right?"

We all admitted that was true. I could tell she was conflicted. I think she really wanted to finish the full game. A funny crooked smile was on her face. After a bit of indecision, she said, "I've got to go, but I will only go if you promise me that I'll get to finish this game."

We were all happy at the prospect. Ginny rose and said, "I'll pick you up tomorrow to take you to Hogwarts. What time should I arrive?"

Beryl and Maggie agreed. "After dinner tomorrow."

Ginny's nostril's flared again. "I will have some time with Wendt after I pick him up. Let's say four, hmmm?"

The ladies grudgingly agreed. I accompanied Ginny out the front door. She shut the door and threw her arms around me. "They are dears. But they have had you too much to themselves. You be completely ready when I show up at four on the dot!"

"Yes, ma'am."

Then she kissed me. When we were done. I was more than half ready to leave with her right that minute."

When Ginny finally let me go, I returned and found the bridge table devoid of cards. I asked, "What's going on? Are you through playing Back Alley."

They looked at each other. Maggie asked, "Aren't we? We have only three players. Don't you need at least four?"

I smiled and looked from one to the other. "I guess I have never taught you three handed cut-throat Back Alley Bridge, have I?"

Hogwarts Redux

Ginny and I walked through the hearth at Maggie's and into the hearth in my office. We kissed while still standing in the hearth. Then she said, "I've never seen your quarters, have I?"

"I'm pretty sure you haven't. But, you know, time really flies when you're having fun. Don't you think it's possible the whole night would fly by and you'd still be there when the sun rises."

She laughed. "Oh, I certainly hope so."

"What about getting to work in the morning?"

She smiled a clever smile. "I've got a change of clothes in my hand-bag."

I nodded, kept an arm around her waist, and led her into my bedroom. "Welcome to chez-moi."

"mmmm."

After a lengthy session of re-acquaintance, we were lying in bed, comfortable, warm in every way, and indolent. Ginny was spooning me. She was drawing loopy circles on my right shoulder with a finger. As she was doing that she asked me some questions such as: Where were you born? Did you know that Dumbledore was gay? What did you do the year that Snape was Headmaster of Hogwarts?

I chuckled at the second question and said, "I didn't know until the year that Snape was Headmaster. Someday, I'll tell you a funny story about Dumbledore being gay."

She gasped and was about to say something when I interrupted her. "Not now. That's for another day."

She whined a little, but I wouldn't change my mind. Then after the next question, I said, "Well, a lot of it is probably still covered by the Official Secrets Act, but everyone covered by that act tells their lover the occasional story that's strictly speaking forbidden. I'll give you the dragon's-eye view of what I did."

She scoffed, "I suppose that's better than a stick in the eye." With that, she stimulated a part of my anatomy that was just recovering from serious previous stimulation.

"All right, all right! I'll tell you one little very detailed story. Now, if you keep that up, you'll never hear the story." She reluctantly let up on the gentle persuasion.

She, in her turn, said, "All right, all right! Go ahead already."

"I'm sure your brother has told you about his exploits in the States help-ing run the refugee camp."

She hummed an affirmative response.

"Then did George tell you that I helped in a small way to set up that camp?"

She kissed my shoulder and agreed.

"All right. He may not have told you that the camp was run by an Amer-ican witch."

"Oh, George told me that there was an old-maid who ran the camp. She was a real task master. He had a hard time getting along with her."

I hooted in response to that exaggeration. "Oh ho. Is that what he told you?"

Ginny nodded. It disturbed the gentle kisses she was applying to my back. I said, "Well, the truth is that she was not that old—definitely older than Fred and him—but not ancient. As a matter of fact, she kind of hit on them for a while."

She interrupted me with a punch to my right shoulder and said, "Hey! Did she hit on you?"

"That is lost in the mists of ancient history." In order to avoid any fur-ther pummeling, I quickly added, "But it really doesn't matter, because she found an American Muggle whom she worked with to be very fascinating. The feeling was mutual. I don't know whether they eventually married, but my bet is that they did."

"Then you're safe."

I went on. "That isn't the story that I was going to tell, though. When she was interested in your brothers, she asked for details about your family. I gave her such details as were readily apparent to anyone. You know, things like what your brothers and father did for a living—when they weren't avoiding Deatheaters. I told her about Ron being on the run with Harry and Hermione. I told her about Percy in the Ministry . . ."

Ginny interrupted me at that point. "You were trying to put her off George and Fred?"

"Not really. Of course, Fred was already involved with Sally. I told her about Bill and Gringotts. I told her about your Mum—that she was kind of a basilisk where her family was concerned."

"Bloody right! It saved my life once, but it was a pain most of the time." Then she thought a minute. "Just what did you tell about me?"

"Oh, not much, really."

Now there was a little steel in her voice. "Come on. What did you tell her?"

I hesitated as I thought about what to say.

A growl emerged from deep in her throat, "What did you tell her?"

She has just enough legilimens about her that it would have been dangerous to stretch the truth, so I said casually, "Oh, just that you kind of reminded me of your Mum a bit every now and then."

She delivered a blow to my shoulder that I was afraid might dislocate it and said, "You did not!"

"I'm afraid that I kind of did."

The growl returned but turned into something more like the sound that my parent's dog made when it wanted something. She resumed stimulation and we turned to non-verbal pursuits.

$$\triangle$$

On the following morn, I was awakened by Ginny rolling out of bed, practically dragging me along with her.

I glanced at the clock on my bedside. "Six thirty! What in Heavens above would impel you to get up at this hour?"

She just threw a pillow at me and said, "Work, you lazy bones. You should try it some time."

"I'll have you know that I'm going to Slughorn this very morning to beg for a class or two."

She laughed and took the bathroom. She was out quickly. She was completely dressed. She walked up to me and said, "What's wrong with me?"

I looked around, hoping there was someone else in the room to whom she was talking. She just said, "How's my makeup? What about my clothes? Do I have something on backwards? Just one earring?"

I said, "Turn slowly." I did a quick 360 look at her. When she had finished the pirouette, I said, "You're absolutely perfect. I wouldn't change a thing." And indeed, her makeup was perfect, her dress fit superbly. I liked the dark color with a slash of green like a sash.

She just frowned. "I know something's wrong. If you can't help, just kiss me goodbye. I'll see you tonight."

I did kiss her. Before I let her go I said, "The beginning of term banquet is tonight. Since I hope to be back on staff, I'll have to be up on the stage. You might as well not come before eight."

She turned to go through the floo connection. Just before she left she turned back toward me and smiled.

I was invincibly up, so I took my own shower and dressed. I went down to the kitchen to wait for Filch and Dursley. I took along the magazines I'd bought during the Christmas break. I realized that I'd have to start up my paper subscriptions again. My Kindle was worthless here.

They were not early risers. I had just gotten well into an article about dark energy when they arrived. I was greeted with excitement. Filch actually threw his arms about me and shouted, "I thought I'd never see you again!"

Dursley clapped me on the back and said, "Me, too."

I just said, "Me, too."

Then we sat and ate. Afterwards, I went up to Slughorn's office. Sally was there, of course. She greeted me with a hug. She shook her head and said, "I've finally stopped being surprised by what you do. I suppose that I should have long ago. Are you planning to teach again?"

I nodded. "That's why I'm here to see Slughorn."

"Go on in."

I did. Slughorn wasn't surprised that I was here. He smiled. "I knew that you'd be back eventually. You're too good a teacher not to."

"OK. I just want one course this term. Next term I hope for more. But now, just one course."

Slughorn scratched his head. "Well, how about fourth year lit?"

I thought about it. Fourth year lit was where Sissy would be. That would not be good. There were too many memories bouncing around in my head about her and her dad. Jaimie was too close to them for my tastes.

I asked for a different year. Slughorn started to argue that fourth year was ideal—easy and less contact time than other courses. Then he realized why I didn't want the course. He said, "Cecily would be in that class, right?"

I nodded.

He said, "OK. Take third-year then."

I agreed. I returned to my office and started getting my lesson plans together, trying to decide whether starting at the beginning would be better or in the middle or maybe trying to hit the highlights. It felt good to be wrestling with these issues rather than life and death among the stars.

That evening at the beginning of term feast, there were the usual components of the evening. Slughorn delivered announcements. No one was permitted in the Forbidden Forest. Hogsmeade weekends were limited to upperclass students. Professors were required to sign up for chaperone duty for Hogsmeade weekends.

Slughorn was about to sit and let the feasting begin. He turned back to the students and said, "I almost forgot. One more thing. Professor Wendt has returned and will be teaching third-year English literature. All third-years will check the bulletin board in the morning for section assignments. Let's welcome Professor Wendt back to Hogwarts from his sabbatical."

There was a small sigh of resignation that filled the Great Hall. I guess that was about the best result that I could have wished for. I enjoyed the banquet otherwise. The food was it's usual superb sublimity.

After the meal, I started up to my office. On my way to my office. I heard someone shout my name. I turned and saw Cecily running to catch me up. I nodded and waited for her to arrive.

When she did, she said, "I'm happy you're back. Too bad that I don't have you for a class."

"Yes. It is. I'm actually happy I'm back as well." At that, I ran out of things to say.

Cecily did as well. However, she did have a parting shot as she ran off toward her house. "I'll be seeing you."

I muttered under my breath. "Yes, I'm afraid you will."

I proceeded on to my office. When I arrived, I found that the door was locked. I knocked on the door and said, "OK, Ginny. Unlock the door please."

There was a snick and the door handle released. I opened the door. Someone was hiding behind the door. When I was fully in, the door slammed shut behind me. She took my arm and swung me around.

I was surprised, but I recovered quickly, "Well, Aurora what a surprise." I took a step back and asked, "What brings you to darken the back of my door?"

Just then, there was a rustle behind me. I turned and saw Ginny just arrived. Aurora looked from one to another of us and said, "Oh. I see you have a prior appointment. I'll be back later." With that she turned and left.

Ginny had reached me by then. She put an arm around my waist and said, "It never ends does it?"

In answer, I pulled her around to face me and we kissed. She took my hand and pulled me to the sofa. We sat in each other's arms and talked. I told her about teaching third-years.

She nodded and said, "It's a start." Then she talked about her day. We ended by just snogging for a while. Then, I sort of convinced her to slip off some of her clothes. She left a trail into my personal quarters. After a while, she stretched and said that she had to be off.

"Didn't you bring a change of clothes?"

"As you would say, this is a school night. I can't spend the night here." She quickly collected her clothes and dressed.

I lazily got up from my bed and put my arms around her from behind. I implored her, "Just one more . . ."

She laughed. "I've just got dressed. I'm not going to undress and dress another time." Then she turned in my arms and kissed me with enough feeling that I thought she might relent. But no, she broke the kiss from my lips so she could say, "See you tomorrow earlier. Seven?"

I agreed, and she opened her purse to get her hand mirror. She took a quick look at her face and her upper body, nodded, and walked into the hearth. After a quick turn of her head toward me she disappeared. She was gone.

Chess

I was far too nervous as my first class of the term approached. After all, I'd taught this course for over a decade. I knew most of the students. I only had one section today. What did I have to worry about? Right?

Well, I'd not been in a classroom for over a year. As I was waiting for the class to arrive, I was rehearsing all the things that could go wrong. There could be another Fred Weasley who would take delight in using a silencing charm or some other devilish curse on me. There were the normal fears—spitballs, notes passed between students, etc.

What really happened was in a way more disturbing to me than any of those possibilities.

The class started well. I briefly introduced myself and asked for a show of hands for each of these groups:

- People who had had me in class before.
- People who hadn't had me in class but who had seen me in the school in previous years.
- People who didn't know me at all.

I found that about two thirds had had me in class before. Ten percent hadn't seen me at all. The rest had seen me around but hadn't had me in class.

From there, I used a technique that Jaimie had used. I gave the class a set of FAQ's about me and refused to answer other questions.

A few of the FAQ's were:

- Q: Where did you grow up? A: In the States.
- Q: How long have you lived in England? A: About a dozen years.
- Q: How long have you taught Eng. lit? A: About ten years.
- Q: Are you a Muggle? A: Yes.

- Q: What are you grading policies? A: 30% exams, 20% class partic-
ipation, 20% writing assignments, 20% final exam, 10% final paper.
Occasionally, I will grant extra credit opportunities.
- Etc.

That wasn't all, but it gives you a flavor for what I covered. That took up more than half of the class period. I then offered the class the opportunity to ask three questions.

This was actually their first in-class assignment. I divided the class into three groups. Each group was to come up with one question to ask me.

I gave them a couple of cautions: "I don't guarantee that I will answer the question, so you should be careful what you ask. If two groups asked the same question, it's just bad luck. I don't guarantee to answer personal questions, so again, be careful."

I gave them seven minutes to compose their question and why they chose it.

I gave them a two minute warning and then a one minute warning.

The first group offered this question: Why do you teach English litera-ture? They said the answer would tell them something about what kind of teacher I was.

My answer was, "I love English literature and I'd like to interest stu-dents in it. Second, frankly I like England. The only way that I could stay in England was to find a job that paid me a living wage."

The second group asked: How do I get on your good side? Their reason was obvious.

My answer was, "Do your homework. Pay attention in class. Don't dis-rupt class. Have a good time." That last comment brought out some sur-prised guffaws.

The last group had a really disheartening question: Will Professor J re-turn? If so, when? Their reason was that they really liked her and hoped that she'd be back soon.

That had come out of left field, and I'm afraid I let my emotions show on my face. I took a minute to compose myself and decided that, even though I could simply refuse to answer, I would give them an answer.

I said, "You are right that she is a very good teacher and knows English literature." I chuckled. "And she looks a lot better than I do."

I took a deep breath trying to decide how much to reveal about Jaimie's future. I decided, "Jaimie was filling in for me temporarily. I'm pretty sure that she enjoyed teaching here and wouldn't mind coming back." There were a lot of smiles in the room.

I went on. "I too enjoy teaching here and I don't intend to leave any time soon." That was clearly not a cause of happiness for the class.

31

By this time, I only had time to make the first reading assignment of the class. The class left rather glumly. Only one student stayed behind to ask a question. She said, "Don't worry, Professor Wendt. You'll do fine."

I shrugged and said, "Thanks for your support."

△

In my room that night, I was rather glumly working on my next lesson plan. I was so intent that I didn't notice when someone came through my floo connection. She was standing behind me looking over my shoulder when I finally noticed her.

"I take back what I said about your not working. You're so intent you didn't even notice when your girl friend came in."

Ginny was right, of course. I swiveled around and rose, which put me nose to nose with her. She said, "More like it." We then kissed.

I asked her if she wanted something to drink. Her answer was, "How about some of your Blue?"

"You've got it." I hadn't opened the bottle yet. I commented, "You're in luck. Fresh stock."

After pouring, we sat on the sofa and talked about the day. I admitted that I was discouraged about the class's preference for Jaimie over me. Ginny just shook her head. "Kids have such short memories. Once they've seen you in action for a couple of weeks, you'll be their favorite."

I shook my head.

She told me about her day, which was pretty boring. Then we gazed into each other's eyes for a while and ended snogging for a good while. Far too soon, she declared that she had to go. I objected, but I could tell from her demeanor that she really wanted to go.

I agreed but asked her, "How about doing something tomorrow night?"

"Like what?"

"Like a movie?"

She looked to her left and then said, "Sounds great. When should I come?"

"Bring a *Times of London* and come as soon after 7 PM as you can. You might look at the movie descriptions and see if there's one that you like."

She agreed. Then we stood in the hearth and caressed each other for a couple of minutes, and we kissed again. I said, "Oh, Ginny, the time with you is a little slice of Heaven."

She pulled away and said, "If we keep this up, I'll end up spending the night."

I laughed. "Would that be so bad?"

She laughed, too. "My boss would write me up if I were late one more time." But, she continued to hold me for another minute or two and then separated and disappeared.

In the next couple of weeks that was the way things went. We saw each other almost every night—except when she had to work late. We went out a couple of times a week and went out on a real date one weekend night. That night, she stayed over, and we were filled with bliss the next morning.

When she left for home that day, I couldn't keep myself from telling her that I was in love with her. She nodded wisely, "If you're not careful that's going to turn into quite a habit."

I smiled. "It's gone way past being a habit."

She chuckled. "For me, too. See you tomorrow." An all-too-quick kiss followed, and she was gone.

The next afternoon during my office hours, there was a knock followed by someone entering the office. It was Sissy.

Of course, I knew her purpose. I asked her to sit and invited her question. She obliged. "You've probably guessed that I'm here to ask you to be my chess coach."

"Yes, I did guess that. I hear that you wanted Professor J to be your pretty cheerleader. Let me make it clear that that is the wrong attitude to take into this or any other coaching relationship."

She seemed chastened. "Oh, professor, I gave that idea up long ago."

I smiled. "You are a wise young lady. In that case, I think we might work on chess together with your father's permission. Have you asked yet?"

Her face colored a bit, and she said, "No. sir. I wanted to talk with you first to find out if it would be all right with you."

I agreed. "That's fine. But first, I want to do a little interview with you."

That surprised her. "Interview?"

"Yes. Do you have a little time right now?"

"Yes, sir."

"OK. First tell me what your daily chess routine is."

She stared at me for a moment and then seemed to realize what I wanted to know. "Oh, yes. Well, I usually spend about an hour studying the latest edition of MCO. I take a couple of problems and work through my answer to them."

"OK. Do you play with anyone?"

She shook her head. "No, there isn't anyone I know who is real competition for me."

I nodded. "Of course. What about tournaments? Have you entered any?"

"No."

"What about exercise? What do you do?"

She stared at me again and asked, "What kind of exercise?"

I was surprised at the question. "Why, physical exercise."

"You mean like push-ups or weight-lifting?"

"Well, I wouldn't expect either, but yes, that sort of thing."

She colored again. "I know that Professor J suggested exercise, but I never really got into the . . . habit."

I thought a minute trying to decide whether to pretend that I were her coach or just make suggestions. I decided on something in between. I said, "OK. I'm going to pretend for a minute that I were your coach. I'm going to make suggestions. You'll need to talk them over with your dad. Whether he chooses to let me coach you or not, I'd suggest you do these things. He makes the final decisions. OK?"

She nodded eagerly. I went on. "Then, first, exercise is important. Pick something that you can do safely. Here are some possibilities: Walk at least four miles in less than an hour. Or jog gently for forty-five minutes. Or play a vigorous game for the same amount of time."

She asked, "You mean like Quidditch?"

"I'm not sure. I've never played it. I don't know what kind of effort it requires. Your dad can probably advise you on that. Whatever you do, do it every day, preferably the first thing in the morning.

"Second, make sure you do all your school homework completely before studying chess.

"Third, get at least nine good hours of sleep a day. The key is the old Roman motto, 'sano mens in sano corpus.'"

"Sir, what does that mean?"

"A sound mind in a sound body. Then put your hour of study on chess in."

She was gaping at me. "With all those things, how will I have time for chess?"

I smiled, "You're a smart girl. You can do it. Now, do you have any questions?"

"No. I'll send an owl to dad today."

"Good. I'm anxious to see what he has to say."

She nodded enthusiastically, got up, and turned to go. At the door, she turned back and said, "Oh, I have just one more question."

"Sure. What is it?"

She looked down to her toes, as though looking for something. "This may take a few minutes."

"Oh, come back and sit." She did.

"Sir, Do you know if my Mum is coming back?"

I knew in the back of my head that that was coming. I wished to God that I could have a drink right then. But I certainly couldn't under the circumstances. I started slowly. "Sis . . . Cecily, you mean your step-mom, right?"

She was on the verge of tears already. She just nodded.

I had a hard time looking directly at her, but I forced myself to look her in the eye. "There are only a couple of things that I can tell you.

"First, I've known your step-mom for most of her life. I've known her since college, at least. If I know anything, I know that if it were possible for her to return, she would."

"Second, I don't know where she is now. I can't get in touch with her. I don't have any idea if it will ever be possible for her to return. I don't even know if she's still alive or not."

Cecily was obviously not satisfied with those answers. She burst out, "Why don't you know? If you're such old friends, surely she'd get in touch with you!"

"If she could."

"Why wouldn't she be able to? Even prisoners in Azkaban can get in touch with family and friends."

I sat trying to think of an answer that would relieve some of Cecily's anguish but not break any duties that I had. She stood and paced, convinced, I suppose, that I had more I would say. I was doing my best to be able to say something more.

Eventually, I said, 'Please sit. I'm about to tell you the very last thing that I possibly can." She sat. "OK. Here's the deal. You have to promise me not to reveal this to anyone—even your dad. I'll talk with him about it myself."

She asked light-heartedly, "Unbreakable oath?"

I was discouraged by that question. I asked, "Do I have to make you take the Unbreakable?"

She gritted her teeth. "You're really serious, aren't you?"

I just nodded.

She shook her head. "No. If it's that important, you don't have to. I won't even tell Dad anything."

"Good."

I hesitated and took the plunge. "She was involved with a government mission. It wasn't a wizarding government. I can't tell you what government it was. Anyway, she might have been captured and been in prison. I don't know anything more than that."

Tears brimmed in Cecily's eyes. "Wouldn't they let her talk to anyone?"

I shook my head. "You don't understand the kind of people that she was dealing with. They are cruel in a way that only Riddle was cruel."

The tears came. I kept a box of Kleenix on my desk. She used it.

I said, "Get in touch with your dad. Ask him about chess. Tell him that regardless what he says he and I should get together to talk."

She left my room.

The Old Boy's Club

I was having dinner in the Great Hall. The Head had just gotten up. That was a signal that everyone else could be dismissed to their houses or study or their offices.

Slughorn stopped by my place and leaned over to say something to me. "Meeting of the OBC tomorrow for lunch—regular time, regular place. Mum's the word."

I nodded. On the way back to my office, I ran into Filch. He had a broad smile on his face. He winked at me and said, "Tomorrow lunch. No mumbling about it."

I nodded again. As a matter of fact, every time that I encountered a member of the OBC, there was a reminder that we were back in the saddle.

The next day, I went directly to the Broomsticks after the end of my office hours. As I was the first one to arrive, I noticed that several women teachers came in, and instead of taking a table, went up to an upper room that was usually only for meetings. Then a memory bubbled up. This was a meeting of the Hogwarts coven. I wondered if Dumbledore was aware that there was a coven at Hogwarts.

Shortly the rest of the OBC started to show up. Filch was the first closely followed by Dursley. Then Slughorn arrived. Finally, Hagrid came.

Once everyone was seated and we'd got our usual drink order in, I asked everyone, "Do you know that there is a coven here at Hogwarts?"

Filch exclaimed, "What an underhanded thing to do—make a secret club at Hogwarts!"

Dursley laughed. "What are we, then?"

Filch sort of shrugged and shook his head as though to discourage a troublesome fly. "Well, we're different. We're all men."

I laughed. "And they're all women."

Filch said indignantly, "Exactly!"

Slughorn said, "We can't have any gender-based rules. It's a new edict from the Minister of Magic."

Hagrid asked, "Isn't she a . . . well . . . woman?"

Filch said indignantly, "You're right! It's a. . . a. . . tranvesty!"

Slughorn just shrugged, "Nothing I can do about it. Now, let's get down to our business."

Dursley said, "Right. Professor Wendt, what happened when you were out of the country?"

Everyone turned an eager ear to me. I leaned forward and said, "Would you agree that everything I tell you is confidential?"

They looked at each other and each nodded. I said, "OK. Here's what happened. It's pretty boring, but there are a couple of things that you might be interested in.

"I took a repositioning cruise that took me from London to Miami, Florida, USA."

Dursley asked, "Did anything romantic happen?"

I smiled. "Well, there was a crew member who took me to a dance at the end of the cruise."

Filch rubbed his hands together and said, "And . . ."

"And, pretty much nothing. We had a nice evening. She invited me to see her while they were docked in Miami. I declined because I was anxious to travel to my parent's home more than a thousand miles away."

Everyone released a sigh of disappointment. Then Hagrid asked what happened at my parents' home.

I said, "Well, a friend from England showed up and encouraged me to return to England."

That perked everyone up. Slughorn asked, "Anyone we know? Perhaps Ms. Weasley?"

I tried to mask any reaction that might show up on my face, but I was probably not too successful. I simply said, "I don't think that Ms. Weasley has ever been to the States."

The immediate reaction was that everyone nodded knowingly and said things like "Right," "Yesss." "uhuhn."

I said with a perfectly clear conscience, "Ginny Weasley never showed up in the States."

Filch said, "Just keep up with that story. I wouldn't want to cross that Ginny Weasley if she wants to be discretionary."

We then went on to other topics, like what classes I was teaching, what the latest potions projects the dynamic duo (Slughorn & Dursley) were up to, any new creatures that Hagrid had adopted, and how Mr. Filch was doing with the fair librarian.

Filch didn't like that last topic. He declared, "I objectify to that as a topic of dissertation."

I pointed out that what was sauce for the goose was sauce for the gander. After all, he felt free to discuss possible intimate relations I might be having.

Filch admitted that perhaps that topic ought to be out of bounds for the rest of the meeting.

The meeting ended and I insisted on standing the OBC the lunch due to my long absence from the meetings. There being no serious discussion, the motion was accepted by acclamation.

$$\triangle$$

That evening, Ginny showed up and we had a wonderful time discussing the one item on the OBC agenda that pertained to her. She tried to worm more details out of me of the OBC meeting. I insisted that the price for that sort of information was much higher than a little snogging on the sofa in my office.

She replied with a proud flip of her fiery head, "Do you think that I sell my honor for such a paltry price as the top secret agenda of a committee that is so devoid of worthwhile topics that they stoop to the private life of a girl and her insignificant significant other?"

That induced me to ask just what price would cause her to sell her honor. Her reply was, "Nothing less than the pleasure of hearing the insignificant significant other beg her favor."

I asked, "Does it have to be at your feet, kissing your toes?"

She giggled at that and said, "From the tip of my toes to the tip of my nose . . . and you chose what else in between."

I picked her up and carried her into my private rooms and removed her shoes and stockings. Then I began the kissing. I'd not reached her knees when she rolled over and said, "Sorry. It's a school night and it's too late. Besides, you need schooling on the lip routine. I don't have time to do a proper job."

I objected, but she was not a lady with whom to trifle. She rapidly resumed her hose and shoes. I barely reached the hearth before she left.

I taught her a little lip lesson just before she took the floo connection.

The Father

I was in the Teacher's Lounge reading the latest *Times of London* when an owl flew in through the open door and landed on the end table next to my easy chair. It held out its claw for me to remove the note. That sort of operation almost never happened except when a return was expected. I wished that I had some owl treats about me.

Then it occurred to me that Jaimie might have left some in my purse. I opened it and rumaged around in the bottom. To my slight surprise, I found a resealable plastic bag with a number of owl treats in it. I laid several down on the end table and removed the note.

It was from Cecily's father. Its substance was, "Please choose a meeting place and time for this weekend so that we can discuss chess and other topics."

I had no doubt what the other topics would be. I thought a moment and wrote on the back of the note, "Saturday, noon, lunch at any wizarding inn or pub that you prefer."

I retied the note on the owl's leg. It wasn't happy at the operation, but I gave it a couple of more owl treats. How could it complain about that?

That Saturday, I had gotten Dursley to drop me off at a pub that I'd never been to before—the Pale Festral. I gathered that it was somewhere in the North East, perhaps near Sunderland. He'd dropped me off about fifteen minutes early. I got a table and ordered a butter beer.

Cecily's dad showed up at about five minutes to the hour. He immediately picked out my table and came over. He had a dour mien. He quickly sat and came to the point, saying, "I hope you've come to talk about when you'll allow my wife to return."

I wasn't surprised. If I were he, I would probably have thought the same question if not actually saying it. I temporized by asking if he'd like something to drink. His face turned grimmer and he said that he'd go to the bar himself to get something.

When he returned, he simply asked, "What do you have to say for yourself?"

I took a sip of the butter beer, wishing it were Dewars at least, and said, "Well, you know that I'm not going to commit suicide even to give you back your Jaimie. Yes, she is yours, not mine. However, I came here to talk about whether I would be Cecily's chess mentor."

I couldn't tell if he were going to punch me in the nose or break down in tears. "Why not! She gave up her life for you."

I took a deep breath and considered where to begin. "She didn't do it for me. She certainly wouldn't have. She did it for. . . " And there I was stuck.

Brewster jumped on that. "Yes, who did she do it for if not you?"

"I think you know the answer to that if you will only face it. The Ministry of Magic for one wanted me back. Then there were others. I'm not really at liberty to name others. As a matter of fact, I'm not really at liberty to name the Ministry."

He chewed on that for a while. Meanwhile the waitress approached us for orders for lunch. I glanced at the menu and decided that I couldn't go wrong with fish and chips. Brewster waved her off saying that when she brought my order, he'd order.

As we waited, I could tell that Brewster was going through a struggle deciding what to do. He ended up by saying, "If you want to help Cecily with chess, I'd appreciate it. Is there anything else you need?"

It was a major concession, and I wished I didn't have to ask anything else. However, if I didn't ask now, I'd just have to ask later. I tried a smile and said, "My plan is to oversee her training regimen, but I'll try to schedule a couple of tournaments for her this term. Those tournaments sometimes happen in England, and it's possible to get there each day by disapparation, but it's likely that she'll have to stay over a couple of nights on the continent to find some of the very good tournaments. I think she'll be ready for that kind of tournament soon."

He asked, "You're asking me if I'd be able to accompany her to some of these tournaments, right?"

I nodded.

"And what if my job prevents me from doing so?"

Here we'd reached the point of the spear. "I think I could recruit a female professor at Hogwarts to accompany her when you weren't able to."

41

He nodded slowly. "I suppose that would be OK, depending on who the professor was. Can you tell me who it would be?"

"I have a couple in mind, but it would depend on the dates involved and the professors' other commitments."

He smiled. "You haven't talked with anyone yet, have you?"

It was my turn to squir., "Well, I think it's premature to investigate possible chaperons when I don't even know if I have your permission in principle, and I don't have specific dates of tournaments that would be good."

By this time, my fish and chips had arrived and the waitress turned to Brewster for his order. "Fish and chips as well."

Then he returned to me. "Go ahead and eat. This was never anything but a war negotiation. We don't need to observe the niceties of friendship."

Then he turned his full attention to me and barked, "Names. Give me names. Who could you get to help with these overseas tournaments?"

I hadn't spoken to anyone, but the first name that popped into my head was Aurora. I spoke her name.

He stared at me and laughed. When he'd had a good laugh, he said, "I thought the two of you were on the verge of a feud constantly. What in the world would make you think that she might go along with you?"

That was such a good question that I put down an excellent chip to think through the question. "Well, we've always had a rather on-again-off-again relationship. However, in the last year or so, her attitude has changed from being . . . well . . . rather Puckish to being, if anything, contrite.

"You, of course, know the incident that led to this change of attitude. In a way, you could even say that you benefited from it."

I paused to resume eating a piece of fish. Brewster took the opportunity to press a different point. "Yes, I suppose that you might consider my taking the second worst wound that I'd ever suffered as a benefit." He paused for thought and then said, "Yes, I suppose it was none-the-less a benefit."

I followed up. "Do you know that Plato considered that you can't evaluate whether a life has been a good one or not until the end of it."

Brewster replied, "I doubt that Plato ever loved a woman, then."

I confessed that I had no knowledge about that. Then a thought occurred to me. Meanwhile, Brewster went on. "Do you have any other women in mind as chaperons?"

That forced the thought to the front. I said, "What about other women of good repute but not Professors at Hogwarts?"

"Such as?"

"Such as an Auror."

He laughed. It was the first good-hearted laugh that I'd heard from him the entire time we were together. He finished and said, "You made that up, didn't you?"

"No." I objected.

"Yes, you did!" He said more forcefully. "You mentioned Aurora and that name suggested to you a different sort of person—an Auror."

I laughed myself. "Did not."

"Did too. And, I saw you hesitate and look away. That was the moment that Auror occurred to you, isn't it?"

That had me stuck. I couldn't name the Auror that I had in mind and I couldn't offer any proof that I did have a specific Auror in mind without naming her. I just sat there. I would have been open-mouthed if I hadn't had the perspicacity to stuff a chip into it.

Brewster asked me, "How could I agree to such a proposal without knowing that at least one person had agreed to be a chaperone in principle."

I could only say, "How could you not agree to letting Cecily pursue chess seriously simply because all the relevant details had not yet been worked out?"

The grim smile returned, and he said, "I'll give you provisional permission to proceed. You must, though, as soon as possible, present me with at least one responsible woman who would agree to this arrangement."

I extended my hand to signify my agreement to the deal and seal his permission to proceed as well. We shook.

I had nearly finished my fish and chips. His had just arrived. I rose and placed a fifty galleon coin on the table. I kept the waitress at the table and asked if the coin would cover my meal and a reasonable tip.

She smiled broadly. "You should really take some change. I'll get it right away."

I shook my head. "Sorry, I've got to leave. Please keep the change." She did.

Of course, I'd have to hang around waiting for Dursley. I stepped over to the hearth as though I were about to take the floo connection somewhere. Fortunately, I'd only been standing there a couple of minutes when Dursley stepped through the floo, saw me, and asked, "I hope you haven't been waiting long?"

"No. You've arrived just at the right time." He extended his hand and I took it. We walked into the floo and then to the hearth in the Great Hall at Hogwarts.

That evening, I was also going on a date with Ginny. She showed up in a very nice evening gown. Against my better judgment, I'd agreed to go to a wizard club where there would be dancing.

I knew it was inevitable, but I still was not completely comfortable with dancing to modern wizarding music. My worst fears were not realized. The band played some truly dance-able songs. Some even permitted the dancer's victim to be held quite close.

The club had a food service. I had to complement Ginny on an excellent choice of clubs. I mentioned that while we were dancing to one of the slow songs. I happened to have a hand well down on her waist. She replied, "Well, I'm glad that you like my choice of clubs. But even here, there are certain standards of decorum." With that she reached down to her hip and repositioned my hand at a more decorous location on her waist. Then she added, "There are other locations where that will be quite desirable."

As the song finished, I held Ginny close and told her, "You are the most beautiful woman I've ever known."

She laughed. "I suppose you mean in the Biblical sense."

"I mean in any sense."

We ordered a late night dinner and turned to serious discussion. Well, actually, it was just I who turned to serious discussion. I began with a little background. "Did you know, Ginny, that I was a chess mentor for Cedric Diggery?"

She stared at me. "Diggery? Wasn't he a crack Seeker for Huffelpuff when I was just starting at Hogwarts?"

She made my answer difficult to give by a serious kiss delivered at the very end of her question. When my lips where unoccupied again, I said, "Yes. You're right. However, something that you might not have known is that . . ."

The comment was punctuated by a gasp, and she supplied an additional fact, "AND, he was killed by Riddle!"

"Well, you've got that basic fact right. However, it was actually one of his Deatheaters who was wielding the wand. He was just obeying orders. But that wasn't what I was thinking off. He was also a chess prodigy. I was a mentor for him when you were in your second and third years."

She nodded. "I didn't know that." Then she corrected herself. "No. Wait. I remember a eulogy about him. You talked about his chess skills."

"Right. I thought that he was talented enough to become a professional and maybe make a try for . . . world champion. If that had worked out, it would have been my opportunity to go down in history."

Ginny started to say something. I forestalled her by saying, "Oh, I don't think that I'd have been his mentor after he left Hogwarts. I'm not anywhere near good enough at chess, but I could have been a little footnote about his rise to fame. You know, I was the one who discovered him and got him started off in chess."

Ginny said, "Interesting, but what has that got to do with the price of dragon blood in Durmstrang?"

"Amazingly, another chess prodigy dropped from heaven into my office two years ago. She may even be a stronger player than Cedric. She just walked into my office and asked me to be her mentor."

Ginny smiled. "You do seem to have the luck—both good and bad. OK. So, where do I come in? You know, I've got a sneaking suspicion that I might just know."

"Well, here's the deal. In order to mentor her properly, I've got to get her into tournaments. The good tournaments typically take several days and most of them are outside England. She and I would have to stay in a hotel or inn for several nights."

Ginny frowned at that. "I see. You need a chaperone for the young lady. What about her dad or mum? Wouldn't one or both of them come along?"

I grimaced. "Well, both her mom and step-mom are dead. Her dad has a job and might not be able to attend the complete tournament."

She shook her head. "How sad—both mum and step-mom gone." Then she looked up, and the expression on her face changed. "She wouldn't happen to be that Brewster girl whose dad married at the end of last term, and then her mum disappeared without a trace?"

I only nodded.

Then she nodded. "So, is this a commitment for a specific week?"

I shook my head vigorously. "No, no. This is just a commitment to be willing to do it once or twice. You could always beg off for any specific tournament. I'll be looking for other chaperones as well."

She took on a contemplative attitude and eventually said, "I suppose that this could turn into a weekend together in the same hotel room when the dad showed up, as he surely would?"

That made me grimace. "I suppose it might. I'm not sure how I feel about obviously sleeping with someone I'm not married to while in the company of a student—even accompanied by her dad."

She took on a determined grin. "Well, you check that out with Brewster before you commit me too strongly. I don't know how anxious I'd be to spend several days and nights near you and not be able to get away alone with you at all."

I agreed to do that. It was all so nebulous. I didn't know what I'd do if Brewster wanted to hold Ginny and me to a vow of celibacy while we were at a tournament. And of course, I didn't know what she'd do either.

By the time that we'd gotten through that conversation, there was not a lot of time left for dancing. We did dance. Shortly we discovered that we both were interested in a different sort of dancing. We went back to my office and in the wee hours of the morning when we were spooning, Ginny commented that we'd proved an old wives' tale that she'd heard.

I asked, "What was that?"

She sighed, "Oh, just that if you can talk past midnight, you'll have great sex."

The following Tuesday, I screwed up my courage to talk to my other main candidate to be a chaperone for Cecily. I checked her schedule of classes and office hours. 2 PM was free. I mounted the stairs to her tower with shaking knees. When I reached the top of the tower and knocked on the floor (the closest to a door that was available), the worst happened. She was there.

She said, "Come in."

I did. When she saw me she said, "As I live and breathe, you are the last person that I would expect to come to my office."

"Yes, you made quite a reputation coming to mine."

"Well, take a chair and let me know what's on your mind."

I did. "OK. You're aware that Cecily Brewster has a special interest in chess?"

She nodded and agreed cautiously, "Yes . . ."

"Well, like I did with Cedrick, I'm planning on being a chess mentor for her."

She had been sitting behind her desk, facing off to the side. When I started to talk about Cedrick Diggory, she swiveled around. "What do you mean, 'like Cedrick?'"

I shrugged. "You know, I took him to the occasional chess tournament. A few were out of the country." With a bit of pride, I said, "You know he did rather well in those."

"No, I didn't know. Oh, I knew that you had been the faculty adviser of the wizard chess club a long time ago." She thought a minute. "Now I remember about you saying something about chess at Cedrick's memorial service. I guess I didn't pay much attention. Hmmm. Just how well did he do?"

"He had reached the level of International Master. It was amazing that he did that so quickly."

She leaned forward. "Back to Cecily. What do I have to do with her and chess?"

"Well, her father may not always be available to go along on out-of-country trips."

Aurora picked up the idea. "So, you're looking for someone to babysit with Cecily." She paused, considering the idea. Then she said, "How well do you know her?"

"Well, I've never had her in class, but she did approach me about being her mentor a couple of years ago, and I got to know her a little." I didn't add that I had a lot of memories of her that I inherited from Jaimie.

"Then you maybe don't know that she can be a right pill."

I nodded. "Oh, I have an idea of that."

Aurora shook her head. "I'd need a little inducement to get me to volunteer to be her babysitter on one of these junkets. . ." She left the sentence hanging, pregnant with meaning.

Of course, I had a good idea what the meaning might be, but I asked anyway, "Just what sort of inducement would we be talking about?"

"Oh, commitment to go along with my entertaining little masquerades at Halloween."

I shook my head. "I'm not signing on for an open-ended commitment of that sort. Now, maybe year by year. Each year that I need help with a babysitter, I co-operate with your hare-brained schemes at Halloween."

She considered it. Then she suggested, "One for one. Each time that I go along as babysitter, I get a credit. I exchange one credit for one Halloween."

"Two for one."

"You're killing me here. How about this? Two for one, but I get a two credit signing bonus."

I had to admire her. "Did you used to be an agent for Quidditch players?"

She just maintained a steady gaze and asked, "Well?"

I didn't like it that much, but I agreed. I asked, "Don't you usually drink over signing a deal?"

"It's a school day AND night. You may be done with classes today, but I'm not."

"OK. I'll give you plenty of warning when I need a babysitter."

I turned to go. Then I had a thought. "Oh, one last thing. Would you mind helping me send an owl to Cecily's father? I want to give him the names of the chaperons that I've found."

She laughed. "Sure. In for a knut, in for a galleon."

I had to ask for a piece of parchment. I had my own pen. I wrote a simple letter naming Aurora and Ginny as my chaperons and asked him to get back to me at his earliest convenience with his permission to act as Cecily's mentor.

After writing the note, Aurora and I went to the owlery. As we went, she asked if I remembered the last time that she helped me with an owl post.

"Let me see. That was when I was answering a business proposal."

She laughed. "Yes. From Gringotts."
"Now you're not supposed to have known that."
She laughed again tauntingly. "But I did."

The Board

I was having breakfast in the Great Hall one morning when a Great Eagle Owl flew up to my place, dropped to the floor and extended its beak up toward me. It was holding a large manila envelope. I took it, and the Owl flew up and out of the Great Hall. It did it as neatly as you please. The envelope didn't end up on my plate. I didn't even have time to tip the bird with a couple of owl treats.

There wasn't a return address, but I was pretty sure whence it had come. I finished breakfast as quickly as I could. Then I returned to my office. I broke the seal on the envelope and examined the contents.

They consisted, as I knew they would, of:

- A cover letter
- An agenda
- Minutes of the last meeting
- A multi-page financial report
- A magical ticket allowing the holder to use the floo connection to the reception area of the board room of Gringotts

Removing the boilerplate, the cover letter told me that the next meeting of the board of Gringotts would happen the following Wednesday at 7 PM in the Boardroom.

The minutes of the last meeting were standard fare except for Jaimie's report, which had apparently been well-received even though it contained little that Gringotts staff didn't already know.

The financial report told a story of slowly improving vault occupancy rates but not profits.

The agenda had an intriguing item—a report on crypto-currencies, whatever they were. I thought that it might be interesting to attend this meeting if for no other reason than to find out about crypto-currencies.

The only thing left was to get someone to take me there. Of course, I immediately had an idea about that.

⊿

That night, as frequently happened, Ginny showed up in the early evening. She breezed in and strode up to me. I'd only managed to get up from my desk. She planted a quick serious kiss and said, "I've not got a lot of time. Have an early morning meeting for which I have to make some last minute preparations."

With that, she took my hand and practically dragged me to the sofa. We sat. She gave every sign of starting in with a course of serious snogging.

I lifted a hand and said, "Wait. I've got something that I want to talk about."

She showed impatience but said, "OK. Let's get it over with and on to serious stuff."

I said, "I need a lift to Gringotts next week Wednesday night."

"Don't be silly. In the first place you can't go directly to Gringotts. You must mean to your favorite spot, the Cauldron, or maybe a business in Diagon Alley. In the second place, Gringotts keeps . . . well . . . banker's hours. They're not open at night."

I smiled. "I'm a . . ." At that point, I hesitated to name what I really was. Instead I said, "I'm a sort of consultant for Gringotts. I have to meet with representatives of the bank and . . . uh . . . other consultants."

She was the one to hesitate now. She asked, "Just where would I be taking you and how?"

"Well, it's a floo connection inside the bank. I have a special ticket that let's me and whoever is transporting me to use that floo connection."

She smiled, "A single use passport. I've heard of them but never seen one. I'd like to take you just to get to see it and use it."

"Then you'll do it?"

She almost whined as she said, "Wellll, I didn't say that actually. There's a fine point here." She stopped again, closed her eyes and I swear it looked like she were speaking to herself.

After a few minutes, I said, "Well?"

She seemed to come awake and said, "Oh, here's the deal." She shook her head. "I really have been seeing you a lot. I'm starting to use your Yankee slang.

"Anyway, I'm not sure that I can. You see, there's this situation between wizards and Goblins. There's a precarious truce between Goblins and wizards. The terms of that truce are that they get to run their businesses—

like Gringotts. As long as they run them with integrity and basic honesty, they will be fine, and they can have the secrecy they crave. At the same time, we wizards will give them the basic rights of citizenship. That is, access to the courts—including the Wizengemott—protection of Aurors, and so on. They won't have a vote in wizard politics.

"So, that's the fifty thousand foot view. . . God, I've got to stop channeling you. That's the broom's view of the relationship between the Ministry and Gringotts. I don't think that I as an Auror can show up deep inside Gringotts even if it's totally innocent."

"That's OK. I'll find someone else. You just happened to be the first one through the floo."

She laughed. "Speaking of that, you could always have Aurora take you."

"I've already got her to volunteer to be a chaperon. I had to pay dearly for that. I don't think I want to knock on her door for a favor anytime soon."

She smiled. "Good luck! Now, let's get down to serious business." With that, she pulled me close and we did get down to some serious snogging.

The next day, I decided that I should pay a visit to the kitchens for breakfast. I could afford to spend a little of the good will that I had built up with Slughorn by skipping breakfast in the Great Hall.

Everyone was surprised to see me there for breakfast. Dursley and Filch both got up to find a chair for me at the table. I didn't want to get off on the wrong foot, so we had hardly sat when I forestalled the inevitable question; "What brings you down here?"

I said, "I'll tell you why I'm here. First because I want to ask a favor and second because our weekly OBC meetings just aren't quite enough." That brought out a laugh or two.

Dursley asked, "What can we do for you?"

I started to answer when the house elves brought to the table a basket of pastries, a pot of tea, and a tureen of scrambled eggs with sausages. That led to plates being filled, and the meal begining. After the worst pangs of hunger had been sated, I said, "I need a lift down to Gringotts next Wednesday night."

Filch turned a little red and said, "Sorry. I've got an important repair to be done here at the castle that night. I wish I could."

There was a standing fiction that was supported by all the members of the OBC whenever we met. No hint that Filch was anything other than a fully capable wizard was ever voiced. So, I said, "I'm sorry that you're busy. But, I don't have any doubt that I'll find someone who will take me."

Dursley said, "I'd be happy to, but I have great news that I haven't shared with any of you. My girl friend, Pamela, is returning from Canada.

Wednesday is the day. I've arranged to meet her and take her out to dinner. So, I can't help you."

I smiled. "Don't worry. I'll find someone to take me. But tell me more about Pamela's return, Dudley."

He beamed a broad smile. "Well, she'd served her time in reporter purgatory and will take up the city desk for the *Prophet*. It's not the most glamorous assignment, but it's HERE in England. I can see her every day!"

Filch was feeling a little left out, so he asked, "How are you going to get to Gringotts?"

I said, "At our next OBC meeting I'll ask if anyone can take me."

Filch said, "Sure. Old Sluggy should be happy to take you."

The next OBC meeting was the next day. Technically we usually conducted the meeting like a regular business meeting with old and new business, etc. There was rarely any business that we conducted. This time I proposed new business.

Filch waved his hand like a student who for once knows the answer and wants everyone to know that he does. He was recognized by the chairman, the Headmaster. He triumphantly declared, "The new business is that Professor Wendt needs a ride to Gringotts next week Wednesday night. I wanted to take him, but I had other pressing businesses that I'm in contention with. "

Dursley admitted to having other important business as well. Slughorn looked truly disturbed. He admitted, "I've got a Hogwarts board meeting that night. I have to be present."

I commented to myself, "Seems to be a popular day for board meetings."

The only person left was Hagrid. I looked over to him. He said, "I'd love to take yer professor."

Hagrid was about the last person with whom I really wanted to go, but he had offered, so I humbly thanked him and agreed that we'd go together. Hagrid was clearly overjoyed at being able to do a favor for me. I decided that I'd have to do something nice for him to repay the favor.

After the meeting, I pulled Hagrid aside—an amazing feat in itself. I said, "Let me take you to the Cauldron after my meeting for a couple of drinks."

Hagrid beamed. "That's really kind of yer, Professor. How long do y'think the meeting will last?"

"I would say that it could be over in an hour or it might take as long as two hours. I really doubt that it would go much longer."

Hagrid nodded wisely. "Yup. I have some parchments to grade and a little lesson planning to do. I could do that while I wait."

I asked, "Are you assigning scrolls now?"

"Oh, yes. Now that I'm more confident in my writing, I'm grading my students' writing. I've always known how to talk about my animals, but somehow when it comes to putting it on parchment, it's never been easy."

I asked the obvious question, "So, what's changed?"

Hagrid scratched his head and said, "I'm not sure. We could talk about that at the Cauldron after."

I agreed and headed back to my office.

The day of the board meeting I was beginning to regret agreeing to have Hagrid transport me. Would he fit through the opening of the hearth in the Gringotts Boardroom? Maybe worse than that, where would he sit? Gringotts barely had chairs big enough for me—and I was not even a very tall person. What would happen when Hagrid looked for a place to sit? It was too late to change, so I guessed that I would find out.

That evening as soon as we could politely leave the evening meal in the Great Hall, Hagrid and I started for the hearth there and then I realized that I hadn't brought my agenda and associated documents. I asked him, "Do you mind if I go up to my office and get some papers that I need? I'll be right down."

Hagrid just shook his head as if there were a fly buzzing around it that he wanted to shake away. Then he asked, "Don't you have a floo in your office?"

"Sure, but you're . . . uh . . . a little . . . uh . . ."

Hagrid just stared at me and asked, "I was never a little anything. What are you talking about?"

"Well, the hearth in my office is kind of small, and you are kind of large."

Hagrid laughed. "You've been living with wizards for a long time. You don't know that floo's expand as much as they have to for whoever's in them?"

I laughed too. "OK. I buy it. We'll leave through my floo."

We got up to my office. I collected my papers and handed Hagrid the ticket that would give us access to the Gringott's floo connection. "Well, let's go. You know, I'm anxious to see how this will work—both of us fitting in the floo at the same time."

He laughed again. "Easy as pie. Just take my hand and you'll see."

I took his hand. The floo looked awfully small. He took some floo powder and threw it down. Even though I was standing outside the floo, somehow we were both pulled through the hearth and out into the Gringott's hearth.

As I expected, Javeen was waiting. Hagrid gave her a little surprise. She started to send for security, but when she noticed that I was in tow, her mouth opened wide enough to fly a broom through. She recovered herself quickly. She asked, "Who's your friend?"

I smiled. "A fellow professor at Hogwarts. His name is Hagrid. Hagrid, let me introduce you to the executive secretary to the CEO of Gringotts—Javeen."

Hagrid smiled sheepishly and said, "I teach about magical animals."

I added, "There is probably no one who knows more about them than Hagrid."

Hagrid perused his shoes and said, "Oh, that's not really true."

I went on. "Anyway, he's offered to bring me to this meeting and take me back to Hogwarts after it's over."

She made a funny face and said, "I would be extremely happy to give you a lift home. . . " She added softly, "I would have brought you too."

Hagrid, bless him, said, "I brought some homework to do here. After the meeting's over, the Professor promised to take me out for drinks."

I quickly added, "I'm looking forward to it."

She tapped her chin and said, "I could join you for drinks."

I grimaced. "Oh, you know, it's a guy thing. Maybe some other time."

She strode over to me and took my arm, "That's a promise."

Well, it wasn't exactly a promise. As a matter of fact, it wasn't a promise at all. I said, "I make no promises. We'll see how things go."

She nodded and whispered so that Hagrid couldn't hear, "It's good to see that you have close friends who aren't humans."

I was stuck. I sure didn't want to offend Hagrid, but I didn't want to encourage Javeen. All I could say was, "Well, I'm going to go into the Boardroom. I'll see you in a little while Hagrid."

He nodded, "You bet, Professor."

I reached for the doorknob, but Javeen beat me to it. She opened the door and ushered me in, saying, "See you afterwards."

Of course, she would, but it sounded really ominous.

The meeting turned out to be the most boring that I'd ever attended. There was the usual financial report that had nothing unexpected. There was a brief thank you to me for providing the report on the future of money. It had convinced the bank to do nothing rash like investing in bitcoin. I was glad that they'd felt that way because bitcoin seemed to be gaining value with every passing quarter. I'd convinced them that bitcoin was too speculative for their tolerance of risk. It worried me, though.

The meeting ended. Everyone else treated it as a ho-hum meeting. One or two Goblins patted me on the back and asked if I wanted to go out with them for a drink. I said, "I already have a commitment. We can do it the next time."

Then the CEO approached me and drew me aside. He said, "You may notice that some of the board members were more friendly to you than usual."

Fearing I knew not what, I cautiously said, "Well, I did wonder a little at the invitation to drinks afterward."

He nodded. "You were right to wonder at that. Some members of the board thought of you as a flash in the pan. They are the more conservative members. However, your report on bitcoin that discouraged us from investing in such a speculative medium has affected them deeply.

"When they saw the wild fluctuation of bitcoin value, they were to a Goblin convinced of your perspicacity. Not for the first time, you have prevented the bank from following a potentially ruinous course.

"I, of course, was convinced from the beginning of your level-headed business sense. Keep up the good work. You know that I will not always be the CEO and president of the board. Someday, there might be a presidency in your future. You just need to learn the politics of the board a little better. It would really have been good if you could have joined a few of us for drinks."

I said, "Well, it was a matter of honor. I had promised someone that I would drink with him tonight. I know how much you Goblins respect honor. You would not have wanted me to renege on my promise."

He blustered a bit and agreed, but I was pretty sure that he might have made an exception in this one case. He then bid me goodnight and left through his private entrance to the Boardroom.

Outside the Boardroom, the board members milled around and exchanged comments as they left. There were the two people waiting for me. Hagrid was the first to speak, "Ms. Javeen here would like to go with us for drinks. I told her that I guessed that was no problem."

I sighed. Well, it could have been worse. She could have talked him into leaving without me. But Javeen had maneuvered things so that all three of us had to go together to the Cauldron. I replied, "Sure. The more the merrier." I had never meant that more than I did just then. I briefly considered asking one or more of the board members to come along, but by then, they'd left.

So I was left with the three musketeers—Hagrid, Javeen, and me. I decided to take the initiative to keep things from getting out of hand, so I took Hagrid's hand and said, "Please take me to the Cauldron for a drink or two. Ms. Javeen can make it there on her own, I'm sure."

Javeen smiled prettily and said, "Of course."

Hagrid and I arrived and I immediately had a dilemma—to sit at the bar or sit at a table. Sit at the bar and you were the center of attention, which I didn't want. On the other hand, sitting at a table allowed much more intimate conversations. I mentally flipped a coin and came up with table. The fact that I didn't immediately feel nauseous told me that I'd made the right decision. I picked a table near the edge of the room. As soon as Hagrid sat I asked him what he wanted.

"Oh, professor, a half-pint of whiskey would be good."

I nodded, considering his body mass, that would be OK. I went to the bar and asked for a fifth of Jim Beam and a half-pint glass and a shot glass. Tom smiled knowingly and brought out the whiskey and glasses.

Just then, Javeen came through the floo, took a quick glance around the room, sized things up, and walked over to the bar. She looked straight at me and said, "Good. We're having whiskey. Would you be a dear and get a third glass, please?"

I cursed my luck, simply turned to Tom, and said, "One more shot glass please." He smiled knowingly again and got one out.

As he handed me the glass, he said, "Looks like it will be a fun evening."

I just growled under my breath, "Just shut up."

He laughed at that.

Back at the table, I poured drinks. I put the lion's share in Hagrids and filled both Javeen's and my glasses. She picked it up, smiled at me and said, "I propose a toast. To the continued good relations between Gringotts and Professor Wendt." I thought to myself that there was probably one particular associate of Gringotts that she had in mind in particular.

I toasted Hagrid for the favor of taking me to the meeting at Gringotts and pointedly didn't toast Javeen for anything.

Both Javeen and I had taken sips with each toast, but Hagrid had taken a good swallow. Meanwhile, I heard a voice from the past behind me.

"Hello, hello, hello. What do we have here? It looks like three of my favorite non-wizards." The voice moved around the table and came into view. It was Penelope Clearwater accompanied by Draco Malfois. She continued, "It's Hagrid, Mr. Wendt, and an unnamed Goblin."

Malfois said, "Now, Penelope." He gazed down and was clearly uncomfortable.

"No, no. These are some of my favorites, especially that Goblin. She must be from Gringotts, aren't you?"

I couldn't stand it any more. I stood and said, "Ms. Clearwater. I am still a professor at Hogwarts as is Professor Hagrid. Our friend," I emphasized the word "friend" even though it cost me dearly, "is indeed an important employee of Gringotts. I would introduce you, but I don't want our friend to be embarrassed by you any further. Please go pester someone else."

She started to say something, but Tom had appeared from nowhere. He said, "Ms. Clearwater, I'll have to ask you to leave the Cauldron if you can't treat your fellow patrons with courtesy."

She made a face and said, "Come Draco. We can find better people to associate with." They left our table and went to another table."

Hagrid frowned and said, "That was not fun. I'm glad you stood up for us, Professor." Then he took up the challenge of returning us to a pleasant get together, "I want to toast both of these fine people—Professor Wendt and Miss Javeen for this wonderful time tonight! Isn't that right, Professor?"

All I could do was assent, smile, and drink the toast. Hagrid finished his glass and looked meaningfully to me. I volunteered to get another bottle. I returned with the bottle, filled Hagrid's glass, and topped off Javeen's and my glasses.

She commented softly, "I appreciate your defense of us as well. In a world dominated by wizards and witches, it takes courage to stand up for those who are not."

Hagrid asked me when I would begin teaching my full set of courses. I answered, "It's been difficult to get up my enthusiasm for teaching since I returned. I want to return to something like normal. Perhaps it will be next term after the summer holiday."

Hagrid looked at me and said, "You should take as much time as necessary."

Javeen added, "Yes. It's hard being separated from . . . " She trailed off. I realized that she'd placed her hand over mine. This melancholy reflection was followed by Hagrid's deep bass voice beginning a recitation of the ballad of "Odo the Hero". He accompanied his recitation with the occasional swallow of good whiskey. Before long the recitation had turned into singing.

It was good-hearted, and if I'd known the lyrics, I might have joined in myself. When he finished, I decided that the situation called for a recitation (for I would never have dared inflict my singing voice on anyone) of "The Streets of Laredo." It's been around since the early 20th century in the States, but it seemed to me to be appropriate at this point in 21st century England. I spoke,

> "As I walked out on the streets of Laredo.
> As I walked out on Laredo one day,
> I spied a poor cowboy wrapped in white linen,
> Wrapped in white linen as cold as the clay.
> I can see by your outfit that you are a cowboy.

These words he did say as I boldly walked by.
Come an' sit down beside me an' hear my sad story.
I'm shot in the breast an' I know I must die.
It was once in the saddle, I used to go dashing.
Once in the saddle, I used to go gay.
First to the card-house and then down to Rose's.
But I'm shot in the breast and I'm dying today.
Get six jolly cowboys to carry my coffin.
Six dance-hall maidens to bear up my pall.
Throw bunches of roses all over my coffin.
Roses to deaden the clods as they fall.
Then bang the drum slowly, play the Fife lowly.
Play the dead march as you carry me along.
Take me to the green valley, lay the sod o'er me,
I'm a young cowboy and I know I've done wrong."

When I'd finished, the bottle was empty, and Hagrid's head was nodding. I shook my head in resignation. Everything seemed to go wrong this day. I looked over to Javeen and said, "There's no way that we'll get Hagrid to Hogwarts and into his cabin. I'm going to get a room for Hagrid and try to get him into it. So, this is the night."

She shook her head decidedly. "No. I'll help you. And after we're done, I'd like to talk with you—a serious talk."

I didn't know what to make of that, but I decided that a serious talk might be one where I could disabuse her of any suspicion that she had a chance with me.

So, I tried rousing Hagrid. He came semi-awake. I had a second idea. I left Hagrid for the moment and walked over to the bar where Tom was holding sway. I asked him if I could pay for a room for the night. He agreed happily and handed me a key to a room on the main floor, thank God.

I returned to our table and started rousing Hagrid again. He became half-way conscious, and I started to urge him to get up and help me to get him to his room. I wasn't making much headway. He would stand up on one leg and then collapse down again. Finally, Javeen stood, and with a wave of her hand, Hagrid rose and we three staggered off toward the room.

It was difficult getting the door open. Hagrid took up most of the hall. Just getting the key to the lock was a challenge. I had to stretch to reach around Hagrid and fumble with the key. Then, I dropped the key. I could have just screamed. I didn't.

Javeen at this point had stepped back and actually was laughing. I said, "Do you know that is not all that helpful?"

She laughed even harder. "No, no. It's great. You are doing so, so well."

I had to laugh myself. "OK. OK. You don't happen to know the *aloahora* spell, do you?"

Javeen was still laughing but managed, "I was wondering how long it would be before you asked. Yes. I do." Then she performed it, the door unlocked, I twisted the knob, and we managed to get Hagrid into the room and even had him fall back on the bed. I put the key on the dresser, and we left the room, closing the door behind us.

We returned to the bar area and took our table. Our glasses, still mostly full, were awaiting us. I held Javeen's chair for her for which she thanked me. I took my own chair and said, "Well, we're on your nickel now."

She looked puzzled and asked, "My 'nickel'?"

"Oh, it's a Muggle expression. It comes form a time . . ." I stopped. I was just trying to put off the inevitable. I finished, "It doesn't matter, it's just a Muggle expression. Go ahead, please."

Now that it came to it she seemed as reluctant as I to start. She said, "No, go ahead. I want to know what nickel has to do with talking."

You never have to encourage me more than once to tell a story, so I went ahead. "First, do you know about telephones?"

She perked up at that, proud that she could answer, "Oh, of course. We have to deal with Muggles and Muggle inventions at the corporate board level. Sure. They're these little boxes that Muggles use to talk to each other at long distances. They come in two varieties—candy cane and egg shell—I think."

I took a deep breath and decided not to talk about candy bar and clamshell. She was smiling so happily at having such arcane Muggle knowledge that I couldn't disappoint her by correcting what were such minor issues.

I just soldiered on. "Very good. Now, telephones used to be very different. They were connected by wires rather than radio waves." Her forehead wrinkled at the mention of radio waves. "Anyway, the old style telephones were much bigger. As a matter of fact, they were so big and bulky that you only found them in homes, businesses, and on street corners in glass boxes that were big enough for one person to occupy."

That made her laugh. "How silly, to see a man standing in a glass box to use a telephone."

I shrugged and went on. "Anyway, the glass box variety were completely public. In order to use one, you had to pay a fee. The fee in the

United States changed across the years but for a very long time when these phone boxes first were being used, the fee was one coin called a nickel.

"So, when person A wanted to talk with person B about something that only person A was interested in, person B would say, 'It's on your nickel.' That would mean that person A had the responsibility to convince person B that it was a conversation worth the nickel."

She clapped her hands and said, "How funny." Then the realization hit that the rest of the conversation was "on her nickel." She took a sip of the whiskey appreciatively, apparently stalling for time. Then she began:

"You know that I've been interested in you romantically for quite a while."

I nodded.

"Well, from the first time I saw you, I was in love with you. I quickly learned that you had several women in love with you. There was, of course, Minerva McGonagall. She, at least, wouldn't marry you. There was Aurora Sinistra. She pursued you with real ardor, but you eluded her. Later, I discovered there were other women—Muggle women. How many I never learned. That gave me hope. You were not easy to snare and you might, well, even look on other women with favor.

"The years passed slowly, and you didn't marry Minerva. It was as though you really wanted to keep your options open. That gave me even more hope.

"Then, of course, you did marry. You married Minerva after many years of being on the verge. That destroyed my hope of marrying you, but it didn't end my hope that you would perhaps have an affair. And out of that affair, who knew what would grow?

"Then you disappeared as though you'd never existed. You were replaced by that hateful Jaimie. I was sure that she had you under the imperious curse, that I would never see you again, that you were maybe not literally dead (although I wasn't sure of that by any means), but you were to all intents and purposes dead. Those were my darkest hours.

"I'd gone over the years from hoping for love and perhaps even marriage to hoping to be the 'other woman' and finally to being the widow without ever having been the wife."

As I listened to her, I realized that I had felt most of those things myself when I was younger. I couldn't help but think of my high school career when I'd met and fallen in love with a young lady when I was about the age of a second year.

You might call it puppy love or a crush or an infatuation, but it lasted until long after I'd graduated from high school. It lasted until the young lady married. I'd had the ignominy of being invited to her wedding. I went. I went to see her last moments when she was still technically available to fall in love with me.

After her wedding, I couldn't forget her and could not give up my love of her for a very long time.

Yes, I understood how Javeen felt.

She went on. "Then a miracle happened. You returned from the dead. There was still hope while you lived. Then another earth-shaking event happened. The two of you disappeared and after months, you returned, but she did not. Rather, she returned in a shroud. You were available again! You were fully available.

"Then you returned to Gringotts, and you returned without a hateful female escort. What could I hope but that you were truly available to me!"

There it was. I was the one who was loved without hope. I gritted my teeth because I had decided that I was about to pay it forward. I was about to do what I'd so much wanted that other young lady of mine to do. I took a swallow and began, the words coming to me just in time for me to say them.

"You are an amazing young lady. I have to admire you—your determination, your dedication, your undying love. Most of all, I admire your courage in talking about this with me so openly."

She immediately perked up but said, "But . . ."

"Nothing. I will make you a deal." She really perked up at that and drained what was left in her glass in a single swallow.

"I propose a trade."

Her eyes sparkled, but were also wary. "What kind of trade?"

I finished my glass in a swallow. "You trade all your hopes for my love . . . for . . . "

Her eyes widened in disbelief, "For what?"

"For a night with me. This night. Physical intimacy. I don't promise sex. That no one can promise, but I promise anything and everything up to that. If sex happens . . ."

Her smile widened seemingly from ear to ear. "It happens."

She actually laughed. "You, mister, are a Goblin at heart. Only a Goblin would think of that kind of deal." She shook her head slowly. "That is why I love you so much. I knew it. I knew it! You would make such a lover!"

I had to laugh as well. "Then do you accept the deal?"

She didn't say anything, but seemed to think hard about it. "You drive a hard bargain. If I accept it, you could walk away in the morning and never hear from me again."

I nodded. "Yes. Also, you could walk away with my love."

She nodded thoughtfully. She asked diffidently, "Do you want to make it an unbreakable oath?"

I looked disgust at her. "I would trust you with my fortune."

Her smile burst forth again. "And I you. You are a true Goblin."

Her face changed from happiness to that of a practical plotter. "All right. This doesn't make sense unless it is done secretly. I propose that you go hire a room for the night. I'll walk out and pass you once you're done. You mouth the room number to me. I'll take the floo somewhere and disapparate back to the room. You go up alone and meet me there."

"Good. I'll go right now." I did. Tom gave me room 3D. Just as I took the key, I sensed Javeen walk past. I turned and formed the room number silently and expressively with my lips. She nodded almost imperceptibly. She didn't hesitate for a second but walked to the floo and into it. I walked to the stairs and ascended the two flights to the third floor. As I turned the corner into the hall, I saw a flicker in a dark shadow near one of the rooms. I went to 3D and turned the key in the lock.

Javeen was next to me and closed her hand on my key hand as I pulled the key from the lock. I twisted the handle, turned toward her, and plucked her up in my arms. Her smile was radiant. I carried her into the room, closed the door, and locked it behind me after setting her on the bed.

She stretched her arms out in an exaggerated yawn. I put my arms around her and began unbuttoning her blouse in the back. She whispered in my ear, "You take your part of the deal seriously, I see."

I smiled. "Would you have it any other way?"

"Of course, not. Proceed with all deliberate speed!"

I laughed and finished the procedure. While I was doing that, she lowered the lights and worked on the buttons of my shirt. We finished with each other's clothes slowly with many caresses through the clothes. When the clothes were out of the way, we took to the bed.

I held Javeen close. She whispered to me in Gobbledy-Gook. I still don't know what she was saying. She's never revealed her secret message. The real message was in the tone of voice that she used. It was as seductive as any English language pillow talk that I'd ever heard.

She began kissing my cheek. Her lips were the most unusual I'd ever experienced. They seemed to be covered with tiny bumps that made kisses more like caresses than kisses. She seemed to be kissing every part of my head—cheeks, forehead, nose, chin. Finally, they reached my lips. They were fire on my lips.

I caressed every part of her body that I could reach—which was pretty much all of it. Her slight stature made it easy. Her tongue licked my lips and I was soon licking hers and then we licked tongues.

After an immeasurable length of times, she drew back and looked at me with wonder in her eyes. "You go far beyond what our contract requires. Why?"

I smiled. Her eyes sparkled in the dim light. Maybe mine did as well, "It's easy to understand. Your skin is finer than the finest silk. It is a joy to caress you. Your lips burn like fire on mine. Your tongue is eloquent in the language of love. That's more than enough to explain a wonderful meeting beneath the sheets."

She laughed. "Good." Then she drew me close, and we kissed.

After a time, she drew back again and said, "Please, just hug me."

I took her light frame and twisted it. I asked, "Do you know about spooning?"

She shook her head. I said, "That's what we're doing right now."

She formed her body more to match mine and said, "We call that kar-fark."

We spooned for a while and then she said, "Would you let me use the imperious spell on you?"

"Why?"

She turned in my arms to face me, "You haven't made love to me yet. I want to help you."

I thought about it and said, "I think that's included in the agreement."

Her eyes danced, "Only tonight."

I laughed. "As though I could prevent you from doing it longer."

"Oh, contracts like ours where magic is involved have special penalties for those who break them."

I chuckled. "We Muggles know that. We call it bad Karma."

Her dancing eyes nodded. Then she snapped her fingers. I suddenly felt totally light-headed and without any worries. I found that I was going to make love to her.

My body cooperated perfectly. I took my time. I seemed completely without physical limitations. She moaned in time with my motions. We took a break.

She held me close and whispered another Goblin incantation in my ear. It seemed to send me into another frenzy of love-making. Eventually, she said, "You can't imagine how wonderful that is."

"Oh, I think I have a good idea."

She laughed at that and bit my ear playfully. "You taste so very, very good."

"I want another taste of you." I took it and her.

When we had finished, she said, "Oh, I wish I could keep you under the Imperious."

I said, "There's nothing I can do to stop you. You could keep me for-ever."

A tear appeared on her cheek. "I know." Then she snapped her fingers and that lustrous feeling of heavenly lightness left me. It was replaced by a heavy sense of duty. The tears had begun flowing like rain on a sad day. I kissed the tears away.

When we'd finished, the tears had resumed. She asked, "Will we ever be together like this again?"

I smiled. "Only God knows." The night was growing old, but I took her in my arms and spooned her again. I said, "Send an owl in to Gringotts. Tell them that you're sick."

She laughed. "I've never done that before. As long as we're breaking rules, I might as well go the full way."

I was awakened that morning by a thunderous pounding on the door. For a moment, I didn't know where I was. Then I remembered. I said, "I'm up already, Hagrid. Give me a couple of minutes to dress, and I'll join you downstairs for breakfast." I looked around, and all signs of her were already gone. It was a disappointment. As I dressed, I discovered a piece of parchment in a jeans pocket. It read, "Thanks for an incomparable night. Love, J."

Tourney

Ginny and I were playing a game. We were working on a *Times* cross-word together. I never had a lot of luck with them, but I have never given up. We sat at my desk. I sat in my chair. She sat in the old red leather chair and looked at the puzzle upside down. She maintained that she was just giving me a little advantage so that I wouldn't be embarrassed by her getting the most words.

I maintained that it was to give her an excuse for not doing any better with the puzzle than she did. Of course, it was a faux argument. We always kissed and made up with a great show of affection.

This particular day, there was a knock on the door while we were on the sofa making an especially fervent expression of *bonhomie*. Ginny said, "Oh, bloody hell. Just when things were getting interesting." She quickly glanced at the door to my apartment and then to the hearth. She said, "I'll take the floo." At the same time, I said, "Pop into the bedroom."

She smiled and said, "I can see where you head is located."

I thought of an appropriate comment, but she'd stepped into the hearth already and was gone. I went to the door and opened it.

Sissy Brewster entered and said, "Someone was here wasn't she?"

I said nothing and shrugged with a look of surprise. She just walked to the red leather chair and sat. She said, "I can smell her on the furniture. Who do you know who wears Chanel?"

I could claim total ignorance of that because I didn't know what any woman wore. "You've got me. I don't know."

She looked around and said, "You were working the *Times* cross-word."

"I often do."

She said, "Together. It's a brainy girl you were with."

I said, "No more of that. I suppose you're here to urge me to find a tournament for you during Easter break?"

She nodded. "I've been working especially hard. Besides that, a girl transferred here from Durmstrang. She's pretty good at chess. We've been playing together a lot."

I nodded. "So, you think you're ready for some tougher competition?"

"You bet. Get me a solid tournament, not one of these Junior affairs like we've been going to so much. You know I always win them or come in second. Boring."

I agreed. "OK. Just don't whine about not making the cut to the knockout round."

She stood and said, "You worry about the tournament and I'll worry about the knockout round."

△

That next weekend, courtesy of Ginny, I was at an internet cafe in Inverness. She sat drinking tea, and I scoured the tournament listings for something good and close. Of course, I knew of the annual Paris tournament that featured a strong field and was close. It was the last tournament in which Cedric had played.

Ginny noticed my abstraction. She asked, "Got one? Let's go. These internet thingees always give me the willies. It's so spooky how you type in a question and it comes up with an answer that is usually sort of right, but never right on the money of what you want."

I replied, "You're one to talk about spooky. You live with a ghoul in the attic."

"Well. . ." She drew out the "well". I suppose she was trying to come up with a snappy answer. All she got was, "It's never bothered anyone other than the occasional early morning wakeup due to . . ."

I finished the sentence for her, ". . . a blood-curdling scream."

She nodded her head. "Well, I guess I just find it easier to . . ."

"Spend the night in my apartment rather than be awakened at the crack of dawn by a ghoul?"

She glanced at the ground and said, "Maybe." Then she added, "Well, are you ready to leave already?"

"Now that I've found a tournament, I have to submit an online application. That will take about twenty or thirty minutes. Why don't you just zap over to Diagon Alley and do some shopping or whatever?"

She just shook her head. I got out my parchment of information about Sissy to use on the application. It didn't take as long as I feared. By this time I'd got almost all the information they wanted down by heart. I used my credit card to pay the application fee.

I asked if Ginny could help me send an owl to Sissy's dad to get permission for her to play in the tournament. She dug deep in her handbag for a piece of parchment and a quill pen. I got out my ballpoint. She huffed, "You know that that ball-peen of yours does a terrible job on parchment. Just use the quill."

I groused a little but secretly admitted to myself that since there were now quills with a supply of ink built in there was no good reason not to use them all the time. After I wrote my letter, we went to Diagon Alley to hire a owl to deliver it. As always, witches seemed much more easily able to tie notes onto owl legs.

Gold

I was having a breakfast of hot oatmeal, eggs, and orange juice when a large owl swooped into the Great Hall, flew over to my vicinity, and dropped a large package squarely into my bowl of hot oatmeal. At least it used to be a bowl of hot oatmeal. It was now a bowl of manila envelope. The oatmeal was now decoration for my robes.

Hagrid leaned over toward me and said in a loud stage whisper, "Professor, it looks like you've done some'at to make the owls angry with you."

I just nodded and finished my glass of orange juice and headed up for my office. After changing into clean clothes, I opened the envelope. I immediately realized that it was not from the chess tournament organizers. It was from Gringotts. That was a surprise. It was almost three months to the next meeting of the Gringotts board. I almost never got mail from Gringotts on other issues.

So, I set it on my desk and stared at it deciding when to open it. It surely wasn't good news. I shook my head and decided that I just had to go ahead to read it right now. I got my pocket knife out of my pocket. I slit the large manila envelope open and pulled out an inner envelope. It was melodramatically labeled, "Top Secret—Eyes Only". I'd never seen that before.

I slit the inner envelope and found inside the typical things that would come from Gringotts in preparation for a board meeting. There was a cover letter. It said that an emergency meeting of the board had been called for next Wednesday. The attachments were:

- The ever present ticket to the Board floo connection.
- A strange agenda that only had two items: Greeting and Business Issue.
- An exhortation that this was possibly the most important Board meeting in decades.

How could you possibly prepare for such a meeting? I just hoped that I could find a ride to the meeting with someone other than Javeen. It wasn't that I was afraid to see her. I could hardly avoid that. It was just that I wasn't entirely sure that I could trust myself to be with her. Would I make a pass at her? Would she at me?

◿

I was entertaining Ginny with an account of how hard it was getting a lift to Gingotts. She was shocked that I'd had to fall back on Hagrid.

"I'm afraid so. No one else was available. That actually brings up a point. Could you give me a quick lift down to a Muggle bookstore that I know in London? Maybe tomorrow at lunch time?"

She gave me a queer look and asked, "What's wrong with Flourish & Blotts?"

"Well, what I mostly want to do is make a telephone call. For that I need to be away from magical locales. I like bookstores, so . . ."

"I suppose so. Just who are you calling?"

Here was the problem. I didn't want to admit exactly whom I was calling, so I said, "Oh, just a banker that I know."

She nodded wisely. "Research for a meeting at Gringotts?"

"As a matter of fact, yes."

She shrugged it off. "Sure. Meet me here at noon. It won't take more than a half hour or so, will it?"

"I shouldn't think so."

"Good. Now. . . " She put both hands on my cheeks and drew my face close—close enough for one or more kisses.

That next noon I was standing in a quiet corner of London with Ginny. I said, "Go on in and enjoy yourself. I'm going to stand out here and call." She shrugged and went in.

I made the call on my cell phone. You might have thought that it was a long-shot. You might have thought that Quinn was having lunch someplace. I knew better. She had working lunches almost every day. There were infrequent business lunches away from her desk—very rare. The phone rang twice, and she answered, "Quinn. How can I help?" That was her through and through—direct, to the point, always ready to help.

"This is Wendt."

She answered, "You know, you owe me a favor. Maybe a couple of favors."

Of course, that was true. I said, "Well, this may be a mutual favor. I have a favor to ask, but you may benefit from it as well."

"OK. What do you want? I'll think about it."

"First, this has to be confidential."

She asked the reasonable question, "If it's confidential, how do I benefit?"

"Here's the deal. The bank that I work for has called an emergency board meeting. I know enough about what's been going on at the C-suite level that I'm pretty sure that it doesn't have anything to do with the profitability of the bank or any hanky-panky at the bank. So, it's got to be something bigger—maybe even macro-economic. Do you know of anything else that would cause bank boards of directors to call emergency meetings?"

She asked, "Could a merger be in the offing?"

"I'm pretty darn sure not."

"By the way, what is this bank again?"

I smiled. "I've signed an NDA with the bank."

There was silence at the other end of the line. It lasted long enough that I asked, "Quinn, you still there?"

I got a curt, "Shut up."

Believe it or not, that was hopeful. I did shut up. After five or ten minutes, she came back on the line. "There isn't anything earth-shaking, but there is a rumor going around among the commodity traders. I want to do a little more checking. Could we get together for lunch in a day or two?"

I frowned. "Can we make it a definite Saturday?"

I could almost see her slow thoughtful nod as she said, "Well . . . OK. I should have it tracked down by then one way or another. Where? By the way, you're buying."

"Sure, sure. Let's make it the Green Man."

"OK. Noon. See you then."

I had approached Dursley to give me a ride to the lunch with Quinn. We had been at a meeting of the Old Boys Club. Hagrid had wanted to take me. I assured him that he could take me to the next Gringotts meeting, which was coming up next week. That news made him happy. He insisted on making arrangements right then and there.

I had to say, "Well, it's Wednesday. I think it's the same time, but I have to check the invite to be sure. I'll let you know tonight at dinner."

Hagrid was very pleased. He commented, "That's great. I guess that nice lady, Javeen, will be there. She really enjoyed having a couple of drinks with us afterward." He paused and added, "We had such a good time that both of us stayed the night at the Cauldron."

Filch asked, "Did you both stay in the same room?"

Hagrid turned red and said, "Well, not exactly. The Professor had a separate room."

Filch asked, "Did anyone stay with Wendt?"

Hagrid scratched his head a bit and said, "Oh, no. He was sleeping so soundly that I had to wake him up. He invited me in after he dressed. He was alone."

Filch nodded and smiled. He then asked, "Well, well. Did you enjoy having pleasant conversation with her? Hmmm?"

I smiled crookedly and said, "It was . . . uh . . . pleasant. She had other business and left the Cauldron before I went up to my room."

Filch only winked at me a couple of times and nudged me with his elbow. I was just about ready to nudge him with a fist, but we all had to get back to Hogwarts for the afternoon.

So, on Saturday, I found myself with Dursley in my office about 11:30. He took me through my floo connection to the Cauldron. Outside, we disapparated to the Green Man. He said, "Well, I leave you to it. Are you meeting up with a certain Gringotts employee?"

I blushed a little and said, "Oh, why don't you stay for lunch. There's nothing special going."

He laughed and said, "No. I'll be back in an hour and a half. That should give you lots of time."

I was about to go in when Quinn showed up. She walked up to me and we shook hands. I turned to Dursley who was leaving. I shouted to him, "Dursley, come over here." He did. I introduced him to Quinn.

He asked, "Ma'am, It's Quinn what?"

She shook her head. "Just Quinn. I don't share my first name—not even on my business card, which tells you that I work for Barclay's and nothing more."

Dursley nodded and commented to me, "Another banker. You do seem to be popular with the bankers." With that he walked briskly off.

Quinn shrugged. "And why not? You're a banker yourself. I've held off on breakfast so that I could eat a good lunch. I've got a roaring appetite. Let's get to it."

We got a table fairly quickly and had our order in. It included a couple of whiskeys. When they arrived and we'd taken the edge off our thirst, she asked the first question. "Do you know anything besides what you told me when you called?"

I looked over the rim of the glass that I still held at lip level. "Well, the only thing I know is that there is an emergency meeting. They are being very tight-lipped about it."

She nodded. "OK. Here's what I know." She hesitated and said, "Just to be clear, what do you owe me?"

I smiled hopefully. "A great lunch?"

"What do you owe me?"

I frowned, being unhappy about having to promise to reveal something that I learned at the board meeting. "Something of comparable value from what I learn at the board meeting. . . AND, you owe me a great lunch in re-turn."

She nodded and began. "Well, I have some friends in the commodity trading business. They tell me that someone is looking for gold—lots of gold—on the commodity markets."

"So, what do you mean by 'lots'?"

She took a quick furtive glance around, I guess just making sure that no one was listening on our super-secret conversation. "I'm talking about mil-lions of ounces. That's millions with an M."

I did a quick calculation. "That's billions of pounds worth—with a B."

"You named it."

"OK. So, what do you know about who's looking?"

She took another less furtive glance around. Apparently, she really didn't want anyone to hear what she was about to say. Then she went on, "Here's the thing. My sources don't know who's trying to buy gold, but there are a few things that they are certain about." Another furtive glance, "It's not governments. The people who buy those kind of quantities are nor-mally governments."

"Gold dealers?"

She shook her head. "It's not dealers, although there are dealers who are interested in fulfilling some of that quantity. Some of them are scrounging around for a piece of that market."

I said, "If you're buying anywhere near that amount, I'd guess there is negotiating on price going on. Have you heard anything about that? Is this affecting the future's market for gold?"

She sighed. "That's the funny thing. There doesn't appear to be any talk of price or negotiation going on. It's as though someone were just trying to find out if those kind of quantities are available for sale."

I asked, "OK. Who has got that kind of quantities that could sell to these mystery buyers?"

She shifted her shoulders. "Well, governments for one, but, of course, they normally only sell for their own purposes—not because someone wants to buy from them.

"There is always the black market, of course. I don't have any idea how much gold is available on that market."

That made me think of my experience of the black market in gold. I said, "Well, I know one dealer who bought a fair amount of gold a couple of years ago."

She stared at me. "Really! Just what do you mean by a fair amount of gold?"

Just then, our food arrived. Neither she nor I were going to talk with a waitress nearby, so we started in on our lunches. The food was good enough that we made significant inroads before I answered. "Well, he bought about a half billion dollars of gold from ISIS. I'm pretty sure that he ended up regretting that deal. It was really beyond his resources."

Her expression turned from surprise to incredulity. "You're kidding. How did you ever learn about that kind of deal? You couldn't have been involved."

"No, I wasn't. Let's just say that at the time, I was working as a consultant for a major government. We were trying to follow the money trail on someone who needed that much money and had a source of gold."

Quinn was skeptical but was willing to suspend doubt to query a little closer. "Look, I'm pretty sure that I'd have heard about that kind of deal even though commodities are not my specialty."

I shook my head. "The group involved had probably the smartest set of people that you or I have ever heard of. They were very good about keeping the deal quiet."

She still looked skeptical. "How did you walk away with your skin? You must have been reading reports about that."

"No. I was part of the team that interrogated the dealer."

She scoffed. 'Now I know you're pulling my leg."

"Believe as you will."

We worked on our meals some more and then I asked, "Would you consider knowing who is looking for that much gold sufficient trade goods for what you've given me?"

She practically jumped out of her chair, "Are you kidding? Of course. Do you really have that?"

I motioned for her to calm down. This time it was I who took a quick reconnoiter of the neighborhood. No one was near. "I don't know that now and I don't know that I will know it ever, but if I did happen to find that out, would I be in your debt, or would you be in mine."

She quickly answered, "Oh, depending who it was, I might definitely be in your debt."

"OK. I'll definitely give it my best shot."

She winked at me and said, "Do that and you might just get a little bonus besides a good meal."

I took that with a grain of salt. We finished lunch. I paid, and we went outside. She asked if she could give me a lift anywhere, since I evidently didn't have a car.

"No, thanks. I've got my friend Dursley who ought to be along any minute now. He is going to give me a lift."

She clicked her tongue and turned to find her car in the lot. She had just disappeared when Dursley showed up. He nodded appreciatively and said, "Nice. All business, right?"

I shook my head and said, "Ninety-Eight percent business." We went back to Hogwarts via the Cauldron. Dursley dropped me off at the floo connection in my office.

I was waiting for Hagrid to show up in my office. He arrived with plenty of time to spare, and he was actually anxious to leave immediately.

As before, I gave him the ticket, and we took off from my floo to the Gringotts floo. As before, Javeen was waiting for us. To my immense relief, we had no more than arrived when Hagrid began chatting her up. I did have to ask about entering the Boardroom.

Javeen came to the Boardroom door, stuck her head in, and told me that I could go ahead and enter. She opened the door fully and smiled at me as I entered. And that was it. I breathed a sigh of relief. I had passed that particular test.

I was the first one to arrive. I took my seat where my name tent was located. I looked around the table. There were more seats than normal. There were name tents for all the regular members of the board. There were also seats with no name tents. That seemed ominous to me. Were there people so . . . so. . . what? that they couldn't be named? I'd never been to a meeting like this. We were so early that I had quite a lot of waiting and wondering before the big show started.

It eventually did. People started filtering in. All were people that I knew.

When everyone had arrived, there was lengthy real conversation. Everyone wondered what the meeting was about. After some discussion, a couple of board members turned to me and asked, "What is this all about?"

I took a chance and gave my speculation. "Well, I've been doing a little research. Somebody is trying to buy up gigantic amounts of gold. My bet is that it has something to do with minting galleons and . . ." At that moment, the chairman of the board entered the room followed by four other Goblins. I would have said that they were distinguished looking if I had any idea of what made a Goblin distinguished.

Gorblaz took his seat and said, "You're probably wondering what this meeting is about."

One of the other board members said, "We know what it's about. It's about buying gold and minting galleons."

A lot of the time it's hard to judge from the body language of Goblins what they're feeling. Gorblaz's expression was clearly one of shocked surprise. He immediately turned on the four strangers in the room and asked, "Who gave that information away?"

One of them replied, "You know very well that no one did. We were all sworn to secrecy with the Unbreakable Oath."

That answer did not please the chair, but he had to live with it. He asked the person who'd provided the answer, "How did you find that out?"

The answer was that everyone had just heard it from me. Gorblaz turned to me and glared (I guess it was a glare), but he didn't say anything other than something mumbled under his breath that might have been, "Should have known."

He leaned back and said, "I'm going to suspend the normal niceties of board meetings because this is an emergency meeting. So, no minutes, no financial report, no new business except this one item. I will begin by introducing the guests in the room.

"To my left is Rognaroz, chairman of the board of the dominant bank in North America. To his left is Deftel, chairman of the board of the dominant bank in South America. To my right is the chairman of the board of the dominant bank in Asia and Australia, Laurez. To his right is the chairman of the board of the dominant bank in Africa, Todalz.

"They are here because the entire magical economic system is on the verge of tragedy. Simply stated, there is a liquidity storm brewing. It will arrive soon. The first squalls are already here."

Gorblaz paused for effect. I was preparing to ask the obvious question. Fortunately one of the other board members asked before I did. He asked, "What is a liquidity crisis, and how does it affect us?"

Gorblaz was pleased that someone had asked that question, He turned to me. I suppose that he saw this as an opportunity for payback for my spilling the beans before Gorblaz had the opportunity to make his announcement.

I knew just enough to be dangerous. I proceeded to exhibit my ignorance. "Liquidity refers to available money supply to conduct business."

I took a drink of water to give me a little time to think. Then I went on, "In Muggle societies, liquidity crises happen when the interest rates charged by banks and others to businesses is too high to allow businesses to borrow enough money to expand, buy inventory, and so on.

"On the other hand, in magical society, loans are rare, so the main source of money to conduct business is simply the galleons in circulation.

Now, if there aren't enough galleons to conduct all the business that people would like to do, you get deflation, a recession, possibly even a depression."

Gorblaz and some of the other chairman were nodding silently. I went on. "So, that raises the question of how more galleons get minted and why people are not minting more. I don't know the answer to that, but I imagine those sitting around the table can answer that."

Gorblaz took over. "You've outlined the problem fairly well. As almost everyone else around the room knows, galleons are minted by the dominant bank in each economic region. It's no surprise that the chairmen from those banks are here now."

One of them raised a hand and began speaking, "The way that works is that each regional bank buys gold from magical miners and uses it to mint galleons. We buy using our own galleons and then replace them with the newly minted galleons. It's a public service."

Rognaroz commented, "And we take a tidy little profit in the transactions."

I asked, "So what's the problem? That's been happening for quite a long time, I suppose without problems."

Gorblaz shook his head. "You are right, but the supply of magically mined gold isn't enough to keep up with magical demand for increased supply of galleons."

I asked, "So, you've been making discreet inquiries about the availability of muggle gold?"

Gorblaz shook his head sadly. "Yes. Surely you see the problem."

I thought hard about it and said, "My guess is that you don't have enough muggle money to pay for the gold you need."

Deftel said, "Yes, that's it. Magical businesses are running a slight positive balance of payments surplus with muggles but not enough to buy the gold we need."

Just as a matter of curiosity I asked, "What are your main exports to muggles?"

One of the board members said, "Oh, mainly exotic food stuffs. We do a fair trade in exotic metals that are scarce like Germanium but that's about it."

Glorblaz said, "That's the purpose of this meeting. We need to devise a way to buy gold from muggles. The floor is open for discussion."

One board member asked, "It would be easy enough to steal gold, wouldn't it. You just diapparate into a gold storehouse like Fort Knoxville and disapparate out with what you need."

That idea was greeted by a general round of "boos" and "for shame." Goblins are, if anything, very ethical—at least in their own peculiar fashion of ethics.

The one who had suggested that just said, "Well, this is brainstorming, isn't it? It was just an idea."

Gorblaz replied, "Brainstorming or not, unethical suggestions are right out the door—along with the people who suggested them."

There were a couple of other suggestions that were hardly better, like using a *confundus* charm to trick muggles into thinking they were getting more money than they really were, stealing from criminals and rogue states, and my personal favorite—using lepricorn gold to buy muggle money that would be used to buy real gold.

The person who suggested stealing from criminals defended his idea by saying, "I'm sure that I've heard of muggles doing that."

I didn't mention the one case that I was very familiar with involving that. Gorblaz's response to that idea was, "What! Would you have us descend to the level of muggles and wizards?" He quickly added, "No offense intended to present company, whom I know to be quite ethical."

I responded, "None taken."

The suggestion about lepricorn gold gave me the germ of an idea that I wanted to think about before presenting it.

Having run out of ideas from the Goblins present, Gorblaz turned to me and asked, "Don't muggles have this kind of problem? What do you do?"

I nodded and began, "You're right. Money is money wherever you go. The problems with money are universal. There was a time, a couple of hundred years ago when the only money was specie—that is, metallic coins made from precious metals. A rather famous muggle scientist, Sir Isaac Newton was in charge of an English mint in the Eighteenth century. He had a rather different problem than you do. People were shaving the rims off of coins and selling the trimmings while pretending that the shaved coins were completely genuine."

That caused one of the chairmen to say, "What an idea! We could mint coins with less gold in them and shave off gold from existing coins." That only won him a glare from Gorblaz.

Someone asked, "What could he do to prevent that?"

I answered, "Oh, he made the edges of the coins minted in his mint serrated so that it would be obvious when people had tampered with coins. Take a look at your galleons. They all have serrated edges—I hope."

Goblaz asked, "That's not our problem. What did muggles do about our problem?"

"Well, about the time of Isaac Newton, muggles began using paper money widely. The advantage of paper money is that you can easily increase the supply of money."

I was almost immediately interrupted. "That wouldn't work for us. Almost anyone can duplicate printed paper. It's as easy as pie. That would destroy the value of paper money."

"Yes, even for muggles, counterfeiting has been a serious problem. We have largely solved the problem with various anti-counterfeiting schemes."

Another board member said, "I don't see how that would be possible."

I went on, "Well, that isn't the end of the story for muggles. A couple of decades ago, muggles invented a way for people to increase the money supply with an easy way to get small loans. I'm talking about something that you all are familiar with already."

There were puzzled stares around the room except for Gorblaz and another chairman or two. He said, "You're talking about credit cards."

"Right. They are very widely accepted by muggle businesses but not by a lot of magical businesses. They could be, though."

One of the board members said, "Oh, all that paper is hard to deal with. It's not worth the bother."

I shrugged. "Oh, lots of muggle businesses dealt with it until paper was partially replaced by electronic records."

One of the board members said, "You know perfectly well that ekeltrical things don't work around magic."

I had reached the point where my idea could come out. I asked, "Tell me why galleons can't be easily duplicated by magic."

Gorblaz smiled, "That's easy. There are certain things that can't be duplicated. Food—with special exceptions—is one. Valuable metals is another. If you try to, the duplicate doesn't last long. There was a famous case during the 1995 Quidditch Cup. Lepricorns threw out literally tons of lepricorn gold into the crowd at the finals. Most people realized that it was fake immediately. There were a few cases of mature wizards trying to fool others with it. The case of Ludo Baggman comes to mind."

I nodded. I think everyone in the room had heard of that incident. I said, "Good. I'd like you to bear with me as I talk about an idea that muggles have used to prevent counterfeiting of paper money. One of those schemes was to put colored threads into the paper that money is made from."

Laurez said, "Colored threads would be duplicated as easily as printed images."

I smiled, "But suppose those threads were gold-colored." I paused for effect, "Or actually were gold."

I let that sink in to the collective consciousness of the people in the room. Someone said, "Ohhhh."

I smiled. "Yes. It would be lepricorn gold all over again. If anyone duplicated that kind of paper money, the gold threads wouldn't be visible for long."

78

At that moment, Glorblaz jumped up and said, "Remember that you all are bound by the Unbreakable Oath. You would die if you passed that idea along to anyone." Then he sat with a satisfied expression on his face.

Everyone became excited by the idea. Some raised objections. "People aren't used to the idea of paper money. It would take a long time before people would accept paper money as being as good as galleons."

I said, "You're right. It took decades for that change to happen with muggles. You'd have to start working on publicity campaigns immediately. It wouldn't solve your current problem, but it would be a long term solution, I think."

Someone asked, "Do you have an idea for a short term solution to our current problem?"

I shook my head. "Sadly, not at the moment. I will keep thinking about it."

Gorblaz said, "Well, this is a decent start. We should all be thinking of solutions. Report results directly to me. When anything promising comes to light, I'll convene another meeting. For now, without objection, I'll adjourn the meeting *sine die*."

People began to leave. Gorblaz asked me to stay behind for a few minutes with him. When everyone else had left the room, he said, to me, "I had all the other chairmen do an Unbreakable Oath to protect Gringotts from intellectual property theft. I didn't make board members take that same oath because any ideas that come from us, we need to be able to discuss freely. Also, they are all Goblins . . . uh . . . unlike. . ."

I supplied the missing word, "Unlike me."

He nodded. Then he said, "I think that you've always found that we treat you fairly."

I said, "For the most part."

"Well, this idea is worthy of a bonus. Also, if Gringotts ends up printing money, we'll make a profit on all the money we print. You deserve a portion of that profit. Can we say, the same portion as comes from your other inventions for us?"

I nodded and said, "Let's shake on it."

He agreed. Then we left the Boardroom. Everyone except Javeen and Hagrid had left already. Gorblaz drew Javeen and me over in a corner where Hagrid couldn't hear. He said, "Ms. Javeen, please arrange for a transfer of one hundred thousand galleons to the account of Professor Wendt. He's done a great service for the bank and should be rewarded accordingly."

A broad smile came over her face, and she said, "I'm sure it's fully justified. Of course, I'd be glad to take care of that." She hooked her arm in mine and led me over to her desk in a very possessive way.

When we reached her desk she beamed and commented, "Yes, you are a real Goblin in your heart! A real Goblin."

I didn't know whether to consider that a compliment or not. I just smiled sheepishly and looked over to Hagrid. He came directly over and asked if I were ready to go. I was. He asked, "Is Ms. Javeen coming with?"

I shook my head. Hagrid looked glum and gazed down at his shoes. He looked up and said, "Your office?"

I nodded, and we were gone.

Paris in the Springtime

I was having lunch in the Great Hall when an owl swooped down toward my spot at the head table. I quickly pulled my plate back. Unfortunately, it had a bowl of soup on it. The soup sloshed, and a fair amount of it ended on my robes. I grabbed the sandwich on my plate.

Just then the owl landed on the edge of the table near me and dropped a large envelope onto the table. I had my sandwich and my envelope and started toward my office to deal with each.

When I was off the dais, I was approached by Cecily Brewster. She looked at the envelope and asked, "Tournament?"

I said, "I hope so. But then, the last time I got an envelope like this, it turned out to be something completely different. If you'd like to know what it is, and have a free period, why don't you come up, and we'll open it and see what's inside. I must warn you that if it is not about a tournament, you'll have to leave."

She shrugged and said, "Sure."

We walked up to my office. When we arrived, she shut the door. I said, "I think you should leave that door open please."

She opened the door and sort of pointed in my general direction and said, "Do you want to do something about that?"

I realized she meant the soup on the robes. I nodded, opened the door to my apartment, and said, "I'll be back in two minutes." I was. When I was back in the office, I invited her to sit in the red leather chair, and I slit open the envelope. Inside were two copies of several documents.

One of each pair was in French. The other was in English. I handed the English copies to Cecily and kept the French copies to struggle through with my college French. The gist of the cover letter was that Cecily had been accepted as a player in the tournament. It included congratulations, a day by day schedule of the main events of the tournament, and a list of attachments.

The attachments included a detailed schedule of events, a list of hotels that were approved for contestants, and a list of all contestants. She pored over the documents. As time went on, she was not ecstatic or even excited. As a matter of fact, she seemed depressed if anything. I asked her, "You'd think I'd just returned a parchment to you marked with an "A" for awful."

She finally looked up from the papers and said, "No, no. It's good. It will be a good tournament." With that she got up and started to walk away with the papers.

I said, "Cecily, please leave the papers, so that I can make arrangements with your dad." She put them back on my desk and left my office. I immediately got out a piece of parchment and composed a letter to her dad asking for a meeting to discuss the details of the tournament. I caught up with the headmaster at dinner. He agreed to send it off by owl immediately.

△

The next day I was in my office grading papers when an owl perched on my windowsill and tapped on the window for admission. I recognized Mr. Brewster's Boreal Owl. I let it in. It dropped it's cargo on my desk. I now keep a bag of owl treats at my desk. I gave it a couple. It hung around, so a response was expected.

The note was addressed, "Professor Wendt, Hogwarts School of Witchcraft and Wizardry, Professor Wendt's desk in his office." I opened the note. It simply asked, "Is lunch on Friday noon at the Broomsticks OK?" I simply wrote, "Fine, see you at noon." I didn't even have to tie the message onto the owl's leg. He took it in his beak and was off.

On Friday I arrived at the Broomsticks well before noon. I wanted to be sure that I didn't keep Brewster overlong. I ordered a tea and got a table. Brewster arrived precisely at noon. He joined me at my table. I signaled for a waitress. She took our order and returned with a tea for Brewster.

I handed Brewster the tournament registration papers and said, "Cecily was accepted for the Paris tournament over the Easter Holiday. We will have to arrive on Wednesday night. I'm ready to make reservations for two rooms for the tournament. I assume that you'll be there for the entire tournament."

Brewster grimaced and said, "I have a commitment that will keep me occupied until Friday." He paused, apparently for thought. Then he said, "I will give you permission to accompany Cecily to the tournament. I know that you have in you the memory of Cecily and me somewhere. I know you can absolutely be trusted."

He studied the papers and said, "I see that the knockout round starts on Friday night. I can certainly be there for that and maybe for the last match of the first round."

About that time our lunch arrived. I said, "I hope you can make at least one game of the first round. I can't guarantee that Cecily will make it past that round."

He nodded and said, "I'll try to get away early. Help her win. Oh, don't forget that this permission depends on your getting one of your ladies to be Cecily's chaperone."

"I will do whatever I can. I'll get someone. Also, you know that I'm not a chess master. One of those papers is a permission slip for her to travel with me to the tournament. Uh . . . by the way . . . could you give us a lift to Paris?"

He laughed. "Of course. We'll go to the Cauldron, and from there we'll disapparate to Paris. Just tell me where the hotel is."

We finished our meal. As we were about to leave the Broomsticks, Brewster said, "You know that you are the reason that my wife is dead. I know that the two of you can't co-exist. It's really not your fault. However, just remember that I will never completely be your friend."

I sighed, "I know. I appreciate that you can overcome what I've done to your family. Of course, you're doing it for Cecily to follow her dream—not for me." We shook hands.

Foreign Aid

I was sitting in the Teacher's Lounge listening to the monthly teacher's meeting that Slughorn had instituted. The meeting consisted of each department head's reporting whatever that was significant that had happened in their department, followed by Q&A. There was hardly anything interesting that came up. I not only had to attend, but since I was the department head of the English Department, I had to report. The one saving grace was that I was the sole member of the department, so I only had to report for myself. Hardly ever did I have anything to report. After all, the subject of English literature changes only slowly as do teaching techniques.

For that reason, Slughorn usually saved my report for last. This time, the only things that I had to report was that my 3rd-year class was doing excerpts from "Midsummer Night's Dream" as our class play. Rehearsals were going pretty well. Also, my chess club of one was going to Paris over the long Easter weekend for a tournament.

That occasioned some grumbles from some Professors that their clubs never went overseas for an excursion. I didn't even have to defend myself from that complaint. Slughorn replied that if any other departments came up with reasonable field trips that went overseas, they were welcome to submit them for approval which would be given in due course.

While I was pretending to listen to the ho-hum complaints about my ho-hum field trip, a thought had occurred to me. I was going to foreign parts. There were foreign parts undoubtedly coming here. That gave me a great idea about the problem with galleons.

The rest of the meeting consisted of the headmaster's report. He always had a financial section in which he talked about Hogwart's solvency and how large the scholarship fund was. He usually talked about the open houses that were coming up in the next month. Apparently, parents sometimes sent their kids to overseas magical schools. Currently Beaux Batons and the

American schools were popular. He had instituted open houses to show off the school for prospective parents. This time there was nothing new in his report.

As soon as I got back to my office, I got Ginny's special business card that she gave to all of the people with whom she wanted to stay in contact. By pressing your thumb into the Auror shield on it, the matching business card that she always kept would light up with a color that was unique to the person who had pressed the shield. She would then get in touch with them—however was appropriate. In this case, because it was now after both our normal working hours, she would come to my office to enjoy what was left of the evening.

In less than a minute, Ginny was walking out of my floo connection. We walked into each other's arms and kissed. Her conversation began with the following comment, "It's been a hard day. I just want to do something mindless. Let's snog for a while."

We did, but when the edge was off, I said, "Gringotts has a problem. It's big enough a problem that I think the Ministry would be concerned about it."

Ginny asked, "Well, give. What is it?"

"You know that I can't discuss Gringotts problems freely. If you want to find out, get me an interview with the Minister, and I'll insist that you be included in the meeting. Then you can find out without anyone breaking confidence."

She ran her deceptively delicate hand along my cheek and said, "I'll bet that you might just include me in that confidence."

I thought, "Two can play at that game." I upped the ante slightly and she sighed appreciatively. She said, "OK. The only thing that will come of this is that we'll both have a wonderful evening. You won't tell me will you?"

I shook my head, and she said, "Then I see no reason that both of us shouldn't have a wonderful evening."

We did.

Late in the evening as she was collected some clothes that had accidentally been discarded in the course of the evening, she commented, "I'll do my best to get you a meeting, but without at least a topic, it will be difficult."

"Tell the minister that the topic will be gold."

Ginny looked over her shoulder at me and said, "Fascinating. I think that will get you a meeting."

△

The next day during lunch, an owl swooped in like a missile and landed across the plate from me. It extended its neck and offered a parchment to me. It was still clutched fiercely in the owl's beak, but when I touched it, the owl released it and took off.

The note was from the office of the Minister of Magic. It said, "You are cordially invited to meet with the Minister of Magic and representatives of the Auror office and the Ministry of International Co-operation. You will be escorted to the Minister's personal floo connection in her office suite by Ms. Ginevra Weasley. Please be prepared at 2:45 PM tomorrow in your office. Sincerely yours, Pamela Moertl, ac."

I was pleasantly surprised to see the prompt attention my request had gotten. Apparently, the Minister considered that such a summons didn't require a response—it would be obeyed implicitly. I did not intend to disappoint her in that belief.

The next day at 2:45 PM, I was sitting at my desk considering what I would say, what I would reveal, and most importantly what I would under no circumstances reveal. Ginevra walked out of the hearth looking as fresh as ever with a mischievous smile on her face. She said, "Well, not only did you get an audience with her highness, but I got an invite as well. Let's go. We don't want to keep her worshipfulness waiting."

I took her lips, and she took my hand as we walked into the hearth. We emerged in the office of the Minister herself. She was seated at her desk, a huge mahogany affair surrounded by yellow upholstered guest chairs. She looked up a minute after we entered. She said, "I'm glad to see that you're prompt. I want to have a brief chat with you two before we go into the Conference Room for the official meeting.

"Please sit and give me the brooms-eye view of what this is about gold."

I held a chair for Ginny and took one next to it. Both women watched me expectantly. The Minister noticed Ginny's attention and asked her, "You don't know what this is about?"

Ginny shook her head. The Minister seemed surprised and then returned her attention to me. I began. "I need to establish a few preparatory facts before I go into the high level overview."

I prepared my elevator speech, knowing that what I said here would probably be more important than what I said in the Conference Room. "First, I am a sort of a consultant for Gringotts. Because of confidentiality oaths, . . ." I conveniently left out the fact that the oaths were not Unbreakable. That way I would be less likely to be pressured by the Minister for information that I didn't want to reveal. ". . . I can't give you the full picture.

Second, I am here to investigate a possible deal that I will propose to the board of Gringotts if I receive a favorable hearing here."

The Minister stared at me incredulously. "Do you mean to say that you are offering to act as an intermediary between Gringotts and the Ministry on a deal that you haven't discussed with Gringotts yet?"

I hadn't really thought about it that way, but that seemed to be the gist of it. "Yes, that is essentially the case."

Moertl ran a hand through her shoulder length blond hair. She seemed to come to terms with that and asked, "Go ahead. This should be interesting if nothing else."

I nodded and began. "Are you familiar with the term 'liquidity crisis'?"

Both the women shook their heads. I went on. "Well, the brooms-eye view will not let me explain what it means, but I can tell you some of the consequences of liquidity crises. First, the economy affected by one is in for some very rough times. That will affect everyone. It will affect Gringotts, it will affect the Ministry. It will affect the everyday businessman and laborer.

"In order to avoid the one that has already begun in the magical community all over the world, it will be necessary to buy large quantities of gold. That is an endeavor that is too large even for Gringotts. I have an idea about how to bring it about. That's what I'm going to present in a few minutes."

The Minister's mouth was agape. Even Ginny was staring in the distance trying to take the enormity of it in.

I watched my watch to see how long it took the ladies to absorb what I'd said. It was forty-five seconds for Ginny and a minute ten for Moertl.

Moertl said, "OK. I guess I can't ask for more in the few minutes we had. Let's go into the Conference Room. I just wish I understood more about this before we met. There's no help for that. I guess that's why I get paid the big galleons."

We all rose and moved next door to the Conference Room that I'd been in quite a few times. There were already four people in the Conference Room. I recognized the Minister's personal assistant. Apparently everyone else was acquainted with her as well because she was not introduced. She offered us coffee, tea, pumpkin juice, water, and biscuits.

The other three were introduced as the head of Aurors, Richard Ryan, the head of the Ministry of International Cooperation, Melissa Macron and her deputy, Sam Gosling. Ginny took a seat next to the head of Aurors. I sat next to him and the Minister at the head of the table. On the other side were the International Ministry people.

Ginny was known to all and apparently I was as well. The only thing that Moertl did as introduction was to announce that the only item on the agenda for the meeting was to hear a presentation by Professor Wendt.

I stood and went to the white board. I did that for a couple of reasons. I feel more comfortable walking as I talk. I suppose that comes from teaching habits. I was actually going to use the white board to illustrate my point. As I spoke, I drew on the white board various things like wolves, dragons, and so on.

I began, "I hope you will bear with me. The topic that I want to talk about is both complex and . . . well . . . honestly, boring. So, I've decided to tell you a muggle fairy tale to illustrate it. Like all good fairy tales it begins, 'Once upon a time in a kingdom far, far away . . .'"

There was a good king named Hoover. His kingdom had been extremely successful until recently. As with all kingdoms, the common people had good years and bad years. Recently, the years had been very, very good. Everyone was making money.

Then a bad year came. It came because there was a monster ravaging the land. It was called a Bubble—an economic Bubble. The bubble burst, as all bubbles do sooner or later. Everyone was hit by the bursting bubble because it had grown so large. You might think that this Bubble bursting was a good thing. Of course, it was.

But the Bubble had grown so large that quite a lot of people were hurt badly by the explosion that had burst the Bubble. The chaos caused attracted out of the deep forest the wolves of economic recession. The good king called in his economic wise men. He asked them, "How can we best help the people recover?"

The wise men huddled and declared, "These wolves of economic recession are fierce and terrible, but there is a worse monster. We think this monster is in the deepest part of the woods and is forcing the wolves out. We call it the Monster Inflation.

"We must call upon the great defender against Inflation, Deflation, to vanquish this Monster Inflation."

The king didn't know what to do, so he took the advice of the economic wise men and called upon Deflation. Deflation did its grim work, vanquishing the Monster Inflation. In later times, the economic wise men of the time declared that the Monster Inflation was nowhere to be found and the havoc that Deflation wreaked among the wolves of economic recession turned them wild with fury. They became the wolves of economic depression.

What eventually happened to the wolves and the kingdom and the king? Well, there was a coup, and the new kind king did what he could to help the people, but he didn't understand the problem either. Eventually, the kingdom was invaded. The entire economy was turned to resist the invaders. The wolves died in the battles that ensued. and new economic wise men were hired who kept the pre-war tragedy from being repeated.

I finished the "fairy tale". Ginny immediately raised her hand and asked, "That wasn't a real fairy tale was it? That is real history."

I smiled. "Go to the head of the class. You're right, Ms. Weasley. The fairy tale was a retelling of the Great Depression that affected the entire muggle world in the 1930's."

She then asked, "And the invading army was Hitler's, wasn't it."

"Ten points for Griffyndor. Yes, it was Hitler." There being no more questions, I went on to my point. "To move forward to the present, the problem caused by the economic advisers who wanted to deflate the money supply is upon the magic world now.

"I am a consultant for Gringotts. I can't tell you anything that I learned in my consultancy with them, but I can tell you that from a completely independent source I learned that someone is investigating buying a gigantic amount of gold. Considering that the magical money supply consists almost entirely of gold, what do you suppose is the purpose of all that gold?" No one even raised a hesitant finger, so I said, "Here's a hint, they are looking for gold in quantities of millions of ounces."

There was a gasp in the room at that amount. Ginny raised her hand. I purposely ignored her. The other people in the room were pointedly staring down at their feet as though someone had dropped a million ounces of gold on the floor.

I was becoming inpatient. I said, "You might consider my fairy tale as a hint to what the answer is." By that point Ginny was wildly waving both her hands in the air. I said, "Any answers? Any at all? Any guesses?"

Moertl raised her hand tentatively and asked, "Does it have anything to do with . . . uh . . . oh, never mind."

I finally turned to Ginny and said, "Go ahead Ms. Weasley, please."

She said, "Well, you're saying, I think, that there aren't enough galleons to do business, and somebody probably wants to make a lot more galleons."

I nodded. Then everyone else's hands went up. Moertl said, "Well, everyone knows that Gringotts mints galleons. What's wrong with them? Why can't they just buy gold and mint galleons?"

I asked, "A good question. Anyone have any ideas about why they don't do that?"

It was like pulling teeth getting them to think this through. I wish I could just have provided answers, but I didn't believe that I could ethically tell them things that had come up only in meetings at Gringotts. I could help them think through the issues using information I'd gotten from Quinn and other sources.

The Minister of International Cooperation had an idea. He asked, "That's an awful lot of gold. Can magical sources provide that much?"

We all thought for a few minutes, and Moertl said, "I don't think so. Let's suppose that's true. What about muggle sources?"

Finally, she asked a question that I could answer straight-up. "Yes, I'm quite confident that they can. I was working as a consultant for a government a couple of years back. It was clear that muggles have that much gold available for purchase."

The under-minister for International Cooperation asked, "What's the problem then?"

Ginny immediately said, "Oh, that's easy. How would Gringotts pay muggles for gold?"

Gosling immediately shot back, "They'd just pay with galleons, wouldn't . . ." Then he stopped in mid-sentence and said, "That wouldn't work, would it?"

Ginny looked ready to provide a scathing reply. She had been holding quite a lot of comments in during the meeting. I beat her to it. "No, it wouldn't. I've been doing quite a lot of thinking about that question, myself. I've come up with an answer, but I'd like you to work through all the other ways and convince yourselves that none of them would work."

Gosling seemed to think that he had a brain wave. He threw up his hand and asked, "Why couldn't the Goblins pay for gold with galleons? Isn't that what they do now?"

I chuckled. "One point for Gryffindor. That is true, but that wouldn't work. Does anyone know why?"

Ginny was determined to get her two knuts in, so she just started explaining why that wouldn't work, "When Gringotts buys gold from magical sources, the galleons that they spent stay in circulation and the new galleons go into circulation as well. But the galleons that are paid to muggles are effectively out of circulation. There is no net increase in galleons in magical circulation." Everyone sighed a sigh of regret.

Ginny went on. "First, trading gold for magical things. If we did that we'd break the rule of . . . "

Moertl said in unison with her, "Magical Secrecy."

Ginny grimaced and said, "Right. What about confunding or plain theft or . . . oh, I don't know."

Macron shook his head, "All those are dishonest. Have we become no better than muggles?"

I agreed. "No, I hope we haven't become a band of robbers."

Moertl was obviously unhappy at the direction the conversation was going, but she said nothing. Ryan started to say, "What about magically duplicating galleons?" He only managed to get out "duplicating" before he fell silent. He quickly added, "I know, I know. You can't duplicate precious metals. Sorry."

There was a lengthy period of silence. Then Moertl said, "How about it? Does no one have another idea?"

Everyone shook their heads except me. Moertl said, "OK. I guess we're ready to hear your idea. What is it?"

I started with a disclaimer. "Well, I've done a lot more thinking about the problem than you have, so I want you to know that I'm not feeling particularly proud about this idea."

Moertl said, "Oh, just can the false humility and give it to us."

I shrugged and began. "It's really pretty simple. Up until now Gringotts has been the sole mint for coins in Europe. In most muggle countries now, governments mint coins and print money."

Macron jumped in. "You know perfectly well that printed money would not work in magical commerce!"

I sighed. "Yes, you're right. I didn't mean to suggest that the current problem could be solved by printing money—yet." The last word was said under my breath. I didn't want to get into a battle yet over that issue.

Macron just nodded as though I'd yielded a huge point. Anyway, I went on. "There is a way to pay muggles for gold fairly and transfer the responsibility for minting coins to the Ministry."

Everyone, including Ginny, stared at me incredulously. I remained silent for about ten seconds to increase the suspense. Moertl said testily, "Just come out with it."

"Well, muggle governments loan each other money—muggle money."

Macron asked, "Enough to buy millions of ounces of gold? That's unheard of in magical politics."

I sighed again. "Actually much more than that. You would have to convince the loaning government that it's for a good cause. Avoiding economic catastrophes is a common reason."

The room became very silent as everyone seemed to consider the consequences of that idea. The silence seemed to go on for hours, but I knew it was a much shorter time. Eventually Moertl said, "We'd have to get that approved by the Wizengemott. I think there are a lot of people who are proud that we don't have to borrow money from Gringotts, but muggles!"

Ryan asked, "I don't quite see how that gets us out of troubles." Everyone else nodded their heads in agreement.

I said, "OK. I'll spell it out in detail. Here's the way it would go:

"First, the Ministry borrows . . . oh . . . let's say one hundred million pounds, to have a round number, from the English government.

"Next, It goes on the international muggle commodity markets and buys gold in that amount.

Ginny interrupted me. "But we've never minted coins. Do we have to do that?"

"No, just be patient and bear with me. Next, the Ministry hires Gringotts to mint that gold into galleons.

"It allows Gringotts to keep part of the galleons as payment for the service of minting the galleons."

Moertl interrupted and started to ask, "How much would we have to pay for that?" However, Ginny interrupted her and said, "Just let the man finish!"

So, I went on. "So, then the Ministry has tons of galleons and a hundred million pounds of debt. It immediately starts buying muggle currency using the newly minted galleons. There isn't a lot of muggle currency in the hands of wizards, but there is always some. It uses that currency to start paying back the loan.

"Now, the main problem for the government is how to get that new gold into circulation. There are a couple of ways. One is to start a program of public works. Another is to cut taxes drastically. That will get the gold out into circulation and increase economic activity, which by the way, was the objective of all this.

"That will probably increase commerce between muggles and wizards and thus provide more muggle currency to use to pay off the debt. But, there's another way that we can do that. It's a way that muggles have used for a long time."

Everyone stared at me. I took a deep breath. I was about to jump off the deep end. I started, "Suppose. Just suppose that someone invented a way to make paper currency that couldn't be counterfeited."

That was stirring a hornets nest. Everyone started talking at once. Even Ginny slid her chair back and talked with me behind the back, literally, of her boss. "That's not possible, is it?"

I shrugged. I waited for the hubbub to subside. Then I said, "I'm not saying that it's possible. I'm just saying what if it were possible? There are a lot of ingenious wizards and witches around. Suppose someone invented a way?"

Moertl shook her head as if trying to rid herself of a pesky fly and then said, "OK. Let's just suppose that. Does anyone want to say what might happen?"

Everyone appeared to be in deep thought. Ginny was gazing off into space to her upper right. She sighed and said, "Oh, you've obviously done a lot of thought about this. What do you say could happen?"

I smiled. "Well, muggle governments have been in control of the money supply for over a hundred years. They mint coins and print paper money. They expand it when they think it's necessary."

"Sometimes they even decrease it, as my little fairy tale shows. If you could get people to trust paper money—and I admit that that would take some time—you could print money and use that to buy back galleons. Those galleons could be used to pay off the debt that you'd incurred to get gold to mint galleons in the first place."

I was interrupted by Ginny. She asked, "But, muggles wouldn't accept wizard money. Also, paying the muggle governments in galleons would break the Secrecy Code, wouldn't it?"

Then her eyes widened and she gasped. "Of course, you wouldn't pay them in galleons. You'd convert the galleons to gold bricks." She chuckled. "I'm sure Gringotts would be happy to do that for a fee."

I nodded. Ginny grinned widely. "Gringotts has a way of making coun-terfeit-proof paper money don't they?"

I frowned and said, "Now, you know that I can't comment on that one way or the other!"

She laughed. "They DO, don't they? You . . ." She didn't finish the sen-tence.

Meanwhile Moertl had gasped and said, "If we did that, we'd take the control of the money supply out of the hands of the galleon-grubbing Gob-lins of Gringotts! Oh. . . " I think everyone was thinking the same thing that Moertl was.

She said, "So, you want us to get the Wizengemott to approve getting loans from muggle governments. Of course, eventually, we'd have to nego-tiate with the Goblins." She stopped dead at that moment. Then she went on. "That's lots for us to chew on right now. I'm adjourning this meeting."

We all got up to go. Moertl came over to me and said, "I want to talk for a minute with you and Ginny before you leave. Meet me in my office."

We left the Conference Room and went to Moertl's office. Moertl had a few words for the other attendees. Inside Moertl's Office Ginny started to say something, but Moertl came in the door and closed it magically behind her. She walked up to me, threw her arms around me, and said, "I love you!"

Ginny started to reach into her purse. That left me in a difficult position. She must think that she could do anything as MOM with impunity. She could rape me, fondle me in public, and who knew what else. Was it time to unmask her publicly?

Moertl said, "Don't get your dander up. I just mean that you've done a great service for wizards—and me. I just want you to know that I appreciate that."

Ginny seemed not entirely mollified, but Moertl rushed on. "Have you discussed any of this with the Goblins?"

I opened my mouth to protest that I couldn't tell her that.

She just waved her hand at me and said, "Spare me your ethics. It doesn't matter. I want you to discuss this with the Goblins. Tell them that we are in favor of this scheme that you've discussed and are proceeding on our end."

I nodded. She approved and sent Ginny and me off. We went straight into the floo connection and landed in the Cauldron. I glanced at my watch and understood why. It was almost 7 PM. I gave Ginny a quick kiss and said, "Brilliant! We need to eat."

We were hardly seated and had placed our meal orders when Ginny brought The Subject up, "Well, what are you going to do?"

"I suppose you mean with Gringotts?" I was hoping that she wasn't thinking of the affronts to my dignity by Moertl.

She scowled at me and said, "Of course. Don't be tedious."

I asked, "Do you have some parchment with you?"

She scowled again. "Have you ever known me to be without parchment?" She reached in her purse and out came a half-sheet. I took it and wrote this simple message on it, "CEO of Gringotts, I have spoken with our friends in the Ministry and have news concerning our golden problem. Please schedule a meeting of the board at your earliest convenience. Prof. Wendt."

Of course, Ginny was looking over the parchment. I didn't do anything to prevent it. After all, she was an officer of the Aurors and my lover to boot. Ginny snatched it out of my hands and said, "You were wordy enough."

"I am a professor of English literature after all."

She folded it, took the candle on our table, and poured hot wax to seal it. Then she took the ring off her right hand ring finger. I hadn't paid much attention to it earlier, but now I could see that it had the Auror symbol on it. It was a signet ring. She pressed the ring into the soft wax and commented, "This should get some attention to it."

We finished the meal. As we approached the floo connection, she hesitated in thought. I asked, "What's up?"

She frowned. "I think we should get this in the owl post as soon as possible. Let's go to my home, and I'll use my owl." Then she took my hand,

94

and we stepped into the floo and out into the Weasley living room. Her dad was sitting in a lounger, reading that miserable rag, *The Prophet*.

He glanced up and said, "Nice to see you, Ginny, and, of course, you Wendt."

I shook hands with him. He called his wife. She came in and threw her arms around Ginny and then me. She asked, "Are you staying the evening?"

Ginny didn't give me a chance to answer. She just dragged me up the stairs and said over her shoulder, "Auror business. We'll be down in a few." Upstairs it turned out that it wasn't ALL Auror business. We had a quick passionate snog, and she called her owl Cedric. When I heard the name, I blanched. She wrote an address on the folded parchment and stuffed it in Cedric's mouth. She said, "Go with haste, go with care, go with God."

She turned back to me and saw the expression on my face. "Oh, I forgot about the other Cedric. I'm sorry."

I shook my head and said, "Don't worry."

We went downstairs. Ginny said, "I've got some work to do back at the Ministry. Wendt can't stay either." I gave her a quizzical look at that. She just nodded.

Mr. Weasley said, "Well, then, can't Wendt stay? I want to show him something that I picked up in a muggle junk yard. It's like a fancy shield. It has a big A painted on one side. I was hoping he could tell me what it was."

Ginny said, "Sorry, Wendt has a ton of homework to finish. I'll drop him off."

She dragged me into the floo connection, and we were gone. We did indeed land in my office. "I don't remember having a lot of homework. . ." I didn't finish the sentence because my mouth was smothered by a kiss and there was an extra tongue in my mouth. After she removed it, she quickly said, "I do have work at the Ministry. God, I wish I could stay." With that, she turned and headed for the hearth. When she arrived, she turned back and added, "I really want to take you to your next meeting at Gringotts. I'll be available regardless." She then disappeared in the hearth.

I awoke the next morning and prepared for the first and final class of the day. It was over well before noon. That left some time before lunch to think about what I would say to the board of Gringotts. I was starting to write some notes when there was a tapping on the window of my office. I wasn't too surprised. It could be from Gringotts.

Having retrieved the note from the owl, I found that a reply must be expected by the owl. The note was brief and not at all what I expected. It said,

"Professor W, please be prepared to attend a business dinner tonight at 6 PM. Javeen will arrive at your floo connection shortly before that to take you. Best regards, Gorblaz j".

That sort of put an end to Ginny's wish to take me out the door. I wondered who was going to attend the meeting. I supposed that Gringotts could cater a meal in the Boardroom or even hire a meeting room in a restaurant.

I soon found out. Javeen arrived at ten minutes until six that evening. She commented that we couldn't seem to avoid each other these days. I would have made a cynical remark about that except that her body language was open, and she seemed not to have any ulterior motives.

She took my hand lightly and we walked into the hearth. We came out in a room that seemed like any other restaurant. There was a bar area and a larger room that had a number of tables and booths. It was decorated mainly with what I supposed was Goblin heraldry. I supposed Goblin because the majority of the patrons were Goblins. There might have been a table or two exclusively made up of wizard diners, but I didn't notice them.

The *maitre d'* immediately approached us and said, "Please follow me." We did. He led us to a room that was at that point not in use. It wasn't a private meeting room. Instead, it appeared to be a part of the main dining area that just wasn't in use. The lighting was dim, but it didn't make the room seem dingy. We were led to a booth. Facing away from the door in the booth was Gorblaz. He rose and shook hands with me. I sat.

Javeen was forced to sit next to me because Gorblaz wouldn't yield any of his side of the booth for either of us. I had hardly sat when a waiter arrived to take drink orders. I asked for hot tea. While we waited for our drinks, I perused the menu. It had lots of dishes I'd never heard of. I asked, "Since I suppose that you are familiar with the restaurant, do you have suggestions for what is good on the menu?"

Gorblaz said, "I think the Boeff Borgingon is good and if you like fish, the Salmon Hollandaise is as well." The waiter had our drinks almost as soon as Gorblaz had answered. It appeared that both the other diners were familiar with the restaurant. They ordered immediately without consulting the menu. I asked for the Salmon Hollandaise. The waiter disappeared without writing anything down.

Gorblaz got down to business. "Professor Wendt, this is your party. What have you got?"

As usual I started with a disclaimer, "First, let me make it clear that I have not revealed anything that I learned at the recent board meeting. Believe me, it was not easy getting where I got to only using publicly available information, but I did."

I paused to let that sink in. Then I went on. "I'll not bore you with all the coaxing, cajoling, and nudging that I had to do. Instead, I'll go directly to the results. I went to the Ministry of Magic." The expression of disgust on Glorblaz's face was unmistakable even across the species and cultural divide between us. I said, "Don't jump to conclusions. They agreed to a deal that I think is beneficial to everyone involved. Nobody gets everything they'd like, but then who ever does?

Gorblaz urged me on. So, I got into the details, "Here's the deal that the Ministry will agree to. First, they provide the muggle money that is necessary to buy the gold from muggle sources."

Gorblaz said, "OK. When do the other shoes drop?"

"Right now. Because they're providing the gold, they own the coins to be minted from it, less of course, a reasonable fee for minting them."

Gorblaz asked, "And just what fee would they offer?"

"We didn't get into that. That would be a subject for future negotiations."

Gorblaz said, "Great. It's not awful."

I sighed. "That's not all."

Gorblaz exclaimed, "Of course, not!"

I went on. "There's some good news. Taxes will go down, probably substantially."

Gorblaz had become glum. "What do we have to 'pay' for that?"

"First, the control of the money supply would be exercised by the Ministry."

Javeen commented, "That's obvious from what you already said."

I went on. "That's not all. The ministry would like to start issuing paper money. That would make the control of the money supply a lot easier for them."

Gorblaz blustered. "Did you reveal to them that we have a way to print money that can't be counterfeited? If you did . . ."

"No, I didn't. I just asked a question, "What if it were possible to print paper money?' They went the rest of the way to understanding the advantages for the Ministry of printing paper money."

Gorblaz smiled for almost the first time that evening. Our dinners arrived then. That gave him and me more time to reflect on such a development as we ate.

In a break in eating, Gorblaz asked, "How would we work printing the money? Would we do it? Would the Ministry do the printing? We could license the use of the process to them. We could do it ourselves and charge them per bill printed."

I reflected as I chewed on some grilled vegetables and said, "I don't see that there's any particular advantage to either. If you have copyright protection on the process, then whether you do the printing or the Ministry does, in the end, the result is the same. When the copyright expires, if they want to print money, there's nothing to stop them in either case."

Gorblaz objected, "If we license the process, then that's true, but if we keep it as a trade secret without copyright, we could keep the franchise of printing indefinitely."

Javeen said, "Oh, I don't think so. Everyone will understand the principle immediately when they see our paper money. Copyright is the better way to go and the sooner the better."

Gorblaz sighed. "I suppose you're right. It would just have been nice to have it indefinitely in our control."

I went on. "Now, there's something else that I need to mention. I'm not at liberty to divulge details. However, I can say this. The Ministry doesn't have a huge horde of muggle money. They have a way that they're going to try to obtain it, but there's no guarantee that it will work. Consequently, they want an agreement in principle that this proposal is agreeable to all parties before they proceed. Again, let me emphasize that there's no guarantee this will work."

Gorblaz was glum. "Oh, well. I suppose that I couldn't expect much better. Well done."

By this time, we'd finished eating, and the waiter had returned for dessert orders. Gorblaz suggested, "I'm not interested in dessert, but I would like a liqueur. If either of you want something, go ahead and order."

Javeen said, "I'd just like a glass of Jim Beam whiskey."

I agreed on a glass myself. Gorblaz ordered a glass of port. When they arrived, Gorblaz said, "There's another item of business that I'd like to take up."

I shrugged. "Why not? Go ahead."

He looked at me and said, "I'd like to propose a merger. I'd like to see you and Javeen marry."

I exclaimed, "What!"

She exclaimed, "No! Dad, I want to choose my own husband."

I exclaimed, "Dad!"

Gorblaz stared at me quizzically and said, "Of course, I want my personal assistant to be loyal to me as only a daughter can be."

I commented, "Apparently, you've not read *Lear*."

Javeen started to laugh and then squelched it. She said, "I suppose this is a way to secure the loyalty of someone who has been a good business partner?"

Gorblaz shrugged. "Of course, but I know you really like Wendt. What would be wrong about securing him?"

She shook her head, "Do you think I would marry someone whom I've not spent enough time with to prove our mutual love and respect."

Gorblaz grumbled, "Oh, very well. Date him. Have a dozen dates. Have a hundred dates. Let this be the first."

She smiled and whispered, "Not the first." Then she went on. "Don't you think you should consult the man involved?"

I said, "I completely agree, but I think that even before you consult me, Ms. Javeen and I should consult—privately."

Gorblaz shook his head and sulked. "This isn't the way things were done when I was young. But go ahead. Go consult. Leave me by myself to become a solitary drunkard."

I said, "Let's go before he begins to feel too sorry for himself." I stood and pulled the chair back for Javeen. We walked to the hearth. She took my hand a little earlier than was absolutely necessary for use of the floo.

She asked, "Where to?"

I thought. I didn't want to go to any place that I frequented. I asked, "How about a Goblin bar?" I immediately reconsidered that. "No. how about . . ."

She muttered, "We're going." With that we got stretched out through hyperspace or wherever you go when you use the floo network and landed in my office. I suggested that she take the red leather chair. Instead, she sat on the sofa and patted the spot next her. I took it.

I said, "I want to make one point first. You are a desirable person. You're lovely. You're smart. You've confident. You're actually pretty good in bed."

She said, "I'm damn good in bed, and you know it." Then she added one word, "But."

"Yes, but I don't love you. I like you. You are damn good in bed, but that's different."

She said, "One snap of the finger and you'd want me."

"Yes, I've been there. You're right. I suppose I would even be happy."

She said again, "But."

"Yes, but you have integrity. You wouldn't do that."

"No, I wouldn't. You know that Daddy will be very disappointed."

I nodded. "Better that he be disappointed for a while than that you be disappointed for the rest of your life."

She sighed. "I'll tell Daddy. He doesn't have to know the bad news tonight, but I'll tell him tomorrow." She sighed again and looked around my office. Then she asked, "Could I have one night with you in your apartment? I've heard rumors that you sometimes entertain unlikely partners there."

I sighed. She was really good in bed. I said, "We now know that I'm not going to love you at the end. Also, if I agree, there will be no imperious to help out the sex. It either happens . . ."

She nodded enthusiastically. "Or doesn't."

"Of course." I took her in my arms and we kissed. She put everything she had into it, including her tongue. I caressed her. After a while we mutually broke off the kiss and entered my apartment.

At the end of the night, she said, "If only life together could all be like this." We stood, I took her hand and led her to the hearth. I released it. She backed into the hearth, took up a handful of floo powder, and disappeared in a flare of green.

Tournament

We were sitting at a cafe in Paris near our hotel, where Mr. Brewster had just delivered us minutes before. We had dinner there and discussed the plans for the next day. At this point we only had general information, morning and afternoon game times, all the participants, rules of the tournament. We decided to be up early and go to the tournament at the earliest possible time, 8 A. M.

Cecily asked her dad if he would stay the night. She argued, "You could leave early tomorrow for work and make it on time. I'd really like for you to stay the night." He agreed to that.

Then he turned to me and asked, "Have you got a problem with that?"

"Of course not. I'll go back to the hotel, and you can enjoy being together."

Mr. Brewster looked at me intently and said, "No. I'd like you to come along. Let's walk along the Seine." So, when we finished dinner, we walked down to the river and walked along it in the failing light of the evening as the lights of the city began to shine. We were mostly silent. It was a pleasant evening in early April. We were wearing light jackets and were quite comfortable.

Eventually we reached the Eiffel Tower. We walked underneath it as the lights went on. Cecily oohed and ahhed about the lights of the Tower from the bottom. We then headed back to the hotel because tomorrow was an early day. Our two rooms were adjacent. Brewster and Cecily went to their room. I went to mine.

Too early the next day, Brewster knocked on my door and got me up. He asked to come in. I put my jeans on and opened the door. He came in and began talking immediately. "I have to leave almost immediately. Cecily is sad. I think it's because. . . well. . . search your memories. I think you'll know why."

I asked, "Enough to affect her play?"

Brewster nodded and said, "I'll see you tomorrow as early as possible. Good luck. Take good care of Cecily."

I agreed. Then Brewster disapparated directly from my room.

I showered, dressed, and checked on Cecily. She was slow about getting moving, but promised through the door that she would be ready to go in ten minutes. It was more like fifteen, but I was just happy that it wasn't longer. She looked pretty presentable but had apparently been doing some crying. We went down to the street and found a street cafe to have some breakfast.

I insisted that she have something substantial to eat. I got her to have most of a slice of quiche. We got to the hotel where the tournament was being held in advance of 8:30. I was happy with that. The first game was at nine. That gave us time to sign in, find her table, and set up. The schedule that we'd gotten showed that the first game was with a relatively weak player, but Cecily would be playing black.

Her opponent hadn't arrived yet, so I sat opposite her and tried to pretend that I was her opponent. I said, "OK. I'm your enemy playing white." I picked up the queen's pawn and moved it to position three.

She just stared at it. I chided her. "Come on. I've opened. What do you do?"

She listlessly played with a piece and moved it. This did not look great. I decided that play acting was not a great idea. I just put my pawn back and said, "Cecily, it's your game. Play it like you mean it."

She seemed to perk up a bit and said, "Yes, sir. I'll try my best."

I said, "There's an old movie where one of the characters answers that by saying, 'There is no "Try". Either do or do not.' For the face of your father, 'Do.'"

She seemed a bit perkier still and said, "Yes, sir."

I left the table but stayed nearby. Her opponent showed up and reset all the pieces on the board to his liking. It was looking bad to me. They shook hands and waited for the signal to start."

The tournament director gave the signal, and things started. Cecily's opponent actually opened P-Q3. They followed one of the standard lines for a number of moves and then diverged. From then on it was downhill for Cecily. I didn't realize it immediately but Cecily analyzed her play afterwards at lunch. She knew that she wasn't playing her game from the first questionable move onward.

After lunch, we had nearly two hours before the next game. I said to her, "We're going to take a little walk." I led her out to the Seine. We walked slowly along it. After we'd covered a little distance I asked her, "What happened in that game?"

She said, "I did the analysis. What more do you want?"

"I don't want analysis of the game. I want to know why you aren't playing YOUR game."

She seemed on the edge of tears. After a few minutes in which I didn't pressure her she said, "It's just where we are. My Mum and dad and I spent their honeymoon in Paris not far from here. Every step I take outside reminds me of the fact that my Mum is dead."

I let that sink in for a while and then I said, "No one will ever know what that's like. Do you want to withdraw from the tournament? You could do it and no one would think less of you."

She shook her head and said in a small voice, "No."

I said, "I didn't hear you. What did you say?"

She repeated it slightly louder.

"Sorry, I'm getting old, I just didn't get it."

She almost shouted, "No!"

I took a deep breath and said, "Then, you've got to learn how to take a hit."

She shook her head and said, "What do you mean, 'take a hit'?"

I smiled. "In the physical sports—you know—football, Quidditch, Rugby, you get hit and you sometimes hurt a lot, but the players who love their sport get up and keep playing.

"The coaches have an expression, 'Walk it off.'"

Cecily asked, "What does that mean?"

"It means you walk, you stretch the muscles that hurt, you learn to not care that it hurts."

"How can you do that?"

"I don't know. You just do it, and you either learn how to do it or you don't."

We walked back toward the tournament location. On the way, I talked about her next opponent. "This game will be against a woman, one of the top twenty players in the world. You will be playing white."

Cecily whistled, "What do you know about her?"

I said, "When playing black, she likes the King's Indian defense, when white opens p-q4"

"Well, then, I guess I'll open p-k4 and try to get her off her game."

I didn't make a comment. We arrived at the hotel where the game was being held. Once inside, I asked her, "Need to visit the WC?"

She said, "No, I'm OK."

We then found her table. Cecily's opponent was there already. It was only then that I realized that I recognized her. Cedric had faced her twice in this very tournament. She seemed to recognize me as well. She asked me, "I know you don't I?"

I was forced to admit it. Then she went on. "I don't recall where we met."

I said, "I'm afraid that it was in this very room a number of years ago."

"Were you a player?" She still was puzzled but then her eyes widened and she remembered. "You were the coach for that boy who beat me. What in the world happened to him? I expected to be playing him in the future, but he seemed to drop off the face of the world."

I agreed. "He did. He died in a sporting accident."

Her smile disappeared. She said, "How tragic! He might have had a great career in chess."

"You don't know how pointless and tragic. Yes, I hoped that he would become a great chess player. But we will never know what might have happened. By the way, good luck in your game."

She looked at Cecily for the first time and asked, "Is this your new protégée?"

I nodded. I made introductions. "Helene Du Bois, this is a student at my school, Cecily Brewster. Cecily, please meet Helene Du Bois." They shook hands. They took their seats. Neither touched a piece before the tournament director signaled the start of play. As the play proceeded I wished that Ginny could have been here. This would be the make or break game for Cecily.

Where was Ginny anyway? She hadn't shown up last night but that had turned out all right because Brewster had stayed the night. What about tonight. I pondered whether or not to try to communicate with her. How would I communicate with her? I could get Cecily to send an owl. If I did that, she'd know that I was worried. I didn't what to screw with her fragile attitude at this critical junction. I decided to wait until closer to the end of day.

I forced myself to think about the game at hand. If she lost, I didn't see how she could make it to the knockout round. Even a tie would make it quite difficult. It looked like Helene was trying a variation on the King's Indian. Both sides seemed to be opting for caution. I wondered if that might be a characteristic of woman vs. woman play.

However, as play proceeded, I could see that there was a positional advantage developing. Cecily hammered away at the defensive position of Helene. She seemed to want to exchange down to very sparse resources. Was she trying to force a draw?

Then there was a rapid exchange of forces. The position turned into something that looked like one of those chess endgame problems that you see in chess magazines: Can you force a mate in eight with this position?

Play stopped for a long time as though Helene were trying to solve just such a problem. Then she made a move. Cecily's rapid response showed that she had anticipated that move. They were only a couple of moves away from the 40 move limit. I didn't see a path to a mate for either, but after a minute, Helene nodded, tipped her king over, and extended her hand to Cecily. She said, "Tres bien. Congratulations, Ms. Brewster."

Cecily took Helene's hand and thanked her for a good game.

Helene turned to me and said, "I think you have another Cedric here. As a matter of fact, Ms. Brewster may be a better player. Where *do* you find them?"

I shrugged. "They come and knock at my door."

Helene laughed. "Then you have a very lucky door."

Once we got outside, Cecily was bubbling over. "That was a great game. I thought that I'd have to settle for a draw, but you noticed that long hesitation. I wasn't sure that there wasn't a way for her to force a draw, but that move settled things."

I suggested that we take a walk to loosen her up before dinner. I didn't want any upset tummies during the next game. The next game Cecily played was as black against a strong player, but not rated as high as she after her victory over du Bois. Of course, Cecily hadn't played enough games against rated players that I really trusted the rating much. I tried to play down her win so she wouldn't be overoptimistic.

Cecily was anxious to get back to the Tournament Hall as soon as possible. I tried to slow us down so that she wouldn't arrive too early. My goal was to arrive about fifteen or twenty minutes early. We actually arrived a little less than a half hour early.

The game itself was routine. Even though Cecily was playing black, she took a very strong offensive position early in the game. There was a continual chipping away at her opponent's position. He was hemorrhaging pieces constantly. The end came well before the forty moves had been made.

Cecily asked the inevitable, "How does it look for my getting to the knockout round?"

I tried to nonchalant it. "Well, every win improves your chances."

She was pretty cocky. "Just say that tomorrow at this time."

"I hope I can."

There was the problem of Ginny. She'd not shown up yet, and I was getting worried. When we arrived back at the hotel after dinner, we discovered Ginny waiting for us in the lobby. I released a sigh of relief that I hadn't known I'd been holding. We all came together in the center of the lobby. Ginny and I hugged. She sneaked a little kiss on my cheek on the opposite side from Cecily.

Ginny said, "I'll bet you were sweating . . . oh, what is it that you Muggles say?"

I supplied, "Sweating bullets is the appropriate phrase."

She chuckled. "Oh, yes. How could anyone possibly sweat bullets. Anyway, I'm here now. I had some urgent business with the Ministry concerning the golden problem. Cecily's dad sent me an owl saying that he was staying the night with you, so I wasn't needed until tonight."

I groused. "It would have been nice if he'd let me know that."

Cecily said, "I guess you're my roomie for tonight?"

Ginny smiled one of her radiant smiles and said, "We are going to have a wonderful sleep-over tonight."

That made Cecily smile. I said, "Don't forget the training regimen. You girls need a minimum nine hours sleep."

Ginny replied, "Oh, pooh. Don't be a spoil sport. We girls are just about all adults now." By this time, we'd reached our rooms. Ginny and Cecily entered theirs.

I appealed for a little conversation with Ginny before we parted. She just shook her head and said, "Not tonight. This night belongs to us girls."

Phooie.

△

The next morning, it was business as usual. We had breakfast. Cecily played her game. She was playing white. There was a point where I thought she might end up with a draw, but she pulled the game out.

The afternoon game as black was going well, when someone tapped me on the shoulder gently. I didn't notice at first because I was watching the game so intently. Eventually I did notice. I turned and found that Mr. Brewster was there. He put a finger to his lips. I agreed completely, the last thing Cecily needed was an interruption like seeing her dad.

She won her game. She had the double delight of finding her dad in the audience. Again I offered to let them go off on their own provided that we get back together for dinner and the game afterward.

Ginny said, "I really have pressing business at the Ministry. Since Mr. Brewster is here, you don't need me. I'll see you when you get back to Hogwarts."

Cecily hugged Ginny and thanked her for a wicked sleep-over. I would have liked to have shown Ginny a really wicked sleepover, but of course, I couldn't say that. At least, I did get a hug. I whispered to her, "When will you and I have a sleepover?"

She just replied, "Walk it off." I longed to tell her what she could "walk off." With that she walked out of the main entrance to the Tournament Hall. I didn't see her again during the tournament.

Both Cecily and her dad insisted I stay with them. We walked off into the warm late afternoon sun of Paris. Almost all the conversation was Cecily and her dad talking about the games of the last two days.

At dinner the inevitable question came up—what were Cecily's chances of getting into the knockout round? I had been watching the results of other games. It was pretty clear. "Well, here's the story. If Cecily wins, she's in for sure by winning her division outright. She beat the person she's tied with right now—du Bois. So, the tie-breaking rules would make her the winner of the division. On the other hand if she draws, it depends. If Helene draws or loses, she's still the winner of the division.

"However, if du Bois wins—as is quite likely—then a draw by Cecily is probably enough to get you into the knockout round. With a loss it could easily go either way. So, the bottom line is just win."

Cecily said, "I'm playing white tonight, so I should be in good shape."

Her dad cautioned her about making assumptions. Then we were off to the tournament. After the game started, he drew me aside. "What do you think about Cecily's chances?"

I said, "I think they're very good for getting into the knockout round. After that, it's brutal. The tournament is single elimination. Each round you have to win against one opponent. There are two games in each round. Each player gets to play both black and white. It's hard to recover from a single slip—unlike in the round robin phase."

He took that in his stride and we returned to the hall to watch Cecily's win that I had begun to regard as inevitable. We went out afterwards to celebrate by disapparating onto the Eiffel Tower to see the lights of the city from altitude. We didn't bother to buy a ticket to ride up to the observation level. I decided that I had to make some sort of donation to the Tower.

The upcoming knockout games were somewhat accelerated. The first round games were played in the morning and early afternoon. The second round games were played in the late afternoon and the evening. That way, losers didn't have to stay an extra night to finish second round games. Finally, the title round games were played in the morning and late morning. The games were to finish by 1 PM when the final banquet celebrating the Champion and Runner Up would be held.

Cecily's first game of the day was against a man only into his twenties. His official rating was higher than Cecily's, but I assured her that I wouldn't pay too much attention to that if I were she. She was playing black. It ended a draw.

At lunch, Cecily commented that she wished she could just play him again right away. I understood her feeling. I'd have liked to take that feeling of victory into the next game immediately before it waned.

Playing white proved harder for her than playing black against this opponent. She eked out a win. That was enough to move on to the next round.

That next round started almost immediately. Once again, the opponent had a higher rating. Cecily took that in her stride. She played black again. This time, she took the King's Indian defense. The game reached the forty move limit. Both players had time left on their clock. She had quite a bit of time, her opponent had about a minute. He decided to ask for a draw, which Cecily accepted.

We went to a hurried dinner. We had hardly an hour to dine and get back for the deciding game of this round. Mr. Brewster asked what would happen if it were a draw as well. I'd studied the rules of the tournament as had Cecily. She answered, "It goes to a pair of ten minute blitz games. White is determined by coin toss. If those games don't decide it, the winner is determined by coin toss."

Her dad and I were part of a crowd around her table. There were a couple of players that we'd seen before in the crowd. The game looked even at the beginning, but Cecily seemed to have the better nerve. Her opponent's defense fell apart around the fifteenth move, so Cecily was on to the Championship round.

That night no one got much sleep. Her dad told me that Cecily had been up very late studying her game with Helene and was deep in chess references. That made me worried, but there wasn't much that I could do about it.

I'd been afraid to find out who her opponent would be. She knew, though. It was Helene. She walked directly up to us and said, "I guess I can't escape you two. The director told me that since you had beaten me before, you would play white first. Good luck."

After Helene had returned to the board, Cecily told us that she wished she could play black first. I couldn't blame her. No matter what happened, you could go into the second game with hope. Her dad whispered something to her before she went to the board.

I said, "Do well, regardless what happens."

She agreed.

The game was different from all the others in that there was a large flat-screen monitor displaying the current position, and no one was allowed near the table where they played. There were chairs set up but few sat for any period of time. Both players had intense expressions on their faces.

I could hardly force myself to watch the game, but every time that I turned away, I found my eyes drawn back to the board. The board seemed even to me throughout the game. Near the end of the forty minutes, Helene had forced a draw by repetition of position. That was bad.

All three of us realized the seriousness of the situation. Of course, a win for Cecily in the next game would be a win of the tournament. Even a draw was not tragedy, but playing black against a player like Helene would be brutal. Trying to even eke out a tie would take all of Cecily's strength and determination. Helene knew it too. Her expression had relaxed some.

We had an hour until the next game. I made sure that Cecily was hydrated and had visited the WC. I had her eat a protein bar. Who knew what might help her?

She asked for advice. I simply said, "Don't ever give up." It was trite but in this sort of situation is there anything but trite expressions?

They resumed their seats. Cecily moved each of her pieces slightly. Jitters, I guessed. Then the game began. I never took my eyes off the board. The crowd was supposed to maintain absolute silence, but nearly every move brought a quickly suppressed gasp from the crowd. I had become so focused on the position that I didn't pay any attention to the time. When I did, I realized that Helene was in time trouble. She had eight moves left but only ten minutes left on her clock—bad, of course, but not terrible.

Two more moves and Helene was down to three minutes. Cecily's moves came quickly. She wasn't going to give Helene any of her precious time to analyze the position. Helene's clock reached forty-five seconds with four moves yet to make. It had become speed chess for both of them.

After fifteen seconds had ticked off Helene's clock, she touched a piece and then gasped. She had seen something. She dropped the piece and then deliberately toppled her king, extended a hand, and said, "Congratulations."

I was stunned. I didn't notice what the crowd reaction was or even the players' reactions. I sat. I was probably the only person in the hall who was. We were already a half hour late for the award ceremony. Brewster slapped me on the back and brought me to full consciousness. He exclaimed, "She's done it." I could only nod.

The awards dinner was an anti-climax. There were some pointless speeches, some decent food (certainly not Hogwarts quality), and a small trophy. The trophy was a statuette of a queen. It would be engraved with her name and delivered to her.

The one memorable speech was a brief dialog between Helene and Cecily after the awards ceremony. Helene said, "It's been an honor to play against you. On a similar occasion, I told Cedric Diggery that we would meet again. As it turned out, I lied to him.

"I tell you now that I *will* meet you again. Don't make a liar of me one more time."

Cecily replied, "Believe me that I *will* meet you again. Don't you make a liar of me." She turned to go and then turned back to say, "Oh, one more thing. I count on one of those meetings to be the first all woman Chess World Championship."

She replied, "Count on it."

I couldn't help laughing at the mutual hubris even as I hoped that their mutual prediction would come true.

The rest of the day was a blur. We returned to Hogwarts in the late afternoon. We arrived in the Great Hall floo. There were already some people there for dinner. I couldn't eat a bite. I went up to my office.

I found Ginny waiting for me there. She came up to me and took me in her arms. "I hear you've had a tough day. Brewster informed me that he was able to be Cecily's chaperon, so I knew that I didn't have to come."

All I could say was, "Yes."

She said, "Let's go have a quiet meal at the Broomsticks." We did. Afterward, I had a headache and had to call snogging short.

Ginny just nodded and said, "We'll have a proper celebration tomorrow."

The Best Laid Plans

I was having a rare dinner with the Weasleys the following weekend when the owl caught up with me. I had just finished a fine Yorkshire pudding when the owl landed in front of me and dropped a letter on my empty plate. The amazing thing was that it had yet another letter in its beak that it dropped at Ginny's foot.

I bent down, picked it up, and handed it to Ginny. She said, "It's from the Ministry. Yours?"

A glance showed that it was from the Ministry. I nodded and slit the envelope open. Inside was a mysterious note. It read, "Prof. W. please arrange transportation with Ms. Weasley to the Minister's Office tomorrow morning at 8 AM." It was initialed P. M.

I looked up at Ginny and asked, "You too?"

She just nodded. Then she turned to her parents and said, "Professor Wendt and I have been summoned to the Ministry early tomorrow. May the Professor stay the night so that I can take him there?"

Mr. Weasley immediately agreed. Mrs. Weasley said, "Why don't you take your usual room?"

Ginny flung a hand up like a student asking permission to answer a difficult question. Mrs. Weasley instantly said, "Not on your life what you're thinking."

I think everyone in the room knew what she was thinking. I just said, "Percy's room would be fine."

Ginny said, "Why don't we play a board game like Gringotts Monopoly?"

I am not a great fan of Monopoly, so I suggested a card game. I said, "I have a great card game. You've probably never played it but it's pretty easy to pick up."

Mr. Weasley said, "I'll cut you a deal. You tell me what the shield thing is, and I'll go along with your card game."

I quickly accepted. Ginny said, "You two go ahead and look at it. Mum and I will clean up after dinner." The deal was struck.

Mr. Weasley took me out to his shed where he kept the odd collection of lost and unwanted muggle artifacts. Over the years I'd identified the function of quite a lot of them for him. This time, he led me to a table where an aluminum curved disk that looked like a shield was resting. A glance at it told me what it was. What it didn't tell me was how to explain it. But I soldiered on.

"Well, Mr. Weasley, this is part of a costume that a young boy might wear."

He asked, "But what does the big A stand for?"

I started in on the hard part. "The character who uses that is featured in graphic novels. . ."

Mr. Weasley interrupted, "What's a graphic novel?"

"Oh, yeah. Do you know about comic books?"

He nodded a little uncertainly. "They're picture books that have dialog in bubbles that float over the heads of characters."

I smiled. "Good enough. They're popular with young boys and sometimes grown men. Anyway, the character who uses this shield is called Captain America."

Weasley said, "The A stands for America, then?"

"Right."

He nodded wisely. Then I amplified. "The original version of that is supposed to be made of the core of a neutron star or something like that. Pure fantasy. It's supposed to be impervious to all known forces."

Weasley said, "Too bad it's fantasy. It would be neat to have a piece of a New Town star."

All I could say was, "Yeah."

We returned to the house and found Ginny setting up the card game. I looked over her shoulder. She'd written the pairings for the game on the score parchment. Ginny & I were opposed to Mr. & Mrs. Wesley. When Mrs. Weasley saw that, she said, "No way are two people who know this game going to play two who don't. It will be girls vs. boys."

I scratched out the original pairings and put the new ones in. I commented, "This is better. I get to sit next to Ginny rather than across from her." We then began teaching the Weasleys the game. One game includes 26 hands when played with four players.

We were about half way through when the sound of someone coming through the floo caused Mr. Weasley to get up and start to walk into the living room. Before he'd gotten far, Percy Weasley came through the kitchen door. Mrs. Weasley jumped up and threw her arms around him. She said, "It's about time you spent a little time with your family."

Percy looked like he was going to say something when he saw me. He held out a hand and said, "What brings you here this evening, Professor Wendt?"

Mrs. Weasley answered for me. "Well, if you spent any time here you'd know that Professor Wendt and Ginny have been stepping out."

Percy gawked and asked me, "Isn't that like robbing the pram?"

Ginny was immediately on her feet and in his face. "Percy Edward Weasley, I'll have you know that I've been an adult for more than a half dozen years, and I'll step out with whomever I like."

I leaned back and thought, "I've not seen Ginny's temper in a while. Good. Let her get it out of her before it goes off in my direction."

Percy blustered a little about how he was just being a good brother and subsided into a chair that he'd pulled up to the table. He quickly changed the subject. "I just wanted to drop by and spend the evening. I thought we could get caught up a bit on family news."

Ginny sniffed. "Well, you've gotten some of it right off the go."

I asked if they'd like me to give them some privacy in case they wanted to talk family business. Everyone insisted that wasn't necessary. As a matter of fact, the family news except for Ginny and me was pretty much boring.

Ginny brought it to a close by saying, "Well, now that Percy's staying the night, Wendt can't stay in his room. I was thinking. . ."

Mrs. Weasley interrupted. "You just leave off that thinking. He can stay in Ron's room."

Ginny objected. "But Ron is such a slob. Who knows what's growing in that room?"

Mr. Weasley said, "None the less, Ron's room it is."

Ginny pouted a little and said, "Then I'm going to go up and help him straighten things and get him some clean linens and things. Come along, Wendt."

I followed her up with alacrity. She stopped at a linen closet and picked up some clean linen. When we got into the room, she said, "Help me get these dirty sheets and blankets off the bed." I did. In the process, somehow she slipped and fell onto the bed. When I extended a hand to help her up, somehow she pulled me down on top of her. We had a very enjoyable half hour making the bed comfortable.

The next morning we were up before 7 AM so that we could have a quick breakfast, dress, and get to the Ministry by eight. We arrived about ten minutes before the hour. Moertl was there waiting for us. She urged us along saying, "Everyone else has been here for at least a quarter hour."

We joined them in the Conference Room. It was the same team as the last meeting. We were seated without any ceremony. The personal assistant delivered drinks and biscuits as she had the last time. Moertl looked over to Macron and said, "Go."

Macron started straight in as though there had been no elapsed time since our last meeting. She said, "Here's the deal. We have been in lengthy discussions with the British government. We've also made initial inquiries with the Americans. So far, the Brits are reluctant to commit any large amount of money to us." She nodded at her assistant, who handed out sheets of parchment around. There were figures printed on it in neat columns.

Macron went on. "Here's their commitment. They'll give us straight up as foreign aid one million pounds. They'll loan us without much ado ten million pounds at a nominal interest rate. Beyond that, we pay prime rate and they won't promise anything more than an additional ten million pounds.

"That's hardly enough to begin the project you're talking about. The Americans are more cagey than even the Brits. I'm not sure that they'd loan us anything."

That was a head-scratcher. Moertl stared straight at me and asked, "Have you got any ideas?"

I thought a moment and said, "Well, these are just off the top of my head, but I think they're worth a try.

"First, there are at least two other countries that I'd approach—Germany and China. China is usually pretty willing to loan money. They have lots of surplus money lying around.

"Second, I'd work on the Americans more. Maybe if you brought the American Secretary of Magic in on it, they'd be more willing. I guess that goes for the other countries as well."

Macron said, "You've got some good contacts in the States, don't you? Could we bring you in on the negotiations?"

I reluctantly agreed if they were really desperate. Ginny said, "Maybe a delegation consisting of Wendt and me could make a difference."

Moertl turned the evil eye on Ginny but didn't object. Then she asked me, "Shouldn't you get in touch with Gringotts to keep them up to date on things?"

I sighed, "So far I've only told them that you are trying to get the muggle money together. I don't know that it would be a good idea just yet to reveal how you're raising the money."

She nodded. "None the less, tell them that we will take some amount of time to scrape it together."

I was not happy about it, but I agreed that I really needed to keep them up to date. Moertl added, "Oh, and have Ginny take you and insist that she be present as a representative of the Ministry."

That seemed a little odd, but it would be nice to have her along in any case for a number of reasons. That ended the meeting.

When we arrived at my office, Ginny insisted on writing the letter to Gringotts right then and there. We did. It said that I wanted to report progress on the golden project and that the Ministry wanted to send a representative who would take me to the meeting and attend. She then rushed off to home to get it sent by owl post.

It took a couple of days for a reply to arrive. When it did, I showed it to Ginny that evening. She read it with a puzzled expression.

"OK. They want to meet at a restaurant? What's that about? I thought Goblins were 100% hard-nosed business all the time."

I contemplated the various answers that I could give:

- honest—the CEO wants me to marry his daughter.
- Innocent—the CEO likes to conduct the most important business over meals in a private restaurant.
- Ignorant—I don't have the slightest idea what the CEO's up to.

I said, "The CEO has an eccentric idea about business relationships. I think it will be better for you to see it in action rather than have me try to explain it to you."

Ginny wasn't entirely happy with that explanation. As she would say, it was an explanation didn't explain anything, but she was willing to take a wait and see approach. The meeting was the next evening. Everything was as before—same restaurant, same time, same cast of characters (plus Ginny).

The next day, we arrived at the appointed time and place. Javeen was waiting for us at the bar. As soon as we walked through the hearth she approached, hugged me, and kissed me on the hand.

Ginny stared and mouthed a silent "What!" I shrugged a surprised, "I don't know."

Javeen led us to the same back room where we had met before. Gorblaz rose and shook my hand. He said, "I see that the representative of the Ministry is Ms. Weasley. This is an unexpected pleasure." He held out his hand to her. She touched it, and we all sat.

I decided that I needed to clarify some points. So I said, "I know you all have some questions. I think it would be good if I try to address them all at once. So, I'll list some questions that I think would be frequently asked and answer them.

"First question: what are all the relationships here? Answer: Gorblaz is the CEO of Gringotts and the father of Javeen. Ginny is my girlfriend and vice versa.

"Question: What is each person's objective in this meeting? Answer: I want to give some bad news to Gorblaz about galleons.

"Ms. Weasley wants to make sure I don't give away the store to Gringotts. Oh, and by the way, that includes me.

"Mr. Gorblatz wants to get the Ministry to give away the store—including me.

"Javeen wants to get the Ministry to give away the store including me."

Of course, I didn't bring up the deeper issues about Gorblaz's and Javeen's wish for us all to become one happy family.

At that point, everyone except me exploded in shouts. I'd achieved my goal. First, I wanted to get a lot of important information out in a hurry. Second, I wanted to get the other three in the room to direct most of their anger at me rather than each other. Finally, I wanted to keep my integrity intact. As I saw it, mission accomplished.

Of course, there was some reaction to work through. Ginny wanted it known to everyone that she was not there to cheat anyone. Javeen wanted it known that she would never cheat me. Gorblaz wanted it known that he just wanted to fix the money supply as a good citizen.

So, we got started by ordering. After ordering, we got down to the hard work. Gorblaz asked what the bad news was that I'd promised. I started, "Well, because of confidentiality I can't give you full details, but the Ministry is having trouble getting muggle money together to buy gold for you."

Gorblaz asked how much short of enough for a million ounces we were.

Ginny who is frequently blunt said, "Really short. So short that Wendt here weighs more than the gold that it would buy."

I was quick to add, "But, they've not done putting together the money. I wouldn't give up hope by a long shot."

Gorblaz turned to a different subject. "I have some good news, at least. We've done some experimenting with printing paper money. Your idea seems to be working out. There is some tweaking necessary to prevent short-term counterfeiting, but we've been having some good results cutting down how long short-term counterfeiting can work. We hope that it might be reduced to less than a quarter hour."

I congratulated them on their successes. Then Gorblaz suggested that we discuss fees for minting galleons. He said, "We've never done that for anyone else, so we've not got any history to review to help us set a fee."

Ginny jumped into the conversation. She said, "You should just bear in mind that you might not be the only people that the Ministry could approach for that service."

Gorblaz wrinkled his ears. I'd never seen that expression before. I dearly would have liked to know the significance of it. He leaned back for thought. At that moment our food arrived.

I suggested, "Let's eat and we can think about that as we eat." Everyone agreed and then proceeded. When we'd all appeared to be past our hunger, I asked, "I suppose, Ginny, you mean that there are a variety of governments around the world who already mint coins, possibly including gold coins. They might bid against Gringotts for the right to mint galleons?"

She nodded and added, "I think that the Ministry is already approaching governments for bids. However, there are also private firms that will mint coins. We've only begun to do such searches."

Javeen said, "That raises an interesting question. Who owns the design of the galleon?"

We all looked at one another. Apparently no one had considered that question before. I said, "Let's talk a little about the history of the galleon. When did it first appear, and who made it then?"

Gorblaz cleared his throat and said after some thought, "Well . . . uh . . . I don't know, and I doubt that anyone does. We at Gringotts started minting them in the seventeenth century."

I said, "And . . ."

Gorblaz made a funny expression with his face. "Well, a Goblin artist designed the first galleon. It bore the image of a ship—a galleon—which brought gold from the New World. Over the years, various Goblin artists changed the design. Now, it's just a very stylized image of a ship, of the stern on one side and the prow on the other."

Javeen pounced on that. "We could copyright the image and thus own the right to mint them."

Ginny stared her down. "But, the government could design a new galleon and mint all that it liked!"

I interrupted. "Let me suggest a reasonable way to come up with a bid. Calculate the cost of minting them in large quantities. Then add on a profit of 10 percent. It think that's a fair bid to start negotiations."

Everyone except me had sour looks on their faces, but we weren't negotiating yet, and I didn't want to get into those details here. It might not have been above my pay grade, but I was pretty sure it was above Ginny's. I suggested that it was probably a good point to end the meeting. That seemed to meet with general approval except . . .

I asked for the bill. Gorblaz seemed split about whether he wanted me paying the bill, but he didn't object very hard. As the waiter was going to get it, Gorblaz said, "Wendt, I'd like for you to stay for a little while to talk about a non-business issue."

I objected that Ms. Weasley had agreed to take me home. Javeen interjected eagerly, "But, I could do that."

I said, "Sorry, Ginny and I have to consult right away."

She gave a puzzled look and said, "I don't know that we do."

Javeen quickly said, "It's settled then. I'll take Wendt home and see he gets to bed safely."

Then Ginny made a face and said, "Maybe we should consult privately . . . Yes. I'll take you, Wendt."

By that time, the waiter had come with the check. I glanced at it and gave him a generous tip. Then I told Ginny, "Right. We should leave right now." Gorblaz and daughter saw that there was no appeal from that decision. So, Ginny and I got up and headed for the floo.

We didn't come out at either my office or the Cauldron. Instead we arrived at a bar that I'd not seen before. We stopped at the bar and ordered a couple of Dewars and then found a secluded table. She asked me, "What was all that business about consulting with them on a non-business issue?"

I took a sip and said, "I'm afraid that father Gorblaz and daughter would like me for a trophy."

She squinted at me quizzically and then laughed. "Oh, you don't mean it! They can't want you to marry her. . . Can they?"

"I'm afraid so. He wants me in order to secure his empire. He figures that I've made a bunch of contributions to Gringotts and would like to be sure that I don't go to work for a competitor."

She was still chuckling. "And she wants you for . . . "

I shrugged. "I'm pretty sure she wants me for bed."

She drilled me with her gaze, "You two haven't . . . uh . . . experimented, have you?"

"It's a long story, but one night when we got pretty drunk with Hagrid as a chaperone, we did spend most of a night together."

The idea was so repulsive to her that she didn't seem to know how to take it. "You and she?"

I said, "I don't kiss and tell."

She said, "Good. Whatever it was, it was a one-off, right?"

"Yes."

She finished her whiskey and asked, "How long ago was that?"

"Weeks."

"Good." Then she leaned across the table and kissed me. She repeated, "Good." It was.

The PAK Are Back

Ginny and I had just arrived at the Ministry. She had been very closed-mouth about what this summons to the Ministry was all about. It had started a couple of days before. Ginny had showed up in my office in the middle of the afternoon.

◿

I looked up at the sound of someone coming through the floo connection. I was surprised that it was Ginny. I thought that I could count on the fingers of my hand how many times Ginny had shown up during the day. I was up and coming around the desk to meet her before she had gotten two steps into my office. Her kiss was quick. She said, "We've got to talk seriously."

I didn't release her from my embrace but nodded and said, "Sure. Sit on the sofa." We did.

She said, "I'm on a break, so I have only a few minutes. Tomorrow or the day after at the latest, I'll be sent here to bring you to a meeting at the Ministry."

I asked her if she knew why. She replied, "All I know is that there have been meetings in the Minister's Office with people from the States." She thought a moment and added, "and I know that I saw General Parker there."

I thought about that. I wanted to think of a question that could give me a hint as to what was going on. I came up blank, though. The rest of the day I was very distracted. It was really hard conducting the one class I had.

The next morning, an owl delivered a letter into my bowl of Wheaties. I shrugged it off. It could have been worse. I switched to scrambled eggs and toast on a fresh plate. I decided that I wouldn't rush up to my office to open the envelope that didn't have a return address.

Hagrid asked, "Aren't you going to see what that letter is?"

I shook my head decisively. "No, I'm not—not at this table—and I'm not going up to my office to do it before I've had a good start to my day." Then too, I was pretty sure I knew who sent it. I had a bad feeling about what its contents. Ginny's cryptic warning and the lack of a return address was troubling.

I reached my office. I locked the door behind me, not that it would have kept anyone serious about getting in out. However, it would at least keep the idly curious out. I slit the envelope open. The contents were not ominous other than the lack of any detail. It just said that I was requested and re-quired to attend a meeting in the Minister of Magic's Office the following day at 9 AM. Ms. Ginevra Weasley would accompany me. There would be other interested parties present.

And that was it. That was something to ruin your sleep at night. That night I was up about five times dreaming about being in school without any clothes on. I finally couldn't get to sleep again, so I was in the Great Hall about 6:30 AM having showered and dressed. I was trying to enjoy the typi-cal Hogwarts breakfast.

Ginny walked in and took the seat beside me, which was empty. Hagrid was a late riser as I normally was. She dug into the oatmeal and filled the bowl at her place. I had an omelet. She asked, "You don't like oatmeal?"

I answered, "I like oatmeal well enough but not splattered over my robes by a letter dropped by an owl."

She smiled. "I guess that's happened to me once or twice. You just have to have fast reflexes to catch the mail before it reaches the oatmeal."

I laughed. "I'm a man and can concentrate on one thing at a time. At breakfast it's eating, not keeping a sharp eye out for raptors."

She nodded and said, "I'll keep an eye out for raptors for both of us."

No letters were delivered by raptor or any more normal way. We fin-ished breakfast and went to my room. It was still before eight. I asked Ginny, "Any idea what it's about?"

Her answer was disturbing. "All I know is that there is an Auror Secu-rity Team assigned to protect the Minister's Office for the morning. That has never happened before."

I shuddered and said, "Really? Surely, there were guards when Riddle was around?"

She agreed but added, "Of course, I was never there while Riddle was around."

"I guess we might as well go."

She shook her head. "We're not supposed to arrive before 8:45. We've got to kill more than half an . . . hour . . ." We both looked back in the general direction of my apartment and smiled.

We walked into the floo connection at 8:49.

I looked around and found that the Minister's Office was packed with Aurors. Everyone was wearing the uniform with the insignia.

Moertl commented, "Good, you're the last to arrive. Let's go." She led us to the Conference Room which was also packed. There were several people that I recognized and several people whom I didn't recognize. Those I recognized were Moertl, her personal assistant, General Parker, and Ginny. There were four others.

Moertl was determined to get the meeting going quickly. She simply said, "Everyone will introduce themselves by name and responsibility. Let's go. I am . . ." We went around the room quickly. The four unknowns introduced themselves as:

- Richard Baker - assistant DCN, USONO
- Jerome Michelson—assistant Director, Hubble Science & Technology Institute
- Frederick Smithe - Minister of Defense, Great Britain
- Vasilly Roskopf—Cultural Attaché, Russaia, assigned to the London embassy.

After the final guest self-identified, Ginny leaned over to whisper in my ear, "What is a Cultural attaché doing here?"

"An Attaché in the Russian embassy could be anything—a nuclear physicist, a chess champion, a spy, or all rolled into one."

She replied, "I suppose that's why the Aurors are guarding the room—to protect us from him."

"You'd have to ask the Minister of Magic."

Moertl cleared her throat and said, "Baker will do the main presentation. Please start." There was no further introduction of the man, no introduction of the subject matter, no introduction of the level of seriousness. It was as though she wanted to be rid of the topic and end the meeting as quickly as possible.

Baker introduced himself. "I command the communications network for the navy. It was in that connection that I learned about what we are talking about.

"Four days ago, the naval air station in Dallas, Texas picked up a transmission that was coded with the latest highest security encryption that we use. The base commander was mystified by it. Not only was it from an unknown source, but a great deal of it described events that seemed fantastic to him. His initial evaluation was that it was some sort of elaborate hoax perpetrated by someone in his command.

"However, he forwarded that message up the command chain. We are lucky that he did. He might well have discarded it as a prank."

"I sent it to the NSA, which verified the main points made in the message. The urgency of the message caused them to forward it to the NSC. They briefed POTUS, who . . . "

Moertl interrupted the presentation to ask, "You're throwing around this alphabet melange as though everyone in the world knows what you're about. How about giving us a primer on this magical alphabet?"

Roskopf seemed to be having a jolly time with this reasonable request. Baker sighed. "That's reasonable. Let's start off with my position, DCN of the ONO. DCN is the Director Communication Networks. ONO is the Office of Naval Operations. I'm responsible for maintaining the US Navy communication network.

"The NSA is the National Security Agency, which is generally responsible for keeping a watch on hostile foreign actors. The NSC, which sounds a lot like the NSA, is the National Security Council, which is an advisory board that keeps the POTUS, that is the President of the United States and the VPOTUS. . . "

Moertl interrupted again. "I think I'm getting the hang of this. The VPOTUS must the Vice-President of the United States."

"Right you are. The National Security Council keeps them informed about threats to the United States and recommends actions that the POTUS could take to thwart those threats.

"Now, I want to make sure that you understand that I knew nothing of the incident that we're going to talk about shortly until this message came through. I say that because half of the people in this room are better informed about it than I am. I might not be the best person to field questions, if questions arise.

"Anyway, to get back to what was contained in the message, I'll just say that under consultation with the POTUS and VPOTUS, it was decided to try to implement the request sent to us in the message.

"Now, down to the message itself."

Ginny leaned over and whispered in my ear, "Finally."

Baker went on. "The largest part of the message was a review of recent interstellar history. It included the following points;

- The group of aliens known to themselves as the "Souls" have been proceeding on a program of conquest through as much of the galaxy as they could reach at sub-light speeds.

123

- They encountered a second race of aliens who had achieved inter-stellar, trans-light travel before the Souls encountered us. That encounter was one of very few setbacks that the Souls had had in their career of Galactic genocide.
- They encountered us shortly thereafter and almost added us as one more genocide complete. It was not lost on this other race—the originators of the message—that we too had defeated them.
- The second race set off on a program of genocide of their own—but only one race was involved, the Souls.
- That program was hampered by the fact that the Souls have been very clever in keeping their home solar system completely hidden and also minimized the number of conquered solar systems whose locations were documented. In effect, only the frontier of their empire was known to the ships on the outer rim.
- This second alien race devised a plan to locate the home planet of the Souls. It involved us because we had a sort of peace treaty with the Souls. The plan—at the 100,000 foot level—was to turn over a ship with FTL drive to the Souls, ostensibly to be used to research the plague that was affecting planets on the outer rim of the Soul empire. Once the trust of the Souls was obtained, they would give their home world location to the crew of this ship.
- The pilots of this ship, aliens . . .

At this point, Ginny interrupted. "Can't we give a name to this second group of aliens. I'm tired of referring to them by circumlocution. Anyone have any ideas." No one did.

I raised my hand and said, "I suggest the name PAK."

Everyone except Roskopf and Michelson exclaimed variations on, "What!"

I looked at Michelson and asked him, "Can you suggest why I've chosen that name?"

He chuckled. "Of course, you're referring to the famous aliens from the center of the galaxy who are virtual supermen. They were invented by the author Larry Niven. They were brilliant with quick reflexes, great strength, and one serious character flaw. I didn't know of the existence of such a race until this meeting."

Roskopf nodded and asked me, "What are the significant differences between these aliens and Niven's PAK?"

"Well, these aliens don't appear to have the character flaw of Niven's PAK. Would you care to explain that flaw, Dr. Michelson?"

Michelson looked around and said, "Niven's PAK had a genetic imperative to defend their direct descendants above all other considerations. They

124

also had a very acute sense of smell that would allow them to detect these descendants across many generation. Niven wrote a number of stories that showed that despite their intelligence, they only left their home world when it was threatened with destruction. They couldn't leave their home world because they couldn't co-operate with other clans of PAK long enough to build interstellar spacecraft. Most notably, they never developed FTL travel.

"From what I've heard here, I don't think Wendt's PAK have any such genetic disposition. They probably aren't quite as smart or physically powerful as Niven's PAK. Does anyone object to calling them the PAK?"

No one did. So Baker went on with his points. He restarted, "To continue:

- These PAK piloted the ship.
- When they had the co-ordinates of the Soul home world, they mutinied, took over the ship and prepared to destroy the home world in a sort of super suicide attack.
- They were thwarted by the humans on board. The PAK don't know how that happened. Also, they don't know where the Soul home planet is.

At this point Baker stopped and asked for questions. Ginny asked the obvious one. "How is it that the PAK pilots didn't send the location of the Soul home world to the rest of the PAK?"

Baker said, "That's a good question. We don't know. However, there are some speculations. Before I talk about them, I'd like to know if anyone in this room has an idea?"

I stood and said, "I've got an idea. I'll need to use the whiteboard to explain it."

Moertl said sarcastically, "By all means, the whiteboard is yours."

I went to the board and searched for a marker. Moertl shook her head and conjured a marker for me. Then I drew a picture. I explained as I talked. "I'm drawing circles on the board to represent the Soul colonies. They are all connected by wavy lines that represent laser beams of specially prepared photons that are quantum mechanically linked so that information can be transmitted instantly between the endpoints of the lines.

"Now, I'm drawing a square that represents the PAK world. Notice that they haven't set up any laser beams with the Soul worlds. There are two reasons for that. One is that the laser beams have to travel at the speed of light, so there hasn't been time for the PAK to set up these connections. Of course, the other reason is that until very recently, the PAK didn't know where the Soul worlds were.

"The PAK have to communicate by physical messages delivered by space ships flying much faster than the speed of light, but not instantaneously. There was no messenger to send back the location of the Soul home world."

Ginny asked, "When they found where the home world was, why didn't they just go directly to the PAK world?"

I shook my head. "I don't know. I suspect that they felt so superior to the Souls that they didn't think there was a chance of this suicide mission failing. They only had to destroy the home world once. It didn't matter where it was after that destruction."

At this point, Moertl interrupted us and said, "It's time for a biology break. Also, I think that Professor Wendt should explain for those of us who don't know it the storyf of how the PAK were defeated."

Ginny rose and said, "But first, it's time for me to remind all guests here that your hosts don't appreciate our existence being known more widely than absolutely necessary. If you've managed to bring electronic spying devices, you should understand that they will not work here.

"If you attempt to break faith with us, we will detect it and eject you from the meeting without recourse. So, if you hope to learn more from this meeting, please respect our confidence in you."

Moertl then added, "You should have no trouble finding the loo's. If you do, our Auror guards will be happy to accompany you directly into them. When you return, my personal assistant will have the side table set with beverages of various sorts, such as water, tea, pumpkin juice, and so on. There will also be snacks for those whose blood sugar is dropping."

I was glad to have a little time to plan what I would say. Ginny went out with me and asked me, "Would you like to have lunch with me in my cube?"

"Of course." Then we managed to sneak in a little snogging and were off to the WC's.

I returned to the Conference Room and picked up a couple of graham crackers—classic Nabisco graham crackers. I was back before most of the others. When they had all arrived, Moertl started the meeting up again and turned to me. "Go ahead, professor."

"Thanks, Minister. The party of humans had two witches and two muggles—that is, normal humans.". Ginny kicked me under the table and whispered, "We're the normal humans." She was becoming more and more like Minerva all the time.

I soldiered on without comment. "The witches were married to the muggles. That afforded the opportunity for a lot of pillow talk including ideas for how to overthrow the PAK pilots.

"In the end, we had only one workable plan. It was a real long shot. To explain why it was such a long shot, I have to explain that the PAK breath hydrogen sulfide, which is a rather potent poison for humans of all stripes. They also can tolerate a great deal of hydrogen cyanide in the air.

"Their ace in the hole was that if we tried a revolt, they would flood the compartment with those gases. Bye, bye humans."

"Now there were very efficient spacesuits available, but they were locked in a cabinet. Long before we could get into the cabinet and suit up, we would be dead."

Roskopf said, "Seems hopeless."

I agreed. "Seems."

Roskopf asked, "What is the 'but'?"

"The 'but' is that the witches had a couple of capabilities that the PAK hadn't guessed at. One is the ability to disappear from one place and appear in another instantaneously. The second was that they could paralyze or even kill with a seemingly innocuous wooden wand.

"Then too, we muggles had secreted in a hiding place a Glock with cartridges. One of the witches, my wife, disapparated into the spacesuit locker and back with spacesuits in seconds. We all held our breaths and put on the spacesuits. There was one casualty—my wife.

"Then, the other witch and I disapparated into the Control Room, and I killed both pilots.

Roskopf clicked his tongue and said, "Too bad that you didn't keep them alive for interrogation."

I sniffed. "What you really mean is kept them alive in order that they would kill us and complete their mission."

Michelson asked, "Do we have the plans for that FTL ship?"

Ginny sneered. "Are you kidding. They were lucky to get back with their lives."

Baker picked up where he had left off. "Let's get back on track. The second part of the message from the PAK was the 'ask'."

Roskopf nodded. "I knew we'd be getting to something like that. What is it."

Baker said, "They want to demonstrate their planet killer." There was a tumult of shouted words signifying nothing. Baker regained the floor and went on. "They aren't talking about demonstrating it on the earth. They just want to show us that when they say they mean business, they have the business end of a very large stick."

127

Smithe spoke for the first time. "I'm willing to stipulate that they have that stick. They don't need a demonstration."

Baker grimaced. "I'd agree with you, but they insist on making the demonstration."

Michelson said, "I think this is where I come in. They will make that demonstration on a planet that is close enough for us to observe clearly from earth—through the Hubble telescope."

I said, "There's got to be something more. Why are we here if they're just going to do something on the moon?"

Michelson replied, "Oh, they're not going to use the moon for several reasons. One is that it's too close to the earth. There would be collateral damage to consider.

"Second, the demonstration requires there to be a fairly large supply of water available. That rules out the moon and rules in Mars. There are other technical reasons, but those are more than enough."

Roskopf said, "Mars is pretty far away. How can we be sure that it is their weapon and not a natural event like an asteroid strike?"

Michelson said, "That's where things get sticky. They want a witness to be on-board the ship that makes the demonstration. The witness will actually direct the exact time and place of the strike. The Hubble telescope will verify that it happened where and when the witness directed."

I was beginning to have a bad feeling about this. I decided to try to exercise the Zen art of Invisibility. Of course, it was a complete failure. Baker said, "The PAK also insist on the witness being one of the people on the original mission."

I rose and said, "They just want revenge. They're going to drop me on Mars and fire their super-weapon directly at me."

Baker said, "I don't think so. They really do want to have a witness who can return to earth and testify to us. If you were vaporized on the surface of Mars, you couldn't give that testimony."

Roskopf changed the subject by saying, "Why do they care whether or not we believe they have a super weapon. They must want something more from us. They must want to convince us that they can exact a terrible toll if we don't cooperate."

That seemed so right that I found myself agreeing that whatever reason they had for having me witness the weapon in action, it was something other than exacting revenge on me.

I still didn't want to go on this errand. I said so, "Look. I don't want to go on this mission. I won't."

Michelson began coaxing me. "Look. They can travel at trans-light speeds. They will have you back here in less than a day, maybe much less."

Smithe said, "Look. You've been in space before, and you've traveled on one of their spaceships. This should be a snap for you."

Baker came back with a tough point to argue against. "We're on the clock. The PAK have given us three more days to get you to the rendezvous point where they will pick you up. If we don't, . . ."

He left the 'or else' unstated. Maybe the PAK would decide to demonstrate their weapon on the earth after all. He went on, "There's just not time to train someone else and get him there."

I growled. Everyone took that as assent.

By this time, it was lunch time. They had laid out a nice lunch for us. I guess they thought the meeting would go longer, but it didn't. The lunch was there. We were going to have it.

Ginny grabbed a couple of sandwiches and bottled waters and fruit cups. She put them in a paper sack, gave it to me, and dragged me out of the M-suite. I'd been in the Auror offices a few times, so I had a pretty good idea of where we were going when she dragged me down a flight of stairs in the fire escape and into the large open room full of cubicles where Ginny and other Aurors had offices. However, I was surprised when she opened the door of a real office and pulled me in.

She quickly said, "This is the office of my boss who is on vacation. We won't be interrupted. Now shut up. We don't have much time before they take you off to that rendezvous from which you may not return."

All I managed to say was, "Thanks for the cheery . . ." I didn't finish the comment before she had smothered me with a kiss. I participated enthusiastically. After some serious snogging and necking, she said, "We've got to get back." She handed me a kleenix and her compact mirror, "Clean yourself up. I don't want it too obvious what we've been doing."

We reversed our path and arrived in the Conference Room just as Moertl reconvened the meeting just to dismiss us. She said, "Smithe will get you to the rendezvous. I imagine you've already said good-bye to Ms. Weasley, so you needn't waste any time with farewells."

I was hustled off by Smithe and an Auror. We went down the elevator to the main Atrium then through the floo network to a business that I didn't recognize. Outside, we were picked up by a limousine that took us to an airport, Gatwicke I think. An RAF helicopter was waiting for us. That flew me to what I guessed was a naval base. There was a submarine waiting for me that bore a remarkable resemblance to the Ohio.

Wainwright was waiting for me on the deck. He hustled me down to officer country and gave me the cheery information that I was to bunk in with him. In his quarters there was a change of clothes into fatigues that might have been US Army and several changes of underwear.

The captain stuck his head in our quarters and said, "Ready?"

Wainwright agreed. The captain left. There were sounds that I guessed were undocking, and we were moving. Wainwright commented, "We're going to be going to the rendezvous at flank speed. The captain wants to be there at least twelve hours early, but he'd prefer being a full day early."

I supposed that the rendezvous point was the same as the last time that we'd met with the Souls, but no one would admit that that was true or false.

Wainwright seemed to be assigned to me as my personal servant. He never left my side except when I went to the head. Where he thought I could get to on-board this ship I couldn't imagine. I engaged him in conversations but they never strayed away from topics like what the Cubs were doing this season or who was going to win the college football championship.

Incidentally, the Cubs were doing awful. Alabama was going to win the national championship.

After about thirty hours cruising at flank speed (I suppose), we came to a stop. Wainwright took a call from the bridge. We were on station more than twenty-four hours ahead of the rendezvous.

I asked him, "Now that we're here, can you please tell me what you know about this mission."

His answer was a curt. "No." Then he smiled, "But, maybe I will tell you what I don't know about this mission.

"I don't know with whom we are rendezvousing. I don't know if this is a one-way trip for us or whether we're supposed to pick you up at some point. I don't know what your mission is.

"Incidentally, if I don't have a chance to say so later, best of luck."

The next thirty or so hours went easier. We had made our rendezvous time and place. The captain came down and wished me his best as well. I taught them Back Alley Bridge, and we played cut-throat. Apparently, no one else on board could see me. I didn't even see the cook or any other officers.

The captain admitted that he felt useless. "All I have to do is make sure that we stay on station with the radio mast up. The navigator and "sparks" can do that."

The clock had counted down to one hour before rendezvous.

Wainwright took me up to the conning tower. On the way, he said, "There's one thing that I am allowed to tell you now that I couldn't before. You won't need a change of clothes. You can go just as you are. Except for one thing. Empty your pockets."

A moment of panic went through my body. Then I emptied my pockets —pocket knife, handkerchief, purse. I tried to be as casual as I could. Maybe Wainwright would figure that the flat purse was empty and let me keep it. No luck. He wouldn't even let me keep the Kleenex.

The rest of the hour was torture. I just wanted it to be over. Eventually, the captain came down and said, "They're here. Good luck."

Wainwright took me outside on the deck. A vehicle that was pretty indistinguishable from the other one that I'd traveled in before was hovering over the deck of the sub. A ramp lowered. It was about an inch above the deck. I stepped up and walked into the ship. It was just like the other ship on the inside as well. There was one difference. No one was on-board. The ramp closed, and I went to the Conference Room to sit.

The monitor showed the surface of the sea and at first the sub. It rapidly decreased in size and shortly disappeared. The intercom came on, and a voice said, "Put on a spacesuit. Make sure it's sealed well." I assumed that the spacesuits were in the locker from before. They were.

After I put it on, and the self-check assured me that it was safe for outer space, a voice came on the monitor. It said, "The ramp of your ship will open. Your ship will flood with hydrogen sulfide. From here on out you will keep you spacesuit on. Please come down the ramp and follow the crew-man."

I obeyed the orders. The area we were in was like a large bay in an aircraft carrier. We walked to the end of it, went through a hatch and entered into a much more confined space. It was a corridor. After a turn we reached a hatch. It opened. My guide motioned me in. Inside, was a much larger Control Room than in my ship.

In it were a number of workstations that reminded me of a photo that I'd once seen of NASA mission control. Instead of a large monitor at one end of the room, there was what looked like a simple curved window. It commanded an impressive view of Mars. I was met by another of the aliens. The first had been in a spacesuit like mine. This one was dressed in what might have been the equivalent of fatigues. There were three other aliens in the room sitting at monitors.

He spoke, and the translation sounded in my helmet. "Welcome. We are in position for the demonstration." He paused and seemed to reconsider. "First, let's walk down to the weapons bay and view the armament we're going to demo." I almost laughed at the translator's use of colloquial English. He led the way back to the hatch that gave access to the corridor. We walked down a different path, took a flight of stairs to a different deck, and went through another hatch to a much more confined space.

Inside it were a dozen objects mounted on a rectangular holder. My guide walked to one and patted it much the same way that I patted my dog

131

when I was a boy growing up in Ohio. He said, "Come take a closer look. He pointed at different parts of the missile. "The front and rear sections are propulsion. The forward propulsion unit also doubles as the weapon's . . . uh . . ."

I supplied a word, "Warhead?"

He nodded in agreement. "Yes, that's a good word. The center section is the brains of the weapon."

I noticed that there were some sort of markings that I guessed were in the alien's language. I pointed and asked, "Does that say, 'Handle with care'?"

He made a discordant sound that got translated in my helmet as something like human laughter. He then said, "No, that one says, 'Dear John'. The one above it says, 'Hi there!'"

I stared at him and asked, "You know Dr. Strangelove?"

That seemed to puzzle him for about a second and then he said, "Oh, you mean the video. Yes, I do. We have studied your culture for quite a while before approaching you. My field of expertise is Science Fiction and Fantasy."

I replied, "Then we have something in common. My field is English literature."

The alien, whom I had decided to call Larry, twisted his head and said, "I thought you were an astronaut."

"I guess I am now. That wasn't my vocation."

He shook his head in a strange angular circuit and said, "In that case, I will tell you that I think that Steven King is the best novelist in the English language."

This bizarre conversation hadn't ended yet. I said, "I think a lot of people would suggest Jane Austen for that title."

Larry laughed again and said, "I know. Our specialist in serious literature would agree with you. I have the occasional argument with him about that point."

To bring the conversation back to earth, so to speak, I asked a serious question, "You seem to regard this monstrosity with pride."

He laughed. "Oh my! I've got to say that you remind me of one of those characters in Steven King who kills with humor."

"Right. Much better than killing with a missile."

He actually bent over with laughter, "You kill me." He broke out into laughter again.

I mumbled, "I only wish I did."

"Stop! Stop! I think you are that guy."

He looked directly at me and said, "I do. I didn't invent it. That is not my field, but I wish I had. You've seen the weapon that we will demo today.

It's 'Hi there!'" Then we returned to the Control Room. On the way, he commented, "The shuttle that you flew up to this ship will be the weapon that we use to destroy the Soul's world. We've done a lot of work since you flew in the other model. We've used weapons tests to validate simulation models of the way that these weapons interact with planet atmospheres and stellar atmospheres. We're quite sure now that the ship you flew in can initiate an extremely high yield nova."

What was there left to say? We reached the main Control Room. He led me over to an empty workstation. The monitor flashed to life. He said something that the translator didn't handle, and a view of the southern hemisphere of Mars appeared. It was natural color except for an irregular region right around the pole. That area was green.

Larry said, "You can use your finger to select a target point for the weapon. When you touch it, a cross will appear. Go ahead and try it. Pick a spot in the green."

I did. A faint blue cross appeared. Larry said, "You can drag that cross around to position it exactly where you want it."

I grumbled. "I can barely see it."

Larry was silent for a moment and then said, "Of course, different color sensitivities. Wait a second, I'll make a change to the targeting system profile." His fingers flew over a corner of the screen. Different profile boxes showed up and disappeared more quickly than I could see them. Then the small cross was red. He asked, "Better?"

"Perfect!" I said with bitterness.

It was not translated perfectly. Larry smiled and said, "We mean to please." He then went into instructions for firing the weapon. "Once you're satisfied with the target point, just double-tap the cross when you' want to fire the missile."

This time, I looked carefully. I touched the cross and dragged it near the edge of the green area. I was about to double-tap it when Larry said, "Good choice. It will be interesting to see what happens.

"You are quite close to the edge of the subterranean ice. The weapon is much more effective where there is a lot of hydrogen. Fire when ready. Take as much time as you like."

I intended to take my time. I watched the display rotate the image as Mars rotated on its axis. My selected point stayed where it was on the surface. I wished they had left me my watch. I had to estimate time by the rotation of Mars. Eventually, I double-tapped the red cross. For about two seconds I thought nothing had happened.

Then my eyes were attracted up to the real window. There was a momentary blast of light. The window almost instantaneously darkened, but I could still see an intense bright ball of fire rising slowly. There seemed to be a shock wave that swept rapidly across the surface. I glanced down at the monitor in front of me. It showed in colors. The shock wave was much clearer and the ball of fire had different colors in it.

Meanwhile several of the other aliens came over to Larry. I heard various comments, such as: "congratulations", "stupendous", "Wonderful", and he said, simply, "Isn't it beautiful?"

I thought about giving him my opinion, which would have featured words like: hideous, grotesque, horrendous. Finally, I said, "I suppose you're proud of this monstrosity you've created."

He simply said, "I didn't create it. I tested it. Let's take you home." We walked back to the hangar bay. "The pilot will take you back where your people are waiting for you. When you arrive, he'll open the ship to the exterior. The atmosphere will exhaust at high altitudes. By the time you reach the sea level, the atmosphere ought to be earth-normal. You can take off the suit. Please leave it in the ship."

That was it. I sat in the Conference Room and watched Mars disappear from the screen as though the test had completely destroyed the planet. A moment later, the Earth was growing larger in the screen. When the sphere had expanded to fill the screen completely, I heard the scream of air escaping from the ship. The suit adjusted to the lower pressure. Then I saw the Ohio appear as hardly more than a dot. It expanded until it filled much of the screen. By this time, I was taking off the suit.

The ramp lowered, and I exited. Wainwright was waiting for me. He actually hugged me. "I had no idea if you'd ever return. The Souls, bless their hearts, were a known quantity. You could trust their promises if given straight up to you. On the other hand, these PAK are a total unknown. I was afraid that they would kill you to keep them unknown."

We went into the tower. The captain shook my hand and said, "Thanks for your courage. Now, there's a helicopter coming for you. It will be here within a half hour. You might as well stay up here." Indeed, I could already hear a helicopter approaching. It had pontoons. It landed on the deck and I was hustled in. Just before the hatch on the helicopter shut, Wainwright reached in with a paper bag. He handed it to me and said, "Your stuff. Good luck."

I put on the headphones but nobody had anything to say except that the pilot spoke a few indecipherable words to the control tower of the aircraft carrier on which we landed. I was hustled into a small cargo plane, and we were in the air before I even learned what ship I'd been on. I was pretty sure it was Brit.

We landed at Heathrow, where I was hustled—paper bag and all—into a 747. I wondered what would happen wherever we were going. They'd dropped a boarding pass into my hand. I was in coach. I didn't mind that. I minded that the name on the boarding pass wasn't Wendt. It was somebody named Wilkie or maybe Wilkin. The last letter was smudged. The destination was Kennedy.

There was a news show available on the monitor in the seat arm. I put on the headphones and listened. The third item up was something about an asteroid that had hit Mars. There was a photo of the area taken by one of the satellites orbiting Mars. The news woman said something like, "There was a surprise collision today between a huge asteroid that had come from interstellar space to hit Mars. It almost missed it, striking a glancing blow near the South Pole of Mars. We have the director of the Hubble Institute here to tell us more about it."

And doggone it if Michelson didn't appear on the screen. He was asked a question about how NASA had missed such a large asteroid, since there had been no warning of its arrival.

Michelson, bless him, was prepared for that question. He said, "Well, Maureen, it's pretty simple. All of our efforts at finding asteroids are directed at the plain of the ecliptic, that is the line in the sky where all the planets are concentrated. Nearly all asteroids and comets come from some direction along the ecliptic. From the angle of incidence and the size of the resulting crater we've estimated the speed, energy, and makeup of the asteroid. It was twenty kilometers (that's about twelve miles) across. It was what we call a stony asteroid. It was traveling at several times the escape velocity of the Solar System. So, it was definitely from far outside the Solar System."

Maureen asked what were the chances that such a fluke asteroid would hit the Earth. Michelson cracked a small smile and said, "Very small. You might even say astronomically small." I had heard all that I wanted to know about it. I was sure that wherever I was going, I'd know a lot more than Maureen had gotten out of Michelson.

We arrived at Kennedy. Before the seat belt sign was turned off, the captain came on to say, "Would everyone please stay in their seats? The sky marshals are going to accompany a passenger off the plane before anyone else."

A sky marshal did appear, wielding his shield. He walked straight to my row and said, "Mr. Wilkin, please accompany me." I nodded and squirmed over a couple of passengers. We went to the front of the plane where first-class passengers were being jostled out of the way. In the jetway, the sky marshal opened a door that led to a stair down to the tarmac. The marshal said, "The FBI is waiting for you down there."

Sure enough, when I got to the tarmac, there were two men in dark suits. One flashed an ID for about three tenths of a second and hustled me into the back seat. I asked, "Where are we going?"

The driver turned on the siren and we were quickly on a freeway. The agent who wasn't driving said, "We're going to the nearest AMTRACK station where you'll board a train for Washington. Here's your ticket." He handed me a ticket that didn't have a seat assignment. "When you get off, take the Metro to the Pentagon station."

I asked, "Do you have a subway ticket for me?"

He just stared at me and said, "Don't you have money or a credit card with you?"

Of course, I did. It was all in my purse in my pants in the paper sack that I was still clutching in my right hand for dear life.

The FBI agent asked, "Are you military?"

"No."

"Then get out of those fatigues as soon as possible."

I was ready to give him a piece of my mind about the last ten hours, when I'd been picked up by an alien space ship. That was beyond his pay grade though.

They dropped me off at a small train station in the suburbs. I had to wait a half hour but then I was on the train and well on my way to the Pentagon. In the train station, I went to the men's room and changed in a stall into the jeans and dress shirt that I'd been wearing four days before. Most important, I got into my purse and retrieved some money and my credit card. Of course, the money was all English (and wizard), but having a little in my pocket made me feel better. I used the credit card to buy a Metro day pass.

The ride on the Metro to the Pentagon was the easiest and most pleasant of the whole trip to Mars and back. When I arrived at the Pentagon, I almost walked past my reception committee. They were expecting someone in fatigues, I guess. They ushered me through security quicker than I'd ever gotten through security anywhere. They had already made me an "all access" ID badge using a recent photo. It was waiting for me at the guard desk. Once I was wearing that on a lanyard, I felt like the world was my oyster.

I was conducted to a Conference Room a couple of floors up. It had a view of the courtyard. We arrived at about ten minutes to the hour of three. By three o'clock, there were a dozen name tents set up, and I was one of them. Their owners followed quickly. Michelson and Baker were there. So were the Secretary of Defense, the undersecretary of State for foreign technology. There was a representative of each of the services. Someone from the NSA and the CIA were there. Some old friends were there too. Ballard of the National Science Foundation was there. The FBI was represented by Phil Harris. There were a couple of others.

The Secretary of Defense seemed to be chairing the meeting. He handed out a short agenda for the meeting. The critical points were first a presentation by Michelson about the weapon demonstration. Then came my presentation. I laughed to myself. How much sleep had I gotten in the last 48 hours? Maybe a couple.

Michelson started off by handing out several photos, which were also displayed on an overhead projector. He said, "These are sets of photos of the event. The first is twenty-four hours before the demonstration.

"Pay particular attention to the circled area, the site of the test. What do you notice?"

There was a low mumble of noise. Someone said sheepishly, 'Nothing. It's plain white."

Michelson agreed, "Right. There's nothing there but CO_2 and water ice. It's pretty close to flat as a pancake. Now look at the second photo. This was taken by Hubble shortly after the demonstration. It's at a very much lower resolution, but all you can see is a vast fireball.

He changed to the third slide. He said, "This was taken by Hubble about six hours after the demonstration. What do you see now?"

Everyone chimed in, "A big crater."

"It's approximately two hundred kilometers across."

Someone said, "There's a mountain in the middle."

Michelson smiled, "Right. That's a common feature of large impact craters. I'd say that the test was a success. The only question is whether there is any doubt that it could actually have been caused by an asteroid strike rather than the PAK's weapon. That's where we need Professor Wendt's help."

I could recognize a cue that obvious when I heard it, so I started in without preamble. "I was present on the ship when the missile was fired. As a matter of fact, I chose the exact spot and the time when it was fired."

Someone interrupted. "Could they have influenced those choices?"

"I don't think so. I made them, and I tried to randomize the time and place of impact."

There was silence. Then Ballard asked, "You said that the weapon was a missile. How did you know that?"

I took a deep breath. "They showed me the weapon that they said that they were going to fire. I can't guarantee that they were telling the truth, but I don't see any particular reason to doubt them.

"It looked like a missile. They told me that propulsion was in the front AND rear. Also, they said that the front contained the weapon itself. The middle contained computers and software for guidance and so forth."

The Secretary of Defense asked if there were any chance that I could be mistaken. I shook my head. "No. I believe them. Also, they had at least another ten or so weapons on board."

That caused another lengthy silence. I broke it by saying, "Oh, one last thing. The ship that picked me up was a duplicate of the one that flew me to the Soul's home planet.

"They intended to use that original ship to destroy the home planet of the Souls. The ship in which I flew a couple of days ago rendezvoused with a much larger FTL ship. They told me that it was their intention to use the duplicate ship to carry out the attack on the home world of the Souls. They also said that the weapons development they've done since the failed attempt on the Soul's home world gave them a better prediction capability for the power of these weapons. They were sure that they could destroy the entire solar system of the Souls."

The Secretary of Defense looked around and said, "Any further questions for Professor Wendt?" No one had any. Then the Secretary told me. "We want you to stay for a couple of days for a complete debriefing. Then we'll return you to England." I was doubtful that they'd finish so quickly, but we'd see.

The next two days were intense. If they didn't get every bit of information I had, it sure wasn't for lack of trying. I began to feel like I was a criminal being interrogated or maybe a prisoner of war being tortured.

The ordeal did finally end.

Heathrow Again

I was put on a plane to Heathrow with my passport stamped with an entry visa that was backdated to my real entry into the country. I would have liked to inform someone that I was returning so that I could be met at the airport. The Americans were having none of it. I got off the plane in the early morning in England.

I decided that the best I could do was to send a letter to the London letter drop for mail to wizards from muggles. I took the Tube to my old neighborhood just to see if my old landlord might have my old garret apartment available.

I found the building with little trouble. When I knocked on the door, it was answered by an old friend. She was Pamela from my first year in England. I didn't recognize her at first, and she didn't recognize me, but as I told her that I wanted the old apartment where I'd used to stay, she gasped and said, "You're James Wendt."

I plead guilty to the charge and said, "And you're Pamela. What in the world has happened to you since we were last here together?"

She said, "Just what I was going to ask you. The answer about the apartment is that our landlord sold the building, and there is a new landlord. After trying to rent it for a couple of months, he gave up and decided to use it as storage for his things. But, let's go have dinner and catch up on old times."

I couldn't help but agree. I said, "Let me take you out to dinner at a really nice restaurant, and we can talk until we're both exhausted."

She looked at my clothes that I'd worn for at least three days and said, "Are you sure that any nice restaurant would let you in?"

"Don't let the externals fool you. I'll get us in somewhere. I'll have some new clothes, too. I'll stop in and buy new jeans, a new shirt, and what the heck, a new pair of shoes too."

She laughed and said, "Pick me up at six?"

"Sure."

I called a cab on my infrequently used cell phone. I had them take me to Harrods. I bought a new wardrobe, including new shoes. I wore my purchase out of the store, stuffing everything else into a Harrad's shopping bag. Then I went by cab to the nicest hotel in the area and checked in. I guess the Harrad's bag stood in for a suitcase.

Then I showered and went down to the lobby to buy a *Times of London* to see what the world was making of the Mars asteroid. Apparently, not much. The follow-up to the incident had receded to the last page of the main section. It occupied about five column-inches. There wasn't anything new in the report. Apparently, the cover story was holding up pretty well.

I almost missed my appointment with Pamela. I'd gotten so intrigued by the *Times*, which I'd not seen in a week, that I only barely caught a cab in time to reach Pamela's five minutes late. When I rang the door, she opened it immediately and said, "I was beginning to think that you would stand me up."

My face fell. She quickly assured me, "Just kidding. Five minutes late isn't bad. Where are we going?"

"Pick a spot, any spot. And when I say 'any', I mean 'any—in the world'."

She laughed. "Well, I limit us to London and suburbs." Then she admitted, "You really set me a hard task. If I pick someplace too nice, we'll end up waiting for hours for a table. On the other hand, I do want to test the limits of what you mean by 'any'. Hmmmm."

In the end, she said, "I'll tell you what. My boss once took the office out to a really nice spot. I'll not tell you what it was, but I will tell the cabby."

I agreed. I had held the cab that I'd come in. She whispered the destination in his ear. Apparently, he recognized it. He smiled and said, "Yes, mum." Then we were off.

You might have mistaken it for a hole in the wall from the exterior. There wasn't even a proper sign, but when we were inside, it was obvious that we were lucky that the wait was only a half hour.

Pamela said, "This seems like a date, so I should be able to have you tell me about yourself first."

I shrugged and agreed to the terms with one *proviso*, "Even if I don't finish, you have to tell me about you when I say so."

She agreed. I began. "OK. You have to allow me to think a few minutes to get my story straight before I begin. I promise to begin before we're called to our table."

I took more than a few minutes thinking through my speech. But I began before the *maitre d'* arrived to take us to our table. "OK. Pamela. I'm going to give you a choice about how I tell my story. One, you can get the absolute straight story provided that you don't interrupt me. I'll tell you some pretty crazy things. You don't have to believe them, but you do have to let me tell the story straight without interruption.

"The other choice is that I tell you a sanitized version that will be plausible but not true in a couple of major ways. However, you can interrupt and ask questions which I'll answer mostly truthfully. Which one do you want?"

She spoke immediately, seemingly without a second thought, "Who would want the sanitized version. Give it to me straight."

I said, "OK. Don't complain when you decide that I'm crazy."

"No way!"

"OK. Remember the story that I told you when we met by accident that summer after I'd been away for a couple of years. That was a sanitized version. What actually happened was that I was hired by an exclusive finishing school." I hesitated and then said, "It was a magical finishing school." She didn't blink an eye. I went on. "I taught English literature. I was the only teacher in the long history of the school to teach any English class.

"While I was there, the magical world was rocked by a figure more or less equivalent to Adolf Hitler. As a non-magical in this world, I was in fairly constant danger—sometimes it was intense and sometimes it was far in the background." At this point, she seemed ready to say something, but she kept her promise. I went on. "This man is no longer a threat. He died several years ago." She sighed noticeably.

"Before he died, his followers and I interacted several times. The first was trivial, and I won't even talk about it. The second time I was kidnapped. They didn't want to hold me for money. They just wanted to torture me, and when they'd finished with that, kill me."

This was too much for Pamela. "You are crazy or I am! How could you possibly stay with your job after an attempt was made on your life?"

"Yeh. I guess that I was crazy. I was in love and wouldn't leave the witch that I loved despite the danger for me." She again seemed to be dying to say or ask something but held her peace. I went on. "During this time, I had the extremely good fortune to have a chess genius as a student, Cedric Diggory. He wanted to improve his chess. I wanted to help him. We went to a number of tournaments. He won some, finished well in most. I thought that he would become a force in chess. Before that time, he died in an incident involving the Adolff Hitler of magic. I suppose I should tell you his name because it makes talking about him easier and there's no danger in it. His name was Riddle.

"After Diggory's death, I sought out Riddle. Frankly, my intent was to kill him. I succeeded in finding him, but he escaped unscathed as did I. That was the beginning of nearly open warfare between Riddle and his followers and me. They almost captured me the next year in the States. I didn't come away unscathed. I was injured and spent weeks in a variety of hospitals. I was rescued by my lover. . . "

I was interrupted by Pamela, who asked, "Were you rescued from a hospital or had Riddle's followers caught up with you again?"

"Oh, it was from a hospital alright. That's a story in itself, but for now, let's just leave it that my rescue was one that took a lot of ingenuity and determination. The next school year ended with the death of the headmaster of the school that I worked for. With that death, my protection at the school was gone. My lover threatened me. She forced me to resign my position and prepare to return to the States. However, it didn't work out that way.

"The British government recruited me . . . uh . . . perhaps better to say *shanghaied* me to help them in the resistance to Riddle. It was a long underground war. I can't tell you much about what happened because it's still under the Official Secrets act. I can just tell you that Riddle did lose and died in the effort. I was involved in tracking down the last of Riddle's surviving followers. In that last struggle, I may have killed one of Riddle's last followers."

She was understandably confused by that. "You don't know whether you killed him or not?"

"It's even worse than that. I don't know if she's still alive or not. I fired a bullet at her." I hesitated, trying to decide if this was the point to talk about pure magic. "She disapparated—that's a magical term that means to disappear from one place and re-appear elsewhere. We never found the bullet, which you might think was pretty strong evidence that I hit her."

I weighed my next words carefully. "However, it's not decisive. The bullet could have been disapparated as well to wherever she went. We don't know where that was."

Pamela started to laugh and then caught herself. "Are we talking science fiction or magic?"

"Magic, I'm afraid." She took it stoically or maybe she was just reserving comment for later. "I was put on trial for what in English law would be considered attempted murder. It was actually a near thing. There were both circumstantial evidence and eye witnesses. It finally came down to a question of intent and whether the court believed my self-defense plea."

Pamela jumped up,."Surely there could be no doubt! I can't imagine you willfully killing anyone for any reason other than self defense." She added, "As a matter of fact, I can't even imagine you killing someone in self-defense."

"Well, it almost happened. I found Riddle and came pretty close to blowing the both of us to kingdom come."

She interrupted again. "OK. I've just about had it with this take-it-or-leave-it policy. There is far too much here that screams for comment or objection or just elaboration."

I gave in. "Sure, my request was probably unreasonable. Go ahead. What have you got?"

"OK. You, of all people, almost blew yourself up!! How in the world did that happen? Why did that happen?"

"I guess the how is something that I want to keep to myself mostly. I'll just say that I built an IED like a suicide bomber. I won't tell you more to protect the mostly innocent. The why is more straight-forward. I had seen a lot of people who were injured by Riddle. I knew that he wanted to kill and conquer many more—maybe the entire world. Then he had someone kill a student whom I was helping to build a future. It broke my heart.

"Did you know that Dietrich Bonhoeffer helped with an assassination attempt on the life of Adolff Hitler?" I didn't wait for agreement. "He did. Bonhoeffer was a fully committed Christian. I don't argue that I am as moral or good as him, just that we shared the same impulse."

She looked at me quizzically. "Why didn't it work?"

"Oh, Riddle was amazing at self-preservation. He had a magical talent called Legilimency. He could read people's minds. He saw death in mine."

She nodded slowly, comprehension dawning. "So, he disparated somewhere else?"

"Yes, it's disapparated, but yes, he fled. I never saw him again. I was close to him one more time, but never in a position to try to kill him."

We were both silent for a while, and then she asked, "Can you tell me anything about your help for the British in this secret war?"

"I'll tell you what I can. I was mostly a liaison between the British forces and the magical resistance, which, by the way, was called the Order of the Phoenix. There were quite a lot of people who were treated as the Nazi's treated Jews and minorities. They were either on the run from Riddle or had been herded together in a concentration camp called Azkaban.

"I helped the Order of the Phoenix smuggle people out of Britain. I also helped with a raid of Azkaban that freed a lot of political prisoners."

She just shook her head. "God, if I'd known half of this . . ." She never finished the thought. I don't think she had figured out what she would have done.

I went on. "Well, after the war was over, I went back to Hogwarts. My lover was the headmistress. That was inconvenient. Anyway, then the Souls arrived."

Pamela shuddered. "I was unconscious through most of that, of course, but it still gives me the willies to think about the fact that I almost died without even realizing that I was in danger." She hesitated. "I know that most

143

people think about that experience of being . . . oh . . . out of body as too personal to talk about, but I can't help asking. How did it happen for you?"

I wondered if she'd hate me for what I was about to say. "It actually didn't happen to me."

Her jaw dropped. "Get out! How is that possible?" She answered her own question. "Of course, you were with the wizards." A little more reflection led her to ask, "I suppose they saved the human race?"

"Not by themselves. As a matter of fact, it was a pretty even co-operation between the wizards and muggles that saved us. To answer the next obvious question—yes, I was involved in a liaison role between the muggles and the wizards."

She shook her head. "You get around a lot, don't you?"

I shrugged. "Well, to quote the Minister of Magic who is rather like the Prime Minister, 'I was Minerva's tame muggle.'"

Her face turned downcast. "Minerva. Was that your lover's name?"

I nodded. She asked, "You used the word, 'was'. Does that mean that something's happened between you?"

"Actually, a lot of things. I guess this is the time to talk about that. First, let me tell you why we were lovers so long without getting married."

She smiled. "I supposed that was because you were . . . uh . . . averse to commitments."

"No. She had been married to a muggle before. He died in the first war with Riddle."

She was astonished. "This Riddle sounds more like Napoleon than Hitler. What happened at the end of the first war? Was he banished to Elba?"

"No. He disappeared. I mean that literally. His body and soul got separated. The body died, but his soul continued to hang around somehow."

She said, "See. You talk a fair amount of sense, and then you say something like that. How. . . how . . ."

"Oh, I don't know. I've never had a wizard give me a good explanation of it. It's something to do with breaking your soul in pieces. I know. I know. That doesn't make any more sense. It's just what they all say."

She made a face and said, "OK, we'll let that pass for the moment. So, her first husband died in the first war, and she was gun shy. She was the person who had commitment issues."

I shook my head. "I don't know. I suppose you could say that. The bottom line was that she wouldn't consider marriage before Riddle was completely out of the picture."

"So, the two of you got married as soon as Riddle died? Or at least, fairly soon afterwards."

144

I was the one to make the face. "No, we didn't. It wasn't until after the Soul invasion was repelled that we were married."

She clicked her tongue. "Did you become gun shy after your Minerva became available?"

"No. I don't know why we didn't get married then. It wasn't until the end of the Soul war that she was ready."

"OK. Something else happened, didn't it?"

I paused for reflection and then said, "Yes. I guess I can tell you about it. It was never classified 'Secret'." I hesitated again.

She said, "Then why don't you go ahead and tell me?"

"Well, something happened that really had practically nothing to do with that war. Minerva says that she had some sort of vision of herself being married. I don't understand it.

"Anyway, soon after the wedding something really strange happened. Parts of it are really more incredible than wizards and witches and all that. I just have to think about how to tell it."

"It must be an amazing story."

I frowned and said, "Yeh." Then after a little more thought I started, "OK. Here's what happened. What I'm going to tell you will sound a lot as though the Souls returned, but that wasn't it at all. As a matter of fact, it was almost the opposite.

"A couple of people had shrapnel made from meteor fragments in their brains. They got the wounds while being special forces in Iraq. The fragments had RNA or DNA or something like that in them. That took over their . . ."

She stared at me in confusion. "What did it take over? Their wills?"

"Sort of. It left their personalities and memories intact. They became extremely brilliant and committed to a mission. We got involved as consultants when the US government figured out that something very strange was going on."

"What was their mission."

"That's the thing. I don't know exactly. It certainly involved building a Faster-Than-Light space ship. It involved kidnapping several children who were disabled. They left the earth in this spacecraft. That's really all we know."

She was exasperated again. "Did you try to stop them?"

"Are you kidding? Of course, we did. It proved impossible."

"Oh, you just didn't try hard enough."

I laughed. That didn't improve her attitude any. I went on. "We tried as hard as we could. We involved the FBI, the US military, wizards. None of it made a difference."

"Really!"

I shrugged. "Yes, really. I can't tell you some of the more amazing things. Let me just say that you have no idea how formidable they were. Here's just one minor example. One of them landed in Brazil to get something out of the rain-forest that was necessary for their project. He didn't know any Portuguese when he arrived. In two days, he was fluent. The locals thought he was a native Brazilian."

She shook her head in disbelief again. "Come on. Maybe not impossible, but really!"

"It was one of the least amazing things that they did. You haven't thought about what it would take for a couple of people to build a space ship of any sort, let alone one that can travel faster than the speed of light."

She shook her head again. "That caused your marriage to break up? Were you seduced by one of those superhumans?"

I laughed. I'd not laughed that hard in a long time. "No, our marriage survived that perfectly well. It was . . ."

She interrupted me. "Wait a minute. You said that they kidnapped some children. You got them back, right? That was just to get money or something for their project?"

"No. We never did. They didn't have any problem with money. They were rolling in it. No, the kids were the heart of the project."

"Never! You let them get away with that?"

"You don't have any idea what it was like with them. The closest that we got to ending the project was near the end. They offered to shut down the project IF we really wanted the children back."

Her eyes bugged out, and I thought she might slap me. "And you didn't!!"

"No, we didn't. They showed us that they had cures for all the kids' disabilities. It would have broken our hearts to send them back to what they had come from."

Her expression was grim. "I'd have divorced you if I'd been Minerva."

I shook my head. "Minerva was there. She agreed."

There was a long silence. Finally, she said, "OK. That wasn't what ended your marriage. What did?"

It was really hard talking about what came next. I had to struggle to hold back tears. "What happened next was that the Souls returned."

Pamela slammed her hand down on the table top. 'Impossible!"

"No, I'm afraid it actually did happen. Everything is top secret about that, but I'm going to tell you some of it. You won't understand what happened to Minerva otherwise."

"Go ahead."

"Well, to start with, I had disappeared."

146

She spit out her words. "I can't stand it. How could you disappear? What happened to you?"

"I did disappear. I was unconscious, and I might as well have died. I can't tell you where I was. It would be to break a trust. I won't tell you anything more about it. So, don't ask."

I had forgotten that I had a drink sitting in front of me. I took a deep swallow and went on. "The Souls were losing a war that they didn't even realize was going on. In desperation they came to us for help."

Pamela laughed. "I've stopped applying logic to these crazy events, but I'm curious. How did they not know they were in a war?"

"Oh, it wasn't quite as strange as you might think. They were the victims of biological warfare. A disease was being used against them. We helped them because we were as clueless as they were about what was going on. It seemed like a good investment in good will. Who knew? We might be next."

She actually laughed. "I suppose you were the liaison between aliens and wizards?"

"Well, sort of. I went with a small team that was sent to investigate. It certainly seemed like a disease."

"But it wasn't, was it?"

I agreed. "No. It was actually another alien race that . . ."

She shook her head violently. That sent her blond locks flowing. "No. No! No! Not another alien invasion."

"No. Not an invasion of us anyway. They were trying to exterminate the Souls. They came darn close to doing it too. We were on a spacecraft with them and the Souls. Minerva died saving us. I killed the second group of aliens on the ship."

Pamela demanded, "You single-handedly killed a ship full of aliens?"

"Well, it was a small ship. There were two witches, two muggle men, two Souls, and two aliens. So, it wasn't as hard as you might imagine, but it was plenty hard enough as it was."

"Where were you?"

I shook my head in disbelief myself and said, "We were in the solar system of the Souls. Their nemeses almost succeeded in destroying the home planet of the Souls."

"How did you get back? Did the Souls know how to fly the ship?"

"Oh, yes. The truth was that the other muggle was a genius. He'd figured out how to control the ship and did a fair amount of the flying at the end."

Pamela leaned back in her chair. She closed her eyes and seemed to be forming words with her lips. Then she leaned forward and asked, "So, you're a widower?"

147

I nodded, afraid to speak.

She said, "I had no idea. I'm sorry." She gazed into my eyes with evident compassion. She asked, "Surely that's the end of the tale. There can't be anything more that could happen to you?"

I wondered how I could deny that and not give her information that she shouldn't have. I didn't have to say anything. The long gap in our conversation told the tale. She said, "That's not the end, is it? You have something that you can't talk about, right?"

I was still mute. She said, "OK. I understand." Then she had a lengthy silent period. Finally, she asked, "Is there any chance that I might see you after whatever it is that's going to happen to you happens?"

I said, "I don't know. If there's anything that my life has taught me, it's that predicting the future is a losing proposition."

"You know what I mean. If you come out of whatever is going on now alive, do you want to see me again?"

I replied, "This life has taught me not to hang hopes on the future. If you have something you really want to do, do it in the present."

She reached across the table and pulled me toward her. She kissed me. I found myself responding. She then said, "You were looking for a place to stay, preferably in our old rooming house. You've found it."

I nodded. I couldn't refuse such generous hospitality. During the course of my talk, we'd been seated, ordered and were well along toward the end of the meal. I said, "Why don't you start telling me your story?"

She agreed and began. "I eventually finished design school. I bounced along between a couple of jobs. Some were regular full time. Some were little more than short gigs. I eventually found a good graphic design company in the City. I did a little bit of everything there. It was a great job. I learned about layout of magazines, brochures, even newspapers. I did website design. I designed logos. It was wonderful."

I said, "And then. . ." However, I was interrupted by the waiter with the check. By mutual consent, we decided to put off the sequel until we reached the rooming house. I paid the check with hardly a glance. She was surprised that I only looked carefully enough to figure the tip.

She asked, "How much was that dinner?"

I shook my head and said, "You shouldn't want to know. It might affect how we get on this evening."

Her mouth opened wide and then snapped shut. "OK. I think you're right. I don't want to know. I can pretend that I don't feel any obligation to you when we decide who gets which side of the bed."

"Wise." I called a cab, and while we waited, I asked, "Is there a Starbucks close here?"

"I think there's one about three blocks away. The cabbie will know. Do you want tea? I can brew some at home."

"No. Starbucks always has decent desserts. I thought I'd get something for us."

"Good idea, but I have to have something to contribute to the evening. I'll get it."

The cabbie arrived. We stopped at Starbucks just long enough for Pamela to run in and buy something. Then we were off to our building. I paid the cabbie, and we reached the door to the rooming house. I hadn't penetrated that door in so long that I'd no recollection of when the last time was. Pamela rummaged around in her purse and found her key. She handed me the purse saying, "The lock is a little tricky. I need both hands."

She struggled with it for a few minutes and turned to me. "Would you mind?"

"Not at all." I took the key and gave her the purse. It was a little tricky, but not as tricky as you might have thought would stymie an accomplished young woman.

After I'd opened the door, I was about to return her key. She said, "Why don't you keep it? You never know when you might need . . . or want it."

I agreed. I slipped it into my purse. She gazed at it in wonder. Noticing, I explained, "It's a magic thing. It's a good bit more capacious than you might think. When we get in your room, I'll amaze you with the amount of stuff I have in it."

Inside, we navigated to her room which was really nice. It was an efficiency, complete with portable refer, a gas stove, a sofa that must be a sleeper sofa, a flat screen TV, a nice hardwood dinner table that would seat six in a pinch, and what looked like a cherry wardrobe in a corner. I couldn't help saying, "I think you've made this old dump of a rooming house into a really pleasant place."

She blushed a little and said, "Well, it's all in the choice of furniture."

We sat at the table and divided the Italian cream cake between us. She brewed a pot of hot tea, and I encouraged her to tell me the rest of her story.

She demurred and suggested that we wait until we were more comfortable. Dessert was good. We found that we didn't need to talk as we ate it. Then, she invited me to the sofa. We sat, and she began her story, "A couple of years ago, I left the graphic design business to start my own. The thing that I didn't appreciate was how important sales is. It was a struggle for me to learn the skills. I thought that I could get sales purely with my talent and experience."

She sort of snuggled close to me. I put an arm around her shoulder and she rested her head on my shoulder. She went on. "There was one point when I had so little faith in myself that I seriously considered going back to my old company. I could hardly muster the courage to walk in a business's door to try to sell myself."

I smiled at her and said, "I would beg you to come through my door if I needed graphic design." I chuckled. "Even if I didn't need it."

She smiled too. She said, "I see that you don't have even a change of clothes. There must be a story behind that."

I found myself twirling her long blond hair. She said, "Let me move so you can run your fingers through my hair. With that she shifted to my lap. Her hair fell down over my face. I would have pulled it back, but she was kissing me first.

After a while, we broke, and I said, "God, if this had happened when I was here the first time, I'd never have done any of the things that I was talking about."

Her laugh was infectious as she said, "And I wouldn't own my own business. . . Maybe I'd own you, though." That infectious laughter had infected me. I agreed. "Maybe you would."

Certainly she did for the rest of the night. All good things come to an end. Pamela's alarm clock went off at 6 AM. I rolled out of bed. She was already in the shower. I rummaged around to find my clothes. I found my underwear and my socks and shoes. Where was my shirt? I wondered. I found it under a pile of pillows at one end of the sofa.

Then, I heard a muffled cry. "What?" I asked.

She said, "Come in here. There's something you've got to see."

I chuckled. "It wouldn't have something to do with a view of twin peaks."

She laughed outrageously. "No. No. Ho. Ho. Hurry before it's gone."

I wondered what "it" was. In a couple of steps across the room I was at the door to the bath. I opened the door and looked around. Pamela was holding a towel in front of her. What I heard was a pecking. Pamela let part of the towel drop as she pointed with one hand to the glazed window. On the other side was a bird that was pecking on the glass. It suddenly hit me what was pecking. It was an owl.

I told Pamela, "I think I know what this is about. Would you mind if I let the owl into the bathroom?"

Her mouth opened wide, but nothing came out of it. I said, "Well, I'll take silence to betoken consent. I assure you, there won't be a problem." I unlatched the window and opened it. The bird on the window ledge was indeed an owl. It hopped in and landed on the radiator. It had a note tied to its leg. I untied it. It remained. I decided that it must be waiting for a return. So, I said to it, "Just a minute. I'll find you a treat or two."

Pamela stared at it and asked, "Does it understand English?"

I was continuing to rummage for my pants. "Oh, I don't know. Sometimes I wonder." Then I found them. I pulled my purse out of a pocket and went into the bathroom. Pamela was toweling herself off. I'd probably have found it pretty distracting if I weren't trying to find the ziplock bag of owl treats that I always keep in the purse.

Pamela commented, "That's a nice purse you have. It seems to have an amazing capacity." By this time, I'd pulled out some loose coins, bills, and the box of bullets. I looked up at her and tried to think of something to say to her, but I was at a loss for words.

I just said, "I'll explain that later." Finally, I found the bag of owl treats. I pulled out three because of all the trouble it had had. It picked them off my hand. There was another gasp. Then I said, "If you don't mind, I'll read this out in the living room. Umm. . . don't mind the owl. It's very tame."

In the living room, I unsealed the note, unfolded it, and read, "Wendt, I hear you're back in England. If you want a lift anywhere, just return the note with time and place to meet. Love, Ginny. PS. I'm tied up for lunch today, so it will have to be after work. Dinner would be nice."

I looked around the room for a pencil. I grimaced and went back to the WC to ask Pamela for a pencil or pen. She laughed. "Don't you have one in your deep pockets purse?"

I dug into it again. I didn't want to, but I had to take the Glock out. Pamela's eyes bugged out at the sight of the Glock. She asked, "Is that the . . . the gun that you used to . . ."

"Yes. It wasn't the first time that I'd used it in self-defense, but it was the only time I used it in a rage of anger. That may have saved our lives. The creatures I killed were extremely smart and had amazing physical capabilities. I'm not at all sure that we could have kept them from destroying the planetary system that we were in without killing them. The question became moot because I didn't consider it. I was just wreaking revenge."

She seemed to be struck dumb. I found a pen in my purse and retreated to the main room to write a quick note. "Ginny, I'll meet you at the entrance to the Cauldron at six. See you soon, Wendt." I tied it on the ever-patient owl's leg, and it took off.

That seemed to loosen Pamela's tongue. She asked, "Is that owl a homing pigeon?"

"Oh, it's far more versatile than that. If no return message is required it does go home. If there is a return required, it returns to the sender. Somehow, I don't know how, it knows how to find someone even if the sender doesn't. Like so many other magical things, it's spooky."

She shook her head. "What's really spooky is that you killed a couple of aliens somewhere in space. How far away were you?"

I shrugged. "A couple of hundred light years."

She shook her head again, "I don't believe it."

I shrugged again, "I don't either."

"Look, how can you say that? Have you been on another planet?"

I sighed. "Three actually. Although one almost doesn't count. I was only there long enough to toss a corpse off the ship and take off before the Souls tried to killed us."

"Bloody Hell, I wish I had time to hear more, but I've got to get to work. I'd call in sick, but I've got an important initial meeting with a new client this morning." She came back into the main room and quickly dressed. She was practically flying when she went through the door and shouted over her shoulder, "Lock the door on your way out."

I did. I also wrote her a note telling her that I had to get back to school. I struggled over what else to say. I was anxious to see Ginny for dinner even though it had been a wonderful night with Pamela.

There was a time when I'd have loved to give her a taste of the pain that I had when I longed for her and couldn't get the time of day from her. That was long past. I finally decided to say that I didn't know what the future was for us. I gave her the address that she could use to send letters to me by owl post. I simply signed it, "Wendt."

I left the old rooming house, reflecting that you really couldn't go back home. I went to the British Museum, where I spent the day walking the exhibit halls. I hadn't been there in a long time. It was like getting re-acquainted with old friends.

That evening, I went to the Cauldron as arranged. It wasn't a long wait but an uncomfortable one. I wasn't sure what would happen with Ginny. I wasn't sure what I wanted to happen. Memories of the previous night were still strong.

Ginny walked out of the Cauldron, strode up to me, and breezily kissed me. She took my hand and said, "Come on, I'm ravenous. Let's get something to eat."

We entered the Cauldron. It was packed, but Tom was able to find us a table that had just been cleared. She was gaily talking on about the minor politics of the Auror office. It was punctuated by occasional footsie under the table. Her happiness was infectious. I said, "Well, it's a good thing that things are going well in the Auror office. I am scared by what I saw. I can't talk about it here, but I'm afraid of why they've done this demo. It certainly wasn't to prove to themselves the effectiveness of their . . . uh . . . device." I wasn't going to use the proper word, weapon, in a crowded restaurant.

Ginny was clearly disturbed by not being able to talk about it openly. We were interrupted by our meal being delivered. It was good that we could concentrate on eating. When my appetite was nearly sated she said, "I'm dying to talk with you more about what happened."

"You mean that you haven't heard much about what happened . . . uh . . . on the ship?"

She looked down and muttered, "I don't know whether the Ministry has had a report, but I sure haven't seen one."

I was stuck for something to say. I wasn't going to give her any details here. I wasn't even sure if I could give her details at her office. She'd been involved from the beginning, but if they hadn't shared anything with her, would it be proper for me to share?

Suddenly Ginny brightened. Her face seemed to glow as she said, "Why don't you get a room for the night. I could take you to Hogwarts tomorrow morning before going in to work."

I was dumbfounded for a minute and could just say, "Well, yes, but why . . ." I never finished the thought because Ginny kicked me in the shins and growled at me. I finally got it that she wanted to spend the night here with me. I said, "Oh, yes. Sure. What a great idea. I might fall asleep while going to Hogwarts tonight by floo. Who knows what might happen."

She laughed. "Yes, you'd better just spend the night here, hmmm?"

When Tom came by with the tab, I said, "Have you got a room where I could spend the night?"

He looked from me to Ginny and smiled himself. He said, "Sure, I do. Very comfortable bed, too."

I said, "Thanks. If you go get the key, when you return, I'll pay you for the meal."

He agreed. After he left, Ginny asked me, "What's in the paper bag?"

"Oh, it's the clothes that I took on my little trip. When I got back, I didn't have a clean change of clothes. Maybe you'll change your plans for tonight."

She laughed. "Since you don't secure your floo connection, I'll drop by your apartment and bring back a change of clothes." She hesitated and added, "That's really a good reason for me to pay a little visit to your room."

Tom returned with the key. I paid him for both the dinner and the room along with a good tip. Shortly after he left, Ginny left. I went up to my room. She returned so quickly that I was startled by the knock on the door when she arrived. I asked, "How did you get to my apartment, find some clothes, and get back so quickly?"

"Oh, I know your apartment better than you think. It took about thirty seconds to pull a change of robes, shirt, socks, and unmentionables for you and throw them in my handbag." She pulled them out and hung them up in the armoire in the room, pausing to use some sort of spell to smooth them. Then threw her arms about me, and we kissed seriously.

After a bit she said, "Now about what happened to you in space . . ."

I put my hand over her mouth and said, "Before you say anything, we need to get one thing straight."

She nodded slowly and said hesitantly, "O. K."

"I'm going to give you the brooms-eye view, but we'll do it before anyone's head hits the pillow. I want you to know that this is not pillow talk."

She made a funny expression with her mouth and said, "I was hoping to worm it out of you, but I suppose that if you insist, you can tell me without the worming."

I smiled, and she did too. "Don't worry. You can worm away at me to your heart's content—just not for this information."

"So?"

"OK. Here's the short of it. As you know, the PAK wanted a human witness to a demonstration of their weapon. As a matter of fact, they wanted someone to actually pull the trigger so that there would be no doubt of the reality of the weapon. I did that at Mars."

Ginny's mouth opened wide enough for a banshee to fly in. "I wondered whether or not to believe the public story that it was some giant meteor."

I nodded. "That was the cover story. And it was asteroid not meteor."

She closed her mouth and was deep in thought. Out of that thought came the question, "Why do they care whether we believe they have this enormously powerful weapon?"

I agreed. "Yeah. Why?"

And then it came to her, "They want us to do something, don't they? And they don't think we'll do it without a big threat?"

"That's the way I see it."

"Do you have an idea what it is?"

"No, I don't. That scares me."

She took my hand and pulled me to the bed. We sat. She asked, "If they're so smart and have Faster-Than-Light travel and everything else, what could they possibly want from us?"

I didn't say anything. We hugged and lay back on the bed. She pulled my hand across her belly. I rolled over her, and we kissed. Then we helped each other out of our clothes. Once under the covers we kissed again. I asked her, "Don't you have any idea?"

As I caressed the nape of her back she chuckled softly, "Well, I probably really shouldn't tell you this, but you're on the team, and you'll find out in the next day or two, I'm sure."

I didn't say anything. She hesitated, and as I continued to caress her back, she said, "Oh, hell. We're going to have a meeting at the end of the week." She quickly added, "I don't know anything else, I swear. You can worm as much as you like. There's nothing more to worm out."

The rest of the evening was spent wordlessly worming.

The next morning, we left the key to our room on the dresser and walked down to the bar. I told the bartender on duty that I was checking out and had left the key in the room. He nodded and waved Ginny and me out. We went to the hearth and took the floo network to my office. I kissed Ginny good-bye.

I changed clothes again and went to the Great Hall for breakfast. The one class I had was in the afternoon. That was good because I needed a nap before it.

The next couple of days were uneventful except that on the second day Cecily came to my office during office hours. Of course, I didn't need to ask her why she'd come. So, I gave her the answer to her inevitable question, "I'm sorry. I've been really busy. I've not had a chance to look for tournaments."

She expressed her disappointment openly. "If I knew anyone else who could help, I'd be with them in a real hurry."

I was lost for something to say. I couldn't deny that I'd been too busy with other things to help her. I couldn't tell her what they were. I just smiled and said, "You're right. I've had other things that were more important. I wish I had more time for you."

It was pathetic, but somehow she seemed satisfied that I'd admitted having limitations, and even that she wasn't my highest priority. She sulked a bit and said, "It's not as if you have classes every day to keep you busy."

"Right again."

She thought about that a minute and asked, "Do you want to work with me at all?"

I sighed. "Yes, I really do. It probably doesn't seem that way, but I do want to keep working with you. You know something about my history with Cedric. It broke my heart when he died. Part of that was due to my desire for him to reach his full potential at chess. If you'd told me at that time that I'd find another student with comparable abilities, I'd have told you that you were crackerbox.

"When you showed up in my office, It was like a miracle. I wanted you to be the real McCoy so much that I couldn't sleep properly for days. I may not have seemed excited to you, but I really was."

"Then when you played in a tournament and did well, I was ecstatic. I would never willingly do less for you than my best."

Cecily thought that over. Then she asked, "Couldn't you have done more if you were doing your best for me?"

155

I said, "I can't tell you why I say that, but I can assure you that I took a week off after your last tournament and from then on I've been slammed with . . . well, with really important things." It still sounded lame, but it was true.

She said, "Well, what about now? Can you look for something?"

I was in an agony. I knew that I'd have a meeting with the Ad Hoc Council on Extraterrestrial Affairs or whatever we were in a couple of days. I quickly thought through the question, "Do I need to prepare for it?" The answer that came immediately was, "No. I'm not even supposed to know that it's coming." Should I though?

I was still pondering that when Cecily interrupted my thoughts with a question. "More high level work?"

I answered, "I will do some looking this week. If I come up with something, I'll write it up and send it to you."

She planted her hands on her hips, "Send it to me! Aren't you going to be here?"

I answered honestly, "I don't know."

She shook her head and got up to go. I called to her before she reached the door, "Cecily?"

"Yes."

"I really will look."

She frowned and said, "No offense, but I really wish that Professor J were back." Then she left. I wondered if she would say that if she knew what it would cost to have Professor J back.

The next day, I left for my favorite internet cafe with Dursley during the lunch hour. We went to the Cauldron by floo, and he dropped me at the cafe. As he left, I asked him, "Is it OK to pick me up before dinner at Hogwarts?"

He said, "Sure, I'll leave at five to get you. We'll have loads of time to get back to Hogwarts before the 6 PM start of dinner."

I started to scan through the usual sources of tournaments on the web. Of course, I already had some from the last time I'd looked, but I wanted to see if any new ones had been added since I looked before Easter. There were a couple of new ones, but they were far away or minor junior tournaments nearby. I circled one on my notepad from before. It was the last week of May in Germany. I'd have to get permission from Cecily's dad and the school because she'd miss a couple of days of classes.

I started filling out school trip permission forms—one for her dad and one for the Headmaster. When I finished, it was hardly 3 PM. I needed to kill some time, so I found a bookstore nearby and bought a *New York Times*. I took it back to the internet cafe and ordered another hot tea.

When Dursley arrived, I asked him to take me to the Ministry where I could send an owl. He reluctantly agreed. He said, "Look, I don't want you to be late for dinner. Why don't we just go directly back to Hogwarts and then you can send it from the owlery there?"

I was stubborn, so we went to the Ministry. I went directly to the Owl Post Office. Dursley was surprised that I knew where it was. I smiled. "You forget that Jaimie sent a number of owls from there." I sent two owls—one to Brewster and one to Professor Slughorn.

The next night before dinner was even over, I had a visitor walk right up to the head table. Ginny hand-delivered a note. When I saw it, I asked her, "Are you moonlighting as an owl?"

She replied, "Don't be funny. Read the note before you make jokes."

"OK. Let's go." We walked out of the Great Hall, and I immediately opened the letter. It was from the Minister of Magic. My presence was requested the next day all afternoon for a meeting in her Conference Room in the Ministry of Magic. I asked Ginny, "You know what's in this note?"

She raised an eyebrow and asked with total innocence, "I?"

"Oh, give me a break. You certainly do."

She smirked. "OK. Let's suppose that I do know what this is about."

"Well then, are you invited?"

"I suppose you are angling for a lift to the meeting?"

I realized that she was pulling my chain. "You know perfectly well that I am. And you know perfectly well that you're gong to the meeting too. And you know perfectly well that you're going to give me a ride."

She smirked. "Well, if you know all that, why did you waste your time asking me all those question?"

I grimaced. "Just pick me up at lunch tomorrow." Then I relented and said, "Better, I'll take you out to eat."

She said, "Well. . . It would be nice to eat at Hogwarts for a change, but I suppose . . . "

Then I had an even better idea. "I'll take you somewhere you've probably never been for lunch."

"Sounds scrumptious. Where?"

"Just show up in my office at a quarter to noon, and you'll find out."

Her face lit up and she looped her arm through mine. "Maybe I can worm it out of you in your office."

I nodded, "Maybe." Despite some serious worming, nothing came out that evening.

Tales From Mars

I was waiting in my office at 11:30 that morning, having just finished grading my 10 o'clock class's quiz. I had opened the *Times* and begun reading the sports page. As usual the Manchester teams were fighting to lead the top five of the Premier League. I heard a rush of air, looked up, and found that Ginny had just arrived. We embraced and kissed. She took my hand and started to pull me toward the hearth, saying, "Where are we going?"

I dragged her the other way and said, "Not through the floo."

She raised her eyebrows and said, "And yet, obviously not in the Great Hall because you said that I'd never eaten there before. Also, obviously not in your office. I've eaten here. So, lead on."

We walked down the stairs to the main level and then started down to the next level down. She immediately realized where we were go. "We're eating with the house elves, right?"

I laughed. "Partly right."

We entered the kitchen and found the table where I used to eat with Dursley and Filch. They were there. As we approached, Kreachur came up to us and asked, "Two more for lunch?"

I replied, "Yes, if that's all right."

He nodded merrily. "Professor Wendt and guest is always welcome to eat with the Dursley, the Filch, and the house elves."

Ginny thanked him. Then we joined Dursley and Filch at their table. Filch asked, "What good luck brings Wendt to join us for lunch."

Dursley asked Ginny, "You aren't here to take more revenge on me, are you?"

She smiled. "No, I'm too happy for anything like that. I'm just here to have lunch with Professor Wendt."

Filch said, "Ah, yes. I remember the good old days when Professor Wendt joined us for lunch every day. It was almost as if it were only days ago."

I said, "Well, it wasn't that long ago—a couple of months."

Ginny remarked that she'd never had detention with Filch. She asked, "How do you suppose that happened?"

Filch scratched his chin and said, "That's a good question. You didn't seem to me to be any better than any of your brothers and worse than some."

She went on, "Of course, during the year with Snape as Headmaster, I had plenty of detentions. It was just that they all were with the Carows."

Filch grumbled, "Yeh, They had all the fun around here. That Snape was such an odd bird. On the one hand he had all these great rules, but then he'd let lots of students off without even sending them to the Carows."

Dursley asked, "What does bring you here, Ms. Weasley?"

"Oh, I'm just giving the Professor a lift to the Ministry for a meeting."

Dursley looked hurt, "I'd have been happy to give you a ride there, Professor."

Weasley just shook her head and said, "This is special." She left it at that. Everyone else did as well. When we'd finished lunch, Ginny went over to the house elves to thank them for lunch.

Filch asked me, "Well, Professor, you seem to have a new friend."

Dursley added, "Isn't she a little young for you?"

"I don't know. I really don't know how she got interested in me, but it wasn't through any attempt on my part to pursue her."

Filch sort of grumbled, "Some guys have all the luck."

I agreed. "Some do."

We left. Ginny said, "Well, I'd never been down here before despite the fact that the twins often were. It's an interesting place to visit. Does this mean that you're willing to be more open about dating me? Because, if you weren't, you've sure opened the bag wide now. "

I thought about it. "I guess you're right. It never really was a secret but now . . ." I left the thought incomplete.

"Does that bother you?"

I laughed at the reflection that struck me. "Well, it didn't bother me that I was dating and eventually married a witch much older than I. It's kind of a drastic switch to one much younger, but I guess I can suffer through an immature . . ." I didn't get to finish because she slapped my wrist with her wand.

She said, "Consider yourself lucky, mister."

I assured her that I did. By this time, we'd reached the main floor. She took my hand and led me off toward the Great Hall, saying, "If you're going to go public, you might as well go public in a big way. We're taking the floo connection here."

There were a lot of students and some teachers still eating. We strode up to the hearth as bold as brass and walked in as she took a handful of floo powder and sent us on our way to the Ministry in a green flash.

The next instant we disgorged into the Minister's Office floo. She looked up and said, "A bit early, but that's just as well. I want to talk to you, Wendt." Then she added as an afterthought, "I suppose you might as well stay, Ms. Weasley."

She motioned us to chairs. "OK. Here it is straight from the Pegasus's mouth. Wendt, your muggle friends haven't been keeping us up to date on what happened on your mission. All the muggles in this meeting have the inside info. No wizard or witch does. I want it before we go in. Those damn muggles can't keep us shut out." She glanced at me and said, "Present company excluded. No offense??"

I said, "None taken."

Ginny glanced at her wrist and said, "Don't we have a meeting in just a few minutes?"

Minister Moertl smiled for the first time. "It's my house. I make the rules. The meeting starts when I say that it does and not before. They can just cool their wands in there until we arrive."

At that moment Moertl's assistant knocked softly on the door to the office and entered, "Uh . . . ma'am . . . everyone else has arrived."

Moertl whirled around and said, "Oh, just tell them we'll be there shortly, and breakout the mid-afternoon treats. Have they been offered something to drink?"

"Yes, ma'am."

"Good. Off you go. Chop, chop." And she did go off.

Moertl turned back to me and said, "Now, give. What happened to you?"

I said that I didn't mind giving them a high level overview of what had happened. So, I began, "The PAK rendezvoused with the submarine. They were flying an almost identical copy of the ship that we flew in before. This time, we only flew in it up to a sort of aircraft carrier of space."

Here Moertl interrupted. "Aircraft carrier?"

This might not be as quick as I hoped. "Yes, on the earth aircraft carriers are huge ships from which airplanes can take off and land. They have lots of space underneath the main deck to store airplanes. The ship that we met was like that. It had a lot of storage space for small spacecraft like the one that I flew up in."

She was nodding as though she was getting it. I was surer about Ginny, who seemed to pick up the idea immediately. I went on. "Then this space-craft carrier flew to Mars. It took us less than an hour. When we arrived, the captain of the ship took me on a little tour of it. We returned to the bridge."

Moertl interrupted again. "What's this about a bridge? You weren't on a real sea or river."

I nodded. "Right. It's a nautical term. It refers to the command center of any large ship. Anyway, they sat me down in front of a control monitor where I could select a target and actually fire the weapon."

Moertl was shocked. "You mean that you could fire at any target in space!"

I shook my head. "Oh, no. It had to be somewhere in the South Pole of Mars."

She released a sigh of relief. Then she asked what happened. I said, "You mean to say that you didn't hear about the giant extra-solar asteroid strike on Mars?"

Ginny said, "It wasn't in the *Prophet*."

Moertl asked, "And you heard about it?"

I answered that. "She reads *The Times of London* as part of her job."

"Well, will one of you tell me about it?"

I answered, "Well, it was reported that a giant asteroid had struck Mars."

"What really happened?"

I said, "The weapon that I launched blew a giant crater into Mars."

Moertl leaned back in her chair and closed her eyes. She opened them and said, "I don't want to know the answer to this question, because I'm pretty sure I know what it is. Why did the PAK do that? Answer: They want to convince us to do something for them. Question: What?"

I agreed. "I can't imagine what we could do for them, but I think you're right."

Moertl shook her head slowly and said, "Let's go. I don't think I want to hear anything more." She led us down the corridor to her Conference Room.

On the way, Ginny came close and whispered into my ear, "I've got a bad, bad feeling about this."

All I could say was, "Me, too."

We arrived and found that in addition to all the participants from the last meeting there were two new ones. There was the Secretary of Magic from the United States, Alexander Baker, whom I had met before, and there was someone else whom I didn't recognize. He was introduced as the Under Secretary of the US Air Force, Pete Treats. Treats seemed to have replaced

Richard Baker of the US Navy. When I heard Treat's last name, I thought that I'd have to be careful pronouncing that name.

Moertl took her seat at the head of the table without any apologies for making everyone wait for her. Instead she said, "Secretary Baker, you requested this meeting, causing me to reorganize my schedule for the entire week to accommodate you. Also, you gave no reason. What is the purpose?"

Baker turned to Treats and said, "This is your show; go ahead."

Treats said, "I've brought copies of the debriefing report from Professor Wendt's mission with the PAK." He opened his briefcase and brought out a dozen manila envelopes with Eyes Only stamped on the outside. He personally handed them out around the room. There was even one for me. He went on. "The first page is an executive summary which should be good enough for the purposes of this meeting." Most of the people in the room opened theirs and glanced at the top page. Even I did. Moertl did not.

Treats asked her, "Aren't you even curious about what's in the report?"

She smiled a wicked smile and said, "I'm a quick study. Let's just go ahead."

Treats shrugged, but a couple of the participants asked for a moment to complete reviewing the executive summary. When they'd finished, he proceeded. "What's not contained in the summary or the full report is that we've been contacted by the PAK. They have a rather unusual request."

Moertl rolled her eyes and said, "Here we go."

Ginny nudged my leg and whispered, "I've got a really, really bad feeling about this."

Treats went on. "Here's the thing. They are mounting an expedition to attack the Souls at their home world, and they want help."

Moertl broke in. "How can we possibly help them?"

Treats replied testily, "I was just getting to that. They want us to help them find the Soul's home world. They want the crew of humans who accompanied their first expedition to come along."

At that Ginny banged a hand down on the table. Her mouth was open to speak, but a glance at Moertl showed that she didn't want Ginny to speak. Ginny closed her mouth and sat back.

Parker said, "We don't have the original crew. One of them died on the mission."

Treats said, "We told them that. They said to send all the surviving crew. . . and that we should choose a fourth member for the team."

Moertl asked, "How in the world can this be a help?"

Treats just replied, "They won't say, but they are adamant."

Ginny spoke up. "It's unfair that Wendt should have to go with them a third time. He'll be killed for sure." She touched my knee with hers as she said that.

Moertl said, "They'll use their weapon against us if we don't cooperate, won't they? That was the point of the demonstration, the point of having him pull the trigger."

Treats appeared surprised that she was so familiar with the report. He shrugged. "I suppose. It doesn't really matter. The important thing is that we need. . ." Here he referred to the executive summary, "Professor Sinistra, Mr. Brahms, and of course, Professor Wendt. . ." He paused and added with a chuckle, "and a player to be named later to be ready to take ship with the PAK.

"One of the things to be determined or at least discussed in this meeting is the player to be named."

Ginny kicked me in the shins—gently—and whispered, "What is this player to be named thingee?"

I answered, "We can discuss it tonight." She squeezed my thigh which I took as consent.

Meanwhile, there were various names raised by the wizards and witches for good players-to-be-named-later. I had been thinking about it while these names were batted about. Ginny even suggested Kingsley Shacklebolt as a good candidate. The muggles were mostly silent. Then I cleared my throat.

Moertl looked over instantly. "Yes, Wendt. Do you have a suggestion?"

"I do. I nominate Dudley Dursley."

Moertl scratched her head. "I've never heard of any magical Dursleys."

Then Ginny actually laughed. "Sure you have. Don't you remember that he published an advanced potions text with Headmaster Slughorn a few years ago."

Moertl eyes narrowed. "Oh, yes. I thought that was some kind of joke putting his name on as an author. Why would you suggest someone who never went to Hogwarts or any wizarding school?"

I replied, "Because he has a very special wand. I'm one of the few who have seen it doing what it does best. You should think about him very seriously."

Moertl looked around the room. "Has anyone else knowledge of this Dursley's capabilities?"

Ginny cleared her throat. "Yes. I once tangled with him over his brutal treatment of Harry Potter. He is formidable and really did participate in a big way in the publication of that potions book. I don't know about his wand, but if Wendt here. . ." She rubbed my knee with her thigh at that point, "says that it's special, I'd believe him."

Moertl said, "We'll think about Dursley seriously. Are Aurora and Brahms still associated with the school?"

I nodded. She went on. "Then get in touch with them, and we'll have a little private conversation with them about volunteering for this mission with the PAK."

I agreed, but then I said something further. "You haven't asked me if I agree to go."

Everyone stared at everyone else except Ginny. She just squeezed my arm and said, "You stick to your wand on this one."

Treats asked, "Surely you're joking. You've got to go. The fate of the world is on your shoulders."

I answered, "Let me make something clear. IF. . . and I do mean IF . . . I decide to go, it will be under my conditions."

Moertl said, "You know that we can force you to go."

I smiled. "You can force me to go, but you can't force me to cooperate. There was an American general who put it very well. He was going to be nominated to run for President of the United States. He said, 'If nominated, I refuse . . .'"

At that point, another voice, Treats joined in, ". . . refuse to run. If elected, I will refuse to serve. General Tecumseh Sherman after the Civil War." I nodded.

Moertl said, "Well, don't keep us in suspense. What are your conditions? What do you want?"

I smiled. "First, I don't want money or anything for personal gain. I am a consultant for Gringotts." At that point pandemonium broke out. The magical people expressed dismay that I would work with the Goblins. The muggles were astounded that there was any such thing as a Goblin. I let the uproar die down some before speaking.

Then I said, "Actually my conditions are not really onerous. All that I ask is that England and possibly other interested parties such as the United States make loans to another government."

Everyone's jaws dropped except for Ginny and Moertl. They both nodded. Roskopf, who had been silent up to this point and seemed to be trying to be the proverbial fly on the wall, asked, "What government are we talking about?"

Moertl surprised almost everyone by saying, "Mine." Then she went on. "It's way past time for a biology break. Will Ms. Weasley, Professor Wendt, and Ms. Poynter please join me? Now."

We did. Moertl started the conversation on a negative note. "You are barking mad. Do you think you can blackmail these guys into giving us a loan?"

I had to laugh. "Sorry, it doesn't matter whether I do or not. I want to. I don't lose anything if I don't succeed."

Moertl said, "You don't know these politicians. They'll promise you anything and then find an excuse or no excuse for weaseling out. . . Oh, no offense, Ms. Weasley."

She smiled too. "None taken, Madame Minister."

Moertl said, "I suppose that you have a way to nail them down to a binding commitment. . . OH, you're thinking of the Unbreakable Oath! Good idea. The problem is . . ."

Ginny interrupted. "The problem is that they're muggles. They won't believe it unless they see it demonstrated. And then you've got a worse demonstration than that big asterism on Mars or whatever it was."

I shook my head definitely. "No Unbreakable Oaths required. Just trust me. . . Oh, one thing you could do. Would you bring in the Minister for . . ."

She supplied, "International Cooperation."

"Right."

Moertl started to say, "Ms. Poynter get the . . ."

Ms. Poynter finished, ". . . Minister. Yes ma'am." And she was off.

We returned to the Conference Room. Everyone was present except Ms. Poynter and Ms. Macron. Treats asked what the delay was when everyone was seated and nothing was happening.

Moertl said, "We're waiting for an expert to arrive. It shouldn't be more than a few minutes." There was a little battle over whether new attendees could be added without vetting. Moertl won that by stating that Ms. Macron was the equivalent of the US Secretary of State.

It was a little more than a few minutes. When they arrived, Moertl introduced her. Then we resumed with my demand. Moertl said, "I've brought in the Minister for International Cooperation to fill in details of the loan for any interested party. Minister Macron, please explain."

Macron said, "Well, it's a loan of four billion pounds sterling." The British Minister of Defense gagged.

I stepped in before he could say something. "Four billion pounds is a lot of money but compared with other loans that you've made to the militarys of other countries, it's hardly ground-breaking. Wouldn't you say that this is a real defense issue?"

Smithe blustered and said, "I don't see how . . ."

I broke in. "And, you could hardly have a safer loan. I can guarantee that you will receive it back with interest in a couple of years."

Macron seemed nervous but she agreed.

Treats asked, "What are you going to do—print money?"

I smiled and said, "Something like that."

He laughed.

Then there was a completely unexpected happening. Roskopf spoke up, "I think that I can get Russia to loan you whatever the money-grubbing Westerners won't."

All the muggles looked at every other muggle. After a moment of staring, Smithe said, "You came to us first. I think that I can guarantee loans from us and . . ." He looked around. The undersecretary of the Air Force nodded. Then he grunted a grudging, "Yes."

Moertl asked, "How can we be sure that everyone will keep their commitment?"

Roskopf chimed in. "Yes, the western democracies have a long history of breaking promises to give economic support. It happened to Russia and to many a Muslim country."

He smiled and turned to Melissa Macron. "You do have at least one Swiss bank account, don't you?"

She nodded.

Roskopf said, "I say that we set a limit of one week for the so-called democracies to deposit the four billions of pounds Sterling into your account. The Swiss are notorious . . . er . . . famous for their scrupulous ethical behavior with respect to moneys left in their care. Once deposited, only the account owner can get any out."

Macron chuckled. "Yes, you can say that again. I'll be happy to provide the information required for wire transfers to any interested governments."

There was grumbling a-plenty, but in the end, all three governments present received wire transfer instructions.

Moertl assured us that until the money was deposited there was no further point in discussions. She went on. "We will have meetings with wizarding authorities to select a fourth member of the team. I trust that every muggle has a wizarding companion to get them back home."

Everyone did. The Americans went together, the Brits went with Macron, and Roskopf went with Poynter. That left Ginny to take me home. However, Moertl asked us to stay to have dinner with her. Ginny shrugged and said, "I'll take you home afterwards."

The prospect of Ginny staying for dinner was not totally endorsed by Moertl, but she knew that I would be a pain in the ass if she didn't agree to a third.

Moertl said, "Very well. I suppose you might actually be helpful, Ms. Weasley. We're going to Col. Ander's restaurant. Do you know how to get there?"

Ginny agreed and said, "Good. I'll take Wendt". It was another disappointment for Moertl.

We arrived at the hearth of an intimate restaurant with a number of small rooms. Some had only one table. We were taken to one of these. There was no printed menu. The waiter recited the limited offerings without prices. The table chose an entree and everything else was determined by that choice. We chose Bouef Bourguingon. Servers appeared with soup and the meal was started without any delay.

Moertl cast a *Muffliato* spell so that we could speak without being heard. Moertl assured us that even without the spell we were safe from being overheard, such was Ander's reputation that had been developed over decades. After we had finished with the soup, and the salad was delivered, she brought us to the point, "Wendt, are you absolutely sure that you want this Dursley? How old is he? How much experience does he have?"

I shrugged. "To answer your questions in order, yes, I'm sure that I want Dursley, about the same age as Potter, and a couple of years as a wizard."

She gaped at me and turned to Ginny. "Can't you talk some sense into him? Surely someone like Shackbolt or Carrington or even Lockhart would be better."

Ginny just smiled at me and said, "Believe me Madame Minister, if Wendt wants something, he has a very good purpose for it."

She grumbled. "Do you give him everything he wants?"

Ginny's smile changed, and there was a glint in her eyes as she said, "Not everything, but if I'm going to give him something, I give him exactly what he wants. It always turns out better that way."

By this time, the main course had arrived. The Boeuf Bourguignon was wonderful indeed. That put an end to our discussion for a bit. Then, she returned to it and to me. "Are you going to tell me that I have to provide Dursley or you won't go?"

I shook my head and said, "No, even if you insist on sending Lockhart, I'll go. It's just that I think that there's a lot better chance of my coming back alive if Dursley goes."

Ginny squeezed my arm as if her hand were a pneumatic press, but she didn't say anything.

Moertl agreed. "OK. It's Brahms, Aurora, you, and Dursley. I'll talk Treats into it somehow." That allowed us all or at least Ginny and me to enjoy our dessert worry-free.

After dinner, Ginny and I took the floo to my office. We started to do some serious snogging. However, she stopped and said, "I've got two questions for you."

"Shoot."

She pulled back a bit so that she could look in my eyes comfortably. Then she asked, "What is this 'player to be named later' thing?"

I chuckled. I thought it was going to be something difficult. "It's easy. In professional baseball, players get traded from one team to another occasionally."

She said, "OK. That happens in Quidditch too, but I've never heard that expression in Quidditch."

"Well, in baseball teams have twenty-five players. It's not unusual to have multi-player deals. In Quidditch, you've got more like fifteen players on a team. Multi-player deals are rare."

Ginny said, "I don't think I've heard of any."

"Right. Well, when you do multi-player deals in baseball, sometimes, the deal would be one-sided if there weren't an extra player besides the ones that one team is willing to give up, so an extra unnamed player lets the deal be made and the details will be worked out later. Usually, the unnamed player is not very good."

I was happy to have gotten past that question easily. Then the hard one came. She asked with a definite attitude of indignation, "How could you agree to go on this crazy mission, and if you had to go, why didn't you ask for me to come along?"

I took a deep breath and said, "Well, it's far too dangerous for me to let you come along."

"Then why the bloody hell did you agree to go!"

I looked to my feet for inspiration. She repeated the question. "Well?"

I said, "Ginny, they were going to force me to go anyway. You could see that, surely."

"Well, you sure bargained hard for the Goblins. Where was I in all that!"

My jaw dropped as I thought. Finally, I said, "Look, it wasn't only for the Goblins. It wasn't even mainly for the Goblins. All of the people who use galleons for money will benefit."

She started crying. "Well, that's just fine for all the rest of the witches and wizards. What about this witch?"

I said, "I'll come through it. I always do."

She gasped at that. Then she spoke in a defeated tone, "That's it. I've got this terrible feeling. I don't think you will." Then she pulled out of my embrace and walked toward the hearth. "I've got to go."

I was truly surprised. "No good-bye kiss?"

She seemed surprised. "Oh, yes. How appropriate. A good-bye kiss."

That troubled me, but we embraced and the kiss was as alive as any that we'd shared. She then turned and was into the floo network.

The next morning dawned bright and early. I went through my daily routine until lunch. At that point, I went down to the kitchens to meet with the Maintenance Engineering staff.

Filch and Dursley were there but hadn't begun lunch yet. Filch cackled, "Find you like dining with the engineers more than the professors, do ye?"

I had the philosophy that anything I could do by smiling I would. Filch didn't need anything more to ratify his opinion. Usually, he didn't even need that. Dursley took a more practical approach, asking, "What can we do for you, Professor?"

Just then the house elves delivered a plate of sandwiches, a pitcher of pumpkin juice, a bowl of fruit salad, and condiments. I took that opportunity to procrastinate. We cut the edge off our hunger. I took that chance to begin my elevator speech. "Mr. Dursley, I have an offer to make you."

He excitedly asked, "What is it? You've done me lots of favors. I owe you a ton."

I started to give my spiel, but hesitated a moment and started with Filch, "Just one thing—this is confidential."

Filch's face brightened, and he said, "You can absolutely trust my regression."

I was dumbfounded for a moment and then realized what he meant, "I knew I could. Thanks. Okay, here's the deal."

Filch leaned forward so that we could talk softly.

I looked back to Dursley and said, "You know that I was on a mission for the Ministry last year. It was the mission that Minerva died on."

He nodded slowly. "Yes, I know exactly that much and nothing more. So, where is this going?"

I simply stated it up front. "We're doing a sort of repeat. I don't know how dangerous it will be, but my bet is that it won't be any less dangerous."

He stared at me in incomprehension. I didn't say anything more. I needed him to figure it out for himself. Eventually, he said, "Oh. OH! You want me to sort of replace Minerva?"

I struggled to resist the tears. I succeeded. "No one can replace Minerva, but are you willing to go in her place?"

He stared at me and closed his eyes. When he opened them, he said, "Can I sleep on it?"

I smiled that he had made such a wise choice. I said, "Of course. I don't even know how much time you have to think about it, but I'll tell you my advise." I paused for him to respond.

When he did, he just said, "Give it to me."

"Sleep on it. When you wake up, you'll have an answer. It will be the first thought that comes to your mind. If that thought is, 'Oh bloody hell, how can I say no?' Then your answer is 'no' and I'll be happy to get it. On the other hand, if you wake up thinking, 'Let's get going before I change my mind.' Then, the answer is 'yes.'"

He nodded and said, "I'll sleep on it."

We finished the lunch, and as I left, I heard Filch trying to talk Dursley out of helping me. I liked Dursley so I wasn't disappointed. As a matter of fact, in a way, it was a no-lose situation. If Filch succeeded, then Dursley was "safe." On the other hand, if Filch failed, I'd have Dursley along, which was a bonus for me.

That evening Ginny didn't pay a visit to me. That was another no-lose event. If she came, it would be wonderful. If she didn't, and if she were sep-arating from me, it would be better for her long-term.

The next day, Dursley caught me in the Great Hall just before lunch and asked me to come down and lunch with Filch and him. I hoped that Dursley would announce his decision, so we walked down to the kitchens. Filch was waiting for us. He got up when we arrived.

Kreacher came over to us. He greeted us and asked if there were any-thing he could get us. Then he turned to leave but swung around and said, "There being one more thing. Is you going away, Mr. Dursley?"

Dursley was obviously surprised. He asked, "Where did you get that idea, Kreacher?"

Kreacher just looked down at his feet. Filch did too. I said, "Well, since the elephant has just stepped into the room, we might as well deal with it right now. Kreacher, would you please sit down so that we can talk about this and keep everyone on the same parchment?"

Kreacher turned as red as a beet and said, "Kreacher is not feeling good about sitting with wizards." Filch perked up at that.

I said, "Please sit with us Kreacher." He silently did so. I breathed a sigh of relief. I would have hated to sit and discuss this while Kreacher stood.

We all looked toward Dursley who said, "I took your advise professor. When I got up this morning—and believe me it was in the early morning hours—I wanted to go. I could hardly wait to tell you."

With those words Filch's countenance fell. He looked up and asked, "Why? Why do you have to go?"

Dursley said, "I've lived a life without courage. I had to prove to myself that I could do something that requires real courage."

171

Filch exclaimed, "What are you talking about? Didn't you and Wendt risk your life by going to save your girlfriend from that crazy guy who wanted to keep you from publishing your book."

I couldn't believe that I was adding arguments to Filch's. I said, "Mr. Filch, you didn't realize it, but during the entire year that Snape was Headmaster, the Dursleys were pursued by Deatheaters. I don't know how that story ended, but I'm sure that there were many brave acts that you did."

Dursley dropped his head to the table and said, "Those weren't acts of bravery. They were acts of desperation. It was either flee and even fight the Deatheaters or die. Pamela is dearer than life to me. When she was kidnapped, I had to try to save her. It was just desperation not courage."

Even Filch was moved. He just shook his head. "I will miss you. If you die while you're gone, I'll never forgive you."

I couldn't help laughing. "I won't forgive you either. We'll probably both be dead."

Kreacher only said, "Mr. Dursley, please come back. I will be missing you at meals."

Dursley said, "Believe me, I have every intention of returning." He then turned to me, "When are we going?"

I had to admit that I didn't know, but I added, "It will be soon. Before the month is over, I'm sure." By this time, lunch had been placed on the table, Kreacher had excused himself, and we had a quiet lunch.

The PAK Leave A Calling Card

I was doing some lesson planning in my office when there was a sonic boom that shook the castle. Sonic booms were never heard at Hogwarts. I wondered what was happening. About an hour later, I found out.

Ginny popped into my hearth and virtually ran to my side. She grabbed a free hand and dragged me to the hearth. She said, "You've got to come now!"

I started to ask a question. She just hissed, "Not now." Then she dragged me into the hearth, picked up some floo powder, and we reappeared in Moertl's office. I'd been there so often that I walked directly to her main guest chair and sat. Moertl was still standing, but took the cue and sat as well.

I frowned in concentration and decided to start with a reasonable deduction, "This is about something that happened, resulting in a sonic boom over Hogwarts and probably a lot of other places."

Ginny and she gaped at me. Moertl grimaced and said, "OK. I'll let go of the need to know what magic gave you that idea. Let's just proceed.

"You are right. In about ten minutes there's going to be an emergency meeting that will include the American Secretary of Magic, the Prime Minister of England, and the American ambassador to England. We're going to have it at number 10 Dowley street."

Ginny cleared her throat and said, "I think that's Downing street, ma'am."

Moertl just shook her head and said, "Whatever. The point is that something happened on the edge of the Antarctic ocean south of India that caused that . . . what did you call it?"

I said, "Sonic boom."

She went on. "Yes. Well, we've got to go. There's a floo connection in ten Downey street, and I have to take us. I'm the only one who knows the password to get in." She held out both her hands for us to take. She asked Ginny, "Be a good girl. Throw some floo powder down for me."

Ginny did, but I could tell from her body language that she was not happy about "being a good girl".

I'd only been in ten Downing once in my life. It had been redecorated in the intervening years. I hardly recognized it. The PM stood when we materialized out of the hearth in his office. There was one other person in the room. The PM said, "I'm expecting another before we start, so we'll just hold off introductions until that person's arrival.

We took seats and within moments two people entered the door. Pam commented, "Since when is one person, two?"

The PM said, "I think there may be a couple more on the way." Indeed the door opened, and two entered at the same time. One more person came through the floo connection. He looked around and said, "I think that's everyone." Then he did do introductions. I couldn't keep track of the various people except by title. There was the American ambassador. He was accompanied by a woman who was described as a Scientific Attaché. There was a representative of the British Geologic Society. There was the Minister of Defense along with a some sort of technical expert. There was the American Secretary of Magic, Baker. It was fairly crowded in the PM's home office.

The PM then asked the American ambassador to report on what had happened in the South Indian ocean. He turned to his associate, the Scientific Attaché, Helen, to report. She stood and asked if she could use the projection screen with her laptop. The PM looked around for guidance. No one among the top brass seemed to have an idea. He looked at me and asked, "What do you think, Professor Wendt?"

I rolled my eyes. "Sure. Just let her hook it up. You must have a remote control for it."

He did. He dug around in his desk, commenting, "I rarely use this myself, but if you can set it up, you can use it." Helen placed her open laptop on the PM's desk, connected a VGA cable and used the remote to fire up the projector. While it was warming up, she said, "The first thing I'm going to show you is an ordinary Google Map of the Indian Ocean and the Antarctic Ocean."

Moertl, who was sitting between Ginny and me asked me, "What is this Goggly Map thingee?"

I reported, "It's just a map of the world, probably like every one you ever saw at Hogwarts."

She wrinkled her nose and said, "I don't think I ever saw a world map at Hogwarts."

I sighed. Meanwhile the projector was warmed up, and the first thing that showed on the screen was a regular Mercator projection of the world, centered on the Equator at the Prime Meridian. Helen used her mouse to reposition the center to somewhere north of Antarctica directly below India. She said, "American satellites detected a gamma ray flash approximately ten hours ago. There was an accompanying neutron decay flash shortly after that. The satellites localized it to an area on the border of the Indian ocean and the Antarctic Ocean approximately where my pointer is located. At the same time the NOAA weather satellite stationed over the subcontinent of India recorded an extremely strong optical flash, and infrared picked up what appeared to be a bubble of very high temperature on the ocean. We would have much better data from that satellite if it weren't that the event was only a couple of degrees from the horizon of that satellite.

"Geologic stations around the Indian Ocean recorded a seismic signal several hours later. Their interpretation was that a 9.4 magnitude earthquake had occurred near the ocean bottom at that area. There is a tsunami warning posted to all coasts of the Indian Ocean and the Pacific Ocean. The tsunami will probably circle the world but not cause damage outside those areas. Estimates are that there will be thousands of deaths due to the tsunami in areas that don't receive the warning.

"Based on previous large volcanic explosive events, we will probably hear the shock wave for a dozen or more times before it dies out. We were extremely lucky that there was no shipping within two hundred miles of the event. Of course, there is very little shipping that travels as far south as seventy-fifth latitude.

"The Americans and the Russians are sending aircraft to sample the air for radioactive isotopes to try to identify the perpetrator. Initial results are that no one detonated a nuclear munition. All fusion bombs have a fission trigger. So far there have been no unusual actinide radioactive fallout downwind. The vast majority of the radioactive debris is tritium.

"We've been trying to interpret all that for the last ten hours. Here are our results:

- There was a nuclear explosion that we estimate to be about three to five thousand megatons.
- The amount of radioactive debris is relatively small because only seawater was irradiated. Most of the radioactive nuclei created were tritium. Most of that will be limited to the far south circumpolar jet stream.
- The explosion didn't affect the sea bottom due to the depth of the ocean at that point.
- We don't know how this explosion happened. Even an asteroid impacting the surface wouldn't create that much radioactive debris."

With that she had run out of things to say. She backed up to her chair.

The British Defense Minister sat and said, "We are aware of the cause of this explosion. Everyone at this meeting should be aware that the subject matter is covered by the Official Secrets Act. It is not to be revealed to anyone who is not authorized to receive Top Secret information.

"Now, we know what has happened because the aliens responsible for the detonation have contacted us. They made it quite clear that no further dragging of feet would be tolerated. I am not aware of what is causing our feet to be dragged. Can someone fill me in?"

Moertl said, "The problem is complicated."

The American Secretary of Magic shook his head and said, "It's simple. One of your people is refusing to cooperate."

Moertl came back quickly. "Look, he's a Yank. That puts it more in your bailiwick than mine!"

The British Defense Minister chimed in. "We're burning sunlight. Who is it?"

Moertl was surly in her response. "It's Professor Wendt of Hogwarts, who is here and can speak for himself."

I said, "It's very simple. I am willing to co-operate on one condition. Americans and Brits are quite aware what it is. They just have to make loans to the Ministry of Magic amounting to four billion pounds sterling. That's petty cash for the defense departments of both the Americans and the Brits."

The Defense Minister harrumphed. The American ambassador said, "Well, I've been informed that there are Senators who object to another dime of foreign aid and have threatened to filibuster any special spending appropriation for mystery foreign aid. God knows what they would say if they knew that it was to go to a 'magical' country."

Helen cleared her threat and said, "Uh. . . actually . . . I have some responsibility to the DOD—a dotted line connection."

Ginny whispered a question, "DOD? Dotted line?"

"US Department of Defense. Dotted line means that she doesn't report to the DOD but is closely connected to it."

Meanwhile Helen said, "I can tell you that the DOD has . . . uh . . . some discretionary funds that can be used for developing issues. I don't think that the DOD is aware of the criticality of the deployment of funds to the MOM. I can't promise anything, other than that I am about to step outside number ten and make a phone call to my dotted line contact concerning the importance of foreign aid."

With that she got up and walked out of the room. Meanwhile the Defense Minister blustered a bit and said, "We are not the American DOD. We don't have money flowing like the Thames. I will have to consult with . . ."

The PM cut him off. "Consult with me. We'll put up a half billion if the Americans put up the rest."

The American ambassador blustered some as well. "That's hardly fair. You have a fifth the population of the US."

The Defense Minister shot back, "But our per capita GDP is smaller than yours!"

The PM tried to get control of the situation by interjecting. "Let's wait and see what the DOD has to say before jumping on each other." Just then the "Science" Attaché returned to the room. She sat beside the ambassador and whispered in his ear.

Ginny whispered in my ear, "Oh, to have an extensible ear!"

The Ambassador nodded several times and said, "Uhm, Helen has talked with the Secretary of Defense. He has authorized us to make up the additional three and a half billion. Does anyone have the proper details of where to wire transfer the amount to the proper account?"

Moertl said, "We've already provided that information. As soon as we have notification of the money from both countries being in the account, we will provide all interested parties with the approval to communicate with the PAK our readiness to assist them as they desire."

The PM looked around the room and asked, "Is everyone satisfied?" There were nods of agreement. "Then this meeting is adjourned. Everyone should get moving. We're burning daylight as the Yanks say."

We all left. The American Secretary of Magic left by floo first. Then we left next. In her office, Moertl commanded, "Sit, Wendt." I did. She then asked, "What in the world were you doing? You were playing the highest stake poker hoping that everyone would back down."

I said, "It worked." She stood and reached in her handbag. I went on, "I'd have backed down if everyone was obstinate."

She paced for a while and then said, "You'd better never do that again!" I didn't say anything. Then she sat and said, "The two of you, get out before I curse someone."

Ginny and I wasted no time going to the floo and dropping into my office. She said, "You were pretty arrogant there, holding the entire world's population for ransom."

I had to admit the truth of that—to myself. What I said was, "That only worked out to half a pound per person. We can afford it."

She had sat at the sofa. I guess she expected me to join her. I was sitting on the guest side of my desk. She picked up a pillow from the sofa and threw it at me. I jumped up and jumped onto the sofa, picking up a pillow en route. We had a little pillow fight. It was approaching dinner time at Hogwarts. Ginny suggested that we eat at her parents' house.

I demurred. "I've got to put in an appearance at the head table. Sorry."

She shook her head sending her hair flowing. "Don't worry. I'll come back after dinner. You know, when you're defying the combined forces of the British and American muggles and wizards, it's pretty sexy."

"That was my secret plan to get you into bed tonight."

She nodded silently. Then she rose, we kissed, and she left via the floo connection.

◿

The next evening Ginny appeared in my office, smiling broadly.

I asked her why she was so happy. It was that marked a change from before. She said, "I come from a meeting with the Minister. She gave me a special full time assignment—you. I'm to be the liaison with you. There are several things that we need to discuss before we get to my personal assignment with you."

I agreed. "Let's get finished with the meat and potatoes before we get to dessert."

She smiled at that and started, "OK. First, some really good news. The Brits have thrown more than five hundred million pounds into the Swiss account. They haven't even had us sign any agreement. The Americans have pitched in to the tune of four billion. Why do you think they've done that?" She hesitated for about a half second and then answered her own question, "I think that they've gotten even more pressure from the PAK who are hot to leave. That ultimatum is close enough that there isn't time for negotiation."

I considered it. "It sounds reasonable. Why haven't we heard about that date yet?"

Ginny grimaced. "You know those muggles. They always want to have an advantage. They keep everything away from us that we don't absolutely have to have."

I thought to myself, "Yeah, those damn muggles, you can't trust any of them." What I actually said was, 'I've got some news for you—good news."

She took my hand in hers and said, "Quick, what is it?"

"Dursley has agreed to come."

She shook her head. "You just knew he would."

I gazed into her eyes and said, "You were still hoping to get onto the mission?"

There was a quick nod that you might miss if you weren't watching her eyes carefully. Then she turned away and said, "Well, I guess that's it isn't it."

She threw her arms around me and said, "We've got to talk to the Brahmses. I guess there's still a hope they might refuse to go."

"OK. Let's try the Shrieking Shack. He works late a lot." She agreed and we walked down to the main floor of the castle. As we went I said, "It's ironic, isn't it. If we were anywhere else in England, we could get there in a few seconds. Here, we have to walk."

She took my hand and said, "Lazybones. You just don't want to do any work. You're worse than most wizards."

We passed some students on the way. One of them was a sixth year. She recognized Ginny. She said, "Ginny Weasley! Do you recognize me? I was in Griffyndor in your fifth year. Of course, you were always running around with upper classmen, like that Harry Potter." She seemed to notice our hands for the first time. "Are you. . . with Professor Wendt?"

Ginny said, "My business, not yours." She turned to me and asked, "Don't you have some points to subtract from Griffyndor?"

I smiled at the sixth year. "Not if she can respect confidences." The sixth year nodded vigorously.

As we left the castle Ginny commented, "You know she won't."

"You didn't seem to care much one way or the other, but I have to maintain disciple while you don't."

We reached the Shrieking Shack and found both the Brahmses there. The Boy Genius was working hard at a laptop while the less disciplined half was grading student scrolls. She looked up first and observed, "Well, well. Have you come to plan our next Halloween? Are we going to have accomplices?"

At that Nicholas looked up. "Guests. Let's see. Weasley with Wendt. Well, we've got the W's covered. Must be the Ministry that brings you here. What could it be?" Then his mouth opened wide. "I'm afraid to guess. Tell us."

Ginny said, "It's the Souls."

Aurora asked, "Not again! What do they want?"

Ginny answered quickly, "It's not exactly the Souls. It's their mortal enemies. We've decided to call them the PAK."

Aurora asked, "What in the world could they want from us? They're about a million times smarter and are physically far better than us!"

The BG's face hadn't changed a whit. He said, "They want us to guide them to the Soul's home world don't they?"

Aurora repeated, "How in the world could they want that from us? We haven't the slightest idea where the Souls are. . . do we?"

The BG said, "First, what else could they want?" He had started ticking his points off on his fingers. "Second, we have been there. We have all sorts of subliminal clues to where we were. They probably hope to tease those

179

out. Third, I actually tried to figure out where we were. There were strong hints that I noticed."

Aurora glared at him. "How could you do such a stupid thing!"

He shrugged. "It was hard to escape the temptation. For example. . ."

Aurora screamed, "NO! NO! NO! Don't say anything." She was silent for a moment. Then we both said at the same time the word "obliviate."

He objected, "You can't do that!"

She said, "I can, and we must." I nodded agreement.

He said, "I suppose you're right."

Ginny exclaimed, "God, I love working with you!" It wasn't clear whom she meant, but I had a feeling it was all of us.

Aurora muttered, "Maybe it's one particular person and maybe it's just plain love." She had her wand out and motioned Ginny and me back. She had it pointed at the BG.

He said, "Is this really necessary?"

She nodded and motioned with her wand. Apparently, she was using a silent spell. There was no apparent change, but the BG said, "Well, that's done it. All my observations are gone. Too bad. They were really insightful —I think. So, when do we leave?"

Ginny answered, "We don't know yet, but I'm pretty sure that it's going to be soon—maybe within a week."

Aurora asked for details of the mission. Ginny turned to me. "You'd better take that question. You've got a lot more information than I do about that."

I agreed. "Here's the deal. The PAK . . ."

The BG leaped up and shouted, "Now I remember. We're talking Ring-world!"

I shook my head. "That's not their name for themselves. That's our nickname for them. If you remember Niven's PAK, you know why."

He chuckled. "Yeh, you're right. Those bloody bastards are a lot like The PAK. I like it. It'll keep us on our toes to think that we're dealing with the PAK. Go ahead."

"Well, I know that you know about the explosion on Mars."

Both the Brahmses looked dumbfounded. Aurora said, "You don't mean to say that the PAK had something to do with that."

I nodded slowly and said, "Not just the PAK. I actually pulled the trigger on that."

The BG said, "No shit!"

Aurora said, "No asteroid?"

Ginny said, "It was Wendt all the way—with a lot of help from the PAK."

The BG said, "Well, we knew they could do something like that by plowing an FTL ship into a planet or the sun, but that would have been much larger. Even on Mars, we'd have been fried by that, wouldn't we?"

I sighed, "They've miniaturized their FTL drive. I saw the missile they mounted it in. It was much smaller than the smallest cruise missile that I'm familiar with." I hesitated before saying the worst. "They claimed that the yield was adjustable. What we saw was not the most powerful yield out of that one missile."

Aurora said, "Shit! How was it that you pulled the trigger on the test?"

I shook my head. "No test. That was just a demo of what they could do —in our solar system."

The BG said, "I see now why they wanted a human observer up close. Did they let you take video?"

Aurora said, "We got it through the Hubble, didn't we?"

I nodded. She said, "That's it. We don't have a choice. Co-operation or incineration." Then she nodded. "That's what the big bang was, wasn't it? I wondered about another Krakatoa type explosion down there."

The B.G. nodded again and added, "Yes, I guess the governments haven't released the info yet, but that was made by a big nuclear explosion in the Indian Ocean. It's so remote that they can probably hide what it really was for a few days yet, but the radioactive debris is going to start showing up in Australia, and then they'll have to come clean."

I agreed. "I think you've got it."

The BG asked, "Did the PAK ask for us specifically?"

I shrugged. "Not by name, but as good as. They wanted the same team that had gone with the Souls.

He asked, "What are we doing about Minerva's seat?" He was always direct about things. By this time, I was pretty inured to the pain of thinking about her.

Ginny jumped in with the answer. "This moron, Wendt, wants Dursley. He's gotten the Minister to go along with it."

Aurora asked me, "Why Dursley?"

I frowned as I tried to give my answer without answering.

Ginny scoffed. "Oh, come on. It's not that hard a question."

I disagreed. "Yes, it is. I would have preferred that it wasn't generally known that I wanted Dursley. That cat is out of the bag, but I'm not going to tell you why. You can guess."

Ginny scoffed. "You haven't got a reason other than not wanting me on the mission."

I smiled. "That's a pretty good reason."

Ginny swung around to put her face into mine. "You don't trust me to come back alive."

The BG said, "Wow, you've got a whole string of good reasons."

Ginny whirled around on him, and you could see the fire in her eyes. She seethed for a full minute before saying, "Wendt and I will talk about this later. It's not settled yet."

I smiled. "Oh, I'm counting on it."

Aurora said, "Well, I think that's a great idea, and I think you two should go and take your nuclear war someplace else." We did.

In my office, Ginny completely surprised me by falling on the sofa and breaking into sobs. She looked up at me through tears and asked, "Why don't you want me on the mission? We make a great team! Those PAK don't stand a chance against the two of us."

I sat beside her and took her hand. "Look, Ginny, if it were just the two of us, I'd be with you 105%. There's a problem though. It's not just the two of us. It's the whole human race and maybe all the Soul's race."

She opened her mouth to object. I touched her lips with two fingers. I said, "You know I'm as stubborn as you are. I don't want to argue the night away. Especially since we might not have that many nights before the mission starts."

She ripped my hand away with her wand and smothered me with a kiss that would ignite a star.

The next morning when the sun woke us, Ginny said, "We've got to get the Goblins going with the money that we've got in that Swiss account. If you're not going to be back here for a while, we need to grease the skids while we've still got you.

"OK. What do you suggest?"

She smiled. "A Hogwarts breakfast first. Then we can start looking for places to buy a hundred million galleons worth of gold."

I agreed. It was earlier than Hogwarts breakfast even when we had showered and dressed. I took Ginny's hand and led her down to the kitchens. Not entirely surprisingly we found Dursley there. I asked him where Filch was.

He stared at me and asked, "How long have you known Filch?"

"Oh, more than a dozen years. So?"

"Then how can you not know that he patrols the halls late into the night. That's good because he never was a morning person. On the other hand, I am a morning person. Voila! I normally breakfast alone. Of course, when he's up and has his breakfast, I join him for a tea break."

He pointed to the bustling kitchen and said, "They'll have some breakfast up for us shortly. I don't remember that you were ever a morning person when we roomed together. What gets you . . .up . . . so . . . ." At that point his mouth opened wide. I guess it had just occurred to him that Ginny was here and probably had been all night.

Ginny filled the empty space with a question for me. "You roomed with Dursley for a while! How did you two get along?"

I answered, "Oh, you remember the first year that Dursley was here. You were, too. That little incident with the love potion caused both Dursley and me to be sent to Coventry. We had to room together until Minerva was satisfied that we'd suffered enough."

Ginny ran her hand up my arm and said, "I'd never ever send you to Coventry." Then she laughed good-naturedly. Fortunately, the house elves delivered some breakfast, and we could eat without speaking.

After we had eaten enough to satisfy, Ginny asked, "Where do we go to find gold?"

I said, "The only time I dealt with large quantities of gold was in the Middle East. It was almost as scary as being in space with the PAK. I'd like to find someplace safer to buy. Why don't we start with General Parker. He should know where to start looking if not actually point us somewhere."

She said "I suppose that you have to get away from Hogwarts so that you can use your pheletone as Dad would say."

"Right."

We walked out of Hogwarts. When we reached the midpoint between Hogwarts and Hogsmeade, I tried my phone. I used Parker's personal line. No answer.

Ginny said, "Maybe he doesn't want to talk with you."

"Yeh. Maybe. I'll send him a text." I did. Then I said, "We've got to stay away from magic to wait for an answer."

She said, "Oh, pooh! What else can we do?"

I thought about it and decided that we should really get in touch with Gringotts. "Let's go send an owl to Gringotts and set up a meet. We really have to let them know to be ready to start up their mint."

Ginny said, "Back to Hogwarts." We walked back through the brightening morning. Though it was spring, it was still chill. We held hands and walked, arms touching, on the way back to Hogwarts. The owlery was still chill as we ascended the stairs.

I commented that Hogwarts was designed to keep people healthy. Ginny laughed. "You mean that you can't get anywhere without using stairs and usually lots.

"Right."

It took me longer to compose the letter than I expected. I didn't want to raise their hopes too high, but I did want them to start thinking about how to get the gold to their mint.

At my suggestion, we took the floo network to the Cauldron and then disapparated to a good library. She smiled. "Excellent. I can read the muggle newspapers and do a little research on the criminal scene. I suppose you're going to be using the innernetwork."

I simply agreed.

At the Cauldron, when I offered to buy Tom a round, he just shook his head and said, "You've got a lifetime pass to my floo. You've given me so much business that I should pay you every time you use it." He laughed that distinctive hoarse laugh that I've never heard anywhere else.

At the library, my phone rang. It was Parker. I started to explain what I wanted to talk with him about, but Parker interrupted me. "Just can it. The damn Americans listen to the Hottentot bargaining over fish shipments to his marketplace. If you want to do anything quietly these days, you have to do it in person. Let's have a late lunch at a fish and chips I know near the Cauldron. Who else is going to be there?" He immediately added, "Oh, I don't want to know or actually, I don't want the Americans to know."

I said, "OK. We'll find your fish and chips. What time?"

"Let's say 1 PM."

We showed up at the fish and chips shop which turned out to be a fairly nice restaurant that actually had tables and wait staff. Parker showed up ten minutes after one. We had gotten a table and ordered drinks. He talked with one of the wait staff on his way to our table. He commented, "I eat here fairly frequently. I know that waiter. I just told him that I wanted my regular. So, what do you want?"

Ginny started the story. "You Brits have served up a nice down-payment on your loan. We need to buy a large amount of gold from muggle sources so that we can start processing it. Have you got suggestions where to go for. . . oh. . . say a hundred million pounds worth of gold."

Parker smiled. "You don't believe in starting small, do you? Well, I knew that this request might be coming, so I made some discreet inquiries. Just how fast do you need it?"

I said, "ASAP."

He nodded. "Of course, you magic types think everything can be done with the flick of a wand. Well, if you really want that kind of quantity quickly, you'll have to be prepared to deal with . . . shall we say. . . shady sources. Is that all right?"

Ginny nodded. Parker asked, "This is a change for you, Wendt. Since when do you let other people make the decisions?"

"Oh, come on. You know that I've always cooperated with others."

184

He chuckled. "Well, I suppose I can't blame you. Seriously, how are you going to transport that much gold? That must be at least ten metric tons."

Ginny smiled. "Don't worry. That will not be a problem."

"Good. Well, I've been talking to someone at MI6 just in case you needed to deal with shady types. He has someone that he wants you to meet. I'll get back to you by text when we have it set up."

"That should be fine."

The End of English literature

We returned to Hogwarts. I decided that it was time to have a discussion with Slughorn. I asked Ginny where she was going. She stared at me as though I were a nincompoop. "Why your office, of course. I wasn't kidding when I said that I was assigned to you for the duration."

"OK. I'll be up in time for dinner, I hope."

Slughorn usually kept a class period free just before dinner. So, I wasn't surprised when his personal assistant, Sally, ushered me directly into his inner office.

Slughorn rose and rounded his desk to shake hands. "Good to see you. How's your class going?"

He offered me a drink as I took the red leather chair. I asked for a hot tea and said, "I usually hold on the hard stuff until after dinner. That's what I've come to discuss with you."

Slughorn buried his face in his hands. "You're about to tell me that you're resigning."

I felt sorry for all that I'd put him through. I tried to let him down gently. "Here's the thing. The British government and the Americans are forcing me to help them. Believe me, I'd rather not. I don't have a choice."

He leaned back and asked, "You couldn't just wait until the end of the term? It's hardly more than a month away."

I shook my head. "Sorry. I don't know when I have to leave, but it will be a lot sooner than later."

As we were speaking, Sally opened the door. An owl flew in. She said, "I didn't verify who it's for. It's got to be one of you." The owl landed on the side of the desk that I was beside. I looked at me and dropped the letter that it was holding in its beak into my lap. I looked up at Slughorn.

He said, "Oh, you might as well use my office. Go ahead and open it."

I did. It was from Gringotts. Its substance was that I was to meet the CEO to discuss gold. The place and time was lunch the next day. He invited me to use Javeen to conduct me to the restaurant—the usual one. Of course, it had been dictated to Javeen. I wrote a brief note in response. It read, "I accept the meeting time and place. However, I must use my own transportation."

I folded the note and put in the owl's beak. It took off and flew out the door that Sally had left open.

I turned to Slughorn and said, "Sir, you're right that the term is almost over. I propose that I will submit the current effective grade as the final grade for the students. The chances that any of these students will improve their grade significantly is small.

"The chances that some will worsen their grade is a definite possibility. I submit that no student will be sorry to have my class end early. I don't think that parents will be grieved either."

Slughorn closed his eyes and pursed his lips in concentration. Finally, he opened his eyes and relaxed his lips so that he could deliver his decision. "Fine. Please draft an explanation to be distributed to the parents and students. Fill out the grade reports for your students, and submit them to Sally. Oh, please don't include the real reason."

I agreed to the terms. I went to the door, but before I left, he asked me a question. "Oh, one more thing. Are you going to be at the evening meal tonight?"

I agreed that I would. He nodded and said, "Then in that case, I'm going to announce your sabatical. I want you to tell your students that all your classes are canceled as of this day. You may add anything by way of explanation that you like."

"Yes, sir. It will be a brief version of what I write to be given to all the stake-holders."

When I got back to my office, I told Ginny what was going to happen. "You can have dinner in the kitchen or in the Great Hall. If you decide on that, please sit at the Griffyndor table. I'll be giving a brief farewell speech at dinner."

She decided to sit in the Great Hall. I seated myself at my usual spot. Ginny was at the very front of the Griffyndor table. Slughorn started the meal as usual. Before anyone was dismissed, he called the Great Hall to order. He said, "I regret to have to announce that Professor Wendt, our English literature professor, will have to end his teaching assignments early. I've asked him to say a few words to his students and the rest of the school."

I stood and said, "This last year has been very difficult for me. Recent events have forced me to end the term early. I apologize to all my students. All students will receive the grades that they've earned so far. I only want to say that I dearly wish that this were not necessary and thank my students for their patience and efforts throughout the term." With that I sat. Ginny stood and applauded. She was followed by the rest of the Griffyndors and eventually the entire hall.

That night, I worked on computing final grades and writing an explanation of each student's progress. When I finished, Ginny asked me, "Will you return after the end of your mission?"

We were sitting on the sofa in my office. I leaned back and closed my eyes. I said, "God, you can't imagine how much I wish I could answer that question and answer it yes."

Her arms encircled my shoulders, and she pulled me close to her. I felt tears on my cheek. She just said, "You have to come back." It was a quiet night in my apartment.

Gold Pays Galleons

We had breakfast in the kitchens. Filch was there early while Dursley, Ginny, and I were still were eating. He said, "I understand that you're done at Hogwarts."

Ginny gagged and I said, "I don't know. I know I'm finished for this term. If God wills it, I'll be back."

Filch said, "I don't know about God. He always seems to come around a day late and a galleon short. But you'd better just . . ." That was the end of what Filch had to say. I think he was choking on tears.

It was a sad meal until Dursley said, "You know, when I was running across Canada with my parents trying to escape Deatheaters, I'd not have given a brass knut for our chances."

Filch looked up from his plate, "You were being chased by Deatheaters!"

"Yes, didn't I ever tell you about it?"

"Well, I think I'd remember if you'd told me that you escaped those Deatheaters. How'd you do it?"

Dursley leaned forward and said, "Well, they thought they had us cornered in a frozen cabin in Northern Canada. Well, Dad and I . . ." I'd taken Ginny's arm and dragged her away from the table. When we were out of the kitchen, she asked, "Why'd you drag me away? I wanted to hear that story."

I shook my head vigorously, "I want to make sure that Filch has a real story of courage that he doesn't have to share with anyone."

"You're sentimental. Do you really like Filch?"

I smiled. "Don't you?"

She thought about that a long time without ever telling me.

Meanwhile, we went to my office where I collected my grades so that I could turn them over to Sally before we left for lunch.

We arrived at the restaurant just before noon. We were taken to a table in a private room. Gorblaz and Javeen were there waiting for us. We gave drink orders to the waiter who was waiting on us there. He was back quickly and took our order. Then, Gorblaz asked, "What's going on with the gold crisis?"

I said, "We have the first tranch of muggle money from the Ministry. It's worth about three hundred million galleons. We're going to buy muggle gold with a portion of it to start. We are planning to by sixty million galleons worth. How do we get the gold to you?"

There were two reactions in the room. Gorblaz said something in Gobbledygook and extended a hand to me. Javeen was sitting next me on my left hand at the circular table. Ginny was sitting at my right hand.

Javeen leaped out of her chair and threw her arms around me. She exclaimed, "I knew you could do it. You're wonderful!"

Of course, I didn't miss Ginny's hand plunging into her handbag. I briefly contemplated what it would be like to be between the crossing curses of two magicals. Fortunately, it didn't happen.

Everyone felt the tension of the moment. Gorblaz broke the utter silence of that moment. He smiled and said, "Just tell us where to show up and we'll be sure that it gets safely to our mint." That caused us all to laugh. It was clear to everyone that that statement was unnecessary. The Goblins would not let a single galleon slip through their fingers. Sixty million? Only a Riddle could separate them from that.

I returned us to a semblance of reality by saying, "I don't know where we'll find that much gold, but I know that we will somewhere in this world. You need to be prepared to pick it up—and maybe with little time to do it."

I hesitated because I didn't want to make the next point. I needn't have worried. Ginny jumped in. She said, "We may have to buy it from criminals that don't have much in the way of scruples."

Javeen laughed. It was a side of her that I'd not seen before. It was a cruel laugh. She simply said, "If only they would try to cheat us." It was said quietly without any particular emphasis. It made me shudder.

We talked about how we would get in touch with them at short notice with the location. They didn't go into details of how they would get there or how much advance notice they needed. I got the feeling that an hour would be enough. However, I was not going to let it rest at that. "I can't let us leave without more detailed instructions for contacting you and the absolute minimum lead time you need."

Gorblaz turned to his daughter and spoke in Gobbledygook. The conversation went on for quite some time as Ginny and I waited silently. It ended, and Javeen turned to me. "Since you have to get in touch with us from anywhere in the world, we'll give you this." She reached into a pocket in her skirt and said, "You have to keep what I'm about to show you secret. Ms. Weasley should go to the loo while I show it to you."

Ginny's eyes flared, and she said, "I'm the official Ministry representative here. Anything you show Wendt I will have to know about—if not now, then later when we're alone."

With that Javeen's mouth turned into a strange frown. Then Javeen pulled her hand out of her pocket. It contained a strange locket with a photo of Javeen. She said, "If you hold this in your hand, thus." She demonstrated without closing her hand about it. "It will signal all nearby Goblins. At least one will disapparate to you immediately. You can give a message to one of them. We'll get the message quickly. Be sure to include in the message, the date, time, and location where you want the gold to be picked up. Do you understand?"

Both of us said that we did, but she made each of us repeat the procedure and swear not to reveal it to anyone else. She trusted us enough that she didn't require the Unbreakable Oath.

We left the meeting and went by floo to my office. There we discussed the meeting. The first topic on Ginny's agenda was why Javeen was so free with my neck.

I answered, "Look, I've done everything I can to swat her away, but we still have to work with her and daddy. I'm limited in my options."

"Well, if you don't swat her away pretty soon, I'll show you how it's done with my wand."

The afternoon was uneventful except that in the evening, we joined Filch and Dursley in the kitchens for dinner. We were having a pleasant meal when an owl flew above us and dropped an envelope in my rice pudding. I dug it out and said, "I never liked rice pudding."

Ginny urged me to open the envelope. It was obviously from a muggle because it had gone via the wizard mail drop service. I retrieved it from the rice pudding, but before I could open it, a house elf appeared at my side with a towel. He said, "Begging you pardon, sir. May I be opening the envelope for you? Otherwise you will be getting rice pudding all over you."

I let him do it. He opened the envelope magically and reached a dry hand into it, retrieving the interior envelope. I took it from the house elf and used my knife to slit it open. I unfolded the note which I glanced at. Then I began delivering my deductions, "Well, it's obviously from a muggle. The inner envelope was obtained from a British Post Office and postmarked at the Kensington station. The sheet it was written on is plain notepaper such as . . ."

At that point Ginny grabbed it out of my hand and said, "Can't you just read it aloud?" She proceeded to do just that. "We have a mutual general friend. He would like us to meetup. Be at Paddington Station tomorrow at 2 PM. I'll recognize you. I'll tell you that I'm Macduff."

I smiled. "There are you happy?"

She frowned. "I thought there'd be more to it. What does he or she look like? How are we sure that we have the real thing?"

I agreed. "I don't know. I'm hoping that he'll have enough unique information to assure us that he's the real thing. Besides, you'll have your wand, right?"

Ginny frowned at me as though I were a moron. I said, "OK. I know you always do. Still . . ."

◁

The next day, we slept in by which I mean that we were abed until late in the morning. Neither of us were hungry—for breakfast. We had lunch with Filch and Dursley. They both tried to talk us into changing the meeting —to someplace like the Cauldron. Ginny and I were having none of it.

Dursley said, "Well, at least, go early and check out the people hanging around without apparent business there."

Ginny agreed with them, "It's probably a smart idea. Let's arrive at 1:30."

I didn't fight the idea. We arrived early. Before we disapparated there, Ginny disillusioned us so that we'd be invisible. We then walked hand in hand down the stairs to the main floor, out the main door and to the gate.

We disapparated to the ladies' loo. Ginny said, "Just close your eyes and pretend that you're in the guys'." Fortunately, there was no one in the loo that I could run into blind as I was. We navigated outside the loo. Ginny led me to a remote corner and we waited and watched. Every now and then someone seemed suspicious, but he'd quickly find something to do like buy a ticket or go to the loo or enter the Starbucks.

It became close to noon. A typical businessman walked in through the main entrance to the station. I wouldn't have noticed him except that his well-tailored suit revealed a more athletic form than the typical business-man. He walked to the kiosk and bought a ticket. I lost interest in him for a few minutes. Then I noticed that he had bought a newspaper and sat, apparently waiting for a train. He seemed to spend a lot more time glancing around than a commuter waiting for a train.

Just then Ginny nudged me and said, 'It's time. I'm going to undisillusion us."

I said, "I think I might have made our contact. Go ahead."

"Who?"

"The guy in the grey business suit. He looks like he'd be better at running a marathon than running a brokerage." Just then I felt the weird liquid feel of whatever the disillusionment spell did slide down my body. I shivered involuntarily. Then we walked out of the shadows and approached the bench where my candidate sat. We had almost reached him when he stood suddenly, startling me.

He said, "MacDuff of MI6 at your service." in a soft but penetrating tone.

Ginny said, "Fine. Where do we go?"

His eyes seemed to be constantly roving around the train station. He said, "I've got a nice little pub where we'll not be interrupted at this time of day."

I said, "Lead on, MacDuff."

We walked out of the station and went two blocks then turned down a side street. At the end of the block was a pub named, "MacDuff's."

It was small, had about a half-dozen tables and a pool table. Beyond the pool table was a single table. We sat there. I went to the bar and ordered three tap beers. MacDuff or whoever he was shook his head and said, "You should have asked me first. Their beer is piss poor."

He then glanced at each of us and said, "OK. I'll give you the fifty-thousand-foot view, and you correct what's wrong.

"You want to buy one hundred million pounds worth of gold. You need to find someone who can deliver it soon—within a week—and won't ask questions provided the price is right. You need an entree to this person, transportation, and security throughout. Do I have it?"

Ginny quickly answered, "We don't need security."

He stared at her and said, "I've got a bad feeling about this. I'm just this far from walking." He held his thumb and forefinger about half an inch apart.

I said, "Look. I know it sounds crazy. Believe me, we've handled some pretty dicey situations before. All we really need is a contact and help getting to the contact. We can handle negotiations, delivery, security, and payment."

He sighed. "They said that there was more to you than met the eye." What he did next seemed to happen in the twinkling of that eye. He had a gun out and almost pointed at me. I expected him to announce the futility of my security when I noticed that he was frozen in place.

I reached out for the gun, wrested it from his stiff hand, unloaded the clip, removed the bullet from the cylinder, and set the gun on the table. I then said, "Ginny, let him go."

She shook her head and said in an intense whisper, "I didn't do it."

Just then, the paralysis lifted. MacDuff's cocky smile changed to a frown. "How did you do that?"

Ginny was about to say something. I shook my head and said, "I'm not at liberty to discuss that."

His frown deepened. Then he said, "OK. I'll take that as proof that maybe you can handle your own security, but I'm going to be along. I still don't trust you." He retrieved the gun and reloaded it. Then he said, "With the requirements that you have, there are only two or three gold brokers in the world that could possibly satisfy them. I personally prefer Baghdadi in . . ."

I said, "Beirut."

He stared at me. "You know about Baghdadi?"

I nodded. "Yes, We tried to do a deal with him a couple of years ago."

MacDuff asked, "A wheel came off?"

I slowly shook my head. "No. We didn't want to work a deal. We just wanted information from him. We had a lengthy discussion with him and came out with what we went in to get."

MacDuff nodded slowly. "How much did you have to pay him?"

I smirked. "About 100 grams of gold."

He stared in disbelief. I quickly added, "It was probably the most precious gold in the world."

He smirked as well. "If you don't want to tell me, it's OK. Everyone has his secrets. Do you think that he will hold a grudge after that 'deal'?"

I said, "I don't think so. We parted on good terms."

"All right. If you're lying or even just exaggerating, you won't walk out of there alive. You're still determined to go?"

Both of us nodded. He sighed again. "OK. We'll arrange a meet at his business. We'll tell him that you want to buy a lot of gold without specifying how much. We'll tell him that you are good for it. You are, right?"

I nodded. "Yes, we are. We have a Swiss account with the money and can transfer it to his account in seconds."

I then asked, "I'm sure we'll have to offer a premium over the international gold price. What would you suggest?"

His face didn't change in the least as he said, "Offer ten percent. Haggle, but you're doing well if you get somewhere between twenty-five and thirty."

I said, "That's acceptable."

Ginny kicked my shin under the table. It was getting so that I wondered at times if she were channeling Minerva.

He asked, "What kind of delivery do you need?"

Ginny said, "Somewhere in Lebanon, remote. We'll transport it from there to our location."

MacDuff actually laughed. "You are crazy. How do you think you're going to get it out of the country? We can help you, but that's beyond even our resources without a month of planning and even then . . ."

Ginny just repeated, "We'll worry about getting it out. You don't even need to be there. As a matter of fact, it will be better if you're not."

Macduff shook his head regretfully, "Oh, how I wish I could leave it to you, but I can't send you in like that alone. I will come." There was a determination in his eyes that even Ginny wouldn't deny.

I said, "OK. But you have to swear not to tell anyone what you see."

That surprised MacDuff. "Well, that's pretty standard, but it's usually to protect the guilty. I've got a feeling that you don't care about that."

I agreed."No. It's to protect you."

Macduff shook his head, "OK. But you need help getting to the meeting and later to the rendezvous."

I agreed and asked, "How do you suggest going?"

He said, "I'll get you both British passports to travel on. I'll need to get photos of you. I can take them myself in the back room here. We'll get them to you tomorrow. They'll come along with a cover story and background that you should memorize. You probably won't need them, but it's better to have them and not need them than need them and not have them."

We agreed. He said, "OK. We've already got airline tickets for you. We'll deliver them with the passports. Basically, you'll be finishing school teachers going on a holiday together. It's your first trip abroad. You're experimenting with living together, so you don't have to know intimate details about each other."

Ginny smiled and said, "Oh, we could probably make it our second trip."

MacDuff rolled his eyes. "Just stick with the story on your bios."

I asked, "That's not what we tell Baghdadi, though."

"No, you don't tell him anything. He'll probably assume, I guess incorrectly, that I'm your body guard and she's your favorite harim girl. It doesn't matter what he thinks. You just have to convince him that you've got the money. He'll probably want you to transfer half the price before delivery. Do it as soon as possible."

I asked, "How do we rendezvous with you?"

"I rendezvous with you. You've got a reservation at a nice hotel. I'll meet you there."

"OK. Is that it?"

MacDuff looked around and said, "We'll go back and take some snaps and the papers will get to you the same way your invite did. Any last minute questions?"

There weren't. We went to the back room. There was a finicky photographer who took about two dozen photos apiece before he was satisfied. We left by a back door. I insisted that we go back to Paddington. There I said, "Find a desserted corner so that we can disapparate."

"Where to?"

"Make it the Three Broomsticks." She did.

The Broomsticks was pretty quiet. It was almost normal dinner time. I convinced Ginny to eat there. After we were finished, I asked if Ginny minded spending the night there.

Her answer was, "I wondered how long it would take you to ask. Of course."

We paid for a night and headed up to our room. As we were getting comfortable, there was a scratching on the window of our room. We both knew what it was. I opened the window. The owl flew in with a large envelope clutched in its claws. It dropped them on the bed and flew out the window.

Ginny opened it and spread out the booty on the bed—two passports, two fully refundable round-trip tickets to Beirut, two multi-page stapled c.v.'s—one for each of us. Ginny said, "We'll have to read both. I'll start with yours." She tossed hers to me. I quickly scanned it, then read it more carefully. She finished with mine before I was finished with hers. She picked up the tickets. She gasped, "We're flying tomorrow morning!"

I commented, "MI6 is all business."

"We've got to get home. You to your office and me to the Burrows so that we can pack." She already was half undressed. She went on. "Get dressed. We'll go by floo to your office, and then I'll go on to the Burrow. I'll meet you there in time for breakfast tomorrow."

I reluctantly started dressing. She was ready to go before I had my shoes on. She urged, "Come on. This is serious. We don't know when we'll get a decent night's rest."

I grumbled, "Or a decent night's lay."

She laughed. "Come on."

She dropped me off at my office and gave me a very unchaste kiss before leaving. I was always a quick pack. I had my duffel bag loaded with everything except pajamas before 10 PM. I went to bed wondering when the next time that I would get a good night's sleep in my apartment.

The next morning I woke to find Ginny lying in bed with me. "How did you get here?"

She didn't answer but made a statement of fact, "Do you know that you would sleep through an earthquake?" I glanced at the clock. It was six thirty. I asked a one word question, "Time?" She answered with one word, "Yes." After a quick series of things including shower, dressing, finishing packing, we went down to the kitchen."

When we arrived, both Filch and Dursley were laughing their heads off. I asked, "Whatever the joke is, it must be on us."

Filch managed to squeak out. "You should have seen your faces when that MacDuffer pulled that Glock on you."

Ginny laughed too. She asked, "You were there?"

Filch said, "Of course. We couldn't let you two go off alone to that meeting. Dursley dellusioned us. Of course, I could have, but I wanted him to have the practice.

"I told Dursley to keep his wand on that MacDuffer and not let him pull any fifth-year tricks on you. You should have seen that muggle's face when I told Dursley to let him go."

Dursley said, "I thought that photographer was going to take all day getting your photos. We had to get back here and put in a little work."

Ginny broke in. "Sorry to break up this fun time, but Wendt and I have to get to the airport by nine. Let's just have breakfast, and let us be on our way."

Filch said, "Spoilsports. Anyway, you're not going to fly in one of those muggle contraptions, are you?"

I said, "I'm afraid so."

We hurried breakfast, ran back up to my office, took the floo to the Cauldron, and disapparated to Gatwick. With our brand new passports and a little confunding charm, we were at our gate in record time.

Beirut is a Great Place to Visit, but I'd Hate to Die There

We had an hour to wait for boarding. I pulled out my profile and started to review it one last time. Ginny noticed and said, "Hand that to me." I did. She took it with her into the lady's loo, and when she came out, she didn't have it.

"What have you done with that? Did you hide it in your brassiere?"

She smiled. "Do you ever think of anything other than breasts and bras?"

"Sure. It's there isn't it?"

"I destroyed it just as you should have done before we left Hogwarts."

We boarded the plane and took our seats near the tail of the plane. Ginny was playing her part. She asked me, "Couldn't we have at least gone business class?"

It was easy for me to reply in kind. "Look. We agreed to spend our money on a nice hotel. We'll be there for a week. We'll be in this plane for only a couple of hours."

Her mischievous smile broke through, and she pretended to play hard to get. "It would be a lot easier to share a room with you if you weren't so miserly." The giggle was a dead give-away.

I said, "I'll show you that sharing a room with me is one of the most de-lightful experiences that you'll ever have."

We held hands through most of the flight. Even though I'd been there and visited Baghdadi before, I couldn't find any comfort in that prior experience. I had begun to feel like all those previous trips where I was glad to be on the way and not glad that every second passed was a second closer to our objective.

We arrived with less support than I'd had the last time that I'd been to Beirut. We took a cab to our hotel. At least, it was a nice one. The cabbie was just another Lebanese entrepreneur out to make some money. He wanted to give us a guided tour of the Korniche. I told him that we wanted to rest up today, but maybe tomorrow, we might be interested. He gave me his card. There was no secret message, no hint that he thought we were anything but tourists.

At the hotel, we checked in. A bellhop took our bags and us up to our room. I kept hoping for a contact from MI6. There was none. We had a little discussion under the *Muffliato* spell just in case our room were bugged.

Ginny asked, "Could you find Baghdadi by yourself if we had to?"

I tried to remember where his store front was located. It had been too long for me to remember. I finally said, "He has a public business. I don't know what the name of the business was, but most cab drivers probably know his name and where his business is. I think it would be dangerous though to just pick a driver at random and ask him to take us there. He might figure that we had real money—which we do. Then who knew what would happen?"

Ginny chewed on that for a while and asked, "So, we just wait for Mac-Duff to show up . . . and if he doesn't?"

"Someone will show up. If something has happened to MacDuff, then someone else will. If no one shows up, I guess we just play tourists and go home."

After that cheery discussion, we went down to the hotel restaurant for dinner. There were tables outdoors in a sort of courtyard. We ate there and stayed until well after dark, nursing drinks along in hopes that someone would come to meet us. No one did.

After a while, I commented that you could see some stars anyway. She was not amused. We decided it was time to call it a night and headed up for our room.

◁

We got a bad shock when we entered the room and discovered that someone was there. It turned out to be MacDuff. He had some good words for us. "So far you've been acting pretty much like tourists. Good job."

Ginny asked, "When are we going to act like what we really are—gold merchants?"

He smiled. "Tomorrow. We have an appointment in the early afternoon. I'll pick you up at one. Be in the hotel restaurant and ready to go at one. Make sure your profiles are straight in your heads. Wendt, I understand that you've been to Baghdadi's place before. Their procedure hasn't changed much. However, now they check identities more seriously.

"Ms. Weasley, expect to be searched thoroughly. They won't do a strip search of either of you, but they won't be bothered by modesty. During the whole visit, you will say or do nothing other than follow Wendt and I. Of course, if you are providing security, you may have to do something in an emergency. Baghdadi and his staff will assume that you are the favorite of Wendt's harim.

"They will assume that I am the body guard. I hope they let me in to see him with you."

I smiled at that and said, "I think we can assure that you get in with us."

He just shook his head. Then he said, "We already talked about negotiations. As the body guard, I can't help you with that, but you've been there before."

I agreed. He wished us a good night and left.

We then huddled again under the *Muffliato* spell. I said, "Minerva taped her wand to her inner thigh and confunded the man patting her down to avoid detection. I'll have my purse. You could confund whoever tries to search it as well.

"I'd prefer not to have to do anything to Baghdadi. But, if you have to imperious him to get him to give us a reasonable deal on the gold, go ahead. I'll give you the fast ball sign, if I want you to do that."

Ginny shook her head, causing her locks to flow. "You and your baseball! What is the fast ball sign?"

I demonstrated with my index finger.

She asked, "What if a wheel comes off?"

"I'll give you the curve ball sign, and we all disapparate to the hotel room. Then we figure out how to recover."

She scoffed. "Again with the baseball."

I showed her the sign, and we seemed to be ready for the next day—except for getting a good night's sleep in. It was not a great night for sleeping or love-making. I ended up just spooning her, and we managed some decent sleep.

We decided to have a good English breakfast and just hydrate at lunch in preparation for the afternoon. So, we just ordered hot tea and waited. At seven minutes to one, MacDuff showed up. I had already charged the "lunch" to our room, so we just walked out with him. He had a cab ready. On the way to Baghdadi's he gave us last minute details.

"Our appointment is for two. We'll arrive plenty early and cruise until almost two. At two, our driver will drop us. We'll be shown into the outer showrooms and we'll identify ourselves. From there on, we're flying by the seat of our pants."

He paused. Then he said, "I'm going in unarmed, and you two had better be as well. If you aren't now, please leave anything you've got in the cab now."

I just shook my head.

He went on. "Once we're into the inner office, if something goes wrong, stay close to me."

Ginny said, "I'm security. If anything goes badly wrong, Wendt will give the curve ball sign, and you grab me by the arm or body. I'll take it from there."

MacDuff raised an eyebrow and said, "Are you absolutely sure about this?"

We both said "Yes" in unison.

I remembered enough about the streets around Baghdadi's place to feel like we were close. MacDuff confirmed that. I glanced at my watch. It was 1:40.

At 1:50 MacDuff told the driver to drop us.

In a couple of minutes we were in the narrow street that I remembered. The driver stopped, we got out, and the driver took off. I don't know what the point of no return was, but this seemed like a pretty good imitation of one if it wasn't. MacDurff rang the doorbell, after a brief pause the door opened, and we went through the portal that might as well have had the motto above it, "Abandon all hope, ye who enter here."

There were a couple of sales people behind counters. MacDuff approached one and announced us, saying that we had an appointment. The salesperson opened a gate that led behind the counter and opened a door that led into the interior. The interior had been redesigned. It was like the concentric rings of Hell. We had passed the first ring. The second ring had someone who checked our ID's. The guard examined our passports and passed us into the next ring.

The next ring had guards. One examined us individually and several others armed guards stood back. They were prepared to deal with us if all didn't go well. They patted down MacDuff first, passing a sort of electronic wand around his body. Then came me. They had me remove my purse. I said nothing.

The searcher asked what was in it. I said, "Nothing." At that point I prayed for the confundis charm to work. Apparently, it did. The guard rubbed it between his hands and said, "Nothing here." He did not ask me to open it.

He then went to Ginny. He was gentle. He hesitated over one of her thighs and then went on without comment. One of the other guards asked, "What was with the thigh?"

He answered, "Just nice muscles." They all chuckled. I breathed an involuntary sigh of relief. We went on to the next ring.

It was a waiting room. It had chairs, a table with magazines, and even a flat screen TV that was not turned on. I was pretty sure that this was another room where we were being examined—how, I couldn't guess.

Finally, we were ushered into Baghdadi's office. He rose as we entered. There was only one chair on our side of the desk. He and I shook hands and I took the chair.

He stared at me a moment before speaking. "You and I have dealt before, but I don't recognize the name on the passport."

I simply said, "What's in a name?"

He replied, "I suppose your Shakespeare is right. A rose would smell as sweet or a rat as foul by any name. Why not use the same name as before?"

"One choses a name to suit the purpose of the moment."

Baghdadi didn't smile. He said, "Well, let us hope your business is never turning me over to authorities for minor infractions of the law."

I didn't smile either.

He started the negotiations. "You want to buy 200,000 ounces of gold to be delivered within a week?"

I agreed. He continued, "What do you offer for that amount?"

I tried to let the number trip off my tongue without a hesitation. "10% above market value."

Baghdadi pretended to laugh. His mouth didn't twist in the least. "Consider the large amount and the tight schedule. . . and the fact that you are not an established customer. I think that 50% over par is generous on my part."

I replied, "I admit that 10% was just an initial feeler. However, I think that 20% is fair. After all, The amount can all be delivered to one location that can be of your choosing. I would not object to any reasonable location —certainly any place in Lebanon would be acceptable. I would object to the capital of the caliphate. But then, I think you would as well."

Baghdadi scratched his chin and seemed to be actually surprised. He asked, "You really would accept the delivery anywhere—within reason? What about your costs to deliver to your client? I assume that you would not try to deduct from your offer based on our choosing a difficult location from which you would deliver?"

I smiled slightly. "Yes. I am not worried about delivery costs."

That really did puzzle him, but he made a counter offer. "Based on the assumption that we can deliver at the most convenient location for us, I will offer 40% over par."

That caused me a pause. I was ready to go as high as 30%. I wouldn't go higher, but on the other hand, I really didn't want to confund or use the imperious on him. So, I said, "I will offer 25%, and that is it."

Baghdadi closed his eyes and sat. Finally, he said, "If I were certain that you would come back to me for substantial additional purchases, I could go as low as thirty-three and one third."

He was a bargainer. I could counter-offer 30%. He would undoubtedly stand firm. I decided to accept. "I agree." I hesitated to see what he would say. Nothing. I went on. "I agree—assuming that future transactions, which by the way will have much less stringent time restraints, will be at 25% or less."

He said nothing. That was fine with me. I asked the next question, "I can deliver the money to your Swiss account as soon as we have tested the gold to ensure that it is 100% gold. "

He said, "We will not wait for a week for you to test the gold. At the meet, you either accept it and pay or not. We have a standard policy of 50% down and the rest at delivery."

I countered. "That might be all right for modest purchases. For a purchase this large, I'm not turning over half the price sight unseen. You have a right to something down. 25%"

He seemed to be tired of bargaining. "Make it a third."

We were getting really close, but I was tired of giving in on everything. I gave the fastball sign. Then I said, "One quarter."

He seemed a bit woozy and said, "OK. OK. One quarter."

I said, "Give us your Swiss account information for a wire transfer and when you give us the date, time, and location, we'll provide the down payment."

He sat staring at us for a minute. I hoped Ginny hadn't overdone it. I said, "I think that's all we need for the moment. Uh . . . we'll be on our way."

Baghdadi sort of waved us off. I rose, turned as did Ginny, but MacDuff kept his eyes on Baghdadi for a full minute. A guard had opened the door, and we all walked out. We proceeded from ring of Hell to ring of Hell without incident. I had my curve ball signal prepared and ready to give, but nothing happened.

As we reached the door to the outside, I turned to see that all was well. I noticed MacDuff take a cell phone from his suit and hit one button. That must have been the summons for our ride. We had hardly stepped outside when the cab pulled up, and the rear door opened. We got in quickly and were on the road.

MacDuff nodded his head slowly. "All right. We're all still alive. Good. We seem to have a deal. Good. I'll be informed by our contact when we get details to make the down-payment. You two stay in your room. I can't guarantee that you'll be safe, but Baghdadi won't try to kill you anyway."

We decided that MacDuff really meant stay in the hotel, so we had meals in the restaurants, including out on the patio next to the pool. We exercised in the weight room. We even went up to the rooftop patio. I suppose that we could have been shot by a sniper there, but what the heck? That could even happen in our room if we didn't have the drapes pulled.

That regimen chaffed at Ginny more than it did at me, but after three days had gone by, we were getting cabin fever. We hadn't even heard from MacDuff. However, we stuck to our intentions. Mostly.

On the third day as we were having dinner in our room an idea hit me. I asked Ginny, "How far do you think you can disapparate?"

She shook her head lazily and said, "Oh, I guess about 400 miles maybe 500 hundred on a really good day. What are you thinking of?"

I smiled. "Well, we promised not to leave our room or at least our hotel, but surely MacDuff only meant not to travel around Beirut or Lebanon."

She frowned. "I suppose so." Then she became more serious. "Just what do you have in mind? I can't think of anyplace around here that I'd want to go."

I smiled more broadly. "How about Giza, Egypt to see the sun set over pyramids?"

She asked, "Like the Great Pyramid? The Sphynx?"

"Bingo."

She was smiling broadly. "You want to go right now?"

"Sure."

She held out her hand and said, "Let's go."

I pulled her erect, and she said, "On the count of three. Three. Two. One." Then there was a whoosh and pop as we twisted through space. We landed next to the Great Pyramid. We walked around to the opposite side of the pyramid so that we could see the sun set behind it.

When the sun had completely set, we disapparated back. Ginny and I sat in each others arms quietly thinking of what we'd just done. She kissed me and I kissed her back.

We ended in bed making love for the first time of the trip. I said, "I'm glad we did that. You know that we might not get out of here alive."

I could feel more than I could see her nod as she said, "I'm glad we went. I'll never forget it."

I laughed. "If I ever forgot that, I'd deserve to die."

MacDuff knocked on our door the next morning. We'd finished a room service breakfast and were just presentable. I asked him to back away from the door just to be sure that he wasn't accompanied by anyone. He wasn't.

I locked the door while he went to our desk and unfolded a large sheet of paper that had a map on it. We pulled up chairs and huddled around it. There was a spot marked with a red circle near the Darmour River. MacDuff said, "That's it. The time is 10 PM tomorrow night local time. Does that give you enough time to arrange transportation."

I said that it was. Of course, I didn't know exactly how transportation would be arranged, but I knew that the Goblins were anxious for the deal and they were, after all, magical. However, I didn't want any wheels to come off, so I said, "If you've got any idea of providing assistance or additional security, forget it."

MacDuff shook his head and said, "Your security is the lassie here?"

I cringed at what I knew was coming. Ginny sneered, "This wee lassie can provide all the security you need old man."

I quickly added, "We've got a Transportation Team who will be security aplenty. I don't want you barging in and screwing things up. Understood?"

MacDuff wasn't happy, but he agreed.

I took my statement further. "Until we leave for the rendezvous, you are welcome to keep an eye out for us. But after 9 PM tomorrow, I don't want to even see you in the background around here. OK?"

"It's your funeral, but you're in charge." With that he left.

Ginny got out her wand and the token the Goblins had given us. She tapped it. It glowed briefly, and she sighed a sigh of relief. She said, "Well, we should hear from them shortly, maybe in an hour or two."

We did hear from them before lunch. Around eleven AM a Goblin disapparated into our room. I was disappointed by who it was.

Javeen looked around the room, and her eyes glowed, "So wonderful to see you." She was looking straight at me. Then she turned to Ginny and said, "Of course, you, too." She looked back to me and asked, "What have you got for me?"

Ginny motioned her over to the table where the map was. Ginny pointed to the red circle and said, "Tomorrow night at 10 PM local time. Let's plan."

Javeen nodded. Then she said, "Here's the Gringotts plan:

"First, I'll take the map back to Gringotts. We'll prepare a port key that will take us to the location. Incidentally, I got here by taking a port key to the local branch of Gringotts that happens to be in Egypt. I think one of Ms. Weasley's brothers worked there for a while. We have sets of paired port keys that let us travel at any time between Gringotts home office and our branches. I then disapparated directly here.

"The next point is that we have three teams for this operation. There is the Security Team. They will appear at the rendezvous point at least two hours in advance. They will assess the dangers and get in touch with us if there is a problem that should cause us to abort the meet-up. If they give the go-ahead for our meet-up, they will stay on station to defend us should anything bad happen.

"There is the Transportation Team. They will appear when the gold has been verified."

"Finally, there is the Verification Team that will insure that the gold is the correct amount and is pure gold. I am that team. Along with you two, I will show up about fifteen minutes early for the meet-up.

"I've already talked a little about security. If the Security Team signs off on the deal, we go. If something goes wrong, after we arrive, I take Wendt away, and you provide us cover, hon." "Hon" presumably was Ginny. That was the way she took it, and she obviously took it badly judging from the expression on her face.

Ginny said, "I am Wendt's security. If he needs to escape, I'm going to take him, HON!"

Javeen just smiled and then said, "I'll be back as quickly as I can with the original map. Don't you worry, hon, I'll be here the rest of the time to ensure Wendt's safety."

Ginny asked, "Does that mean that you will be staying in this room for the next, say thirty hours?"

"Of course, hon. How could I protect Wendt otherwise. You have a suite. I don't mind sleeping on the sofa. You two can have the bedroom, hon."

Ginny was livid. I'd never seen her so angry that she couldn't say anything. I suppose it was the cognitive dissidence between having to work with Javeen and hating her. Fortunately, Javeen disapparated and we had our suite to ourselves. Ginny insisted that we go down to have dinner in one of the hotel restaurants. It was a little early for dinner but clearly Ginny wanted to talk away from our room where Javeen might show up at any moment.

When we were seated and had drinks delivered, she let go of her emotions. There was not a lot that was repeatable but one point was made very clear. She summed it up in one sentence, "If that *** calls me 'hon' one more time, when all this is over, I'll send her to the moon—and not by disapparation."

I was certainly not going to argue with her on that. We had a very leisurely dinner and eventually decided that we couldn't hold the table where we were seated any longer. I said, "I'll save you the trouble of saying it. I hope Javeen is there when we arrived." Of course, she was.

She exuded self-satisfaction when we entered our suite. "We've got the port key set up. The teams are on standby, ready to move at any moment. The Security Team is at the local Gringotts. They're sleeping over in the back offices. The Transportation Team is at our mint waiting to activate the port key." Then she added modestly, "And of course, the Verification Team is on site with you." Ginny scoffed at that.

We now had the rest of the night to think of things to do to occupy our time. Ginny and I could have gone into our bedroom and enjoyed the facilities of a bedroom. Instead, we just all sat around the telly that no one wanted to watch. I finally suggested playing a card game. It was a variation on whist. Only Ginny and I knew how to play it.

Amazingly both ladies agreed to try a few hands. We played the three-handed cut-throat version. I quickly discovered why they were willing to play it. It was a way to assert dominance without actually trading blows or spells. A complete game involves dealing and playing twenty-six hands, so that allowed us to reach an hour that would allow us all to go to bed and re-tire from the field of conflict. For the record, I ended up with the worst score. Both ladies were well ahead and close enough that they both came away with honors.

Ginny and I went into the bedroom and got ready for bed. We sat on the edge of the bed and started snogging, but almost immediately Ginny pulled away and said, "You know, I just can't do this with her out there."

I sighed. "Yeh, I know what you mean. I guess I can't either."

She said, "I just hate her."

The next morning nobody wanted to get up. Not even Javeen was up. We couldn't hear any signs of movement from the other room. We finally were up and dressed. We got dressed and with some trepidation opened the door and went out to the sitting room of the suite. We found that Javeen was sitting on the sofa staring out the window. She was so absorbed in the view through the window that I had to clear my throat to get her attention.

I asked her if she wanted breakfast. She said, "I don't think that I can eat anything before we're finished with this business deal." Her major change of attitude from her confident even sassy ways the previous day seemed strange. Of course, she'd probably never been in a situation where you need serious security. And it was now less than twenty-four hours away.

Ginny and I ordered room service. It arrived, and we had begun break-fast when there was a knock on the door. It turned out to be MacDuff. We shuffled Javeen into our bedroom and let him in. He explained his unexpected visit, "We have a change in plan. Baghdadi has provided us with a new rendezvous location." He then displayed a new map with a new rendezvous."

I asked, "Is this normal? How does he expect us to adjust to a change with so little time!"

MacDuff sighed. "I'm afraid this isn't too unusual. When you're moving this much gold, you want to take every precaution. And, it's not that hard for us to adjust. The amount of gold is much less that ten metric tons. It would be less than a meter on a side, maybe as little as two feet. You could put that in a step van, except that most step vans aren't rated to carry six tons. A Ford F-350 could handle it easily.

"The real problem would be adjusting security, coming up with a new route that is vetted to take it to wherever you're going to take it out of the country. I wish I knew how you were going to do that."

Ginny looked ready to give an answer. I over-rode her. I said, "It's highly unusual that someone outside government would negotiate this purchase. We, Ms Weasley and I, were called on because we have contacts that can pull this purchase and subsequent delivery efficiently, safely, and effectively. I am not at liberty to discuss ways and means without breaking confidentiality."

MacDuff was not convinced, but we had him over a barrel. He could only say, "You have my phone number if a wheel or several wheels come off. I can't guarantee anything."

After MacDuff left, I went to the door to the bedroom. Javeen opened it before I arrived. I asked, "Did you hear that?"

Ginny scoffed and said, "Of course."

Javeen just sniffed. Then she said, "I hate this. This is just bloody shit." She paused, apparently in thought. "I'll go back and reset the port key if you think we're going ahead with the deal."

Both Ginny and I said that we were. Javeen scowled and snapped her fingers and disapparated. We could only wait for her return. Noon arrived and we ordered a simple fruit and nut platter, I guess we hoped that we could manage to eat something. It arrived, and we picked at it. Ginny finally gave up and said, "I guess I have to admit that I am like Javeen. I can't eat."

About two hours later, Javeen reappeared in the room seething as she came. "Damn muggles." Then she looked up and noticed us. "Sorry, it's just that I had to get the Transportation Team to create a new port key. My dad insisted on doubling the size of the Security Team, and he almost replaced ME!"

Ginny said, "Sorry." At another time that would have been a sarcastic remark, but this time, I was sure she was being genuine in her regret.

Javeen looked over at the platter of dried fruits and nuts. She walked over and sampled it, nibbling for the rest of the afternoon. During that time we discussed detailed plans for the evening.

Javeen began the conversation. "We haven't discussed the detailed plan I have for completing the purchase. First, come look at this map of the area that we're going to." She laid the map out on the table. It was a topographic map. She pointed to a hill close to the circled spot. "We'll disapparate behind this hill, and you two will walk around it to the rendezvous. That way, no muggles will see me."

I immediately asked, "They'll wonder how we got there. Do you have a cover story for us?"

Javeen seemed not to have considered that. Ginny made a suggestion. "We can say that we were dropped there hours before and waited for the meeting time to come out."

I was not totally happy with that proposal, but I didn't have anything better. Javeen went on. "You make sure that they are there with the gold. Of course, I need to test the purity of the gold and look for other problems with it.

"As soon as you've verified the basic setup is acceptable to us, You insist on inspecting the gold in private. I assume that it will come in some sort of vehicle that closes. When you are safely inside, signal me with the token and I will disapparate to the token.

"I will examine the gold and validate its integrity."

I asked, "How will you do that?"

She chuckled, "I'm not at liberty to reveal that, but I assure you that I can't be fooled."

Ginny said, "As long as you accept all responsibility for the gold, I'm happy."

Javeen smiled a wicked smile. "You can count on that."

Then she went on, "After I validate it, I will disapparate away and get in touch with the home office. You will complete the sale with Baghdadi. When that is done, signal me, and I will have the home office transfer the money.

"When they've verified the transfer, you instruct Baghdadi to leave the vehicle with you, the understanding being that you will bring your own vehicle in, transfer the gold, and leave.

"We will insure that they have left the area, then I will send the Transportation Team in with the port key. They will transfer the gold and leave with the port key and gold. When the transfer is complete. We will disapparate to our hotel room."

209

Ginny scoffed, 'OUR hotel room."

Javeen said, "Well, we have to celebrate somewhere."

The next couple of hours were pure torture. We'd run out of things to do, plans to make, and appetite for food. We all took turns pacing, sitting, standing, and lying on the sofa.

At five PM Javeen got word that the Security Team had arrived, surveyed the area and set up surveillance posts. They were prepared to act if anything went awry. Then we waited.

At 8:30 the Security Team reported the arrival of the Baghdadi Security Team. They were ready to handle Baghdadi's team if necessary.

At 9:30 we checked our equipment. I had my purse with Glock and bullets and cell phone. Ginny had her wand taped to her inside left thigh. Javeen had god only knew what.

At 9:45 we had a little difference of opinion about disapparation. Javeen wanted to disapparate all three of us. Ginny wanted to disapparate herself and me. I had to go with Javeen on that one. We all needed to arrive at the same time and place. The only way to insure that would be for us all to disapparate at once together. That meant that Javeen had to do the disapparation because she'd been there before. That in turn meant that she had to be in the middle with Ginny on one side and me on the other. We clasp hands. Javeen looked over at me and smiled while she gave my hand a squeeze. Then we twisted through space and time and landed in a little whirlwind of dust and sand.

I said, "From here on in, I take command of the negotiations. We don't start walking until the stroke of ten."

Ginny objected, "Then we'll be late."

Javeen said, "That's what we want. It establishes us as powerful agents."

At 10:00 we walked around the knoll that we'd landed behind. As we walked, a truck pulled up at the rendezvous point. We arrived a couple of minutes later.

Two guards exited the truck and checked us out. They compared us to photos of us. One had the photos the other had an AK-47. They apparently found us acceptable. One of them called something back to the truck. Then Baghdadi got out of the truck. He said, "Here's the gold. You can check it out. Then transfer the money. But just one thing—where's your truck?"

I said, "That waits for us to verify the gold and complete the sale."

He shrugged and said, "That's your lookout."

"OK. Let's see the gold."

He led us around the back of the truck. He opened the rear doors to reveal three men armed with AK-47's. They were sitting on a tarp. Under the tarp was the gold. Baghdadi said something in Lebanese or Arabic or something. They got out of the truck, and we climbed in. I said, "Close the doors. Don't open them till we ask you to.

Baghdadi laughed and said, "Whatever you like. It's not like you're going to run off with it." Then he added, "Don't you want a lamp or something?"

"Don't worry."

The doors swung shut, and Ginny reached under her skirt and pulled out her wand, saying, "Lumos." The wand lit. She tapped the token with it and Javeen instantly appeared.

The gold was made in small ingots. Javeen asked Ginny to help her levitate them off the top, exposing the lower ranks of them. Javeen then said, "Ms. Weasley, please use your wand to slice a few of them through diagonally. I'll check them." Meanwhile she did the same. As soon as a bisected ingot was cool to the touch Javeen ran a finger along the exposed surface. After sampling about a dozen she said, "They're good. I'm going to disapparate and have the transfer of money happen."

After she was gone, we opened the door to the truck. Baghdadi was cool as a cucumber. He didn't approach us. He let us approach him. I said, "The gold is fine. We've asked our principle to forward your money. As soon as you've gotten notification of it's arrival, we'll signal our transport to come to pick up the gold."

Baghdadi only nodded acknowledgement. He had a cell phone to his ear, presumably talking to someone monitoring his account. So, we waited. I had no idea how long to expect to wait. The wait dragged on seemingly for hours, but when I checked my watch I discovered that it had been less than twenty-five minutes.

Baghdadi nodded, hung up the phone and said, "The payment has come through."

Both Ginny and I smiled—probably bad Karma, but we couldn't help it. I said, "Please leave with your men. We'll leave your truck intact. After all, this is only the first of several transactions this size or larger."

Baghdadi didn't smile. A couple of his guards came close. They held their AK-47's loosely. Both Ginny and I thought to ourselves that this felt like one or two wheels coming off. I hadn't asked her to do it, but I hoped that she had her wand taped to her thigh.

Baghdadi said, "I think you haven't paid enough. I'm instituting a surcharge of 10%. You'll have to pay that before taking the gold."

I shook my head sadly. "You know that I would like to do future deals with you. You're making that very hard. Are you really sure that you want to do this?"

Baghdadi said, "In this business, no one can count on the future. Either pay up or leave." With that he nodded imperceptibly and the guards raised their weapons to the ready position.

I turned my smile to a grimace. "Do you remember another large deal you did a couple of years ago?"

For the first time a little tick showed in his face. He kept the cool in his voice. "I don't know what you're talking about."

I turned my expression into a smile, "Oh, come now. You remember the Lieutenant."

A cloud passed over his face briefly, and then he regained control of his face. He actually managed a realistic laugh. "Nice trick. That's one I've not seen before and I thought I'd seen them all."

I tried to make my smile more relaxed. I said, "Oh, sure you remember it. You tried to cheat another customer, and you paid for it. Let me just remind you that you brandished a knife that you always carry. You found that somehow the only person you could hurt with it was yourself. I think you pressed it to your carotid." Here was the critical point. Would Ginny pick up on the hint for a repeat performance. "I think you'll find that you won't be able to hurt anyone but yourself right now."

Ginny, God bless her, did pick up on the cue. Baghdadi reached into his boot slowly, deliberately. He found a rather nasty knife, curved and gleaming in the dim illumination of the lantern that one of the guards held. He slowly raised it. It came higher and higher, up to and right next to his carotid artery. It would have been better if Ginny had brought a little blood, but this was fine. He stood there for about a minute. Then Ginny apparently released him from the Imperious.

His expression had not changed until he was released. Up to that point his expression had been if anything, relaxed. After release, he gasped and pulled his knife from his throat so quickly that he nicked himself and the blood rolled down his throat. His mouth opened as though to say something. I stepped in by saying myself, "You really don't want to make a hasty decision."

His eyes widened until they were like pie plates. He stood there staring at Ginny and me. He finally muttered, "Get out with your gold. Keep the truck."

I said, "Don't think that you are safe after you leave this meet-up. And the next time that someone from my principal does business with you, its representative will not be so forgiving as I have been."

His gaze shifted from me to Ginny and back. I squeezed my eyes and said, "Go! Now!"

He was still defiant. Whether that represented his real feelings or just meant that he was trying to save face with his men, I didn't know. They all got into a HumVee that drove up. They drove away.

When they were out of eyesight, Javeen disapparated to us. She said, "You shouldn't have let him live. My Security Team was ready to deal with him and his muggles if he'd gone a half step further. He was smart to take all his Security Team with him. They'd be picking up their pieces all over the Middle East if any had stayed."

Just then we heard a thud coming from the other side of the truck. We went around the truck to find a half dozen Goblins sitting on something that looked like a large wooden pallet. They jumped up, levitated the pallet and one of them asked, "Where do you want this?"

Javeen said, "Follow me." They walked around the truck, and she had them drop it behind the truck's lift gate. She then said, "Load the gold from that truck."

One of the Goblins looked at the volume of gold and said, "We'll take it in two trips." Then the Goblins started levitating the gold and laying it gently on the pallet.

Ginny asked, "The pallet is the port key?"

Javeen said, "Sure, hon. We should have this gold out of here within a half hour."

Ginny sneered, "Thanks, hon." Then she turned to me and asked, "Our work is done here. Let's get out."

I said, "No. We need to see this through to the end." Ginny was clearly not happy but didn't argue.

Before long the pallet was heavy-laden. The half-dozen Goblins climbed on and they were gone is a whirlwind. In about five minutes, they were back. The remaining gold ingots lifted—apparently of their own volition—and dropped on the pallet. In less than ten minutes the Goblins had patrolled the area, making sure that nothing was missing and then disappeared. Ginny asked Javeen, "Aren't you going with the gold?"

Javeen just said, "Obviously not. Let's go."

Ginny said, "We don't need to disapparate together. Go ahead. Wendt and I will go together."

Javeen didn't object. She just disapparated. Then Ginny held out her hand to me. I took it. We disapparated and re-appeared in our hotel room. I quickly looked around and asked Ginny, "Any reason that we shouldn't get back to England as fast as possible?"

She shook her head. "No. Let's disapparate our way across Europe."

I growled, "No. We came by Muggle means. We should leave the same way. For one thing, MacDuff would be troubled if we didn't." As I was saying that, there was a disturbance in the air, and Javeen materialized.

She said, "It's time to celebrate! I brought champagne." Indeed, she had. She was carrying a large bottle that almost was as tall as she was.

Both Ginny and I sighed. Sure, we could have sent her away, but we'd worked long and hard on the success of this project. It would have been mean and petty to do so. I took the bottle. Ginny materialized some champagne glasses. I poured.

Javeen said, "To the first of many like adventures."

I said, "To the completion of one with everyone alive."

Ginny said, "To better times." We all drank enthusiastically to that toast.

I got on the phone to the airline on which we were going to return to England. The tickets were fully refundable. I changed the return to the earliest flight I could. It was the next morning. I reported that to Javeen and Ginny.

Ginny urged Javeen to leave and let us get packed for our trip the next day. Javeen just smiled and said, "Don't let me get in the way. Feel free to go ahead and pack." Ginny just shook her head.

It wasn't as inconvenient as it might have sounded. All the things that we would pack were in the bedroom. We could close the door and pack in perfect privacy. While we were doing that Ginny commented, "God, you can't get rid of that Goblin for love or money."

I laughed. "I hope she didn't hear that. She might just offer to leave for love." Ginny just growled at me.

By this time, it was well after midnight. We found Javeen sitting on the sofa sipping champagne. I sat down on a chair in front of her and said, "We've got a flight at 10:30 this morning. We need to get to the airport by 8:30. So, we're going to bed so that we can get some sleep before leaving for the airport."

Javeen is a wonder. She said, "Don't worry about me. I'll just stay here on the sofa." Then she added, "Oh, would you like me to disapparate you to the airport?"

I just said, "No thanks. We'll disapparate directly from our bedroom. Please leave before the room checkout time of eleven."

We went back into our bedroom. I called the front desk and told them that we were leaving directly in the morning. The room keys would be in our bedroom. That night we had a terrible night's sleep. We were up around 6:30.

Ginny asked if we would have breakfast in the hotel coffee shop. I said, "No. Let's just finish packing and go directly to the airport. We can have breakfast there."

She agreed. We were at the airport before 7:30. We checked in for our flight, got our boarding passes, worked through security, and were in an airport restaurant by 8:30.

The flight was mercifully boring. Or would have been had it not been for Ginny's question. "That little story about Baghdadi was just one of your fairy tales, right?"

I just frowned at her and asked, "What do you think?"

Her answer was a glum, "I guess not."

"Why do you guess not?"

"Well, I guess it's too crazy to make up at the spur of the moment." She hesitated in thought. "And. . . uh. . . you have a certain way of getting into bizarre situations. Tell me about it."

I was starting to decide what to say when she added, "Oh! Yes. This is just like those fairy tales that you used to tell Minerva when you flew together."

I asked her, "How did you know about those?"

"I was talking with Minerva once toward the end of the Battle for Earth."

I was puzzled. She quickly cleared it up. "Oh, that's a name that some of us in the Auror group made up for the resistance to the Invasion of the Souls. Anyway, we were talking about some of the adventures that you and she used to have."

I said, "Well, first, those stories were fairy tales. What I'm going to tell you isn't. And, I'll thank you to keep it to yourself."

She droned, "Oh, all right."

"Good. Now, after the Battle for Earth, there was another little adventure that Minerva and I and a few others from Hogwarts had."

"There was a group of ordinary muggle men—a small group, just four. They were soldiers who served in the United State Army. You will remember that there was a political group who wanted to start a country in the Middle East. They called it the Caliphate. The United States opposed them and fought in a couple of local wars against them.

"The four were injured by a kind of explosive called an IED. They were injured in separate incidents. They all received head wounds. Despite the fact that they were injured in separate places at separate times, their recovery from these extremely serious wounds were very similar. Basically, they all should have died, but recovered rapidly, became very interested in unusual fields of study, and—here is the key—walked away from the hospital they were in without permission. "

Ginny interrupted my story to ask if they weren't arrested. My answer was that lots of people tried but failed.

I went on. "They began collecting things—chemical equipment, a warehouse, exotic drugs from the Amazon rain forest, extremely advanced computers of their own design, parts for assembling a large structure."

Ginny again interrupted to ask just how large.

"Large enough that they could build a large house or a small building, something that could be assembled in a warehouse.

"In the middle of that project, the United States FBI brought Minerva, the Brahmses, Sally, Pearson, and me into the investigation.

"We tried to track them down. It was very hard to do—even with magic to help us. They had fake passports and lots of money."

Ginny laughed. "How many times have I heard you say that with enough time and money you could do anything."

"Yeh. Well, they were out to do 'an anything' on the edge of belief. No, actually beyond the edge of belief. "

She asked, "How did they get all this money?"

I smiled. "I'm glad you asked that. That is the main point. They stole a huge amount of gold from this Caliphate."

Ginny gaped and said, "The four of them stole all that gold from a government?"

"Actually, it was one of the four—admittedly, the most brilliant of the bunch, but still just one man. Now, we come to the point."

Ginny was leaning in across the arm of her seat in rapt attention. I said, "He sold the gold to Baghdadi."

She asked, "To that pirate! And he came out alive?"

I smiled. "Baghdadi tried to cheat him. What I described to Baghdadi was exactly what happened. Baghdadi almost slit his own throat."

Ginny shook her head and asked, "Magic—the Imperious."

"Remember that they were muggles. No, not the Imperious." I held up my hands in protest as she was about to object. "I don't know how. He just did it."

She thought about that for a minute or two and asked, "Did he have a Swiss account or something where Baghdadi could transfer the money?"

"No, he didn't. He brought a suitcase and walked out of the dessert."

Ginny objected. "I don't know much about muggle money, but I don't think that one person without magic could carry that much money."

I smiled. "Well, it wasn't as hard as you might think. He carried it out in a brief case. It was all in 10,000 dollar United States Treasury Bonds. They are just like cash. Any bank will take them." After a moment, I added,

"Here's something ironic. Some of those Treasury Bonds were cashed into dollars by Gringotts."

She just gaped at me. Then she asked, "How did you find out about Baghdadi's little adventure?"

"Oh, well, in tracking these four men, the trail led to Baghdadi. Minerva, Aurora, and I went in to do a little business with Baghdadi. I had Minerva use the Imperious to get him to tell us everything he knew about the one that he dealt with. That story came out in the process."

Ginny's jaw dropped again. "You met this guy under those circumstances and came back to give him another shot at you!"

I shrugged. "It seemed the only way to get what I wanted—all that gold in a hurry."

Somewhere during that story, a steward came to offer us food. We both waved him away preemptively. Ginny finally asked, "What were they building and why?"

I chewed on that question for a while and finally said, "I don't think I can tell you that."

She grimaced and said, "I've half a mind to use the Imperious on you to find out." After a little reflection she added, "I guess I can't do that, can I? You don't use the Imperious on people you love."

I just smiled.

Heathrow III

Our flight returned to Heathrow. We disembarked the airplane and worked through customs. When we got past the secured section of the airport we found a dark corner and were about to disapparate when Javeen disapparated next to us.

I was reaching the end of my patience. Javeen was in good spirits, though. She said, "Dad wants to throw a little party to celebrate our success. Would tomorrow night or the day after be better?"

I just shook my head in disbelief. "Let's make it day after."

Then we disapparated to the Cauldron. From there it was on to my office. When we arrived, we found a letter placed prominently on my desk. The envelope was addressed to Professor James Wendt and Ms. Genevra Weasley c/o Headmaster Horace Slughorn, Headmaster's Office, Hogwarts School of Witchcraft and Wizardry. I said, "Since it's addressed to both of us, we might as well read it together." We went to the sofa and sat quite comfortably together as we read the note.

The gist was that as soon as feasible after returning, we should report to the Minister of Magic. No subject matter was referenced. I suggested that since we'd not had lunch and since it was the lunch hour that we stop off at the Cauldron on the way to the Ministry.

At the Cauldron Tom greeted us like long lost relatives. He said, "It's been an age and more since you last ate here."

I had to admit that he was right. I added, "Just bring us whatever's on the menu that you think is the best for lunch. I'll take a Dewar's to drink. What do you want, Ginny?"

She agreed with my choice, although she wondered that I had something hard before dinner. Then she said, "We've got to think out what the Minister wants that she's so anxious to see us."

I said, "It's got to be those damn aliens. They're probably anxious to get their expedition started."

She said, "You know that you don't have to go. I don't want you to go or if you absolutely have to go, I want to go, too. I still don't know why you want Dursley along."

"And you won't. No one will."

We finished lunch and were off to the Ministry. We landed in a hearth near the Visitor Desk. As we passed it, the person manning it, started to ask us—or at least—me to sign in. Ginny flashed her Auror badge, and we breezed by. In the Minister's Office, the receptionist signed us in. She provided me with a visitor badge and said, "Nobody is in with the Minister. You can just go on in to see her. She's been expecting you for a couple of days."

We did proceed to the Minister's office. When we arrived, she got up and shook hands with us. Her first question was, "Was your trip successful?"

We agreed that it was. Then she immediately turned to the aliens. She sat on the edge of her desk on the same side as our chairs. She said, "The aliens have been putting pressure on us to get our team ready to go. They've given us a time limit. We must be ready before next week. We're putting a meeting together tomorrow of all the people from the last meeting. I need to know if Dursley is on-board since you are so determined to have him on the team."

I had some more good news for her. Dursley was on-board. She released a sigh of relief that was short-lived. Ginny started her campaign to get Dursley off the team and, oh yes, herself on. She was everything a debater ought to be—succinct, logical, respectful. She said, "I think that we should find someone else for the team than Dursley.

"First, I've known him since he started his magical life. I admit that I hated him when I first met him and before then because of the terrible way that he treated his cousin, Harry Potter. However, in that year, I discovered that he had become a different person. I won't say that he is morally upstanding, but he is a much better person than he was. That, however, is beside the point.

"He was an adult at that point and had just started practicing magic. Almost every wizard and witch of his age is more advanced than he is. He would be better than any muggle." Here she stumbled and added, "Present company excluded. However, we have some very capable wizards and witches in the Auror group who would be perfect in that position."

Here I interrupted to say, "Present company not excluded."

Ginny went on. "Second, I would nominate myself as much more knowledgeable, experienced, and accomplished as a witch than he could ever be as a wizard. I deal with muggles on a regular basis and work with them quite effectively."

I interrupted her by saying, "Let me agree that at least one muggle thinks she works very effectively with him."

Ginny seemed not to know how to respond to that. She perhaps didn't want to admit that we worked together in other places besides the office. On the other hand our relationship outside the office and inside the bedroom might be a plus for her. She resolved to say nothing about that. What she said then was, "Third, I think that Wendt's choice of a highly suspect partner for this mission should be explained before it is accepted."

I made a simple argument. "I've already made it clear that I will not cooperate in this mission without my choice of partner. I've also made clear that that choice is Mr. Dursley. You can certainly put Ginny on the team without Dursley. I won't accept it and I doubt that the PAK will accept the team without me. So, it doesn't seem to me that you've got any choice. It's got to be Dursley and I."

The Minister was fit to be tied. She had to accept my argument. On the other hand, if she rejected Ginny, she had to deal with a Weasley scorned—not a pleasant alternative. She temporized by saying, "I've been remiss as a hostess. I should have offered you refreshment. What will you have to drink? We have water, tea, pumpkin juice, butter beer, and personally, I want to have something harder." She looked around as though she were afraid that someone would overhear. "I'm going to have a shot of Blue Label."

We all accepted the last-named option. She waved her wand, and a trio of shot glasses wafted into the room from her personal assistant's office. We all gratefully accepted them and immediately swallowed. Thus refreshed, Pam took a different tack. She said, "Both your arguments are cogent. God, if only we could have another wizard or witch on the team. If only we could replace you Wendt."

Ginny enthusiastically agreed. Actually, I wasn't entirely against that option myself. It was just that I could not figure out a way to do it.

Pam almost pleaded, "Wendt, you seem to have a way of coming up with the timely *deus ex machina*. God, don't you have anything?"

I started to shake my head and then a horrible idea occurred to me. I didn't say anything, but both Ginny and Pam picked up on it immediately. They both exclaimed almost as if they were channeling the Weasley twins, "You've got something, don't you!"

I didn't say anything for a long time. The two others in the office held their peace as well, seemingly not wanting to break my concentration. I closed my eyes to help me think. My lips quivered as I thought through the consequences of the idea that I'd had.

I finally said, "I may have a workable idea." There was a perceptible relief of tension in the room. I continued, "I have to do some thinking about this. At the very least I want to sleep on it. To do that I've got to be back at Hogwarts to do some research."

Ginny was completely in favor of that. She jumped up and said, "Well, let's go." I wasn't sure that Ginny was going to like what was going to come next, but the sooner that we got on with it, the sooner we'd know.

I agreed. "Let's go." I turned to Pam and said, "I'll let you know what I decide as quickly as I can."

She nodded. "It'd better be within a day or two." She walked over to her personal floo connection with us, and she actually hugged me. She said, "I have a bad feeling about this." I couldn't bring myself to say anything.

Ginny suddenly turned thoughtful. Although she seemed anxious to go just moments before, she wasn't now. Her eyes were closed, and her lips parted as though in a trance. I had to nudge her. She seemed to wake up. She said, "Right, we've got to go."

Then Ginny and I were gone.

$$\triangle$$

We arrived in my office. Ginny said, "The old witch! She has a bad feeling does she? What reason does she have for having a bad feelings?" Then she said, "I've got some research to do. I've got to spend the night at the office. See you tomorrow."

That was a really unusual disappearance. After clinging to me as though she were my shadow, she was gone without a word of explanation. I could only wait for the next day for an explanation.

The next morning, she didn't show up until almost noon. We had lunch with the elves as usual. Ginny was in a fey mood. She wouldn't give the slightest hint about what had happened.

However, there was an unusual visit to my office that evening. The Minister of Magic herself showed up shortly after dinner. I started to say something, but she raised a hand peremptorily and just said, "You and Weasley, come to my office." When neither of us jumped she said, "Now!"

I got up and looked over toward Ginny. She shrugged. The Minister was already gone through the floo. Ginny and I followed. In Moertl's office, there were a couple of people already present. There was Parker and the American ambassador.

There were barely enough chairs for us. Moertl, who was becoming more incensed by the moment, said, "Amabassador, please repeat what you just told me."

He took a deep breath and said, "The PAK don't want Professor Wendt on the team."

I stared at him and objected. "After forcing me to join this crazy expedition, they want to drop me at the last minute. What the hell is going on?"

Ginny actually jumped up, declaring, "I'll take his place."

Then I did jump up, "No, you will not." I swung her around to face me. She just smiled that smug smile that she sometimes uses when she's gotten the better of you. However, it turned out that she hadn't got the better of anyone.

Parker sighed and said, "Let me clarify the situation. What's happened is that somehow the PAK discovered that you had killed the PAK crew of the first expedition. They don't want to take you along. However, they do want all the other crew of the first expedition to go along."

Moertl spoke up, "Well, they can't have Minerva. I thought we made that clear."

Parker replied, "They had the idea that the Souls on the original crew were responsible for the deaths of the PAK. Now that they know better they think we've been lying to them. They think there's some reason that we don't want Minerva to go."

Moertl thought out loud. "They don't know who is who on that original crew. We could send a whole crew of ringers." Ginny was nodding vigorously to that idea. Moertl noticed and growled.

The Ambassador disagreed. "Whatever their reason for wanting the original crew, I think we should do our best to send the ones that are available—less Wendt, of course."

Ginny said, "Well, that's the Brahmses, Dursley, and me."

I had been thinking this through and came to a different conclusion, but Moertl beat me to it. She said, "No! We can't avoid sending Dursley in place of Wendt, but there is a different witch who could stand in for Minerva."

Everyone asked the question, "Who?"

Moertl smiled. "The one witch, other than Minerva, who was closest to Wendt and knows the most about him—sometimes seeming to channel him." Ginny jumped up, waving her hand, but Moertl had a different idea. She said, "Professor Jaimie Sinistra."

I corrected her. "That's Brewster. She married."

Parker interrupted. "Married? Then why is it hard finding her? She's surely with her family."

I shook my head. "I'm afraid she's disappeared. Nobody knows for sure where she is. Even I, who was as close to her as anyone don't know."

That made everyone react. They ranged from puzzlement to outright rage. I was the only one who recognized the justice of that idea. I said, "I don't know if I anyone can contact her, but I'm the only one who could."

Ginny didn't know how to take that. Her mouth hung open.

Moertl said, "Well, you'd better do that and do it damn quickly. If you can't, we'll have to take Ms. Weasley's offer and hope she doesn't come back in a hand-basket." I fervently agreed.

Ginny turned to me with some of the smugness still on her face and asked, "Where to next, boss?"

My answer was, "Back to Hogwarts."

We arrived through the floo to my office. Ginny repeated her question, "Where to boss?"

I didn't answer directly. Instead, I said, "I have to get Dursley, Slughorn, and the Brahms together for a meeting tonight. Sorry, this is a meeting that you can't attend. I'll find them tonight and try to get the meeting set before the evening's over."

I first went to Filch's office. As usual, Filch was there, and Dursley was off working. I asked Filch to have Dursley go to the Headmaster's Office at nine.

I walked to the Shrieking Shack. It was the Boy Genius's workplace. I knew the code for the electronic lock on the main entrance. I entered and went up to the Main Office/Control Room. There were several employees and Brahms there. They were discussing something about blockchains.

Brahms looked up and asked what was up. I replied, "I've got an important meeting tonight in the Headmaster's Office. Can you and Aurora attend at nine?"

He asked, "Is it about the PAK?"

I nodded. He answered, "Of course."

I went to the Headmaster's Office. I got into the outer office, of course. Sally had left for home already. I was going to try knocking on the door. As I approached the door, it opened. Slughorn had opened it. He said, "What's up?"

"I need to have a meeting here at nine. It's really important. Is that a problem?"

He shook his head and said, "I've got a feeling about it. It's not good."

I couldn't deny it.

I had a couple of hours until everyone could get together and then would come the deluge. I returned to my office. Ginny was reading the *Times* when

I arrived. She looked up and said, "Just catching up on some homework. Did you know that there is a World Cup of Football. The qualifying rounds started this year. Imagine that! The following year is our World Cup of Quidditch."

I said, "Pass the front page."

She did and said, "How long is your meeting tonight?"

"I don't know. It depends. It's a planning meeting."

She laughed, "Planning what?"

"Can't tell you."

The Return of Jasmine

Slughorn's office hadn't changed a whole lot since Minerva had been the Headmistress. I knew that her portrait was somewhere in the office, but I didn't see it, and frankly, I wasn't all that anxious to find it. I wasn't all that anxious to catch up on old times. She probably knew what had been happening in my life, at least the bold outline. Maybe someday I'd find that portrait, and if she wanted, have a talk with her. For now, I just wanted to talk with the invitees to the meeting.

That made me realize that there was one other person whom I couldn't keep out of the meeting. When I entered the outer office, Sally greeted me, "It's been a long time since you dropped by."

I said, "I know. You should probably join the meeting."

"Damn straight. You couldn't keep me out if you wanted to."

I added, "Just leave the outer office doors open, please."

"Why?"

"I've got a feeling that Ginny will want to listen in. You couldn't keep her out of the outer office. But with the doors open, we can at least tell if she shows up."

Sally tossed her head of golden hair and said, "Do you mean that I know something that she doesn't?"

I said, "Shortly you will."

We all sat in the Headmaster's Office while we waited for Dursley and the Brahmses to show up. I took the red leather chair. I thought that I deserved it, especially considering what I was about to propose.

Dursley showed up next, then the Brahmses, and finally Slughorn. He sighed as he walked around his desk to take his chair. He looked around at all of us arrayed around the table. He said, "Well, give me the worst right now so that I can get the shock over quickly."

Dursley said, "It's your show professor. Why don't you go?"

It was a bad start, but I had no choice. "Most of you are aware of the background of what I'm about to say, but Sally isn't, so I'll have to give her the dragon's eye view of the background before starting."

I looked around and decided that I could stand and even pace about and still keep eye contact with everyone, so I did. I said, "Well, first some really old background. Aurora Brahms has had a habit of involving me in Halloween pranks. They always involve using polyjuice potion to disguise me as someone else. Two years ago, that got far out of hand. She got her . . ."

Sally interrupted, "I know about polyjuice potion and Aurora's pranks. What's the big deal?"

The rest of the occupants of the room groaned. Sally looked around and said, "I guess I really am out of the loop. Go ahead."

I did. "Anyway, Aurora got hold of an experimental . . ."

Aurora interrupted here. "Oh, Wendt, let me tell this part. It's embarrassing enough if I tell it. It would be excruciating if you did with your lackadaisical pace." I didn't say anything, so she went on, "I got hold of an experimental polyjuice potion based on Dursley's research into Severus Snape's potions. It was a tremendous improvement—if you can call it that—on the original formula. It is much easier and faster to brew AND it is permanent."

Sally is a quick study, so it took only a couple of minutes for her to realize the consequences of that. She said, "But you," looking at me, "you changed to look like Aurora! It couldn't have been permanent. You're here as you!"

Aurora said, "It was permanent. It was just that the 'new' Aurora had a mind of her own. She didn't want to change back to Wendt."

Sally was having a hard time keeping up, but she is sharp. She asked, "But she had all of Wendt's memories and mind. . . didn't she?"

I said, "This new polyjuice potion changes your genetics, blood chemistry, hormones, the whole shebang. I ceased to exist. A new person came into existence. She was a mature woman. She . . ."

Sally's eyes widened and she gasped, "She was a witch!"

I said, "Yes, she was a witch. She was not Aurora. She wasn't me. She chose to name herself . . ."

Sally again interrupted. "She named herself Jaimie Sinistra! How did we not see it?"

I shrugged. "You see what you expect to see. You didn't expect to see a clone of Aurora. You didn't. Of course, she didn't want you to see a clone of Aurora either. She wanted to be her own witch."

Sally shook her head and seemed about to ask a question several times. I gave her time to think it over. Eventually, she asked, "But how is that possible? This person still had all your memories. How were you not around somehow?"

"It's not that strange as you think." Sally seemed about to object again, so I hurried on. "At least, not in comparison with things that happen in the muggle world."

Sally scoffed. "Give me a break. You don't mean to say that two people in the same body, sharing memories, but not both aware!"

"Nope. Actually, there are much stranger things that happen with people with Multiple Personality Disorder. There are cases where muggles have several personalities. Some don't even know that the others exist. Some have all the memories of all of them. Some have only the memories of some of the other personalities."

Sally mused. "So, somehow, the genetic change changed you completely to a woman—ovaries, uterus, all that stuff?"

I said, "Let's get one thing straight. It didn't change ME into a woman. It created a woman who had some of my memories. When the transition back happened, it didn't change Jaimie into a man. It re-created me. I don't have any of the emotional responses that she had. I just have her memories."

Sally asked, "That still leaves the question of how she disappeared and you returned."

I took up the story again. "As you know, she married and would undoubtedly have continued on at Hogwarts, maybe had children of her own, maybe lived to a ripe old age with her grandchildren and great-grandchildren arrayed around her."

Sally asked, "But where were you when she was around?"

"Nowhere. Literally. Physically there was only she. Oh, she had all my memories, but they weren't hers. For her it must have been like knowing everything there was to know about David Copperfield.

"I would probably have been gone forever if it had not been for the Souls. They returned begging for help. Because people believed that Jaimie had a background with connections to Wendt, she was involved in dealing with them. Eventually, the muggle governments and the Ministry were begging her to find Wendt and return him to help.

"She gave in, and with the help of the Headmaster and Dursley, effectively committed suicide."

At this point Dursley said, "You're probably wondering how we did it. Jaimie still had Wendt's razor that had a lot of his hair in it. We used that to add to the the polyjuice potion. It worked."

Sally filled in some final details. "Then you and Minerva went with the Souls, and in the process of helping them, Minerva died."

I nodded. Then she asked, "OK. That brings us up to date, right?"

I said, "Not quite. Minerva died in preventing a second group of aliens from destroying the home world of the Souls. The pilots of the spacecraft that we flew in were from this second group of aliens. We now call them the PAK."

Sally nodded but asked, "How does that explain why we're here now. . . Unless these PAK have returned and want help in another attempt to destroy the Souls."

I agreed. "That's it. Of course, that still doesn't explain why we are gathered here. The answer to that is that they want the original team of the Soul's ship to help them locate the Soul world."

Sally said, "You're not there yet."

I replied, "Right. The Ministry has agreed to replace Minerva with Dursley on the crew. The PAK somehow learned that I'd been the person who had killed their pilots on the first mission. I was the last person that they would allow on the mission. They also wanted the witch who had been on the first mission.

Sally said, "Problem is that she's gone."

I went on. "The trouble is that the PAK insist on the original crew—as much as possible. The Ministry thinks that that is Jaimie Brewster because she was so close to me. I'm afraid it's Jaimie because she has all my memories."

Sally nodded slowly. "So, boss, they want you to commit suicide so that Jaimie can come back. She has all your memories, so she could stand in for you?"

I agreed. "That's it. We are having this meeting first to see if that is feasible and second to try to come up with an alternative that doesn't require me to die."

Slughorn asked, "How much time do we have?"

I shook my head. "A few days at most."

Brahms asked, "If we say no, what then?"

I grimaced. "You remember the recent asteroid strike on Mars? And then the explosion in the South Indian Ocean?"

Everyone nodded. I said, "Those weren't asteroid strikes."

There was a general moan. The boy genius summed it up. "So, they're threatening to use their weapon if we don't cooperate? Maybe something like lose a continent a week until you go along?"

I said, "I've not heard the details. They may not have made explicit threats, but it's clear that they really want our cooperation."

Everyone thought about that for a while. Slughorn said, "Bringing Jaimie back is feasible. We have a sample of her hair, don't we Dudley?"

He agreed, but he added, "I don't know that I would cooperate. You still have the option of just going yourself on this trip to hell."

I sighed in resignation. "I have to agree with the Ministry. It would be better to have another magical person on this mission. Jaimie gave her life for me. It's a sort of terrible justice if I returned the favor."

Dursley said, "Surely Ginny has something to say about that."

Sally looked from one face to another and said, "Wow, I really am out of the loop. You and Ginny . . . are . . . together?"

I could only agree. "Yes. It's a long story how that happened, and we really don't have time for it. She doesn't know about this, and if nothing comes of this, I'd rather she didn't."

Slughorn said, "Right. Now, two things occur to me. First, we don't need Dudley's sample of Jaimie's hair. Aurora's would do almost as well. Dudley's would be better, of course. Second, we could use any other wizard or witch."

Aurora said, "I don't see how that would help. As a matter of fact, I think that would be counter-productive."

Slughorn agreed. Then Sally had an idea. "What about this? Your problem is that you and Jaimie are mutually exclusive, as long as one lives, the other can't."

I said, "I don't see that that gets us anywhere."

Sally said, "Hear me out. You've shown that the two of you can alternate, right? First there was you. Then there was Jaimie. Now there's you again. We're talking about bringing back Jaimie."

She turned to Dursley. "Is there any reason that the two of them couldn't keep alternating back and forth?"

He was surprised to hear someone ask his opinion, but he did give an answer. "I don't see a problem. Of course, you have to get both to agree to it. They only did it at first because whole worlds would die if they didn't. Why else would someone agree to their own death?"

I said, "There's one problem. How do we negotiate? We can't both be in the same room or even the same world at one time."

Sally provided a suggestion. "No, but Jaimie has a husband. We could negotiate with him. I know him and his daughter; I think he could convince her to trust you to keep your part of the bargain."

Aurora said, "Then the way the deal might work would be that each of you alternates having life—maybe a year or two at a time. Would you agree to that?"

I laughed. "It's better than a stick in the eye."

Slughorn said, "Let's get what's his name, Jaimie's husband. Uh . . ."

I said, "Brewster."

Slughorn continued. "Let's get him in here right now. Does anyone know how to disapparate there?"

I scoffed. "I know how to or anyway Jaimie does, but that doesn't really help us." Then I remembered. "Oh, he has a floo connection, of course, but stepping out of it unannounced would not be a good way to win his cooperation."

Sally slapped her head. "The school has his address in his daughter's file. I'll go get it."

△

Ed Brewster entered the Headmaster's Office accompanied by Aurora. He accepted the invitation to sit, taking a yellow guest chair. His first words were, "What's going on? Is this something about Cecily? Professor Brahms wouldn't tell me what it was about."

Slughorn said, "No, it's nothing to do with Cecily." Then he reconsidered and said, "Well, maybe it actually is. I'm going to let Professor Wendt explain." He leaned back, probably happy to have someone else take that particular burden from his shoulders.

I said, "Please bear with me and let me finish before you speak. This will take a good bit of explaining. But . . ."

With that, Slughorn interrupted and said, "Wendt is right. This will take some time. Can I offer you something to drink? What do we have Sally?"

She named a list of drinks including pumpkin juice, hot tea, and harder beverages. Generally, people selected from the harder beverages. I had a Dewars. Fortified by that, I started the explanation:

"First, let me come to the main point. This concerns your late wife, Jaimie." Brewster drew in a breathe sharply, but he resisted the temptation to speak. I continued, "There is an opportunity to bring her back. However, there are catches, rather serious ones. Do you want to hear more?"

He grimaced and said between gritted teeth, "How could I not want to. Say your worst."

I stood and paced. "Here's the thing. First, in order to give you all the information you need to make an intelligent decision I have to give you some background history. To do that, I have to have your promise not to reveal anything that I tell you to anyone."

He sneered, "Unbreakable Oath?"

"No. You are an honorable man. As a matter of fact, it is that honor that I'm going to have to depend on later, as you'll see. You'll also see why I couldn't use the Unbreakable for that. If I'm already using your personal integrity for the second thing, I should use it for this as well. Do I have it?"

He sneered again, "In for a knut, in for a galleon."

"OK. The last time that we were here talking about this, the Souls. . . "

230

Here he interrupted. "You mean the aliens who almost took over the Earth?"

"The same. Yes, they approached the main governments of the Earth asking for help. Some of their planets were being decimated by a disease." Brewster's mouth opened wide. I answered the unspoken question. "Yes, they did come, and they did ask for help. That was the secret mission that Jaimie gave up her life to support. As you know, that gave me back my life."

I had been pacing, but then I stopped and looked at him. "I'm going to tell you something that hardly amyone else knows. Even though they are my closest friends, they don't know. Minerva and I went on this mission along with the Brahmses. We almost all died on that mission. We didn't because we all worked together to defeat a couple of aliens who were not Souls. They are of a race that we're calling the PAK. The PAK provided the Faster-Than-Light ship that we used. They were the crew of that ship. The Souls had no idea that they were from a race that wanted to destroy them.

"Minerva died in that successful effort to defeat the PAK. We were extremely lucky. We prevented the PAK from destroying the solar system of the Souls.

"I still grieve for Minerva, and I'm sure that I always will. As a matter of fact, I seriously considered returning Jaimie—permanently. I was discouraged from that and . . ."

Brewster couldn't resist commenting. He stood and said, "Why did you bring me here—to torture me with memories of my grief!"

I shook my head. "No. Please let me continue." He sat but looked on the edge of doing harm to someone. I went on. "The PAK have returned. They somehow think that we can help them find the Soul's home world. It may not be totally hopeless for them. They insist that all of our team that went the last time come on this expedition. Their goal is the same—genocide. They want us to help them with it."

I paused and finished my Dewars. Sally noticed and went for another. I went on. "I hope that we can prevent that without the PAK inflicting genocide on us. So, here we come finally to the point. We have to send a team composed of as many of the original team as we can. For our purposes we want as many of them to be magical as possible. We think that Jaimie—armed with my memories—will satisfy the PAK."

Brewster interrupted again. "So, you intend to bring her back and send her on this crazy trip. I was right. You brought me here to torture me."

I objected. "No. . . Well, I guess this is torture for you, but that wasn't our intention. We want your help in bringing her back."

He gazed at us in wonder. "Why do you need my help?"

I sighed. It was going to be harder than I'd expected. "I'm surprised you haven't figured that out yet. Well, I'll take it step by step.

"First, we don't absolutely need Jaimie. We have another witch who is willing, even anxious, to fill in. It might even be the best option for getting the PAK to negotiate with the Souls, which is my personal bet for our best plan.

"Second, since we don't absolutely need Jaimie, without your help, my personal best option for coming out alive would be to not go myself."

"So, my hope is that you will be willing to bargain to get her back. I'll help you out by making the opening offer—which I think is a pretty damn good offer considering that I could walk out of here and not be in awful shape."

Brewster wasn't much impressed. He just said, "Well, bargain already."

I nodded appreciatively. I'd not really expected to get this far before he walked out. I proceeded. "My opening offer is this. Since we've pretty well established that we can return Jaimie and then return me and so on, pretty much *ad infinitum*, my offer is that we take turns being alive. Jaimie gets a year or two then I get a year or two. We alternate back and forth until one of us dies for real."

Brewster thought about it. His lips squeezed tight, and he looked up and to his right. I was not going to rush him. After a while he looked at me and said, "That's not a terrible deal, but I have a slightly different suggestion. Now, I'm going to ask you to bear with me while I lay out my reasons for it."

I readily agreed. I had nothing to lose, and it was just fair play to give him his say. He proceeded. "OK. Here's the deal. One year is OK, two years are better, but four years is nearly perfect. Here's why,

"First, Jaimie and I didn't have even a full honeymoon. We need plenty of time for that." Of course, one year would have been an unbelievably long honeymoon, but I didn't say anything. He had a right to his uninterrupted say.

"Second, Cecily is a fourth year now. She'll graduate in a little over three years. Jaimie should have the opportunity to help Cecily reach adult age and complete school.

"Third, Jaimie and I were planning on having kids. We should have the opportunity to have a couple of kids and at least see the older ready for nursery school. Of course, that would be nice if we could do it for the second, but I'm willing to compromise."

I listened with care to his idea and to myself I had to admit that I couldn't argue too strongly against it. However, I made a counter-offer. I said, "You've made some good points, but I'd like to suggest a variation on it. What about three years? I'd make the following points:

"First, Cecily has almost finished her fourth year. By the time that Jaimie comes back from this mission, it will be less than three years until her graduation—quite likely months less. Second, three years would still leave you ample time to have two kids. Quite likely, your first would be ready for nursery school. Third, if you look at the years beyond the first six year cycle, Jaimie would be home for most of your kids important events. In years seven through nine, your first would be starting school and your second would be as well. In years thirteen through fifteen both would start at Hogwarts if you held them back a year, which is often a good idea. In years nineteen through twenty-two, they'd graduate from Hogwarts."

Brewster was silent throughout and seemed to be thinking it over. I went on. "A slight variation on that would be three years on, three years off and then switch to two on and two off from then on. I'll not work out the details. You can do that for yourself."

He leaned back and said, "How long do I have to think it over?"

I replied, "We are definitely on the clock. We have to field a team by Saturday. But it will take time to bring Jaimie back. I want a definite decision one way or the other from you not later than tomorrow, Tuesday night. We can still negotiate over details of frequency of switching back and forth between Jaimie and me until Wednesday, but that's it."

Brewster considered. Then he said, "I want to talk it over with my daughter. Can she have a one day holiday from school tomorrow?"

Slughorn agreed to that. Brewster went to collect his daughter. That was one conversation that I certainly didn't want to be in on. I had memories from similar conversations that Jaimie had had with her. They were heart-wrenching.

I turned to Dursley. "Would you and Slughorn start brewing the wretched stuff immediately."

Dursley glanced at Slughorn and something passed between them. Then Dursley said, "We should have it ready by Thursday. Let me say something. I really hope Brewster doesn't go along with it."

I asked Dursley, "Let's have a meeting of the Old Boys' Club tomorrow at lunch. Win, lose, or draw I'm in for a rough time. I want to say good-bye, just in case."

No one was happy about that, but then I wasn't either. The meeting broke up, and I returned to my office. Ginny was still there. She was sitting at my desk writing notes for delivery by owl. When I entered, she looked up and grinned. She asked, "How'd your meeting go?"

"Oh, better than I hoped, but I don't want to talk about it today. Tomorrow will be good for that."

She raised her eyebrows. "Hoping for something tomorrow?"

I tried to crack a smile. "You could say that, I suppose."

Ginny's grin disappeared. "I've got a bad feeling about it, whatever it is."

I said, "We'll see tomorrow."

The Old Boy's Club meets at the Three Broomsticks, rarely in a private room. This time, I insisted on it. Everyone showed up—Hagrid, Filch, Dursley, Slughorn, Nicholas Brahms, and me.

Everyone had arrived, and we'd placed orders. We could almost have had a standing order, they changed so infrequently. That completed, everyone's attention was fixed on me. I began. "The reason that I wanted this meeting, besides just enjoying getting together with you all, is that I am shortly going on a special assignment from the Ministry of Magic."

Filch immediately interrupted me, "Is this the same thing that happened a while back?" Then he added, "When your wife died?" That last was in as muted a voice as he ever used. Luckily in the still of our private room no one had trouble hearing.

I nodded my head. "Yes, it was the assignment during which Minerva died. This is really the same thing. Nearly all the actors are the same. Most of you know these details, but I wanted to include Hagrid and Filch so they would know. It's very unlikely that I will come back. I'm going to explain why, but first, I want to give you details that you didn't have before. I'll do it quickly, never fear.

"Here's what happened. The Souls came back for help. They were being decimated by a disease. They were so desperate that they came to us for help. We put together a team—the Brahmses and the Wendts. That was about all the spacecraft would hold. We visited a couple of planets. But there were a couple of sleepers on-board. The pilots were not under Soul control. They were from another race that wanted to destroy the Souls."

Filch exclaimed, "Those stinking . . . uh . . . what did you call them?"

Count on Filch to bring serious topics to their proper perspective. I said, "We don't know what they call themselves. We call them the PAK." I continued. "They were going to use the ship in a suicide mission to destroy the home planet of the Souls. We prevented that. We killed them. In the battle, Minerva died."

Hagrid asked, "So the Souls have come back?"

I shook my head. "No, the PAK have come back. They are forcing us to help them find the Souls. They insist on the original human crew to go with them. I'm putting together the crew. It will be the Brahms, Mr. Dursley."

At that Filch cried, "Bravo, way to go Dudley!" It seemed that Filch had reconciled himself to Dursley leaving and was making the best of it.

Hagrid asked, "And, you, of course, Professor?"

"No, not me. Professor Jaimie Brewster."

Filch and Hagrid went slack-jaw with the statement. Then there was general pandemonium. Eventually they were ready for an explanation. I said, "Some of you need more of an explanation than the others. I'll start with them. Briefly, just before Jaimie Brewster (then known as Jaimie Sinistra) showed up, I disappeared after the Halloween party. That was not coincidental. Aurora can fill you in on the details but the bottom line is that she used a new very improved version of the polyjuice potion on me. It converted me into a clone of her—permanently. The resulting person was not Aurora—she had none of Aurora's memories. She certainly wasn't me. She did have my memories, but she was a witch. She named herself and took over my position at Hogwarts. She'd have been there to this day except that the Souls showed up and asked for help. They explicitly asked for me to help them. She did a very courageous act—she let Dursley and Slughorn use the new polyjuice potion to convert her back to me.

"That would have been the end of the story except that the PAK came back for another go at the Souls. I would have been on the team again but for one point. Somehow the PAK learned about my role in the death of their people on the previous mission. They have forced the Ministry to appoint someone else. Almost everyone at the Ministry wants to maximize the number of magical people on the team. Jaimie is magical. I am not. She has all my memories and will have to do for the team because I will have converted to her and therefore I will be dead."

Most of the people in the room were still partially in the dark, and were asking questions like, "Did Brewster agree to get his wife to trade places with you?" and "Did you hear from Brewster?"

I said, "I've decided that whatever happens, I'm still going to go ahead and let Jaimie Brewster return. If she decides later to bring me back, and by the way, I sure hope she does, fine. Otherwise, I'm still OK with it. She deserves a life too. So, the reason I wanted to get together with the OBC today is that I'm going to be gone for a very long time at the least. I think that the chances that Jaimie will die is one in four. After that, the chances that she will restore me is maybe fifty-fifty, maybe less. This is an opportunity to say good-bye."

On that somber note our orders arrived, and we ate for a while in silence. Filch broke the silence by saying, "I've been thinking." Everyone treated that statement with a lot more respect than they might otherwise. "You know, what you're doing reminds me of a sailor's life. A hundred years ago, sailors went off on journeys that could last years. There was a good chance that they would never return. They said good-bye just like we are. It was sad, but not terrible." That different perspective made the rest of the meal more like the last night reveling before the sailors sail.

We talked about old times. That isn't to say that it was all fun. Filch insisted on re-telling his part in Dursley's getting to edit and publish Snape's revisions to the old standard *Advanced Potionmaking*. It would have been amusing to hear his highly exaggerated version again except that the butt of the story was the Headmaster who was sitting right there. The one saving grace was that Slughorn had broken an unwritten rule when he suggested that it would be all right for staff to have something "hard" to drink. "We normally discourage drinking before the end of the teaching day, but this is a special event, so I'm going to make an exception and have a glass of port myself." Everyone else was happy to join in with their own favorite beverage. Slughorn could hardly be disappointed when some people spoke more directly than they normally would.

After we had finished the meeting, we all returned to our offices or classrooms. Ginny was no where to be seen as I entered my office. I was in a rather unusual situation. I would ordinarily have started packing for the space voyage coming up. As it was, even though some of Jaimie's clothes were still in my closet, I had no idea what she would want. I reflected that she would surely want at least one or two pairs of jeans, right? Further reflection suggested maybe not. However, I could inventory my purse to make sure I had a good inventory of items. That was especially important because I'd not done an inventory in a long, long time.

You may wonder that Jaimie was able to open my purse since she was a completely different person than I was. When she was first able to do that I was not present, of course. I think that the spell somehow detected my memories in Jaimie's brain and decided that was good enough validation to allow her to open the purse.

It took a few minutes to empty the purse on my desk top. There were the items that I knew were there. There was the Glock, the was a spare clip (empty), there was a nearly full box of bullets. I made a note to myself to get a fresh box and replace the one that was there. There was money.

Then there was a miscellany of other things. I reloaded the purse and felt like I'd achieved something worthwhile. Now my purse was ready for interstellar travel.

I picked up the *Times* that Ginny had left and tried to catch up on the news of the world.

Dinner was fast approaching, but before I could leave for the Great Hall two people arrived in my hearth.

It turned out to be the Brewsters. Cecily walked up to the desk and demanded to talk. Her father didn't really want us to, but I decided that it might be a good time to do that. I was sure that she would have things that she wanted to say to me and would be angry if I never returned from this little adventure and thus deprived her of that opportunity. Her father was persuaded.

I asked them if they wanted anything to drink. The father wasn't interested, but Cecily asked what I had. I answered, "Water, pumpkin juice, and some warm soda, I can brew some tea if you would like some."

She asked what soda I had. I replied, "I'm afraid you've not heard of them—Seven-up and Dr. Pepper." She asked for Dr. Pepper. I got out a clean glass and the can. Brewster materialized some ice in the glass.

I hoped that she would be less angry. Her frown softened after a few sips. I asked her to say what she would. She spoke, "Why didn't you give us my mum back after you returned from space! I had a mum for the first time that I could remember, and then she was gone—forever! And you want her to give you back as soon as she's back!" Her nostrils flared at that.

I took a deep breath and tried to maintain my equanimity as she continued. "Well! What do you have to say for yourself?"

I sighed. "I want to live as much as you want your mum to come back. I don't know what you and your dad have decided." At that Mr. Brewster started to speak. I held my hand up and insisted that they hear me out. "I don't care. I've decided that I'm going to bring your mum back. She will go with the rest of the team and the PAK to commit genocide. I hope that your mum and the rest of the team can prevent that. If she comes out alive—and I won't kid you by saying that it's not dangerous—I want her to be around until you finish at Hogwarts. After that, I would like your Mum and me to alternate times to be alive and with the people we care about."

Cecily said, "We've decided to accept your deal. If I am going to have sisters, I'd like mum to be around for them too, but dad really wants to play fair with you." She hesitated, and tears ran down her cheeks. She said, "This isn't fair at all."

I said, "You're right. It isn't fair at all. I wish I had an answer that's fair for everyone. I don't. You're in luck, though. You're going to get something that many kids don't have—a mum who loves you and will teach in your school. You can see her every day, although I doubt that you'd always want to."

She then turned the corner and said, "How about my tournament? Who's going to go with me?"

Mr. Brewster immediately said, "I'll be there."

I added, "I think I can get a good friend of mine to help you get there and be there as moral support." She pressed me on that promise, asking who it was. I said, "I've not asked her yet. I definitely will before I go. She'll get in touch with your dad about it."

I looked up at her dad and asked, "You've been awfully quiet. No comment, questions, or requests?"

He just said, "You've pretty much covered everything. I'll believe that Jaimie's back when I hold her in my arms." I just nodded. Then I invited him to stay for dinner in the Great Hall. We went down together. I went to the head table, and they went to the Ravenclaw table.

After dinner, I returned to my office feeling a lot lonelier than I had in a long time. My office was empty. The sun was nearly set. I looked around and could find comfort nowhere. That hadn't happened a lot lately. I took it as a bad sign. I'd committed to taking hemlock. I'd never done anything like that before. Jaimie had done it, but even though I shared her memories, I'd never realized just how frightening an act it was.

I was sitting at my desk thinking about that until it had gotten fully dark outside. Then there was a whoosh in the hearth. I looked up to find Ginny striding out of the floo connection. I got up, came around the desk, and walked into her arms. We kissed. Then she observed, "You look pretty down in the mouth. I understand that you're probably unhappy because your friend, Dursley, is about to go into the first circle of hell with the PAK. I could still take his place."

I cracked a tired smile. "Oh that would be choosing Scylla over Charybdis."

She laughed. "It's easy. Send me!"

I took her hand and dragged her to the sofa. When we were seated, I started my speech. "In the first place, I'm committed to Dursley. But that's only the first place. There's more. I guess I've got to make a confession or two to explain this."

She seemed pretty sturdy still. I continued, "First, let's talk about Jaimie Brewster."

Ginny went on, "She replaced you here when you dropped off the face of the earth a couple of years ago. I thought you were gone forever. You know, that was a turning point for me."

That was a surprise for me. I asked, "What turning point was that?"

"That was the point when I realized that it made a difference if you were around or not. I've told you that I've had a crush on you since my school days. That dates back to my first year when you were the first one on the scene when we came out of the Chamber of Secrets.

"Of course, I had a crush on Harry too."

I started to object, but she insisted, "Oh, just be quiet and listen. The crush on both you and Harry subsided for a while. Then it got really confusing when Riddle seemed to be in control."

I commented, "For more than just you."

"Yeh. I suppose. Anyway, Potter was gone while I finished my last year at Hogwarts. I was really impressed when you helped that dratted Dursley save his girlfriend. Then there was the way that you beat the Ghosts. I guess my feelings for you had been growing all that time. I suppressed them, of course, when you and Minerva got married. Then you disappeared. That was a real shock to my system. When you were committed to Minerva, I could still kid myself that she was much older than you and you'd probably outlive her by a bunch. Then you'd be available. Understand. I know that was stupid, wishful thinking. It was just something to daydream about when I didn't have anything worthwhile to do.

"But with you off the face of the earth, even that stupid daydreaming was no longer possible. That forced me to realize that if a miracle happened and you reappeared, I'd want to try to win you—maybe even from Minerva.

"Well, you reappeared, and almost immediately you and she were off on your space adventure. When you came back, it was as a widower. Believe me, my heart almost exploded. Then I faced reality. You were deep in grief and seemingly a little . . . uh . . . suicidal."

"That was when I started my campaign to return you to normal and eventually to my arms." She was holding me tight. "Worked pretty well, didn't it?"

I had to agree. That made what I had to say all the harder. I began. "Back to where I started. There is a reason that Jaimie showed up shortly after I disappeared."

Ginny's eyes widened and turned a little wild. She clutched me convulsively and said with an intensity that I knew was in her, but I'd not actually heard before, "Don't tell me! You're back. You're going to be around while someone else deals with a bunch of maniac aliens and pulls the rabbit out of the hat that you always seem to be able to find. Most importantly, we'll be together."

I realized then that this was going to be very, very hard. I started none-the-less. "I've got to keep going." Ginny was steely-eyed but didn't say anything. "Aurora used an untested version of polyjuice to make me a genetic clone of her—permanently. That clone was not Aurora, it certainly wasn't me. She was a witch and didn't want to go away just because I used to be here but wasn't as soon as she appeared."

Her jaw dropped, and she whispered, "And we talked her into bringing you back for that mission in which Minerva died." She dropped her face into her hands. She gasped, "I helped talk her into ending her own life."

I nodded, and she said, "So, you're here because she died."

"That's it."

The point began to sink in. "You said that you had a way that a magical person could stand in for you. You were talking about Jaimie, weren't you?"

"Yes."

She took a deep breath and said softly, "No." Then she repeated louder and louder, "No. NO. NOOO." It ended as a wail.

"I'm decided. It's not that bad. I think that she will let me come back after a couple of years."

Ginny shrieked again, and her eyes filled with tears. "Do you know how the PAK learned that you were their Nemesis on that last mission?"

I was beginning to understand her shriek. I decided to put off the realization as long as possible. I said, "No."

"It was me! It was! I asked Parker to pass the message along to them that you were the guilty party. I was sure that they'd not want you on this mission." She laughed without humor. "I am the reason that you're dying so that Jaimie can return!"

Ginny went on. "And you're wrong. I would never give up my life so that some guy could be with his sweetheart. You can't do this. No. You have to go yourself—with me. We'll come back together, and we'll live together. I don't care how. Married. Living with you. Whatever."

I said, "Look, this is a big surprise. You're not thinking. Think about it. The PAK will never permit that. Besides, put yourself in Jaimie's shoes."

"I won't put myself in her shoes. I'm in my own shoes. I want you alive, here, with me. None of that will happen if she kills you or you kill yourself or whatever it is." She was on the verge of hysteria, and I was not all that calm myself.

I said, "Look." And then I remembered Filch's sailor story. "You're imagining the worst. In the 19th century sailors left home and family. They went on voyages that lasted for years sometimes. They came home and rejoined their loved ones, and all was well."

She didn't seem to be buying it. She had stood and began pacing. As she did, she said, "You've got to give up this crazy idea. Don't do it!"

I was on the point of gagging. I just said, "Let's sleep on this. Things may feel different in the morning."

Her lips formed a tight line as she thought. She seemed to relax and said, "OK. Let's relax tonight and do something that will take my mind off your leaving on this terrible journey in someone else's body."

That was the most hopeful thing I'd heard today. I said, "Sure, What do you want to do?"

Her lips turned up for the first time, and her eyes twinkled. "I've got an idea. We'll take the floo network to the Cauldron, and then I'll disapparate us somewhere."

I was game. When we stepped outside the Cauldron, she took both my hands in hers. She asked me to close my eyes. I did. Then we disapparated somewhere. When I opened my eyes, besides seeing her, I saw a great city from a couple of hundred feet. I turned and realized where we were. It was the Eiffel Tower. We walked around a girder and found ourselves at the restaurant. I had to bribe the maitre'd rather seriously, but I didn't care. I even got to kid Ginny. "Muggle magic. No confunding necessary."

We had dessert and hot tea. It was a warm evening, and we enjoyed watching the City of Light in the evening. When we left and arrived at the Cauldron, Ginny squeezed my hand and said, "Let's spend the night. You know, just like the first time." I agreed.

That night, the love-making was not desperate or intense or world-shaking. It was just the reliable balm that washed away the pain and gave us escape for a time.

We awoke after the sun was well up. We took time to bathe, dress, and go down for breakfast. The presence of Tom was pleasant. It was a hint that some things never changed in this crazy world. Of course, we didn't take his recommendation for breakfast. We had simple fare—eggs, bacon, toast, tea. We wasted as much time as we could justify. Then I paid for the room and the breakfast. Tom left, wishing us a soon return. We walked into the hearth hand in hand, swinging pleasantly.

We walked out into my office. That brought us back to the inevitable conversation that had only been postponed, not finished. We stood there in each other's arms. She asked, "Are you still going to bring Jaimie back?"

I made a clear answer, "Yes."

"There's nothing I can do to convince you otherwise?"

"No."

She stepped out of my arms, and a grim expression crossed her face. She said with all the steel in her voice that I'd ever heard anyone use in saying anything, "This is it. If you do that, James Thomas Wendt, I will never see you again."

I said, "God don't do that."

She said, "I'm leaving." She turned, walked into the hearth, and disappeared without another word or even a glance backwards.

The rest of the day was uneventful. I went down to the kitchens to have lunch with the maintenance engineers. They seemed confident that I'd pull a rabbit out of the hat and save myself from turning into Jaimie. I let their happiness reign. I even joked about what we'd do when I returned from the PAK. Dursley was betting on a wedding with Ginny. I couldn't smile at that.

The next day was the J day. I had lunch again with the engineers. Slughorn dropped in and said that the brewing was finished and that after dinner would be the best time to take the polyjuice potion. There was an agreement to meet at Slughorn's office at 8 PM.

I showed up there immediately after dinner—about 7 PM. The maintenance engineers would be up shortly. Both the Brahmses would be there, not that they had any great desire to watch the beginning of the transformation, but they decided that since we'd be together in close quarters on the spacecraft, it wasn't too early to start getting used to each other.

Dursley arrived and yielded up one of the locks of hair that he'd been given by Jaimie to the polyjuice potion. Aurora thought it would be appropriate that she mix that ingredient in and administer it to me as the last time that I'd be using polyjuice. That was actually kind of a scary thought.

Dursley reminded me that he had to get a sample of my hair so that I could return. Slughorn always seemed to have a sample vial at hand. Dursley used his wand to cut some hair off and put it in the vial. Slughorn took it, sealed it, and filed it in his desk.

At that last moment, the thought of the taste of that concoction was more off-putting than the thought of what came next—which was nothing. I thought about Socrates' slow death after taking the hemlock. I forced the stuff down, half gagging half wanting to throw up. I reached the end.

Since I was wearing dress robes and Jaimie was smaller than I, I didn't have to worry about the fit of my clothes other than having to swim in them. The gross external changes came swiftly, the more subtle genetic changes would come far more slowly. Filch had never witnessed this and was not shy about expressing his disgust at the bizarre contortions my body went through in reaching its final state.

Dursley asked me a question that I'd expected to come up before now, but somehow had never really been broached. He started with something simple. "Are you Jaimie now?"

"No. That will take several hours."

He followed up with the core issue. "How can you possibly become a different person. You still have all of Wendt's memories, right?"

I shook my head vigorously, sending my locks flying. "OK. Here's the deal. It's true that Jaimie has all of my memories, but she also has a very different body. She has a whole different set of hormones running through her blood. The way she thinks about things is different."

Slughorn broke in. "Yes, but a different identity?"

I nodded. "Yes. And, really, it's happened before and without magic and without changed genetics. There was a psychiatrist who documented a case of a muggle woman who had multiple identities—not just two. I think there were seven. It was very strange. Some of the identities knew about others. Some were unaware that there was anyone else sharing their body. Some shared memories. Some didn't.

"How does that work? I don't know. The man who documented the case of the muggle woman didn't know. I just know that when Jaimie is around, I'm not conscious, and from her memories I know that when I'm around, she's not conscious."

Aurora asked, "What happens when the changeover happens? Is it instantaneous?"

I had to admit some ignorance. "It's only happened twice, and one of the times it was when I wasn't conscious. The one time that I was conscious, it wasn't in a sudden rush. It took a couple of minutes. It was like a wave on a beach. As the wave reached the furthest up the beach, I was me becoming less and less me. As the wave retreated, I was Jaimie becoming more and more Jaimie. There was that peak when the Jaimie personality just seemed perfect and right. After that I wasn't any more."

Filch pulled us back to earth. He said, "There's not going to be anything more to see is there?"

Dursley answered, "No. The rest is boring, except for Wendt."

Filch shook all over. He looked at me again and said, "Sorry. I can't stand to look at you and think that you're what's left of Wendt." He got up and left the office.

I realized that everyone must feel that way. I stood and said, "I'm sure that you all must be wishing me gone. I'm going up to my office." I turned to Slughorn and said, "On behalf of Jaimie, I guess I'd like you to keep my teaching post open for her. I'm pretty sure that she'd like to come back to Hogwarts—if there is a coming back from this adventure."

243

Slughorn just nodded and looked down at the floor. I turned to the door and left. Even though I was a dead man walking, I still somehow hoped that something would happen to give me a reprieve. I guess I was more like the man on death row than I'd ever realized.

My office looked just the same. I sat behind my desk. I opened the drawer that served as a liquor cabinet. I selected the lone remaining bottle of Blue Label. There wasn't a lot in it. I found a glass. It didn't matter that it wasn't clean. I poured a shot and was about to drink.

There was a knock at the door. I barely heard it. I certainly wasn't going to answer it. It was repeated a couple of times. Then, it opened. Aurora walked in. I scoffed. "Old habits never die I see. You never had much respect for my privacy."

She took the red leather chair and nodded at the bottle. "Have you forgotten your hospitality? Aren't you going to share?"

I grimaced, scrounged for a glass, and was about to fill it. She pulled it from my hand and said, "Don't you ever wash your glasses." She then used the *Scurgio* spell to clean it.

I sneered, "If you only waited a day, your hostess would be Jaimie. She was a neatness freak. She'd have cleaned all the glasses."

She sneered, too, "I'm not interested in being with Jaimie. I'll be with that bitch all too much. I want to be with you at the end."

"You just feel guilty for getting me into this fix."

She laughed. "You'd be going off with us in any case. We'll probably all end up dead, blown to elementary particles in the Soul solar system."

We just drank in silence for a while. The Blue Label helped cover the rumblings of pain from my interior as it rearranged itself. We sat and finished the bottle. When it was drained, she finished the last partial glass in a single swallow. She stood and said, "Well, no more reason to stay. God, I'll miss you. Regardless what the Ministry thinks, I think we'd be better off with you than her." Then she walked around the desk. I rose. She hugged me, turned, and walked through the still-open door.

I closed the door and decided that it was time to go to bed. I took off my robe and tossed it into the hamper where the house elves would pick up clothing to be washed. I walked to the closet to remind myself of what robes that I'd left there. There were only a couple for Jaimie. I ran my hand over them, appreciating their silky texture. I picked one to wear and hung it outside the closet. It was fast ending. I finished undressing. I decided that I would re-enter the world naked. I slipped under the covers, appreciating the comfort of the sheet on my bare skin as I rarely did.

Return to Space

The light streaming through the window brought me slowly to consciousness. I was lying face down. As I stretched and rose, I realized where I was. I immediately wondered if the polyjuice potion had failed. After all, I was still Jaimie and in the bed where I'd fallen asleep after taking the polyjuice potion. Of course, they might make me take that spaceflight with the Souls instead of Wendt, but . . .

Then memories started to stream in. I was going into space, but it wasn't with the Souls. It was with a race called the PAK.

I had been gone for almost two years!

I'd missed two years of Sissy's life. I'd missed two years with my husband. I sank back on the pillow and almost wished I'd not come back. Then I realized that I never expected to be back at all. I had time. I could get dressed and find Sissy in this very castle! I could take the floo connection to my home.

That was what I did. I hurried to shower and dress. It was still before seven, Ed wouldn't leave for work for at least a half hour. I stepped into the hearth and blessed Wendt for keeping the floo powder supply fresh!

I stepped out of the hearth at home. It took away my breath to look around the living room and find everything as I'd left it seemingly only hours before. I called out to Ed.

I heard motion upstairs. I called again. This time there was a shouted, "Jaimie! Is that you?" I needed no more encouragement, I ran up the stairs and we collided as he ran out of our bedroom.

He immediately (after a passionate kiss) exclaimed, "I knew that Wendt intended to send you, but I didn't really believe it! Are you really going to go on that crazy space plane?"

That caused me to take a deep breath and think. I said, "The short answer is yes, but I . . ."

Ed's eyes dropped, and his embrace loosened. He then said, "How can you leave us again, so soon after returning!"

I thought carefully, "Why was I going to do that? Was it because I thought I owed him something?" I sat on the edge of the bed and thought and remembered. I remembered things from Wendt's memory.

I began slowly. "There are good reasons. First and most important is that I wouldn't be here except for his belief that I would do this. Second, these aliens, these PAK." I paused. It was the first time that I'd said that name out loud. There instantly flowed into my memory a torrent of mental images—the interior of the spaceship, Minerva wearing a spacesuit her face as grey as dirty snow at Christmas, the PAK bodies lying at my feet while I fired the Glock again and again into them, Aurora pulling me away. Strangely, the images were as clear and crisp as if they had just happened, but there was absolutely no sound, not even Wendt's voice screaming at them.

I tried to start again but my throat was so constricted that I couldn't say a word for a while. Then I did start again, "These PAK are as bad as the Souls. Worse, they killed Minerva. I don't want to help either of them, but I know that Wendt's hope was to broker some kind of peace—a peace where there are no victim races—like us. I do want to help with that."

I took a deep breath and said the last and most horrible words, "They have threatened to destroy the Earth if we don't help them."

Ed just stared at me. "You are kidding?"

I shook my head. "I have direct access to Wendt's memories. At the very least he believed it."

While we were talking, an owl landed on our window ledge outside our bedroom. He tapped on the window. I opened it and took the note from the owl which immediately took off. No return for him. I slit it open and read. I said, "The Minister of Magic wants me to come to her office at 8 AM tomorrow. She enclosed the password to it." I glanced at the note again.

As I memorized the password, the note caught on fire and burned without a trace. Ed said, "Will I see you again after you leave tomorrow?"

I opened my mouth to say something, but all that would come out was, "I hope."

He grimaced, strode to our dresser, picked up a scrap of parchment and quill. He wrote, speaking as he did, "Something urgent has come up at home." He smiled wickedly at that and went on. "I may be in to work tomorrow. Otherwise expect me on Monday. E. Brewster."

He was indeed right that something very urgent had come up for him. We did our best to satisfy that urgent uprising. I certainly enjoyed it. We forced ourselves up and out of the house at noon for a lunch at a local pub that was not run by a wizard but was a favorite among wizards and witches because of its excellent fish and chips and craft beer. The conversation was centered around whether we should take Sissy out of school for a long weekend holiday.

I said, "You can't imagine how much I want to be with Cecily, but she's already had a special holiday once this term. Maybe on Saturday."

Ed was adamant. "You may be billions of miles away then, never to be seen again. No, what would I say to her if you never returned, and she hadn't seen you?"

How could I argue against that? I gave in happily. It was so wonderful to have a partner that you could argue with and make up with so easily!

Ed insisted on going to Hogwarts right away to get Sissy. I couldn't argue with him although it would have been nice to visit our bedroom one more time first. We arrived in the Great Hall floo connection. The hall was empty. On the way to the Headmaster's Office we passed a few students changing classes who recognized me. They wanted to stop me to talk about my return, but we were determined to get to see Slughorn immediately.

We walked in the door. Sally was there. She apparently hadn't been informed that I was back. Her face oscillated between surprise, pain, and even happiness. She leaped out of her chair, circled her desk and hugged me. Neither of us could come up with anything to say. There were tears in both our eyes—tears of happiness and sadness, I suppose. I could tell that she was trying as hard as I was to come up with something to say. Eventually she said, "Sorry, Slughorn isn't here. He's in class."

My hubby said, "I want to take Cecily out for a couple of days."

She replied, "Just pick her up. I'll clear it with the Head."

We both thanked her and started to leave when she called after us, "Wait a sec, and I'll look up which class she's in."

It turned out that she was in Professor Binns' History of Magic class. We went to that classroom which hadn't changed since Ed had taken History of Magic. I stayed outside while Ed knocked on the door, then banged on the door, then finally just opened it and walked in. Everyone was doing everything other than paying attention to the lecture. Sissy noticed her dad and jumped up. They hugged, and he said, "I'm breaking you out."

She stage whispered, "Why?"

He turned her around so that she could see me through the door. She shouted, "Mum." Then she was in my arms before I realized it. Everyone in the class—except Binns—sighed, no doubt wishing they could be rescued. Sissy was crying and laughing at once. "I never thought I'd see you again."

I was shedding a tear or two myself. "I didn't either. But . . ."

She held me all the tighter as though she could undo that "But" by squeezing it to death. She said with an intensity that I'd not heard in her voice before, "No. Dad, you have to do something."

I pulled her away from the door. We walked down the hall. I finished the sentence, "I have to go on a mission for the Ministry, but I will come back and I don't have to go again for a long time."

She sniffed her disbelief. "You just say that to make me feel better."

Maybe I was saying it to make me feel better. What I said was, "Let's go somewhere that we can talk privately."

She replied, "What about our home!"

Ed nodded enthusiastically, and I found that the idea of being some-where familiar and safe was good. I said, "Right. Let's go via the floo in my office."

Sissy was suspicious again, "Why there?"

"It's quiet, it's safe, it's a place where we can talk right away." There was no one walking the halls, so we could go unobserved to my office. Once we were there, I locked the door with a spell that would keep it locked. I thought about using the *Muffliato* spell, but I decided not to. I didn't want to discourage Sissy. I said, "OK. Now, we can talk about what's happened and what's going to happen."

She was still unhappy, asking, "More lies?"

"No, but not the whole truth either. I owe secrecy to the Ministry. But I will tell you the most shocking part of the truth."

Ed put his hand on my arm and asked, "Just what are you thinking?"

"I want our daughter to know the most important thing about me. Every-thing else will make more sense when she does—even the things that I can't talk about."

He rolled his eyes. That was one thing I really liked about him. He was honest about his feelings—even when it would hurt, but all he said was, "Go to it, then."

I took both Sissy's hands in mine and drew her to the sofa. We sat. Ed sat on a yellow guest chair. I started in without any hesitation. "The most important thing that you need to know about me is that I love you as much as I would love my own daughter. That will mean a lot more to you when you are older, but I think you may have an inkling of what it means now. I love you as much as I love your dad. I would love to have a baby with your dad. Well, maybe more than one." She chuckled in spite of herself.

"The second most important thing to know about me is that I am living in a stolen body. Your dad can maybe explain in magical terms better than I can, but the dragon's eye picture is that the body that I stole was Professor Wendt's." She jumped up and started to say something. I put my hand on her mouth and with my other hand urged her back on the sofa. I said, "Don't say anything that you'll regret later. Give me a few minutes to explain. Someone was playing a practical joke on him."

Sissy interrupted to say, "Aurora!"

"I'm not saying who. It doesn't matter. She used an experimental polyjuice potion that changed him permanently and completely into a genetic copy of her. Do you know what I mean by genetics?"

She laughed. "Sure I do. Do you think I'm some ignorant kid who never pays attention in Muggle Studies class?"

I went on. "Something really strange happened."

Sissy sniggered. "That's not strange enough?"

I gave her a withering look, at least it was supposed to be withering, and said, "The person that resulted was not Wendt in a witch's body, whatever that would be. It was a completely new person—a witch who had never existed before." I hesitated.

Sissy's jaw dropped, and she said, "No. No. No."

I shook my head sadly. "Yes. It was me. I was around for most of a year. Then I had to give Wendt's body back to him so he could go on a Ministry mission. Now, he has to give me my body back for another Ministry mission."

Her eyes began to tear. She just asked, "How long?"

I answered both "how long" questions, "I don't know precisely when I have to leave on the mission. It could be tomorrow or it could be early next week. Once I am returned, I will be with you at least until you graduate."

Ed quickly added, "And, young lady, you may not try to flunk a term to stretch that out!"

I said, "My suggestion is that we go out to dinner and pick something fun to do today."

Sissy wasted no time with an idea. "Let's just go home and fix dinner together. At night we could go to Harley street and find something exciting to do."

Ed brought out his own idea, "How about seeing a Quidditch match? I think the Chutley Cannons are playing tonight."

That brought the first laugh out of Sissy. She said, "Well, that would be pretty funny even if it weren't fun. The Cannons are just the worst!"

That comment stirred one of Wendt's memories. I pulled it up and said, "Well, the muggles have a game sort of like Quidditch. They call it football. The teams have several leagues. If you are at the bottom of a league, you get kicked down to the next lower league. If you do poorly there, you move down again and so on. I suppose the Cannons would be in the bottom league if they played football."

So, we did exactly that. I wasn't a great cook, but I could follow directions. Ed had become a pretty decent chef over the years as he'd taken care of Sissy. We ended up doing something pretty simple. We had a green salad with grilled chicken pieces. I had Sissy cut up the veggies and some fruit. It was pleasant mindless work that would occupy our attention. We did things the muggle way. We could talk while we worked. The talk was mostly practical: Where's the potato peeler? Do we have a big bowl for the salad? And so on.

Sissy stayed close to her dad. Perhaps she was afraid to get too close, too attached before I left. We laid out everything on the kitchen table. She thought it was a wonderful meal, prepared a la muggle.

After dinner we went to the Quidditch match. Ed had been to the Cannon's stadium before. He disapparated, and we girls went via side-along disapparation with him. The stadium itself was rather grungy. The seats were old and weather-worn. They were up on towers that seemed that they might actually have come from the fifteenth century. The hoops were bright. The pitch itself was yellowed sand. It looked as if it might have come from the fifteenth century too.

The home team, the Cannons, were fairly well represented in the crowd. Their opponents the Slopshire Thrashers looked appropriate to their name They all looked to be eight stone—particularly the beaters. Sissy commented that the Cannons were small and probably fast. Ed said that they'd need to be fast to avoid getting beaten to a pulp by the solidly-built beaters.

The official blew her whistle, and the game started. Quidditch reminds me of what Wendt sometimes calls football, and sometimes he calls it soccer. Football has lots of motion up and down the field with rare scores. Quidditch has lots of motion up and down the pitch with not much scoring. Also, the scoring that happens is less consequential because the big deal that usually determines everything else is catching the snitch and ending the game. Wendt thinks that Quidditch is a stupid game. He doesn't appreciate the excitement of two teams on brooms flying at each other at over 200 mph. It's amazing how fast the action is.

Another great thing about Quidditch is that you can get 100 points behind and then, if you have a good seeker, you can overcome that in five seconds.

The game proceeded as we expected. The Cannons got ahead forty points. Then, the Thrashers scored. That went back and forth for a half hour. By then, the Thrashers were up 120 to 90. It was exciting. There was no quarter given or received. Then the Thrashers' seeker streaked up into the air. I couldn't see the snitch, but it couldn't be a Wronsky Feint because they were going up and up. The Thrashers' seeker was fast! He was more than a broom's length ahead of the Cannon's, but the Cannon's seeker was closing on him. Both sides were cheering at the top of their throats.

Then it was over. The Thrashers' seeker had the snitch. He zoomed down at full tilt until he almost hit the ground. Then he took a victory circuit around the pitch, holding the snitch high in the air.

People began disapparating away. The Thrasher crowd remained and lifted the seeker into the air and gave him another victory lap.

I have to admit that I agree with Wendt that there is an unjustified glorification of seekers when the team wins and an unjustified disdain of the goalkeeper when the team loses.

We, being Cannons fans, went home deflated and with the reality of what I was going to do in a couple of days at most. We arrived home, cleaned up the dishes that we had left in the sink. It was almost therapeutic washing the dishes the muggle way. When we were finishing the last ones, Sissy began sobbing softly.

Ed said, "Your mum has to go to the Ministry tomorrow. You can stay and wait for her to return."

She controlled her sobbing and said, "If they let her come back."

I took her in my arms and just held her for a while, rubbing her back softly.

We got ready for bed. I asked her if she wanted me to sleep with her. She put on a brave face and said, "Tomorrow. I know you and dad wanted to be together . . . alone."

Ed and I spent a lot of time talking. We'd not been together for over a year. The first thing that he insisted on talking about was the agreement that he'd had with Wendt and his gang. Yes, I thought of them as a gang. They were ganged up against me. They made Ed agree to try to convince me to let Wendt return after Sissy graduated from Hogwarts.

I wasn't very happy with Ed either. I'd eventually have run across that memory among Wendt's, but it might have been weeks or longer before I did. On top of that there was the realization that I'd let Wendt return whether Ed had agreed to it or not.

When I'd been alive before, I'd done my best not to think about Wendt and his predicament. After all, he'd died accidentally. I'd not caused it. I was just the unwitting beneficiary of it. I hadn't even thought about how he might return until I was forced to. Oh, if only I could have called back those blessed days. Now, I was doomed to think every day of the fast approaching time when I'd have to give my beautiful body back to Wendt. It just wasn't fair. I didn't know anything that was, but this sure wasn't!

Ed interrupted my thoughts. "Jaim, are you awake?"

In a very real way, I wasn't. I had been focusing on my problem and was lost to the world. I said, "Oh, sorry. I was trying to figure a way out of this mess. I guess there isn't, is there?"

Ed shook his head, "No. I don't see it. I wanted a suggestion from you about how to spend the next few days."

I swallowed hard. I was trying to say something that had just occurred to me. I was having a hard time bringing myself to say it. It just sort of sputtered out of my mouth in little spurts. "I just thought. . . You know, I may not have a . . . have a say after that. . ." Here I gulped hard to get the lump out of my throat. "The meeting tomorrow. I may not return home from it." I felt the hot tears streaming down my cheek. Ed put an arm around me and patted my back. He didn't say anything. What was there to say?

Then he did say something, "Just for the record, I still want to have a baby with you."

I was still kind of weepy. I just said, "Me, too."

I then had a thought that was completely unrelated to anything. I said, "Did I ever tell you about this?" I reached into my purse and pulled out another purse.

He stared at it a moment and said, "That's magic, isn't it?"

I couldn't help smiling at my clever husband. "Yes, it is."

"Is it yours?"

I smiled mischievously. "Noooo."

"It's surely not Wendt's?"

I nodded. He nodded his head slowly and picked it up. He tried to open it. Of course it wouldn't open for him. Then he said, "Mokeskin. . . and an extensible charm on it too?"

I nodded again. Oh, he was such a clever husband. He then asked, "Why did you bring it with you? You'll never be able to open it."

I smiled again. "Here's the funny thing. I think I might just be able to open it."

He frowned at me disapprovingly, "Surely not."

I just said, "Let's see." I then took the purse from his hands, not neglecting to caress them in the bargain. I pulled at the drawstrings and *voilà*. It opened easily.

Ed's mouth dropped. He asked, "How is that possible?"

I shrugged and started to reach in to get whatever was in it out. Ed seized my hand quickly and not in a gentle way. He said, "Wait, Do you know what's in there?"

I stopped to think about that. I said carefully, "Not off hand. I could search Wendt's memory to find out, assuming he remembered everything he put in it." I started that search and commented, "Heck, I don't remember everything I put in my handbag."

He said, "Try to remember anything dangerous that he might have put in it. Surely, he'd remember those things."

It took me no time to remember one truly dangerous thing. Despite struggling with that cursed memory of Wendt's, I could not drag another memory from those mountains of recollections. I wasn't sure that there wasn't another questionable object in that flat purse. I took the purse, reached in confidently and withdrew the one object that I feared.

My hubby stared at it and asked, "What in the world is that? Could it be a firearm?"

I smiled as I released the parallelepiped, caught it in my hand, and turned it upside down to allow the contents to spill on the bed. He stared at them in wonder and asked, "What in the world are those? You handled that thing as though it were second nature."

I retained the smile. I was myself surprised at the ease and facility with which I had released the clip and removed the bullets. I answered his questions. "This is a firearm." I picked up the clip. "This is called a clip. I don't know why." I pointed at the bullets scattered haphazardly on the bed quilt. "Those are bullets. They are held in the gun, which goes by the name, Glock. They are designed to be expelled by exploding gases from the barrel of the gun and are deadly if aimed accurately.

"I think that I handled them so easily because of what the Muggles call muscle memory. I guess it's not lost any more than the higher memory functions are when taking the super polyjuice potion." I mused a moment and commented, "I wonder what other things I can do by muscle memory alone. Maybe I can fire that Glock accurately."

Ed commented, "It's frightening to contemplate. Are you expert in martial arts too?"

I chuckled. "Better not to test me." I lifted my right hand to contemplate it. "Who knows what arcane knowledge is lodged here?"

He hurried on. "Let's get the rest of the things out of that Pandora's box and decide what stays and what goes."

I reached in confidently, looking for the box of bullets that Wendt kept in it. It was easy to identify by feel. It rattled as it came out. I was lucky. I could probably put the bullets from the gun back in the box for safe storage. I then reached into the purse again. Out came a profusion of coins and bills. We sorted through them quickly. The money I had was:

- A roll of US currency in a rubber band—a thousand dollar bill, three centuries, one fifty, five twenties, three tens, no fives, and a couple of ones. I decided I should have at least three of everything except the thousand.

- A roll of British currency in a rubber band—Two hundred pound notes, five twenties, four tens, and half a dozen singles. I decided that was OK.
- Ten one hundred-galleon coins, seven ten-galleon coins, about a dozen single-galleon coins, a few sickles and knuts. I decided that was more than I needed and cut the amounts by half. I put the surplus in a desk drawer.
- A "lucky" silver dollar, about ten quarters, a few dimes, nickels, and pennies. I decided to leave them.

I had Wendt's real US passport, his real US driver's license, his fake British passport that he'd just recently gotten, and a real British driver's license that he'd never used. There was a US VISA credit card, a Barclay Mastercard credit card, and a debit card from a US bank. I decided that I probably shouldn't be carrying the fake British passport, and I removed the debit card as well.

Then there was a miscellany of other things. There was a small notebook, a couple of pens, a mechanical pencil, a Swiss Army pocket knife, a small steel tape measure, a level, and various receipts and other papers. I removed all of those items except for the writing materials and pocket knife. I'd used Wendt's credit card a number of times when I was alive before. What a strange way to think—when I was alive before. I'd never had any purchase denied regardless how expensive it was. Ed asked what it was. I said, "It's a credit card."

His eyes bulged. "I've heard of them but never seen one."

I squinted my eyes in concentration. Had I never used it in Ed's presence? I asked the question. Ed replied, "I suppose you have, but I think you were always paying at the cash register, and I'd never looked over your shoulder. I think I always thought you were using galleons or muggle money. I've always wondered what kind of magic lets that little card act like cash. Is it some kind of *Confundus* charm?"

I couldn't help laughing. "No. There's no magic at all to it. I seem to recall that Wendt once explained to someone how it all works, but I really don't want to spend the effort to try to dredge it up out of his memory. We have more important things to do."

I emptied the rest of the contents of the purse onto the bed. It was a real mess of odds and ends. There were things like a program to a string quartet concert from sometime in 1995. There was an airline boarding pass to a flight to Sydney Australia. There were a couple of crumpled up paper towels, a little card case with transparent windows that had mostly pictures. There were a couple of magic moving photos. One was of Minerva seated on a bench in a park. She was blowing a kiss. There was a picture that

Wendt's memory told me was his family when he graduated from high school.

I gasped as I saw the magical picture of Ginny Weasley and him. She started staring at the camera. Then she turned toward Wendt with lips that seemed to be forming a kiss.

Ed wanted to know what had startled me. I said, "Oh, it was a picture in this little album." I handed it over to Ed. He flipped through the photos and said, "I suppose it was the picture of McGonagall." He quickly corrected himself. "Oh, I suppose I should say Mrs. Wendt." My grunt was non-committal. For some reason that I couldn't identify, I was troubled by seeing Wendt with a woman. Could it have been that I was in some crazy way jealous of Weasley?

Ed wondered what was in the notebook. I opened it and glanced at a couple of pages. There were strings of digits that might have been telephone numbers. There were names of businesses. There was a name and telephone number. I wasn't sure because there was only the first name, but I think Haley must have been THE Haley who had gone to America. With that, I closed the notebook. I said, "It's too creepy looking at someone else's private notes." With that I shoved it back in the purse.

Ed said, "I have a suggestion. Let's put the wizarding and English money back in the purse along with the credit card. Of course, put the gun and accessories in. Don't put anything else in. In case you have to use the Glock, I want it to be easy for you to find. Oh, yes. I suggest that you put your wand in there too."

I agreed, and we put the rest of the things in a bottom drawer of our dresser. Then, we spent the rest of the night enjoying our conjugal rights and duties.

The alarm went off at 6 AM. Both Ed and I groaned. Ed suggested that we get dressed and then wake Cecily. I shook my head vigorously. "No. I have a right to as much time with her as possible. I'll go wake her."

I knocked on her bedroom door vigorously. I used what Wendt used to call his paperboy knock. He apparently used it to get someone out to pay for an overdue paper delivery bill. Sissy mumbled, "Whu . . ." in a half-awake voice and then quickly in a fully awake voice, "You're not leaving already!"

"No. We're just up. As soon as we're dressed, we'll have breakfast."

I went back to our bedroom and the battle for the bathroom began.

I was the first out. I started breakfast, which was a good English breakfast—eggs, bacon, muffins, orange juice, and cereal for Sissy. The mood started pretty somber, but Ed insisted on planning for things to do after I returned from the Ministry. Sissy was convinced that we'd never see each other again. Ed convinced her to tell us what she wanted to do later in the day.

Sissy wanted to go for a picnic in Hyde Park near the Serpentine. Ed and I instantly agreed. Wendt had such powerful memories around that location that I knew that I'd be plagued with them while we were there, but I was not going to disappoint Sissy.

At 7:45, I looked myself over in the mirror. I was wearing my best work outfit. I had my hair up in a tight bun on top of my head. I didn't want to look casual in any aspect of my appearance. I wanted to be composed when I walked into the floo connection. I was wearing minimal makeup. I was afraid that I might cry when we separated. I only wore eye shadow and not much of that.

My worst fears were justified. I managed to kiss Ed good-bye without anything worse than a choked throat, but then Sissy hugged me and started crying. I couldn't stop the floodgates. I tried a joke. "You'd think that this was the first time I'd taken the floo."

Sissy just held me the tighter and begged me not to go. I disentangled myself from her arms and said, "I will be back." I had a certainty that came from some deep well within me. Maybe it was an intuition from Wendt. I don't know, but I was sure. I took a Kleenex from my purse and dried her tears. I then dried my own. A quick glance at my compact mirror showed that I didn't look too bad. It would take a close exam to see that I'd been crying.

I walked through the floo and found myself in the Minister's office. She was standing watching the floo. Her comment was, "Well, you believe in cutting it close to the bone. There are only two minutes left. The rest will be here momentarily." She turned toward her desk. She pressed a small medallion resting on her desktop. She'd hardly lifted her finger when her door opened and several people entered.

I recognized them all. There was that US Naval officer, Wainwright. There was Pete Treats of the US Air Force. There was the British Minister of Defense, Smithe. There was General Parker. Of course, I'd met some, but I'd technically never met Treats or Smithe. I'd have to remember that. Ginny was there too. We all barely fit in Moertl's Office.

Ginny didn't look directly at me at any time. She rarely spoke and never addressed me directly until after the meeting.

Moertl asked, "Has Wendt briefed you on what's going on?"

I frowned. "Fully. I'm supposed to help these PAK find the Soul's home world in some as yet undefined way."

Everyone else looked around at each other, then Parker said, "You have to be able to convince the PAK that you were on the original mission. Are you sure that you can do that?"

Ginny sneered, "Believe me, she has complete knowledge and can report on it thoroughly."

I wasn't sure that I could do that. His memories belonged to me, but I wasn't sure that I could pull up everything from his memories that quickly.

She went on. "Test her."

There ensued a length interrogation. Everyone in the room had knowledge of at least part of the ordeal that Wendt had gone through on that long space voyage. They took turns asking questions. They weren't simple yes or no questions. They were all like the following:

Moertl asked, "What was the name of the alien that you interrogated on the first planet?"

I answered, "I can't pronounce his name. It sounded something like . . ." I made a sound that approximated his name. "We shortened it to Rich for ease of conversation."

Parker asked, "Describe his family."

I answered, "He had a son." I hesitated.

Smithe jumped on that, "Was that the whole family?"

I testily replied, "No. I'm just not sure that the offspring was actually male. I was going to tell you about that ambiguity. He also had a wife."

Someone else asked me to describe the Soul facility that we visited on that planet. I started to, but a vision of the dead bodies scattered around the building came into my head as clearly as though I were standing there at that moment. I realized that I was going to throw up. I jumped up and ran out of the office for the nearest loo. Ginny followed me. I was in a stall bent over the commode when Ginny arrived. I was dry heaving for a while. I finally felt like I was as empty as I was going to be. I went to a basin and washed my face as well as I could. Luckily, none had hit my robes.

Ginny and I returned to Moertl's Office in complete silence. She held the door for me. Inside the interrogation continued as though nothing had happened.

They were finally satisfied. Moertl delivered the verdict. I was sentenced to a round trip excursion to the Soul's home planet. The trip was to begin on the weekend—Saturday morning. I was to report to the beach in Northern Scotland where Wendt had started the last space voyage. The Ohio would be waiting for us. The meeting broke up.

As I walked toward the floo connection Ginny, took my elbow and said at hardly more than a whisper, "Would you have lunch with me?"

I tried to think of an objection to the idea, but I couldn't, so I said, "Oh, I suppose." She took my hand and we walked into the floo connection. We came out in a shop that I didn't recognize. It was empty except for the apparent owner who was behind a counter. Ginny immediately led me outside. We walked down the narrow lane between dark buildings occasionally interspersed with dingy storefronts. I asked where we were.

Ginny made a noise that might have been a laugh and said, "Knockturn Alley. The perfect place for our business."

She stopped and swung around. Her wand was out and pressing into my forehead. She suppressed the scream she apparently wanted to use to say, "If you don't bring my Wendt back, I'll . . ." At that point she stopped and seemed to realize that if I didn't come back, it would be because I was dead. There would be nothing more that she could do to me.

I didn't say anything and was indeed unperturbed by the intensity of Ginny's feelings. After all, I had already died once. What more was there that she could do to me.

She seemed to realize that, for her face relaxed, and she said, "You know what I mean."

"Of course, I do. The only thing left of Wendt are his memories. If they're going to come back, they have to come back with me."

For just an instant her face transformed. It seemed to assume an attitude of fear, though I can't be sure. The transformation was very rapid. I would later learn what had occasioned that transformation, but for now, I hadn't the vaguest idea.

She then totally relaxed and said, "Yes, you know what I mean. Let's really go to the Cauldron and have a late lunch."

My intuition was that she was speaking in earnest, so I accepted again.

She took my hand again, and we reappeared at the rear entrance to the Cauldron. We entered and were almost immediately greeted by Tom. "What can I get you ladies? Afternoon tea?"

I said, "Lunch. We've not eaten since an early breakfast."

He glanced at the clock and said, "It's a bit late for our lunch menu, but you can order from the dinner menu." Then he showed us to a table near the center of the room. However, both of us said that we wanted something in a corner. So, he showed us to a small table for two in the darkest corner. That was to our liking. Tom brought us the dinner menu. Both of us were familiar enough with it that we both ordered immediately.

Ginny had ordered the beef stew and I ordered a chicken salad. Tom then asked for drink orders. She had a gin and tonic. I had a Dewars on the rocks. He cocked his head at us and asked, "A little early in the day for the hard stuff, eh?"

We both answered with a resounding "No." Tom left without further comment other than an over his shoulder, "Hard day, eh?"

Ginny immediately got down to business. "I think we should have a meeting with the other crew members to lay out strategy. If this hadn't been such a hard day, I'd suggest tonight."

I agreed about the hard day, but I was more thinking about how my family must be wondering what had happened to me. I agreed about the meeting as well.

Our food came quickly. The stew undoubtedly had been simmering since the morning and the salad was quick to throw together. It was up to the usual Cauldron standards, that is good, wholesome, and undistinguished. At that moment something totally ordinary was exactly what the doctor ordered.

Ginny picked up where we'd left off in Knockturn Alley. "Are you really going to give Wendt back to me after Cecily graduates from Hogwarts?"

I nodded and said so with my tongue as well. I then looked at Ginny with an eye to assessing her. I held my tongue as we began our meal. At a pause in eating I took a chance. I decided to give Ginny my thoughts about her and Wendt. "Ginny, I totally understand your interest in Wendt."

She interrupted me and said, "Yes. It's so weird being here with you in surroundings that I associate with dates. You replaced him. I see little signs of Wendt every now and then in your gestures and your pet phrases. I'll give you an example.

"Wendt was always using the phrase, 'Oh, one last thing.' I've heard you use it a couple of times today. The way that you like to stand and walk when you are thinking hard is another."

In that instant, I realized that she was right. Those examples were things that bubbled up from Wendt's memory. I adopted them myself. I said, "I've heard that couples who have been together for a long time frequently start to do that sort of thing."

Ginny gave a little start. "Are you saying that you're in love with Wendt?"

I laughed at that. Then I thought about it. I respected and liked most of what I remembered about Wendt. Did I have a little . . . crush . . . on him? That made me laugh again. "That would certainly be the strangest love affair that anyone ever had. I've heard in literature of people falling in love with a painting or an old photograph of someone long dead, but one can imagine being alive at a different time and meeting that person. How can you imagine being with someone who can't exist as long as you exist?"

Ginny frowned. "Are you really so sure that you don't have at least affection for him?"

My answer was immediate because it was sure in my heart. "No, I don't have affection for him. I like him and respect him, but that's all." I paused and went on. "What I really wanted to talk about was someone who really is in love with Wendt."

Ginny's frown deepened, "You mean me."

"Yes, I do." She started to scoff, but I was insistent. "You listen to me now. If you really love him, you should pay attention to what he likes and try to please him."

She said cautiously, "Just how?"

"Well, for one thing, I happen to know." I couldn't help smirking at that, "You know, inside information, so to speak. I know that he likes women who wear their hair long."

She sneered, "Is that why your hair is so long?"

That set me back. Could that be true? No matter. I went on. "Your hair is very pretty. It would be even more appealing to Wendt if you let it grow for a while—say until Wendt returns."

She gagged at that. "That's three years or more! My hair would be down to my hips!"

I smiled mischievously, "That would be a good start."

"A good start! That's longer than it's ever been." She hesitated and asked, "You think it should be longer?"

"Yes, I do. Again, inside information. If it were longer than that, I don't think he'd be able to keep his eyes off you."

Ginny smiled. "Really? He's pretty good at paying attention to me already."

"Absolutely."

"In that case, maybe I will let it grow some. Hmmm."

She asked, "Anything else?"

I said, "I've got to get going. My family will be beside themselves. I was supposed to join them for a picnic after an earlier walk in the park was done."

She agreed that I should get going.

I smiled as I said, "Oh, one more thing. . ." We both giggled at that. I then said the one more thing, "I'm pretty sure that if you had mentioned marriage even one time a couple of months ago, you two would be married now."

Her eyes widened. Her voice became quiet and serious. "Is that really true?"

I nodded. "That is inside information that is as inside as it gets. You may not realize it, but you may be the reason that he . . . and I, come to think of it . . . are alive now. He worshiped you."

She thought about that and said slowly, thoughtfully, "I could have been married to Wendt now. Maybe I would be going along with him and the Brahmses."

I didn't want to disabuse her of that idea. It would be needlessly cruel. The truth was that someone else might well have let the PAK know about Wendt as well as she. She might possibly have been coming along with me, but not with Wendt.

We stood and hugged. I think it was a genuine expression of affection. I asked her to contact the Brahmses and Dursley to set up a meeting tomorrow. She said she would. I paid for the meal, and we parted.

I stepped out of our hearth and called out happily, "Hello, I'm home." Before I'd finished, I realized that both Sissy and Ed were in the living room.

Much to my surprise they weren't unhappy with me for arriving almost at dinner time. Instead, they ran to me and hugged me. Ed said, "We've eaten our picnic lunch here. We had an indoor picnic. It's nice out. We can still go to Hyde Park and have a good time."

I was all for that. We did go. We walked through the park talking. I declared that it was Ed's turn to decide what we did the next day. He declared that he wanted to go to see a movie.

They were both overjoyed to hear that there was a next day. Sissy asked hesitantly, "What about the next day after that? Are you going to be . . . around?"

I happily said, "Yes, I will be around, but not the day after."

That soured the mood. We walked past the boat house. Sissy remembered the last time we'd been there. She apologized. I smiled, "Oh, I'm just happy that you remember. I'd rather be here any day to being anywhere else in the world without you two."

As the sun set, we found a local fish and chips joint and had a delicious very unhealthy meal. That night I kept my promise that Sissy could sleep with Ed and me. We engorged the bed a little to give us room for all three of us to sleep comfortably. She was positioned between Ed and me. That was fine with me.

I stepped out in the morning to get a newspaper with movie ads. I saw that a new version of *Pride and Prejudice* was in the theatres. We had a little discussion. Ed was interested in *Aeon Flux*. They were both set in England, but neither Sissy nor I were interested in science fiction. We wanted a romantic comedy. Ed showed good taste in acceding to our wishes.

We were old hands with the movies. We chose a matinée showing. It was probably the best movie that I'd ever seen. Of course, I'd not seen a lot of movies, but even Wendt's memories informed me that he regarded it highly. He'd seen it with Ginny a couple of weeks before. As a matter of fact, his date with Ginny was a lot like mine with Ed. That is, we missed a certain amount of it due to close consultation on details of the movie. They were so close that we missed some aspects of the movie.

When we left the theatre, an owl hopped up to us and held out a parchment toward me. Of course, I was expecting something of the sort. I relieved the owl of its burden and opened it.

Sissy said, "Uh oh." Ed just frowned. I read it and reported, "I have a meeting tonight after dinner at Hogwarts. That doesn't mean that we can't have dinner ourselves."

We did. This time we went home and fixed bangers and spuds (and fresh vegetables). I insisted that Sissy learn how to peel spuds the old-fashioned way—the muggle way. I cut up the other vegetables. We divided up the other tasks and each took their share. We all enjoyed the meal. It lent a normalcy—at least for a short while—to our life together. As we ate, we talked about the movie.

Sissy wanted to know if the sculpture in the Darcy mansion was real. I asked, "You mean real marble carved in such intricate patterns?"

She nodded. Ed said, "I've seen pictures in a book of carved jade that was at least as fine as that."

I said, "Still, it's hard to believe that it's possible. Is there anyone who could do that by magic?"

That seemed to stump Sissy. Instead of answering, she made a different comment, "I'd sure like to meet that Lord Darcy, wouldn't you?" The question was directed at me.

I said, "I'm very happy knowing the people in this room." We all laughed.

After dinner, we cleaned up, and I excused myself. I gave Sissy a nice kiss on her forehead. I gave Ed a very un-nice kiss. Then I went to the floo connection in the hearth and paused after taking a small handful of floo powder. Sissy asked hopefully, "Having second thoughts?"

"No, I was just thinking about how quickly we become used to the amazing things that we can do with magic—like using the floo network to travel anywhere in England in seconds. I was about to use it without a second's thought to how amazing it is."

I stepped out of the floo connection in my office. There was scant light. I carefully let my eyes adapt to the low light. There was no one present that I could see. I got my wand out of my purse and used the *Revelio* spell to make sure that no one was in my office. I then left and headed for the Headmaster's where we were all supposed to meet.

I found that though it was much later than the normal work day for Sally, she was in the Reception Room along with Dursley and Filch.

Sally invited me to sit while we waited for Aurora and the Boy Genius to arrive. The Headmaster was already in his office. The door to the Reception Room opened. Ginny entered and said, "Quite a little party we have here, and we are still missing some key players."

I asked each who had invited them. I turned to Sally who shrugged and said, "I work here. Whenever the Headmaster has a meeting, it's my duty to be here to take notes." That was not strictly speaking true, but I thought that it would be churlish to exclude her, especially since she had a good head on her shoulders.

I didn't look the question at Dursley, but he volunteer his answer. "Ginny invited me."

I looked at Filch next. He didn't take the hint, so I had to ask, "What brings you here Mr. Filch?

His answer was, "Well, besides my feet, I feel a certain responsibility-like for Mr. Dursley. You know, like I'm a loco parent."

I had a hard time keeping a straight face. I managed to say, "I completely agree."

I looked at Ginny and asked, "You just organized the meeting. You aren't necessary to it. Why are you sticking around?"

Her answer was probably not comprehensible to all the rest of the people in the room, but it was certainly comprehensible to me. She said, "I'm here to protect my interest in certain property."

Shortly thereafter, the two Brahmses entered the room. Sally said, "Good, everyone's here. Let's go in and start the meeting."

We entered and were greeted by Professor Slughorn. He invited us to take seats, which had been laid out in two rings around his desk. Sally redirected a few people to their proper seats. Ginny, Sally, and Filch were in the outer ring. Filch had to be moved from the red leather chair, which he thought he owned as the senior member of the group, to a yellow chair. The other four of us sat in the inner ring of hell. Sally had laid out drinks and some snacks on a side table. After finding our seats, we were invited to help ourselves and return to our seats so the meeting could start.

Slughorn announced, "This meeting was set up by Ms. Weasley. Would you please start us off?"

She stood. Even though she was in the back row, no one had any problem hearing her. She began, "Some of you don't have the full picture, so I'm going to summarize quickly.

"First, you all are familiar with the background.

"There are two alien races now locked in a war that will see one of them annihilated. To quote a phrase that some of you may be familiar with, 'Neither can live while the other survives.'

"Ordinarily, we'd just say, 'A pox on both your houses'. There's just one problem. The PAK insist on our helping them. Why do we care? They threaten terrible destruction on our planet if we don't help them.

"Now, the reason that I called this meeting was for Jaimie's sake. I think we should be planning in advance. I don't want to assist genocide on a galactic scale, and I assume that none of you do either.

"This meeting's purpose is brainstorming ideas to prevent that genocide. Now, before we get started, what questions do you have?"

Slughorn asked, "What do we know about these PAK?"

Ginny let the Boy Genius take that one. He said, "Well, here are the main points.

"First: They all seem to be geniuses. They have far better science than either the Souls or we do. I don't think that's because they've been around for a lot longer than either the Souls or we. As a matter of fact, they seem to have gotten into the space traveling business very recently—maybe a few dozen years ago. The Souls have been at it for at least hundreds of years, probably thousands. However, the PAK are far more advanced than the Souls at space travel.

"Second: They are physically as capable as they are mentally. Saying that they have super powers would be far overstating it, but they have very fast reflexes and appear to be very strong.

"Third: They are perfectly capable of committing genocide. We visited one planet where they had succeeded in eliminating all of the Souls and another whether they were well on the way to that. I don't doubt that they would follow through on threats that they've made to the earth if we don't cooperate with them."

Filch mumbled, "As easy as pie."

Sally asked, "How long will it take to reach the Soul's home world?"

I answered, "Last year when we returned from the Soul's home world, it took almost five weeks. If we could fly straight there, then we might be back in ten weeks. However, I think that is strictly a minimum estimate."

Ginny sat with her head cradled in her hands. She asked, "Why do they need you lot? They seem perfectly capable of wreaking destruction all by themselves."

I started to answer and decided to yield to the Boy Genius again. He said, "They never knew the location of the Soul's home world." He took a deep breath and released it slowly, his head bent low. "We helped them find it the last time. The crew of the ship last time were too conceited. They thought they didn't need to share that information with their home world because they were going to cut the viper's head off, and the rest would follow. Then too, they'd have had to return home to share that information. They didn't want to waste the time.

"So, they need our help again. For the life of me, I don't understand why. None of us knows the location."

Filch stood and shouted, "Dursley wasn't even on the original flight! Why does he have to go?"

Dursley shook his head and said, "I want to go, Mr. Filch"

Filch spoke again. "I'm exercising my rights of loco parent. I forbid you to go!"No one had the heart to laugh although I didn't know whether to laugh or cry.

Dursley just said, "I'm sorry, Mr. Filch. I'm going. That is all there is to it."

I turned to face him and touched his wrist. I said, "We'll do everything we can so that Mr. Dursley returns."

He opened his mouth to object, but nothing came out. Then a tear came out. He sobbed, "If you don't come back, I'll . . . I'll . . ." Apparently, he couldn't come up with a terrible enough thing to threaten. He just stopped.

The B.G. did have an answer to Ginny's original question. "The Souls did have an answer to that question. They did everything they could to obscure the location of their home world and the others as well. The navigation computers of all their ships had a database of worlds. The database was encrypted. Only the computer knew how to navigate there. . . AND only if the home world was one of the destinations of the ship. Most ships didn't even have it in their databases."

Ginny stared at him and said, "How do you think that they will use you lot to find their way to the home world?"

He shrugged and said, "Darned if I know." She didn't release his gaze for a while. I don't think she was satisfied with the answer.

Ginny returned to planet earth and said, "We need to devise strategies for preventing genocide. I will act as facilitator, and we'll have a brainstorming session. The rules are:

"No idea is too crazy. Hold off critique until all ideas are outed.

"Once critique begins, all ideas are treated with respect but evaluated openly and honestly.

"We rank vote the ideas to pick the top two or three to implement." With that she flicked her wand and a whiteboard floated in from somewhere. It was on an easel. She then materialized a marker, and we began. She asked one question before we started in earnest, "How were the PAK defeated before?"

I said, "Minerva got space suits out of a locker room. Everyone got them on safely except Minerva. She died of cyanide . . ." I didn't realize how that would affect me. I couldn't hold back the sobs. Everyone was silent until I regained control and went on. "Then the sole remaining witch disapparated me, uh, Wendt into the sealed Control Room, and he killed the two PAK with his Glock."

Ginny wrote, "Disapparate into Control Room and kill PAK" on the whiteboard. She labeled it "A". She then looked around and said, "Others?"

Filch said, "I'd pull me wand and destroy the ship's engine before we started!"

I wondered how they'd get back home then. Ginny wrote, "Vaporize ship's engine." Ginny labeled it "B".

Slughorn asked, "Couldn't you just use the Imperious curse?"

The B. G. looked ready to say something, but didn't. Ginny wrote, "Imperious Curse." and labeled it "C".

Ginny requested more ideas. None were forthcoming. So, she took us to the next stage—critique. She said, "Now, you get to put your critic's hat on and we look for flaws in these. So, dig in."

I spoke up, "It's about option B. If we blow up the ship's engine, we won't be able to get back home, will we?"

Ginny didn't answer, but wrote under option B. "Can't get home."

The B.G. cleared his throat and said, "There's a good thing about that plan. There's a good chance we'd get killed in the explosion, but if we survive, a thankful Soul government might use their one FTL ship to take us home."

Aurora said, "Fat chance of that. The last time we were there, they almost killed us after we saved their bacon."

I said, "I'd like to offer another possibility. Is there time for Option 'D'?"

Ginny smiled. "The more the merrier. Sure."

I went on. "Well, then. I happen to know where in the PAK ship, their weapons are. We could destroy them without disabling the whole ship." I curtsied after my little speech. I don't know why. It just seemed the thing to do after delivering a great idea.

Ginny smirked at my curtsy and said, "Option D." Then she wrote, "Destroy weapons in storage."

Ginny herself said, "Plan A might work, but I think there are a couple of problems. On the original mission there were only two PAK. They were confined to a single room. In the new ship, there will be many more. They will be distributed around the ship. You might take the first couple by surprise. After that, I think you'd be sunk."

Dursley said, "Plan C has the same problems as Plan A. You could take a few by surprise but . . .' He finished with an expressive descending inflection to his voice.

Ginny turned to the room. "OK. What about Option D? What problems does it have?"

I looked around. Filch raised a hand and asked, "What about Optical D-Dog? Isn't that pretty D-dangerous?"

Ginny had a hard time repressing a chuckle. "Well, yes. There isn't anything we're talking about including just going along to get along that isn't pretty D-dangerous."

It didn't take long for me to think of another issue. "This time, they'll be more careful. If we destroy the weapons, they have two options. One is that they could just fly home and put together a fleet to attack the home world of the Souls. The other is that they could just kill us and use the shuttle instead of their fancy missiles to do the attack."

Ginny added notes to the options, but she didn't have anything more to say. We sat for a while silent and brooding. No one seemed to want to say the obvious. So, I did.

"I don't see that any of thcsc idea have much to commend themselves to us. It looks like there are no new ideas?" I tried to make it a question by the inflection of my voice, but no one rose to the hint. No one said a thing.

Finally, Ginny said, "I suppose we should do rank voting. I just don't see . . ." She trailed off.

I said, "It looks like the only plan without a fatal flaw is B, other than the fact that it probably is fatal for all the people using it. Hmmmm."

Aurora asked, "Does that break your principle of defending your property??? Hmmmm?"

Ginny just shot daggers from her eyes or maybe I should say used the "evil eye." I didn't mind being referred to as "property" because she really wanted to keep me alive for that day years off that I would disappear, and her beloved Wendt would reappear from thin air.

Slughorn broke the painful silence with a practical word. "I don't think that we need to do rank voting. Ms. Weasley has summed things up very neatly. There is a clear winner. Everyone here is well aware of it. I only hope that the crew of this mad expedition come up with a better solution.

Else, I fear that I'll be in the market for an English Professor, an astronomy Professor, and an assistant janitor."

The words had hardly escaped his lips when Filch corrected the Headmaster, "A maintenance engineer."

Everyone rose and slowly began working their way disconsolately out of the inner office. Ginny came over to me and said, "I may not get another chance to speak to you semi-privately." Her voice was almost plaintive as she begged me, "Please, please stay safe."

I assured her that I would. She squeezed my forearm and looked as though she would say or do something more. She leaned in toward me slightly and then thought better of it. She released my arm and stepped back. "Be seeing you." We had reached the door to the outer office. She held the door for me. I walked out, and we parted. I headed up for my office. She walked toward the stairs down. I almost asked her if she wanted to use my floo connection but decided that she knew well enough where it was and she could ask me for permission to use it if she wanted.

I reached my office and again wondered as I had before if I would ever see it again. I didn't hesitate a second though. There were two other people I was much more concerned about seeing again. I walked into the hearth, picked up a small amount of floo powder, and sent myself to the floo connection in my home.

I stepped out. I'd barely coughed the soot out of my lungs when I was enveloped on two sides by the arms of my husband and my step-daughter. My husband, Ed, took priority for my kisses, but I didn't forget Sissy.

It was very late. I wanted to get a good night's sleep before the meeting the next day. Well, at least after a little pleasant repartee in the bedroom.

I kissed Sissy on her forehead and tried to send her to bed. She wasn't going to let go of me. I found that I didn't really want to let go of her either. I looked up with what I hoped were puppy-dog eyes at Ed. He rolled his eyes, shook his head, and nodded assent to Sissy's evident desire to spend the night in bed with us. Luckily a simple *Engorgio* spell allowed us to all sleep in one bed with a little wiggle room for tossing and turning.

That night there was little tossing and turning but there was begging. Sissy amid sobs begged me not to go. I guess it wasn't really so much of a beg as a whine. It went something like this:

"Mum, you can't go. You've had so little time with us."

I said, "I have to go." I couldn't say, "The world depends on it." It seemed way too melodramatic to actually say. Besides, it would be a betrayal of the Ministry. I thought a moment. Maybe I should say it and make a joke of it.

Sissy whined, "Please, please, please. You don't have to go." She was on the edge of tears. That would have changed it from a whine to a wail of pain.

I held her in my arms and kissed her on the cheek. Then I lied, "I'll be back. We'll be worrying about school clothes before you know it." That pushed us both over the edge. I don't know if Ed realized it, but we were both sobbing. I took her by the shoulders and separated us, holding her face close to mine. I decided it was time to reveal my secret nickname for her.

I was able to make a genuine smile as I whispered so that Ed couldn't hear. Ed was being a dear to let us have the space to talk even though we were all in the same (engorged) bed. I actually managed a little giggle. "I have a little secret for you. Nobody else knows it." She didn't giggle. I said, "OK. Did you know I have a secret nickname for you?"

She whispered back, "A secret nickname?"

"Yes. It's . . . Sissy."

She exploded into laughter. Ed finally intervened. "Is someone choking?" He walked around the bed and me to put his hand on her shoulder. "Is everyone OK?"

She was still chuckling, "Sure dad. We girls were just having a laugh." That defused the situation and let us all settle in for a decent night's sleep. Of course, it was sex-less.

The next morning, we were up with the dawn. Like all teens, Sissy's mood swings made you wonder if she were bi-polar. This morning was no exception. We were hardly twenty-four hours from my moving on to my fate. That doom might have contributed to her mood swing. She moped her way through a bathroom visit, dressing, and coming down for breakfast.

Ed had made pancakes. He was no great shakes in the kitchen, but he had one go-to recipe that he claimed never failed him—buttermilk pancakes. He typically had bacon on the side—crispy but not burned in the slightest. He was a genius at that meal. He once told me that he used to have that for dinner half of the time when he was single. The other half he went to the Cauldron. The sight of bacon and pancakes cheered Sissy somewhat. That shows you either how depressed she was or how much she liked Ed's breakfast. I don't know which.

Over breakfast we talked about our plans for the day. I could think of a dozen things that I'd like to do, but would Sissy and hubby both like them? I had my doubts whether a chamber orchestra concert would fill the bill. Sissy was still morose enough that she refused to give ideas. We were saved by Ed who said, "I've got an idea that I think everyone will like."

Sissy's reaction was to stare more deeply into the half-eaten stack of pancakes in front of her. I sighed and asked, "Do I have to guess?"

Ed actually laughed. "No. No. I was thinking the beach."

Sissy perked up a little and lifted her eyes from the flat-cakes to say, "You mean like Brighton?" She perked up a little more.

Ed answered, "No, something a little further south."

I leaped up and waved my hands enthusiastically as I'd seen some students do when they were absolutely positive that they had THE answer. Ed smiled and said, "Yes, Ms. Jaimie."

I gushed, "Ohhh! The French Riviera!"

He shook his head with a twinkle in his eye and said, "Not far enough south."

That set both Sissy and me to puzzling. I asked for a hint. Ed answered, "It's on the Med."

Sissy asked, "The Med? What's that?"

I said, "Young lady, don't they teach you geography at Hogw. . . " Then I realized that they didn't. I corrected myself. "Didn't they teach you any geography before you went to Hogwarts?"

She answered, "Sure, but that was a million years ago. You don't expect me to remember all that, do you?"

I tried to put on a stern teacher's face, but I couldn't quite manage it with Sissy. Instead my face must have looked comical. Both Sissy and Ed sniggered. I simply ended by saying, "Well, I expect you to pick up some geography on your own before you graduate—even if I have to teach you myself."

Ed sniggered again and said, "I'd like to see that. The young lady doesn't have time for anything but magic and chess."

I replied, "We'll see about that. Now, you aren't thinking of Greece. OHHH! Greece would be nice, but it would be a long hike for a day trip."

He shook his head again. In desperation I suggested, "Algiers?"

He laughed. "Too far south. I guess I'll just have to tell you. Barcelona."

Both Sissy and I were suitably surprised. She said, "Where is Barcelona?" She quickly added, "I know. I know. Where is my geography? Just tell me, please."

Ed said, "Barcelona is in northern Spain near France. While we're there we could do a little sightseeing. I'd like to see some of Gaudi's architecture."

So, we ran to our rooms to get bathing suits, sun screen, towels, etc. When we got back together, Sissy held up a tiny bathing suit and said, "This is all I could find. I guess I haven't been in the water in a long time."

I beat Ed to the punch by saying, "Don't worry. We'll buy you something in Barcelona that's both fashionable and modest."

Sissy snorted, but she seemed as anxious as any of us to be on the way. She asked how we would get there. Ed answered that since we didn't want to waste any time, we'd disapparate directly across the channel to Le Havre. Then we'd disapparate to Marseille. He explained, "Since you need to work on your geography. I'll tell you that both are in France, both are on coasts, and you'll tell me what coasts."

She thought a minute and said, "One's got to be the Med."

Ed answered, "Right. That's Marseille. The other is on?"

That had Sissy puzzled. She said, "It's either the Atlantic or the English Channel." She thought a moment and said, "It must be the Atlantic. The English Channel is too obvious."

My face brightened. "Good test taking logic, but the answer is actually the English Channel."

Ed went on. "From Marseille we go directly to Barcelona."

I wondered who was going to do the disapparating, I'd never been to any of those places. Ed relieved my fears by saying, "Oh, I will. You could, too. When you've got a big target like a city, there's no problem if you've not been there."

I asked about a picnic lunch. Ed answered that we could afford to have lunch and dinner at the beach and a nice restaurant when we'd had enough of the beach. We stepped outside. Ed was carrying the bag with beach paraphernalia—towels, bottles for water, sunscreen, sunglasses, and so on. We took hands, I in the middle.

We landed near a dock. It must be Le Havre, I thought. He said, "The next place is Marseille." We landed on the edge of a beach.

I couldn't resist asking, "Did you go to this beach with another young lady one time?"

He smiled sunnily and seemed lost in thought for a moment. Then he said to Sissy, "Your mum and I spent a fair amount of time on this beach before you came along. If you ever have a young man, you might suggest this beach to him."

She smiled. "I'll never have a young man other than you." He just smiled.

He took her by the hand and said, "Since I know this beach so well, I can take us to a little shop where you can buy a swimming suit."

I added, "Me, too! Come on, let's see if it's still in business."

He led us to a little spot that had some swim wear, towels, and so on in a mock display that looked vaguely like a beach. We went in. I took Sissy aside and said, "Your dad will be no good helping us to find something nice to wear on the beach."

She nodded and said, "In the water, too."

I sighed. "If it has to be." She apparently thought that it did. We picked out a couple of swimming suits and headed for the dressing room to try them on. Sissy had sneaked a bikini into the dressing room for me to try on. I turned red when I saw it. It left very little to the imagination. I shook my head vigorously and said, "Not on your life. I'm not stepping onto a beach wearing that."

Sissy just shook her head slowly, "Oh, just try it on, and let Dad see you in it."

I decided that I should humor her as much as possible, so I did put it on and let her lead me out of the dressing room. Ed responded with a creditable wolf whistle. I turned an even deeper shade of red. He responded by saying, "I see you've already got quite a sunburn. Wearing that, I'll have to use all my powers of magic to keep the beach bums away."

I frowned at him and walked back in to put on the sensible one-piece swimsuit that I'd chosen. I walked out again to model it. He nodded appreciatively. I decided that I'd just wear that directly to Barcelona. However, when I got close, he said, "Why don't you just buy that other number as well? I think it would make a nice pair of pajamas."

I stuck out my tongue at him but kept the bikini in my hand for check-out.

Out of the shop, we found a deserted corner and disapparated. We landed near a nice beach that turned out to be the Saint Sebastian beach in Barcelona. We camped out in a quiet area of the beach. Sissy wanted to run into the surf immediately. Ed surprised her by saying, "We have to do a little spell before we leave our things."

She wrinkled her nose at him. "Whatever for?"

"Oh, the sharks around here are all on the beach." He then turned to me and asked, "Would you like to do the honors?"

I was as surprised as Sissy. I asked, "Just what would those honors be?"

He shook his head sadly. "Look around, do you see there are a couple of guys circling, something like sharks?"

Now that he mentioned it, I did notice there were a couple of suspicious characters. It dawned on me what he was thinking of, so I said, "Of course I will." I put my hand into my handbag where I'd left it lying on the beach towel. I took my wand into my hand without removing it from my handbag. Then I said, just loudly enough for us to hear but not for others to, "*Repello Mugglum.*"

Ed nodded approvingly. Sissy just stood with her mouth agape and then said, "Surely you don't think anyone would take our things?"

I replied, "Not now." Then we ran down to the beach in a race to see who would hit the waves first. I wasn't particularly interested in winning that race or even whether I finished last, but I kept up fairly well. Somehow

Sissy won, Ed finished second, and I was a not too distant third. There ensued a grand water battle—Sissy and I vs. Ed. I insisted that magic not be used, but I'm not sure that the request was perfectly honored. At one point a huge wave materialized from nowhere to swamp Sissy and me.

That sort of spelled an end to that game. At least I thought that had ended it until it became obvious that Ed was paying a lot of attention to something on the beach. Sissy and I turned our gaze there as well. Ed commented, "It seems like some land sharks have noticed that our belongings are unguarded."

I nodded. There were several young men who seemed to be circling our spot on the beach. They really did look like sharks circling prey. Once or twice someone tried to turn toward our beach towel. In every case, they veered off and gave up. After they scattered one by one, we turned back to water sports. I swam. Sissy floated. Ed dived into the water and swam I knew not where until he surfaced right under me, lifting me into the air. From that height I saw something I might not have noticed from sea level. There was a man who was not young, perhaps in his early forties, on the ground seeming to slither like a snake slowly toward our beach towel and other belongings. I told Ed that.

He immediately let me down and said, "I wonder." Then he attracted Sissy's attention and signaled her to join us. When she had, he said, "We're going over to investigate. I want the two of you to stay back about thirty feet or so. Jaim, be prepared to disapparate somewhere with Cecily. I don't think anything bad will happen, but . . . safety first."

He started wading to shore. We followed. I decided to hold back more than thirty feet. Sissy wanted to come closer, but I wasn't going to take any chances. Ed seemingly casually approached the strange character. When he was about ten feet away, he asked, "Can I help you?"

The strange character was about three feet away from our belongings—far closer than I would have thought a Muggle could approach them. He was short and thin, almost to the point of being gaunt. He had short curly hair. When he stood, I got a clear look at his face. It was suntanned like the rest of him. He was wearing a pair of jeans and a short sleeve polo shirt. He also wore a slight smile. He said, "Not really." His confidence was quiet and unassuming.

Ed seemed equally confident even though I couldn't see his face. He said, "You looked like someone who needed help. What were you doing so close to my property?"

I didn't sense a whiff of magic about him, but he continued to speak casually. "I was very curious about my inability to get any closer to that bath towel. It seems strange, perhaps almost magical."

I saw Ed nod. He said quietly, "This is a public beach. I can't summon the police to prevent you from walking or even crawling on your belly. However, if you get any closer to what is mine, you will have concerns far more pressing than the police."

The stranger maintained his calm demeanor but asked rather more loudly than necessary, "Aren't you going to ask me if I understand?" He had revealed a slight accent that sounded French to me.

Ed took a step closer to the towel. He bent, apparently to straighten it. He said as he did so, "I don't care."

The stranger backed away about half a dozen yards and turned, disappearing into the crowd on the beach. Ed turned and strode to us. He said, "I think we've had enough time on the beach. Let's do a little touring of the city."

I had to agree. I said, "That guy gave me the willies. I don't know what you think, but I'd like to put a good number of miles between him and us."

Ed agreed. He helped me pack the beach bag and led us off the beach. When we were alone, he said, "Let's go to a cathedral that Gaudi designed."

At this point, I just wanted to get on the way. I said, "Just so long as it's a distance away."

Ed nodded and held out his hands. Sissy and I took them. Momentarily we appeared on a side street next to a MacDonald's. Sissy clapped her hands. "Good! I'm starving. Let's go in and get something to eat." Both Ed and I grimaced, but we did go in. Sissy wanted a hamburger. Ed and I had salads. They weren't awful. Then we crossed the street and spent some time in and around the cathedral. The rest of the afternoon we spent touring other Gaudi locations.

When the sun was approaching the horizon, Sissy had a dining idea that was actually good. She asked, "Can we stop in Paris and have dinner at the Eiffel Tower?" She used her best puppy-dog eyes. It wasn't necessary. Ed and I were happy to do that.

I insisted that we change out of beachwear. So, we stopped back at the beach where we could go into loo's and change into casual muggle dress. I was really glad that I could go into the loo with Sissy. Frankly, I was a little frightened by what happened on this beach in the morning. When we rejoined, Ed took us to Paris directly. We landed near the Tower. Before long we were seated (via a little confunding of the maitre'd).

It was a pleasant evening. We got to watch the sun setting over the Seine. It was cloudy. The failing light of sunset tinted the clouds in pink. I couldn't help feeling that it was a foretaste of my future—my slow inevitable disappearance forever in the vastness of space. We were all affected by that spirit. Soon we were talking about the next day.

Sissy said sadly, "I suppose you have to leave early tomorrow?"

"Yes, but I don't see why you and your dad can't come along on the first leg. I'm going to a beach where a boat will be waiting for me. We can all disapparate there and say our good-byes."

We didn't even have dessert. The crispy "Tower Nut" looked incredible, but none of us had appetite left. I paid for the meal with Wendt's credit card. I hadn't thought about it recently, but he was being very generous with me and my family. I know that he didn't care, but somehow I was still a little troubled by it.

They booted us out at 9:30. Then, we walked about the Tower, After the sun was completely down (about 10 PM) we stood for a moment looking out over the City of Lights and the Seine which reflected them. I briefly was amazed that Wendt hadn't spent more time in Paris.

I was lost in reverie when Ed took my hand. He said, "We need to get going. It may not be after your bed time, but it's beyond Sissy's and it sure is after mine."

I nodded reluctantly. Ed returned the nod, and at that instant, we three disappeared from the Tower, Paris, France, and the continent. We re-appeared in our own back yard. We silently entered the house. Ed did his usual spell to reveal any intruders. Then we ascended to the bedrooms.

THE question came up. Would Ed and I enjoy a last night together or would Sissy insist on joining us. Somewhat to my surprise she broke the silence. "Oh, enjoy your last night for a long time. I'll see you tomorrow morning when we leave for the beach." That word made me think of the morning. Yes, the beach was pregnant with danger wherever you went.

Ed picked me up, magically opened our bedroom door, and carried me in. Sissy giggled, "Go Dad!" Silently, I echoed that thought. He was the most determined lover that I could imagine. He was determined to drive me crazy with desire. He succeeded.

A sound rapping woke me from a deep sleep.

There was a memory from Wendt. He called it a paper boy knock. What did that mean? For a moment I was confused. Where was I? When was it? Was I at school? Then the harsh reality sunk in. I was in my bed with my hubby being wakened by my daughter. She had begun calling in, "Come on, sleepyheads. Get up. We don't have that much time." The last word was cut off by a gasp and a sob—maybe.

Ed and I were up and dressed quickly. I'd packed a couple of days before. There wasn't much to pack—a couple of pairs of jeans, a few blouses, underwear, a few basic cosmetics, socks, shoes. Wendt's purse was always "packed for bear" as the Americans say. I added my wand to the purse. I didn't want anyone to see it unless it was absolutely necessary.

We went to the kitchen, but Ed said, "Let's stop at a Starbucks for coffee and rolls."

I shrugged. Somehow it seemed appropriate. Ed had a specific one in mind. We landed there but had to wait ten minutes for it to open. We all had tea and muffins. The meal went by far too quickly.

When we left the Starbucks, Ed took my hand and said, "It's your show from here on out. You're the only one who knows where we're going."

Both Ed and Sissy took my hands. I breathed a deep breath and nodded. We spun through space and time, arriving on a cold beach in a light drizzle. There was a large inflatable raft standing on the beach. A sailor walked toward us. He gave us a salute and said, "CPO Green, Ms. Brewster. Are these . . ."

I quickly supplied the dead air space with names. "My daughter Cecily and my husband Edgar Brewster."

He nodded and shook hands with Ed. Cecily held her hand out. CPO Green took it, gave it a quick shake and said, "Pleased to meet you. The others are already on the boat." He glanced back at the boat. It had several people in it. They were not very visible in the drizzle.

Ed took me by the shoulders and gave me a kiss that still burned my lips after we'd boarded the sub. Sissy hugged me so powerfully that I wondered if I'd have to use a spell to separate us.

The rain obscured the tears that both Sissy and I were shedding. Sissy's last words to me were, "Come back quickly!"

Ed said, "We'll see you." He said it with such determination that I half felt that we were all going to meet on the sub. The CPO tried to help me board the grounded boat. I was not going to seem like a helpless woman—especially to my family. I got in without embarrassing myself. Two sailors shoved the boat off the beach and we were quickly disappearing in the fog and drizzle. Only when I no longer could discern even a vague shadow that might have been Ed did I turn to the other occupants of the boat.

The PAK in the Flesh

I turned to see who else was in the boat. I couldn't help being happy at seeing Aurora, the Boy Genius, and Dursley. I knew they would be there, but seeing them was a joy. A phrase bubbled up from Wendt's memory. I was so happy that I simply blurted it out, "The Band's back together!"

Everyone laughed. That moment of mutual exultation assured me that whatever happened from now on, we'd get through it together. There was a feeling of exuberance that made me wonder for a moment if someone had used a spell. The B.G. asked, "What kept you? We've been here almost a half hour?"

Aurora responded for me, "Do you think it's that easy to leave your family? Maybe we should rename you the Boy Moron." He laughed the hardest of us all.

Far too soon the dark hulk of the USS Ohio emerged from the fog. Seamen helped us climb the rope ladder that had been lowered over the side of the ship. We walked over hatches on our way to the sail of the sub. Today was full of memories coming up from Wendt. The hatches were, it reminded me, doorways to death of an extremely violent sort.

I walked through the confined interior with an assurance far beyond that of Dursley or even the Brahmses. We were led to Officers' Quarters and the Captain's Mess. Shortly after we arrived and were seated along with the XO, the captain entered the mess. We all stood for him.

He invited us to sit. He had a brief speech prepared for us. "You'll not see me again during your brief cruise with us if all goes well. You all have been here before except, of course, Mr. Dursley. I'm sure you will all help him gain his sea legs.

"You'll be our guest for somewhere between twenty-four and thirty-six hours depending on the whim of the PAK. So, we've provided some temporary quarters for you." With that he signaled to someone waiting in the wings. He and a female officer entered. He then went on, "Mr. and Mrs. Brahms will take the Executive Officer's quarters. Mr. Dursley will bunk with the Executive Officer in the quarters of the Propulsion Department Head, Lt. Commander Perry. Mrs. Brewster will bunk with the Weapons Department Head, Lt. Commander. Roberts."

Dursley asked, "Sir, will that be the case when we return?"

The Captain smiled. "We'll cross that bridge when and if we come to it." None of us felt happy about that answer. The Captain quickly added, "Further questions will be answered by Commander Wainwright." With that he strode to the doorway into his mess. As he started to go through it, he turned back and directed a request to me. "Oh, one last thing. Mrs. Brewster, the quarters are quite confined in subs. I think it would be best for everyone if you wore your hair up in a compact fashion."

All I could say in response was, "Yes, sir."

Wainwright picked up the Q&A. The only question worth reporting was, "How much warning will we get before we have to meet the PAK?"

Wainwright's answer was, "I've no idea. However, I doubt that it will be less than a couple of hours." He dismissed us. Each of us was joined by our bunk-mate who showed us our quarters.

Roberts was really quite friendly. She asked if I'd ever used a ship's head before. She was surprised that I knew the term. I further surprised her that I had been on the ship before and had used the head. Afterwards, she took us to her cabin. It was every bit as spartan as I expected. As we walked, she asked, "Are you a newlywed?"

That question surprised me. "However did you know?"

She smiled. "It's not so hard. You have been fingering the ring and glancing down at it every so often. It must be new."

I smiled in relief. "Yes, you're right. I'm barely off my honeymoon. I was only married. . ." I hesitated. How long had it been in Jaimie weeks? I was confused about the time but finally answered, "About two weeks ago."

She frowned in consternation. "How can you possibly be confused about that!"

I opened my mouth. I couldn't say anything. I couldn't tell the truth. I couldn't come up with a plausible answer that was true. All I came up with was, "It's complicated." She stared at me for at least as long as I had paused over an answer.

Then she asked, "Kids?"

That, at least, was an easy question. I answered, "His daughter. I don't have any."

It was her time to open her mouth for a couple of minutes in silence. Then she asked, "How do you get along?"

My face beamed at that. I said, "Oh, we had rough times early on, but we're really, really close now." I quickly added, "I really am proud of her. I don't have any responsibility for her character, so I can brag about her with real humility. She's a brilliant student. She's a great chess player."

Roberts chuckled. "Are you sure that you're all that humble?"

I chuckled too. "Oh, I'd love to claim her as mine." I stopped for a minute and realized that I had. I went on, "Really. Now that I'm her step-mum, she really is mine, and I couldn't be prouder." I realized that I had turned as red as a beet.

Robers said, "Then you are the luckiest mom in the world. When it comes to re-combined families, the rule of thumb is that you double the age of the child when you became the step-parent. At that age, you will probably be regarded like a parent. How old is your step-daughter?"

"She was thirteen."

Roberts frowned. "Oh, my. I hope you're not living in a fool's paradise."

I actually laughed. "No. We sat together and cried when I had to leave."

She sighed and said, "I hope you're right." Then she added, "I hope you come back for both your sakes." She finished by saying, "Feel free to use my cabin however you wish. Also, please don't leave officer country. That is any of the officer's cabins, the head and the Captain's Mess."

I thanked her and watched her walk away out of officer country. What would I do? I was pondering that as someone gave me a shoulder bump. I turned and heard Aurora say, "Come on into your cabin. Let's get that troublesome hair of yours up in a bun." She sat me down. She materialized a brush and brushed my hair to a lustrous smoothness. The nervousness that I'd been feeling for the last couple of days seeped out of me like sweat after a good workout. She twisted my hair into a tight coil at the base of my neck. It was a strange feel that I'd not experienced in a long time.

She said, "You know, of course, that the captain is not so concerned with your safety as he is with the distraction factor of all that long, silky hair on display."

I couldn't help feeling smug about the distraction factor of my appearance.

$$\triangle$$

We were in the Captain's Mess having breakfast. It was probably good. I couldn't tell. I could hardly taste anything. There was nervous talk about when the PAK would arrive. Nobody knew. Wainwright refused to say anything.

There was a pool as to when it would happen. The day was divided into morning, afternoon, evening, and next day. I bought evening.

In the afternoon we ended up playing card games. I can't even remember what we played.

At dinner, Wainwright finally opened up. He said, "We will arrive on station to rendezvous with the PAK about 8 PM. I don't know how soon after that that they will arrive."

Dursley cracked the first smile of the day. "It looks like you might win the pool Mrs. Brewster."

I just answered, "Somehow it just doesn't seem much like winning." Nobody disagreed. In the end I didn't win. We arrived on station and sat. And sat and sat. By 11 PM we had all given up waiting and headed for bed.

About midnight Roberts got off watch and came in for "a long nap" as she put it. We talked a little bit as we were drifting off to sleep. She talked some about her family—two sisters and a brother. One of the sisters had died in her first year.

Then she surprised me. She said, "What you're doing takes a whole lot more courage than I have. Thanks for putting yourself out there for us all."

Those thoughts kept me awake for a while. I didn't think of myself as courageous. I didn't even think that Wendt was courageous. I had a unique view of him from both the inside and the outside. Oh, he did what he thought ought to be done. But courageous? Not particularly.

And I hadn't even been tested. I couldn't even pretend to myself or anyone else that I had showed courage. I only hoped that I would be able to do the things that I thought ought to be done.

I was shaking violently. What was happening?

I realized what was happening. I heard Roberts' voice calling my name. I was being awakened. What time was it? She was saying, "I know it's God-awful early, but they're here." My throat filled with something. It was either my heart or my guts. She was still talking, ". . . breakfast and then the sun will be up and they will come down."

I mumbled something and stumbled out of the bunk. My clothes somehow found themselves onto my limbs. I glanced in a mirror and found that I didn't look horrible. My hair was drawn back—not into my usual ponytail but into a bun that I'd never bothered to let down. I was about to leave for the Mess when Richards touched my arm. I turned toward her. She said, "Whatever happens out there, I hope you get back to your daughter."

"Thanks. Believe me, if any PAK stands between me and her there will be a battle."

She nodded and opened the door. From there things flowed far too quickly. Breakfast was a blur. I couldn't even say whether the breakfast was better than a Hogwarts breakfast or not. We were ushered up to the deck. The sun had hardly risen. There was a low cloud deck. Out of the cloud deck came a shape that I remembered even though I'd never seen it with my eyes before. Despite the clarity of Wendt's memories, the reality of this huge vessel floating slowly down and coming to rest a couple of feet above the deck of the submarine as though it were resting on solid ground was almost frightening. A ramp lowered to the deck of the sub with a solid clang that cemented its reality in my heart.

The ramp was wide enough for two. The Brahmses went up the ramp first. Dursley and I followed. Dursley had a sappy smile on his face. I couldn't imagine why. He took my hand. I guess it was to give me confidence.

When we were fully inside the ship, I had that strange *deja-vu* experience that I'd had before when I had visited someplace that I'd never been before but Wendt had been many times. I knew what the rest of the ship was like before seeing it. My first words almost revealed that I had intimate access to the memories of Wendt. That would have been OK with my teammates. It would not be OK for any PAK listening to every word spoken, every gasp of recognition, every heartbeat of all of us. So, I changed what I had intended to say from, "I'm going to take Minerva's cabin." to, "Which was Minerva's cabin?"

Everyone showed a little surprise at my question except the Boy Genius. He seemed to catch on immediately. He said, "Here, I'll show you. Of course, this is a different ship though very similar to the one that Wendt and Minerva and we traveled in. "

Dursley seemed to pick up almost as quickly, "Are there enough cabins for me to bunk solo?"

Aurora answered, "Yes, though you'll have to take the one that was occupied by the Souls, or I guess really, the one that corresponds to the one they had."

I was pretty sure that this was the one that Wendt had flown on when he had gone to observe the conflagration on Mars. He had taken what would have been Minerva's cabin. I decided that I'd have to play particularly dumb. I'd have to let them teach me how to use the auto-kitchen and the loo and the light switches. I saw that it was going to be a hard voyage for the first few days. That was without taking the PAK and trying to sabotage their goal into account.

We moved into our cabins and began unpacking when there was a slight lurch and a distant clang. I went out to find someone else who had experienced it. Everyone had. No one else had an explanation. By this time, Wendt's memory informed me that it was our ship being brought into the much larger PAK ship.

We didn't have to wait long for the official explanation. A voice came over the intercom that announced that we'd just been taken into a larger PAK ship. There was no reason for concern. We all looked at each other and rolled our eyes—no reason for concern, indeed. The voice then invited us to go to the Mess Hall Cum Meeting Room.

The projection screen would be showing our departure from the Solar system. A bit of the moon was showing in a corner of the screen. The alien voice, a mechanical translation, explained that we were leaving the solar system and that we might find the departure interesting to watch.

I felt my stomach lurch as the moon suddenly disappeared. The sun, which was near the upper center of the image quickly, grew in size and in a few seconds disappeared behind us. There was no feeling of acceleration but there was a great feeling of speed. It was disorienting and for a minute or two something seemed wrong about the constellations that were visible in the screen. That feeling of wrongness disappeared quickly.

The voice started to explain what would happen on the cruise, "You will have no specific duties for quite a while on this cruise. Please feel free to entertain yourself as you wish. We have provided a variety of games of chance, manual dexterity, and mental dexterity. In the storage spaces around the room there are decks of cards, board games, a strange game called, "Twister", a variety of books that can be read on the several Kindle devices that we obtained before our voyage."

I wondered how they'd gotten these before the voyage. It didn't seem to matter though. They had them.

The view of the exterior of the ship played continuously on the screen in the Mess Hall. After a short while I stopped paying attention to it. Over the first meal we discussed our situation. Dursley started the conversation, "OK. Why are we here at all? If the only thing we're doing is being passengers?" He looked around the three of us. I only shrugged. The B. G. shook his head and said, "I don't know, but I am sure of something. They didn't want us on board just to be a witness to whatever happens."

A light bulb seemed to go off in Dursley's eyes. He smiled and said, "I'm certain you're right about that."

Aurora asked, "How long do you suppose we'll be? Are we just cruising around at random hoping to find a trace of the Soul's?"

I had been thinking about that very question as we talked. I said, "Well, we know that the PAK were aware of several Soul colonies. They would be stupid indeed if they didn't make some sort of conclusions about the general locale of the home of the Souls. . . "

I was about to say more when Aurora jumped in. "Yes! I don't know those locations even though I was on the original voyage that visited them, but you could draw lines connecting them and guess that the home world probably is in the resulting cone shape. So, B. G., do you think that we're just randomly searching that cone?"

His mouth opened as though he'd been poleaxed and then shut. Aurora followed up, "Well?"

He said weakly, "I suppose."

She stared at him as though he were a fractious student and added, "Well."

He looked up and to the right, apparently in deep thought. Then he said contemplatively, "I wonder if we can enter the Control Room."

Aurora gaped and said, "What in the world are you thinking about! Surely the PAK won't allow us in there?"

He picked up the pace of his words and said, "Why not? Why don't we try to see?"

Dursley was excited by the idea. He jumped up and exclaimed, "Spot on! Let's do it right now. What's the worst that can happen?"

I said, "Maybe we release a cloud of hydrogen sulfide into our part of the ship?"

Dursley replied, "Oh, if that were a possibility, the PAK would make it impossible to enter the Control Room. You've been there before."

The B. G. nodded. "Yes. However, before we do that I'd suggest that we do a little safety drill."

Dursley looked puzzled. "Safety drill? What kind of safety drill?"

Aurora said, "I know what you're thinking of. On the last voyage there were spacesuits on the ship. That was one of the first things we did when we boarded the ship was practice with space suits. We should do that in any case."

I agreed. "Yes, and before we try getting into the Control Room, we should all suit up."

Dursley exclaimed, "Hoo boy! Just like *Aliens*!"

I didn't appreciate the reference. Aurora was apparently ignorant of it. She asked what he was talking about. Dursley excitedly replied, "You've seen the movie, haven't you?"

She just shook her head.

"Well, it's about a space freighter that goes to a planet that has a very dangerous alien on it. The heroine puts on a space suit and expels the alien into the vacuum of space."

Aurora smiled, "That would be a good movie to see. Maybe they have it in the library on the ship."

I brought us back to earth. "Let's get back to basics. We need to find the space suits and practice with them first. You and the B. G. should know where they were kept."

Aurora led us to the walk-in locker where there were indeed space suits just as Wendt remembered them. I, of course, wasn't supposed to have been there, so I didn't remember them. I asked, "What in the world are these. Nothing in here looks like a space suit to me."

Dursley agreed, but Aurora said, "Yes, they are. You can put one on over what you're wearing right now, but if you were wearing anything bulkier than form-fitting fashion jeans, and a light blouse, it would probably be uncomfortable. Come over here, and I'll demonstrate with you how to put one on."

I walked over to her, and she explained the four types of space suit parts, the way you put them on, how you sealed them, and the operation of the helmet. She demonstrated with me as a live manikin. Everything came back quickly to me, but I tried to pretend that it was the first time for me. When we'd finished—it had taken over an hour—I was breathing recycled air, had my radio turned on, and was examining the various "heads-up" displays.

Aurora turned to Dursley, "You next."

He blushed and asked, "Could Jaimie do the demo on me?"

We all blushed. The B. G. came to my rescue by saying, "Strictly men with men and women with women. Come here, and I'll show you how its done."

Dursley was a quick learner. He needed hardly any assistance from the B. G. When he'd finished suiting up, the Brahmses had suited up as well. Dursley immediately asked hopefully, "Time to explore the Control Room?"

Suddenly everyone was pointing their eyes at me. I took a deep breath and thought. I was no Wendt. However, I knew what Wendt would have done. He'd have said, "Yes. Let's get it over with." I was afraid to say that. I stuttered the beginning of an answer YES, but I didn't. What I actually said was, "This has been a good practice but it took a pretty long time. Let's take a break and start again tomorrow. We'll suit up and then try getting into the Control Room." I was no Wendt.

The astounding thing, the thing that took my breath away, was that they bought what I said. They just nodded their heads wisely, and that was that. They never noticed the drops of sweat on my forehead. They never heard the gravelly voice I had because my throat was as dry as the Mojave.

So we explored the rest of the ship. We examined every cabin. We played with the food printer. We found all the games that had been so thoughtfully provided. We had supper. We actually played a card game that Wendt had liked. The night brought a restful sleep to no one.

I was awake and couldn't get back to sleep. I was not just drowsing. I was invincibly awake. In the perfect 72 degree Fahrenheit temperature of the ship, nothing more than undies was required in bed. I slipped on a blouse and jeans and opened the door to the main corridor. The lights there were running on automatic. It had to be close to six in the morning, the lights had started to come up a little simulating sunrise. I went to the refrigerator in the galley to get some icy water when the other cabin doors opened.

Dursley came out of one saying, "I was wondering if you would ever get up. Are you about ready to tackle the Control Room?"

I was tempted to beg for breakfast first, but I realized that one more delay was not going to pass muster. So, I nodded mutely and led us off to the space suit locker. I suited up quickly. There was no point in pretending that I was a rookie at this any more. I told people to pair up so that everyone would be checked by a partner. I was the perfect partner for Aurora and the B. G. for Dursley, but Dursley lined up with me. I shrugged and looked him over after he'd finished. I looked over his shoulder to see the heads up display. I had to ask him to kneel down for that. I glanced at it and said, "Go through the various displays."

He touched the outside of his helmet to shift through the various heads-up displays. They were all in the yellow—the color for good for the Souls who designed the suit. I gave him the all clear and let him inspect my suit. I knelt for him. He watched me go through the paces of the displays. Just as I finished he asked, "Are you thinking of letting your hair down anytime soon."

He couldn't see my mouth drop open. I was flabbergasted. I thought of saying something discouraging. It was going to be a long voyage. I decided that I was not going to be touchy—just yet.

As soon as everyone was checked out we went to the hatch into the Control Room. I looked over to the B. G. "Would you do the honors?"

He nodded. He sighed and took the simple hatch handle and tugged on it. The first try didn't budge it. I think we all gave a sigh of relief. Then he said, "This time for real." This time it opened for real. He pulled the door away from the wall. The interior was dimly lit rather like I remember the day Wendt disapparated in.

We all went in. The Control Room could have been that one from before. I looked down at the spot where the PAK had been petrified and Wendt had fired and fired and fired into it. Aurora touched me on the arm, "You OK?"

I nodded. Meanwhile, the B. G. was sitting in one of the command seats. He was looking around the console in front of him. I asked him, "What are you looking for?"

The B. G. turned to me and said, "Nothing is turned on. All the displays would be lit. The computers are controlled by touch screens. None of them are on."

Aurora said, "You can't blame them, can you? I wouldn't want anyone taking off inside my dreadnought."

Dursley said, "Well, at least we didn't die." It was true, of course.

I asked the B. G. "Just a theoretical question, could you start up the computers if you had to?"

He leaned back. "I never saw it done. All systems were running when I was on the other ship like this. I wouldn't know where to start. It might be a simple physical switch. It might be the corner of one of these touch screens. I could fumble around for years and not find it. . . Or I could lean on the console and hit it by accident."

I thought about that answer and filed it for later. We left the Control Room, dogged the hatch behind us and went back to our usual boring occupation—waiting.

The days crept by. The image on the screen showing our current stellar surroundings changed only slightly from day to day. We ate. We played games. We had no idea whether we were getting closer to the world of Souls or not. It wore on us all. There were little squabbles that ballooned.

One day we were playing a card game, Back Alley Bridge. Dursley misdealt. It had been a close match. Aurora had a dab hand that was ruined. She threw the cards across the table at Dursley and screamed, "Can't you even deal straight!"

He clearly wanted to make a cutting remark. He took several deep breaths and just threw his hand down and said, "Well, you can do all the dealing if you think you can do it better than me."

That was the end of the match.

Aurora took to calling me the ice maiden because I rarely showed emotions like that. The B. G. was evidently disgusted with all of us. It didn't matter much. We were doing nothing but marking time.

Then one day, the intercom came on, and we got a message from the PAK. It went something like this, "Tomorrow morning, we will enter the system containing the world of Souls. We're going to invite you onto the bridge of our ship to witness the beginning of the end of their race. Of course, you'll have to 'suit up' as you say because of our atmosphere which is corrosive to your race. Be prepared at 9 AM ship's time." That was the end of the announcement.

At dinner we discussed the next day. I opened the subject on all our minds. "I can think of a hundred ways that we can't prevent this massacre."

Dursley said, "Yeh. That's what I like to hear. How about you, Mr. B. G., how many ways do you have not to prevent this genocide?"

The B. G. frowned. "I'm not nearly so inventive. I've only go a dozen or so. "

Dursley turned to Aurora, "And you."

I shrugged, "I think those two have the market cornered on how not to prevent this."

Dursley said, "That's got me beat." Then he turned to me and said, "How about it. Give. What are your ways?"

I grimaced. "Well, we can't fight to take over the ship. The PAK are physically overwhelming. They have faster reflexes than we. They are far stronger than we.

"We can't out-think them. They are far smarter than we are. We can't challenge them to a duel. They'd wipe us out with any muggle weapon.

"We can't blow up the ship. We don't have any explosives.

"We can't destroy the engines. We don't have any tools.

"We can't change the programming of the ship's computers. We don't have an interface.

"We can't burn holes in the hull. We don't have any acetylene torches.

"We can't . . . Well, there's so many things we can't do."

There was a glimmer of something in Dursley's eyes. "You are a real Johnny Raincloud, you know, Mrs. Brewster."

Then Aurora asked, "What do you suppose we should bring with us in our space suits."

I said, "Well, if you have a lucky charm in a purse, that might be good." I turned to Dursley. "You too. Any lucky charms about you?"

He shook his head. "No, I left all of mine in a purse back home."

Aurora smiled. Then she said, "I think that you ought to help each of us suit up tomorrow. You seem to be so good at it."

I smiled. "Right-o! See you tomorrow in the locker room."

That evening, we played a game of cards and went to bed as contented as we had in a long time. I was looking forward to the next day. We finally had something we could do. It might get us killed, but it was something.

The next morning, we were all up bright and early. We had a quick breakfast. I had eggs sunny-side up. It was amazing that the automatic kitchen could produce that. It did. It was good.

Then we got suited up. I wore a pair of jeans. Inside a pocket in those jeans was Wendt's purse. Inside the purse was my wand and Aurora's wand and Dursley's really magical wand. As I dressed, I took Mr. Dursley's hint from long ago and uncoiled my hair, and put it back up in a bun at the top of my head with a good bit of hair hanging down from it over my shoulders.

I opened the purse and took the three wands out. I inserted each at a jaunty angle into my loose bun.

When we met at the locker, Dursley commented, "I like your hair. I wish you wore it that way more often."

Aurora added, "Me too. I really like those hair pins." She then managed a real blush. She faltered a little as she asked, "Could I have one of those, love?"

I blushed too as I confidently pulled her wand out and handed it to her. I had removed the decorative handle earlier. It wouldn't help her use it much. It wasn't much of a surprise that Dursley asked, "You know I've always admired your hair." He took my hand and said, "Could I have one of those hairpins as a keepsake of you?"

I nodded and pulled his wand out of my hair. I handed it to him and he said, "I think this is going to be my lucky, lucky charm." I nodded again.

Then we suited up. Aurora had twisted her hair around her wand to make a quick bun. Dursley put his wand in his breast pocket. I suppose it was next his heart. I don't know about the rest, but I was finally ready for whatever might happen. Having my wand in contact with me completed a connection that had long been broken. I felt like I could do anything. God knew that what we had to do would require that kind of power.

After we were all suited up and checked out (again, Dursley checked me), we walked to the Mess/Meeting Room and took seats. It was eerily like Wendt's recollection of the last minutes before the battle of the Control Room on the last voyage. We hadn't sat there long when the voice came over the intercom, saying that it would lower the ramp, allowing us to leave our ship and be greeted by an honor guard. I thought, "Honor Guard my foot. You can leave off the word Honor and be more honest about it."

The ramp did lower, and we walked out of our ship. We were indeed greeted by an honor guard of one. I had no doubt that he could kill us all in a second or two if called on to. He led us through the huge volume of the interior deck of the dreadnought to a hatch that led back into the command area of the ship. We walked down two hallways that ended in a large room that Wendt remembered and that seemed to me like a cubicle farm.

Dursley glanced around and said, "This kind of reminds me of the time that I was on the bridge of a cruise ship. The only difference is that you don't have a window that shows the exterior of the ship."

There were a number of work stations where people sat before large video screens. There was one alien who stood alone. He turned and spoke. A translation sounded in our helmets.

"Welcome. You are largely responsible for this memorable day. I thought you should be on the bridge when all our efforts come to fruition. May I direct your sight to the large video screen on the wall? The very bright star in the center is our goal. In the next hour it will grow and become more than a point of light. You can't see it yet, but shortly the planet that is our target will separate from that star's image." If you could tell from mechanical translation, he seemed to be excited, even ebullient. He added, "Do you have any questions before we arrive?"

Dursley asked, "Do you mind if we sit while we wait?"

Something vaguely like a laugh sounded in our helmets, "No! No! Of course. We'll bring comfortable chairs up." While we talked, four wheeled chairs like the rest of the crew were using appeared.

Aurora asked, "How did you find this planet?"

The voice said, "You are the astronomer, right?"

Aurora, surprised at his knowledge of her, shakily said, "Yes, I am."

"Oh, it is really a story worth hearing." He looked toward me, "One of you is a writer, not so?"

My voice was somewhat shaky too as I said, "That would be me."

"Perhaps you might write a chronicle of this campaign someday."

I grudgingly said, "Perhaps."

"Well, it's like this. After your courageous defeat of the first expedition, we decided that the best way to find this elusive planet of ghosts was to use the only people who knew its location, you."

Aurora interrupted. "But we don't know it's location, even now."

He laughed. "Oh, but you do. You far underestimate your native intelligence. You observed your course to the system and away from it on the viewscreen showing the view from outside the ship. That information was buried in your mind somewhere.

"We made a study of your race, of emotional reactions shown on your countenance. Even your businesses use that information freely. We combined several pieces of information—the location of several of the ghost colonies, the radio signals from colonies unknown, your reaction to your view of our course among the stars as we left Earth. There were small course corrections during the voyage as we collected more reactions to your view of our course. We probably only wasted a few days travel time compared with a perfect course.

"Oh, and one more point. We have corrected our stupid underestimate of your capabilities from the last voyage. We have sent multiple messenger drones back to our worlds with the correct location of the ghost world."

I asked a question that had been bothering me during this discussion. "Why do you call the Soul's world a ghost world?"

He seemed puzzled for once. "Isn't that what you just called it yourself?"

It dawned on me that the translation of Soul might be ghost. I nodded acknowledgment. "Yes, it's just a quirk in your translator. It doesn't matter."

During this conversation, Dursley had been spinning around in his seat as though he were bored by the conversation. Perhaps he was. I was beginning to lose interest in the pointlessness of details of how the genocide was going to happen. The captain of the ship seemed not to lose interest though. He went on. "We have a couple of options for how to attack. We have a number of missiles. Each has an advanced version of our basic drive that can compress space by a factor of over a hundred million. We will use one missile to squeeze the top of the star's atmosphere into neutron star density. That will cause a fusion reaction that will be comparable to a nova—at a minimum."

The ship's captain was saying that we'd just entered the solar system of the world of the Souls. With that a series of things happened that required a lot of time afterwards to sort through. What I experienced was a gut wrenching shudder that went through the ship. The lights all went out. There was a rush of wind that I thought would pull me out of my chair. That blackout couldn't have last more than five or ten seconds, but it seemed like five or ten minutes.

When the lighting came back on, it was dim, and I could see Dursley directing his wand in a wide arc. At the end of the arc, the walls of the room separated like the sectioning of an orange. I regained my voice and called out, "What the hell's going on!"

Dursley said, "I'm cutting holes in the ship." I remembered then that Wendt thought that Dursley's wand could drill a hole clean through the moon. It seemed crazy, but his wand certainly seemed to making swiss cheese of this ship.

The B. G. shouted, "I think the crew mostly got out of this room alive, but some of them may have been blown out into space." Dursley was completing his third arc and starting a fourth.

I shouted, "Dursley! Stop! I want to leave something left of the ship we came in. It's probably our only way home."

He said calmly, "Are you sure we've put an end to the PAK's threat?"

290

"I don't know, but I suggest that we start thinking about getting ourselves out alive."

Dursley didn't seem happy about it, but he stopped cutting the ship to pieces. I asked how we got back to our ship. The B. G. said, "We came in through that hatch over there. We could try opening it."

I shook my head. "No. Dursley burn a circular hole in it. If there's air pressure on the other side, it'll explode into this room. Everyone stand back. Oh, and wands ready in case there's anyone on the other side."

Dursley said, "If I burn that hole, I don't think there will be anyone on the other side."

I just tried using my school teacher voice. I said, "No matter. Everyone with wands at the ready." We had trouble getting our wands into our hands. Both Aurora and I had to work them out of our hair and worked through the sleeves into our hands. I just hoped they would work through the suit without blowing a hole in them. When we were ready, Dursley made a small circle with his wand as though he were sketching on a pad of paper. There was pressure on the other side of the door. As soon as the circle was drawn the circle flew into the room and smashed a console on the opposite side of the room.

I stuck my head a little out to see around the hole. There was nothing there. I commented, "God, I wish I had my compact mirror with me."

We ventured down the corridor. The gravity was uncertain, fluctuating. We lurched down the hall to a cross hallway. I said, "Aurora, use the *Petrificus* charm down the right corridor. I'll do it down the left. On the count of three. . . One . . . Two. . . Three." Aurora and I extended our wands around the corner and used the charm. We peeked around the corners. I saw nothing. She said, "A PAK down."

I whirled around and ran down the corridor to the PAK who was in a space suit. I now understood Wendt as I never had before. I pointed the wand through my suit and used the *Avada Kedavra* curse. Nothing seemingly changed. I realized that if I were able to get the Glock out of Wendt's purse and use it, I would have. I felt in the marrow of my bones how satisfying it would have been to see the bullets make his body jump.

Aurora caught up and said, "Oh, no! Why?"

If she didn't understand, there was no way that I could explain. I just shook my head and said, "Let's get going. On to the ship." I strode forward hoping that the rest were following me.

We reached the hatch that would open on the hangar where our ship was. I turned to Dursley, "Would you cut a hole in the door. Please stand well back from the hatch. Oh, one thing more—please try to direct it away from our ship."

Dursley said, "Right." He stood to the side of the hatch and spun his wand, cutting a circle out of the hatch. There was no pressure difference between the corridor and the hangar. The circle dropped inside the hangar. I peered around the corner again. No one was in view. Then I signaled for the team to follow me. The ship was there as we'd left it. The ramp was down, so the ship had no atmosphere. We ran up the ramp and tried the ramp switch. Nothing was working. There were no lights other than emergency lights. I cursed the fact that my wand was still in my suit. Without atmosphere I didn't have an idea how to get it out.

The B. G. asked an important question. "How are we going to get out of here?"

I had been so anxious to reach the ship I hadn't thought about that at all. "I don't know."

Dursley said, "How about cutting a hole in the deck."

Aurora asked, "Without a functioning ship how does that help us?"

The B. G. answered, "The artificial gravity will give us some momentum out. I've got a feeling that it doesn't work outside the main ship, so we would drift away from the main ship."

Dursley didn't need any further urging. He walked down the ramp. Standing on the bottom of the ramp, he starting cutting a circle in the deck of the ship. He finished, and the circle and the ship slowly fell through what had been the deck of the ship. Outside, our momentum kept us moving slowly away from the dreadnought. He was weightless too. He struggled for a while to get a grip on the ramp so that he could crawl back in the ship.

Aurora had a good idea to help him. We were all weightless too, but she could grab a handhold on the wall. She then pointed her wand at Dursley and said, "*Accio* Dursley." With that, Dursley flew toward her, and she was being dragged toward him. Her grip on the wall prevented her from being flung toward him. They ended up hugging. I wished that I had thought of that little trick.

We were still stuck. We were in a dead ship with no power, no gravity, hardly any light, no atmosphere, no food. The list went on and on. We all thought and thought about what to do. There were few ideas except for the B. G. who had an idea why we were stuck.

He said, "The PAK didn't want us messing around on the ship, so they turned all controls off remotely. The power supply must have been cut off by what happened when Dursley cut up the main ship. Now, we can't get anything going. That doesn't lead me to an idea. It just explains the fix were in. If we could get a generator going again, I might even be able to navigate this ship. . . " He paused. "If I knew the security codes."

The speakers in all our helmets came on. The infernal translator voice that we'd heard from the beginning said, "Congratulations. I don't know how you did it, but you pretty well destroyed our ship. Given enough time, we might be able to repair it. We don't have time. I propose a truce. You help us fight off the Souls who are flying toward us and we'll help you."

I said, "Bloody Hell! I suppose they can hear everything we've been saying."

The disembodied voice replied, "Yes."

I mumbled something about how I wished we could read minds. Then I said, "Come close." We all grouped together, and I used the charm, "*Muffliato.*"

Aurora said, "It's worth a try. We'll never know if it works, of course."

I agreed. Then I asked, "What do you think? I've got a feeling that we don't have a lot of time to decide."

Dursley said, "If the Souls are coming, I vote for the PAK over them."

The B. G. said, "But let's try to get some kind of commitment—no genocide for our help."

Aurora nodded and said, "Can we trust them?" Then she added, "Oh shit, the only way we'll know is by trying them."

I had an idea. "I agree with you all. PAK, if you can hear, speak." There was no answer for several minutes. Then I said, "I'll release the spell. *Finito Incantatum.*" I followed that by, "Let's negotiate."

"What do you mean, negotiate."

I couldn't help giggling. "I thought you PAK knew our language."

"We do. What is there to negotiate about? You help us survive. We help you survive."

I seemed to have the lead in negotiation, so I said, "Here's the deal we're offering. We help each other survive but you must agree that you and your ship and crew will not commit genocide."

"That is not binding on my race."

"No, it isn't. I hope that we can negotiate a peace between you and the Souls, but that is not binding on you either."

There was silence for quite a while. Then the voice said, "Agreed." There were sighs of relief on our side. The voice continued, "First, you must restore power on your ship."

The B. G. chimed in, "Right. How do we do that?"

"Are you in the Control Room?"

"No, but we can be. Give us a couple of minutes."

We moved from one handhold to another. Fortunately, we'd left the hatch open to the Control Room. It would have been a chore getting it open in zero gravity. Inside, we all found seats. They gave us secure points from which to work if there were anything we needed to do. The B. G. said, "We're in the Control Room. I'm sitting in the command pilot seat."

"Good. There is a panel with switches on it. It is underneath the main display screen at the command pilot seat. If you apply pressure at four points along that control panel, it will rotate revealing the switches. There are ten from left to right."

I was sitting in what I thought of as the co-pilot seat. I could see the switches. The voice went on. "The left-most is the main power switch. If you press it for about seven of your seconds, it will start the main generator." The B. G. pressed it for at least seven seconds. Nothing happened that we could tell.

The B. G. said, "Nothing doing."

"I see. Then press the one next to it for about seven seconds. That is the APU—the auxiliary power unit. It's only a fraction as powerful as the main power generator, but it would be something."

He did. At the end of the seven seconds, lights came on in the cabin and we all whooped. The voice said, "Good. It will generate enough power for most of the secondary functions. The next switch turns on gravity." And we had gravity. Dursley said, "I'm going to see if I can close the ramp." He left his seat, and we heard the ramp clang shut.

The voice said, "Good. Turn on the atmosphere recycling and other life support functions."

I asked, "The next switch?"

"Yes, Mrs. Brewster." It was spooky being referred to by name by that voice. It was the first time it had addressed anyone by name.

The rest of the process went smoother. The voice said, "Turn on the scanning array." Then, "Turn on the main control computer." With that the display screens in the Control Room flickered into life. It took a number of minutes for that to happen. As soon as the display in front of the B. G. became stable, he started touching points on it. There was some sort of warning message that came up. It was in PAKese though.

The B. G. asked, "What's the master access code for the controls?"

The voice asked, "What are you going to do?"

The B. G. didn't hesitate. "Turn on the weapons array."

The voice actually laughed. "I guess I can't blame you. On the on-screen keyboard, it's 2nd button 1st row. Then the eighth button third row, then . . ." After a while he finished. A screen that Wendt had seen before appeared on the pilot's screen. The B. G. pressed a spot on his console and a familiar screen appeared on my screen. It was the weapons console. The

294

only problem was that there was some sort of warning flashing on the screen.

That didn't bother the B. G. though. He was busy on his own console. I asked him what he was doing. "Tell you shortly, why doesn't someone sample the atmosphere to see if we can take off our helmets?"

I released my helmet and took a quick whiff. It smelled like nothing. I took a deeper breath and said, "It seems OK."

He said, "Good, take off you helmets. We'll confer a little later." He said all of this while he was keying furiously on his console.

Aurora asked what he was doing. He said, "Be patient. I'll tell you in a few minutes if all goes well."

So, we waited in silence. Eventually, the B. G. said, "Take off your helmets and turn them off." When we had, he said, "OK. Do the *Muffliato* again." I did. "I just set up the consoles to translate into English. Look."

I turned back to my console. Now, I saw in plain English, "Insufficient power for weapons use."

The B. G. said, "I'm pretty sure that goes for propulsion too. We're still stuck here. I'm about to turn on the conference radio in here, so we can talk with the PAK. Anything you want to say while we're still under the cloak of silence?"

I said, "We need to find out their status: How many survived? Can they repair our power supply? Oh . . . I guess I have about a million questions."

The B. G. asked, "Anyone else?" We looked around. No one had any secret communications to share. So, I released the spell.

The B. G. turned on the radio, and we heard the voice say, "I was afraid something had happened to you."

The B. G. said, 'Just getting the controls set up the way I want them. So, I think you've got better information that we do. What do you propose we do next?"

There wasn't a second's hesitation. "The ghosts are coming for us. They will come for you first. You should let us come on board your ship to help defeat them. We might be able to take their ship from yours."

I asked, "How many of you?"

"Twenty-one."

The B. G. asked, "How long before the Souls arrive?"

"Not more than two of your hours."

I asked, "How soon do you want to come aboard our ship?"

"We're on our way now. We'll arrive in thirty minutes."

Aurora asked, "Are you coming in a ship's boat?"

"No. We jumped from our ship in space suits. There isn't much left of our ship still intact."

Dursley asked, "How many of them are there?"

There was a hesitation. Then an answer came. "We think there are about five hundred based on the size of the ship."

There was a general gasp in our ship. The PAK heard and said, "It's not so bad as you might think. Have you ever heard of the battle of Thermopylae?"

Dursley said, "Sure, a god-awful lot of soldiers from Turkey attacked Greece. A small number of Spartans held them off for a long time because the Turks had to come through a narrow pass."

The PAK agreed. "Basically correct. The ghosts will try attacking your ship. They will have to come through your narrow ramp, where we can hold them off. Then you will cut a hole in the side of their ship. We will counter attack there."

Dursley asked, "Then won't you be on the Turk side of Thermopylae?"

There was a scary laugh that came through the speakers, "No, because you will make a big hole in the side of their ship."

It went on. "You should probably blow your atmosphere out and put your space suits on again. We will be arriving at your ship shortly. Please open the ramp."

We seemed pretty committed, so we put the wretched helmets back on, turned on our radios and pumped as much air as we could back into the storage tanks. Then we opened the ramp. It wasn't long before the PAK arrived.

The PAK landed on the outside of the ship and maneuvered over the ship as though they were in full gravity. They swarmed through the ramp. It wasn't crowded in the ship unless you considered that there was going to be a pitched battle in less than an hour.

The PAK were wearing the same sort of suits that we were. We'd seen them without suits in their ship. Here, in space suits, they looked even more fearsome than on their ship. I tried to control a twitch in my right hand that kept wanting to pull my Glock out of the exterior pocket of the suit where I'd put it. I wasn't sure whether I was happy or not that I'd not gotten it out of the purse while we still had atmosphere in the ship.

The leader of the PAK asked to come into the Control Room. He did. He motioned me out of my co-pilot seat and began manipulating the weapons console—in English. He nodded once and said, "Twenty-five minutes left."

No one had any problem understanding what that meant. I asked him, "Are you sure that they will attack?"

"Yes." The mechanical voice was even more precise and dead-pan than it had ever been before. The bastard set up a countdown clock on all the video screens on the ship, as though he knew the moment to the second when the attack would come. When it came, I was surprised by how silent it was. Of course we were all wearing spacesuits in an airless environment, but the PAK didn't use weapons other than their bodies. I stood at the entry to the Control Room with my wand in my hand. I understood why the PAK didn't have any sort of weapon. When the countdown timer reached +0:01, the attack came.

It was rapid and silent. An airlock on the Soul ship opened, and a host of Souls in space suits emerged in a steady stream. The PAK counterattacked. shortly they had killed every Soul that left the airlock. The airlock quickly closed decapitating a PAK who was trying to enter it. At that moment, the senior PAK told Dursley, "There at the airlock. Cut the airlock door open." Dursley stepped to the ramp opening and drew a circle on it. The circle didn't explode out, but the PAK knocked it in. He and several PAK followed.

I never learned details of the battle. There were a number that had been captured and confined to the cargo bay. The PAK commander must have had plans for them.

It was all over in a half hour. We were accompanied over to the Soul ship by the PAK commander. He told us on the way, "We were all lucky. The power supply for your ship and the engines were destroyed by your attack on my ship. You were lucky your ship held atmosphere."

I asked, "What is going to happen when the Souls find out what happened to their ship?"

"Oh, that won't happen for at least an hour, probably longer. We'll be well on our way to someplace where we can work on this ship in peace."

Aurora asked where that would be. He answered, "Oh, the equivalent of your Kuiper Belt. There's a fair amount of junk floating around. Looking for us would be like search a haystack for a neutrino. We'll spend a week or so upgrading the weapons systems and stealth systems."

I asked how many casualties there were. He said, "Three dead and five injured."

"Surely that's not possible. I saw at least a dozen Souls die in the assault on our ship."

He answered, "How can a ghost die?"

We were all still in space suits. I could never have discerned his emotions if he weren't wearing a suit. How could I now? I just said, "Then how many are in the cargo bay? How many were on board at the beginning?"

The answer was fast and apparently unemotional, "Seventy-eight in the hold. A total of about four hundred fifty."

I raised another point, "Either we humans or you will have to wear space suits until we leave this solar system for Earth."

"We hope that we will be able to re-work the HVAC of this ship so that we both can have quarters where we don't have to wear space suits. We'll have to see. But for the time being everyone wears space suits."

I asked, "What about the Souls in the cargo hold?"

"The cargo hold was always hermetically sealed from the rest of the ship. There is food, water, and even a sanitary facility. They will be OK."

I said, "I hope so. They may be your ticket out of here." The PAK commander had no response to that. By the way, you may be wondering how I knew who the commander was. His suit bore a triangular yellow mark underneath the helmet. No one else had a mark like that. Two others, I think, had a single horizontal mark at that level.

We were on our way to the Kuiper Belt. On the way, it was decided that we humans would have an area of the ship surrounding what turned out to be the backup bridge. The entire ship had tolerable atmosphere for us. We could take off our suits occasionally to eat, nap, and perform other bodily functions. I don't know what the PAK did.

As it turned out when we arrived in the Kuiper Belt, they had already reworked the HVAC so that there were two independent systems. They told me that there was already a backup HVAC. They had re-purposed and rerouted some of it to allow us to have independent atmospheres. While we were there, we heard almost continuous sounds coming from various parts of the ship. They were at time very loud. Generally during the hours that we slept they were much softer.

Every meal we had a conference on what was going on. One breakfast, I asked the question, "What happens when we leave the outer reaches of this solar system and approach the home world of the Souls?"

The B. G.'s answer was, "If this crew still wanted to destroy the souls, they'd just wait for their navy to show up and finish the job for them. IF we approach the home world it must be to negotiate. What can we do to help?"

Aurora had an answer, "Look, this is not the first time that we have been here and pulled their fat out of the fire. They may or may not recognize my hubby and me, but I would bet they do. If Jes and Frank are still around, they sure would. They've got to realize that they are in no position to dictate terms. They've pretty much got to take whatever the PAK are willing to give them."

I shrugged, "I agree. How can we convince them that's true."

Dursley said, "Just say what you just said. It's simple, easy to understand, hard to argue against. What I'm worried about is how we get back home."

I said, "Well, there are two possibilities and maybe more. First, if they still have the original ship that Wendt went in, they might send us home in that. Second, since the PAK haven't decided to kill us, they may be kind enough to take us home with them."

Dursley agreed—sort of. He said, "Let's see. We have the Souls. All we did to them was lead the PAK to them and seal their fate—whatever it is going to be. And then, we have the PAK. All we did to them was destroy their dreadnought, kill a bunch of them, and force them to make a treaty with their mortal enemies. Sure, the two of them will probably be fighting for the chance to do us a good turn."

Aurora returned us to the realm of the possible. She said, "What can we actually do to influence our fate? Ideas?"

I muttered, "Keep our heads down and try to ingratiate ourselves with both sides."

It was only a week until the ship was repaired enough to return to the inner part of the solar system. The PAK were sending ahead of us the basic outline of a peace treaty that they were bringing to the Souls. The four of us, that is we humans, were seated together in the backup bridge of the ship. We had discovered that the Souls called it the Serendipity. I suppose that it was somewhat lucky for them. They hadn't been annihilated, and we were bringing a peace treaty in it. So far there had been no response.

No one who designed it thought that the backup bridge was ever going to serve the purpose of being a Conference Room. It was small, cramped, and without much headroom. There were really only two duty stations with chairs. We'd dragged two chairs in from the Mess so that everyone could sit.

We were speeding through the inner solar system, hoping that we could talk the Council of Souls into negotiating in person. We were getting to listen to the conversation between the Supreme Soul and the commander of the PAK. I've condensed all the gaps caused by the speed of light out of the conversation.

Supreme: "You are not welcome. We will fire on you if you attempt to come into orbit. We are dispatching four cruisers comparable to yours at this moment to intercept you and escort you out of the system."

Commander of the Pack (from now on to be referred to as ComPak): "We understand your threat. We do not want to kill more of your race unless you refuse to negotiate. If we are fired on, we will return fire and destroy the ships you send to intercept us. Negotiate, and you can have favorable terms."

Supreme: "You think that capitulating to you to be favorable?"

Compak: "To rule your own system and survive without interference in that system is favorable to that system being destroyed."

Supreme: "That is beyond your capability."

The B. G. just shook his head.

Compak: "We will destroy your cruisers. Consider that we will use one of your cruisers that we, a force of two dozen, captured, rebuilt, and now command. When our main force arrives—it will soon—your solar system will be totally obliterated. It will be too late then. The time for negotiations will be past."

Supreme: "Return to your home, and await our arrival."

The commander came on the intercom. "We will encounter their ships tomorrow."

Aurora said, "Those are big promises. Are you sure you can carry them out?"

The commander said, "We have improved this ship. It is substantially more maneuverable. It's weapons are substantially more powerful and accurate."

Aurora answered, "Then please don't destroy those ships—just immobilize them."

The commander didn't answer for several minutes. "We'll consider the request. I will give you warning before we engage the enemy" Then he broke the intercom connection.

Dursley asked, "What do you think? Is that a bluff?"

The B. G. answered, "We'll find out for sure tomorrow."

It was shortly before lunch that the warning came through. In about an hour we'd confront the Soul's fleet. We gathered in the Control Room watching the video screen. I said, "I don't think there will be much to see. Whatever will happen will happen far off."

Dursley's eyes lit up as he said, "No warning when we die?"

The B. G. said, "Probably not. We're talking long range lasers. Like they used to say, you never see the bullet that kills you." He added ominously, "Especially when it's traveling at the speed of light."

The commander came over the intercom. "I'm sending the weapons screen down to you. You'll have no control but can see the targeting, firing and results."

With that the screen changed. It had four green crosses on it. Beside them were text messages. The B. G. commented, "Probably PAK language. We could know which is likely to go first if we could read it."

A yellow box surrounded each of the green crosses. They changed to yellow too. The text changed. Then the cross was replaced by what looked like a short cylinder. The yellow cross reappeared across the back end of it. The thing seemed to jump around as though it were a puppet on the string of a nervous puppeteer. Then the area around the cross turned black.

Dursley said, "I'm pretty durn sure that was a direct hit."

The cylinder started slowly spinning around an axis that seemed to be at a large angle to the center line of the cylinder. I said, "I think that's it for that ship."

Aurora said, "Yup."

Then one of the other ships went through the same terrible sequence. The other ships changed course. Shortly thereafter, our ship turned through a crazy angle. We were flung to a wall by acceleration. We heard the groaning of overstressed metal. Dursley turned to me and said, "I love you." I heard those words again from Aurora and the B. G.

Then another of the Soul ships blazed with light for a second and disappeared. I asked no one in particular, "What do you suppose they hit?"

The B. G. said, "Don't know."

The last ship slowly changed orientation but didn't seem to be hit. Dursley said, "Turned tail." I released a long held breath and said, "The end of the battle?"

The intercom turned on. "The Supreme command has agreed to negotiations."

Aurora said, "Sensible."

There Are Only Two Answers: Yes and No

We arrived in orbit and then things started happening. We received a location to land. We would meet with the Soul negotiators at that spaceport. There would be half a dozen in the Soul contingent. The commander decided that we'd just send three. He wanted to be present, and he wanted two of us to come along. He left the decision of which two to us. So, we had a meeting.

It happened in the Brahmses' cabin, which was the largest for obvious reasons. Dursley opened the conversation by asking, "Are we drawing straws?"

The B. G. shook his head negatively. "There should be two wizards. One should be in a spacesuit to protect him or her from any skulduggery with atmosphere. Of course, the PAK will be in a spacesuit."

All three of us wizards and witches volunteered. I said, "It should be the two witches. You should have Dursley in reserve in case something serious happens."

Dursley responded, "No way, I'm not going to stay behind safe and sound while two women fight my battles. AND I won't see the Brahmses be broken apart if anything happens to the negotiators."

Aurora protested, "Doesn't breaking up the Brewster family bother you if it comes to that?"

The B. G. said, "Nobody's family is going to be broken up if we plan this right."

I agreed. "OK. What are the dangers that we might face?"

The B. G. supplied a list. "Well, they might kill you outright. There's probably nothing that you can do about it. If you get a hint that it's going to happen, then disapparate—each of you. Don't try to go together just go immediately."

Dursley asked, "If that happens shouldn't we try to bring the PAK back with us?"

Again, the B. G. shook his head. "No. The PAK is more than capable of defending himself. He's the one who wants this meeting."

I wasn't convinced, but I don't know what I'd do if the opportunity arose.

The B. G. went on. "The real main risk is that they will attempt to overwhelm the negotiators and insert Souls into them. They might be able to do that by using drugs in an aerosol form or gas to knock you out. I think that everyone in a spacesuit is probably but not certainly safe. The wizard without a spacesuit would be like a pigeon in a mine-shaft warning the rest of the danger of poison. So, who would go without a space suit?"

We two looked at each other. I don't think any of us wanted to admit that we wanted to wear the space suit. I suggested drawing straws. Aurora's mouth dropped open. "Oh, no! You don't want to do that."

I rolled my eyes. Aurora said, "That really is bad luck. The straw would come from a broomstick. The short straw means that your broomstick will fall to earth."

"Well, what do you want to do?"

Aurora had a crazy idea. "Why don't we play wands, broomsticks, and cauldrons."

I stared at Aurora and asked, "What in the world is that game? How does it work?"

"Oh, you wouldn't know about it, since you didn't grow up in a wizard family. Yes. it's a child's game. It's really popular at the 1st thru 3rd level along with Gobstones."

I was getting impatient. "But how does it work?"

"Oh," She seemed surprised that I didn't get it. "It's pretty obvious, isn't it? Wands beat broomsticks. Broomsticks beat cauldrons. Cauldrons beat wands!"

One of those memories bubbled up from Wendt's memories—rock beats scissors, scissors beat paper, paper beats rocks. She said, "Come on. It's obvious. Broomsticks fly over cauldrons, cauldrons cover wands, wands set broomsticks on fire. Get it." Everyone was laughing—even the B. G. I guess I was at least smiling as well.

I agreed. "OK. Then you count three and show one of the symbols. What are they?"

Aurora still thought me a dolt as she explained patiently, "Wand is the index finger stuck out straight. Cauldron is a cupped hand. Broomstick is this." She closed her hand around an imaginary broomstick. "See?"

I nodded. I completed the instructions, "So, you count to three and then make the sign of whichever you choose."

She stared at me again. "No, silly. You count to the magic number seven and then do that."

I was tempted to wonder about how long a game of wands, broomsticks, cauldrons would take, but I restrained myself. What I said was, "OK. Let's get this over."

Dursley counted to seven, and we both displayed the wand. Aurora clapped her hands and exclaimed, "Again!"

Dursley started the count again, but I had an idea before he reached seven. I grabbed Aurora's hand and asked, "What happens with the winner? Suit or not?"

Aurora admitted that she hadn't thought of that. Dursley provided the answer. "Winner is without a suit." We agreed, and Dursley counted again. This time it wasn't a draw. I had cauldron, and she had wand. I was going naked—sort of."

The B. G. raised another point. "Are you just there for security or do you take part in the negotiations."

His wife answered, "We're not going to be doing the negotiating, but I sort of see our role as being referees. If we hear something that seems un-fair, we call the PAK out on it."

I asked, "Then you don't think the Souls will ask for something unrea-sonable?"

The B. G. said, "What do you think?"

"Oh, they've been pretty darn unreasonable so far. I don't see what would make them change."

Dursley just shrugged. "You'll have to play it by ear. Anything could happen."

The PAK commander announced that we would go down the next day shortly after breakfast. It was a sad night as we prepared for a repeat of the last time that we'd been there. I didn't think our preparations were as good as that last time. But, this time we would have a live PAK with us.

After dinner, we decided to make an early night of it. I was the first to head for my cabin. Dursley followed me. At my door he said, "Please come back."

I forced a chuckle and said, "If I don't come back, the chances are that nobody on this ship gets back."

He just frowned and squeezed my arm.

◿

There was a welcoming party that met us on the tarmac where we landed the shuttle.

That shuttle was not that much different from the shuttle where we spent most of our trip here.

The funny thing was that there were seven of the Souls rather than six. We started the talks. Suddenly there was a hiss that was coming from somewhere under the Conference Room table. I almost immediately could tell that there was something wrong. I felt sick and woozy. Aurora shouted, "Gas!"

I stood up and tried to run from the Souls. There was something strange. I could hardly put one foot in front of another. Somehow I got to the door to the Conference Room. I kept thinking, "If I can only get out of the room, there will be normal air. Then I can think and do something—disapparate, anything."

I managed to get through the door just before the Souls who were running after me. But, somehow my legs were moving like I was knee deep in molasses. I could barely put one foot in front of another. Then I felt the fingers grab an arm. I was trying to scream, but I couldn't. They pulled me down but I couldn't feel it when I hit the floor. They were forcing a mask over my face. I kept trying to scream, "No! No!" but nothing came out of my mouth but a muffled cry that was lost in the mask. I felt myself slipping, slipping away. I couldn't stop myself. I was going to have a Soul inside my head.

Wendt always had dreams in advance of these big events. I don't remember having any. Of course, this night was the first real test. I had just awakened from one of those terrifying ones like he used to have.

I heard a pounding on the door of my cabin. Maybe that was what wakened me. I mumbled something. Dursley came in, pulled me out of my bunk, and whispered, "Are you all right?"

"Oh, yes. Yes. It was just a. . a . . . dream."

He nodded. "I think we've all been having some bad dreams. How are you?"

I took a deep breath. "Oh, I'm OK. What time is it?"

Dursley glanced at his wrist and said, "It's at least two hours before breakfast. Why don't you get some more sleep?"

I agreed. I got back to sleep and was awakened by my alarm clock. I woke and dressed. We had set up a makeshift galley. I was the second to arrive. When I sat, I got out Wendt's purse and opened it. I brought his Glock out and the spare click . . . er clip. I removed the clip from the Glock. I was in the process of making sure that both clips were fully loaded.

The B. G., who had preceded me, asked, "You really are going loaded for bear: your wand and Wendt's Glock."

Just then Aurora followed closely by Dursley came in. They went to the food printer and asked what we'd like for breakfast. I asked for two eggs, sunny side up, toast and jam, and two buttermilk pancakes.

Aurora responded, "The condemned woman ate a hearty breakfast."

I agreed and finished loading the Glock. The B. G. commented, "Both guns and wands for Jaimie."

I sighed and said, "Only guns."

Everyone stared at me. Dursley said it, "No wand?"

"Nope."

"Why not?"

I was on the point of tears as I handed my wand to Dursley. "Take good care of it. I can't stand the idea of my wand falling into the hands of those Souls."

Dursley wore a crooked smile. "Really? That would not occur to me."

I did sob a bit as I reached out for my wand. Dursley handed it back. When I had it, I said to the wand in a whisper, "I still love you."

Dursley smile turned to incredulity. "Say what?"

Aurora said, "I understand. There's a close relationship between magic folk and their wands. Even you should know that."

Dursley turned red and said, "Well, sure. But . . ."

Aurora went on. "I'm not quite that close to my wand, but I completely understand it."

I then handed my wand back to Dursley, who took it gingerly.

The rest of the meal was very quiet. We finished breakfast and were wondering what to do when the intercom came on, "Landing party to the shuttle."

Aurora responded, "I still have to suit up. I'll be there in fifteen." There was no answer.

I helped her suit up. Since I wasn't going to be wearing a suit, I could give her all my attention as she donned her suit. When we'd double and triple -checked everything, we walked to the airlock where the shuttle was docked. Inside the shuttle, we buckled into the co-pilot and observer's seats. We undocked and started the landing descent. The view of the planet was superb. It looked vaguely like Mars—if Mars had several oceans and taller mountains.

Shortly we began encountering the atmosphere, and individual clouds grew from little more than dots to huge storm clouds. Where we were heading was pretty clear. Shortly, the small city we were heading for became human-sized. I realized that I only had minutes until we reached our destination.

We landed. There were only six Souls standing on the tarmac waiting for us. We unstrapped and cycled the airlock. This was it. There were only seconds left. The outer door opened, and we stepped out onto the short, narrow ramp. The air had a smell that I couldn't identify. I was wearing translator earbuds. The words from the Souls was full of platitudes.

They led us inside to a Conference Room that was amazing in its similarity to every other Conference Room that either Wendt or I had been to whether it was a University or the Ministry or Gringotts or the corporate headquarters of Barclays or the SAS warehouse.

We sat. We refused refreshments. As we waited nervously for someone to start, I began to feel queezy. The room seemed to be doing a slow rotation. No. No. I shouted inside my head. I reached into the pocket of my jeans and found the Glock. I put my hand on it. Aurora noticed and tried to catch my attention. My hand grasped the hard, cold surface of the handle. I started to pull it out. It was so comforting to know that I could bring it out in seconds. Then a hand closed on my forearm.

Aurora looked into my eyes intently and asked, "Is there a problem?" That was enough to bring me back to earth or wherever we were. The dizziness passed, and I released the handle of the Glock. I said, "No. I think something I ate disagreed with me."

The tension was released from that moment. My mouth was no longer locked in a rictus.

The head of the Soul delegation gave a short speech.

"We have been preparing for this meeting almost as long as we have been faring interstellar space. We knew that we would meet a race that was smarter, stronger, faster, better in most ways than we were. We just didn't think that meeting would happen here on this world. We hoped that we would have a better bargaining position than we actually have.

"We've learned a lot from the races that we conquered, but we learned more from the races that we didn't. From your race, we learned that there is a special kind of contract that you call a covenant. That is an agreement where one side dictates all the terms. I'm afraid that we're in a situation that we never expected to be in—a covenant with the other side dictating the terms.

"We think it best if you dictate your terms, and we work out how we can live with them."

It seemed too good to be true to me. The commander of the PAK presented his terms. They boiled down to the following:

- No expansion to new planets or races other than those not occupied by intelligent races.

- Allow the vast majority of hosts to be freed expeditiously until every colony planet is turned back to its native race.

There was a sharp intake of breath from the Soul negotiators. I was not surprised, but the Souls clearly didn't expect such bold demands. They seemed to be dumbfounded by it. They immediately requested a recess. That was fine with all of us.

I asked the room, "Is there any reason for us to go into a conference."

Neither the PAK nor Aurora could think of one, so we waited. The conference went on for more than an hour.

When they finally came back in, there was a different atmosphere present. Maybe it was body language, maybe it was tone of voice, maybe it was something else. I knew that the negotiations were not going to be smooth from that point on.

The chief Soul negotiator said, "Your demands are out of the question for us. What you're talking about is tantamount to genocide. We have a modest suggestion.

"First, we agree not to expand our colonies." There was a pause. I knew that what followed would be worse. He went on, "Except, of course, for the new colonies which are midway through conversion. But what you want us to do with existing colonies is out of the question!" It was the first time that I'd seen a soul speak excitedly. "It's just plain impossible."

That made me angry. I exploded, "You know that's a lie. On Earth, my planet, your people figured a way to revive the vast majority of people."

The spokesman swung around and said something in a language that I'd never heard before. There was a conversation that went on for several minutes. Then he turned back and said, "I'm told that you are substantively right. However, it was a crash program that cost us immensely."

The PAK was strangely silent, but Aurora wasn't going to be. She almost shouted herself. "Oh, come on. Give me a break. The Earth never received anything except ships full of Souls from the time they started on the project until they completed it!"

The Soul leader spoke. "On the Home World, we dedicated a large fraction of our biology research staff to support that effort on Earth. They would not have succeeded without our efforts. We can not repeat that effort a hundred times or more."

Then the PAK spoke. "We have not talked about the realities on our side yet. Now I will. The Earth citizens have decided to call us PAK. I know why and am flattered by it. That is not the name by which we refer to ourselves.

However, it is such a simple, easy to pronounce name that I will accept it for our purposes.

"I am not a negotiator for the PAK. I was sent here to commit the real genocide that goes far beyond your 'tantamount' genocide. I act now only for my own purposes, which are to save you from the genocide that you are rightly concerned about.

"The negotiations that we are doing are to establish a reasonable offer that I will make to the real PAK authorities to save your race from destruction. They will arrive soon. You have very little time. They will arrive with the intent to succeed where we failed. They will come with overwhelming force and without the hindrance of human intervention on your behalf."

The Soul's expression changed abruptly. He turned to me and asked, "You intervened for us? But . . . but . . . we colonized you."

I shrugged. "We destroyed the ship that they intended to use to vaporize your solar system."

He leaned back and then asked, "Why? How?"

Aurora said to me, "You tell why. I'll handle the how."

I explained. "There are people on Earth who would just as soon see your system vaporized as they would spit in your faces. Most of us are opposed to the destruction of a race as we would be to capriciously killing a dog. That is, provided that the dog is not rabid. You seem to be doing your best to convince me that you are rabid."

Aurora jumped in before he could say anything, "As to how we did it, it's none of your damn business."

The Soul shook his head and said, "I don't believe it. I don't believe it's possible."

The PAK responded, "There is no way to demonstrate to you before my people arrive. If the little lady had not destroyed my ship, it would be easy. Of course, if she'd not destroyed the ship, you'd have received an upfront demonstration, and the whole question would be moot."

The Soul shook his head again. "I can't agree to that without real proof." He seemed to be facing a real quandary.

The PAK commander announced that he was going to go into conference with the PAK on the ship. Aurora would be able to hear over her suit radio, but there was no way for me to. He requested that the Souls leave the room.

They left. The PAK said, "Ms. Brahms, please opaque your helmet and turn on your audio privacy switch."

I could see her mouth drop. "How do I do that?"

"Just focus your gaze on the scroll button for a couple of seconds and blink slowly until the security screen comes up. Then you can turn those on."

I could see the heads-up display flicker a few times, and then the helmets opaqued, and I could hear nothing. Aurora occasionally moved her arms as she would if she were making points. The motions became more and more violent. Finally they subsided and her shoulders slumped a bit. That was not the end of the conversation. As this was going on I wished that we'd been able to have that sort of conference while we were traveling here. It would have made things very much easier.

Eventually, the screens cleared and Aurora came close to my spot at the table. She pulled a small paper tablet from an exterior pocket in her suit along with a mechanical pencil. She wrote a few words on a page, tore it out, crumpled it, and put it in the pocket. She repeated that several times. If you concatenated the entire message it read something like:

"Let Soul into you... Do Unbreakable Oath... They only can see... what you show them." My eyes must have been as wide as pie plates.

I exclaimed, "Are you crazy! I'm not going to do that."

She said, "It's the only way to convince them. Just follow our lead. You can always bail out if you don't like it."

The PAK went to the door and invited the Souls back in. The PAK said, "We've come up with a proposal about how you can see a demo of what we can do. Our human associates on our ship provided the idea."

I swung around to face Aurora. "It was the Boy Genius, wasn't it?"

She shook her head. "He was against it. It was Dursley who came up with the idea."

Then I knew that it was a serious proposal. He would never suggest such a thing if there were any other way.

The lead Soul shook his head in a strange way that I'd not seen before. He asked, "Are you sure that you're agreed on this?"

I answered, "Yes. We are. Aurora will explain."

She said, "Well, here it is in a nutshell. First, we Earthers have already seen a demonstration in our solar system. There was an Earth witness on the PAK ship for the demonstration. It was Jaimie.

"We propose that you or another Soul be inserted in Jaimie. She will show you what she saw."

He gave that strange head motion again. He asked, "Would you really submit to that?"

Aurora answered for me. "With certain precautions, yes. First, you must agree to a little procedure that we call the Unbreakable Oath."

The Soul asked, "What is this 'Unbreakable Oath'?"

Aurora said, "It's simple. You take the oath, and you can't break it. If you try, you die."

The Soul made some sort of sound that I guessed was the Soul equivalent of a laugh. He said, "This is just psychology, isn't it? You make me swear, and then you depend on my honesty to protect you?"

I laughed too. "No. It's real. If you don't believe, you can just try to break it. Then the next candidate following you will be more cautious."

He looked around at the other Souls, perhaps hoping that someone would volunteer to be first. No one did. He turned back to me and said, "All right, I'll do it. Let's get started. Do you need any special equipment?"

"No." Of course, it was a lie. Aurora would have to administer the oath with her wand, but I didn't want him knowing about wands. I pulled the right sleeve of my blouse back and commented, "You might want to remove your clothes from the arm where we'll take the oath. Having the skin free is helpful."

He slumped back in his chair and asked, "Can I be seated?"

"Sure. Just free up some space so that I can sit beside you and grasp your hand."

He nodded at the Soul next to him. That person stood up, backed away, and shook his head when a different chair was offered him. I took the freed-up chair and held out my hand. Meanwhile, the PAK and Aurora came over next to me. The Soul who'd given up his seat had to move to maintain his view of the operation.

The Soul said, "Is there a special way I should grasp your hand?"

"No. Just make sure that we have good contact that won't be broken despite what might happen." I hesitated and added, "You can back out at any time up to the last words of the oath that you repeat."

He nodded. Then he clasp my outstretched hand. Aurora moved a bit closer and stretched out her hand. I could just see the end of the wand clasp in her hand and almost completely concealed by her hand and the sleeve of her blouse. She said softly, "I may have to take my suit arm off but I hope not." I hoped not too.

I did the detail explanation. "OK. The way this works is that Aurora will say the oath in short phrases. She'll pause after each to allow you to repeat. After you repeat each, she'll go on to the next. When you've repeated the last, it's over."

He stared at me. "That's it? How will I know that it's worked?"

I smiled. "Believe me. You'll know."

He nodded his head and said, "Let's get it over with."

Aurora nodded too and began. "I swear that I will not . . . ."

He was slow with the first repeat, but he soon got the idea, and the rest followed smoothly. With the first phrase, a few tendrils of light encircled both our hands and arms. I couldn't feel anything. The Soul was visibly affected. His grip loosened momentarily, but he quickly resumed it. Aurora went on. "examine Mrs. Jaimie Brewster's mind or memory . . ."

The tendrils brightened, thickened and tightened. I felt them for the first time. Aurora went on. "other than what she willingly. . ." The tightening made my arm uncomfortable. The brightening of the tendrils of fire would have allowed someone to read a newspaper by their light. Of course, no one could possibly spare attention for a newspaper.

Aurora continued, "without any form of coercion. . . " Now the tendrils were intensely bright, and the pressure was positively painful. I longed for the oath to be over.

Aurora finished, "shows me." The Soul gasped out the last phrase with an explosion of air. Then it was over. The tendrils disappeared. The terrible pressure that had almost made me wish that I wasn't involved with this oath was gone. I was not the only one to release a held breath.

The Soul quickly released my hand, turned to another Soul, and said, "Bring what we need to transfer me into her." That Soul rose quickly, and left the room.

Aurora asked what he was bringing. The Soul said, "Some anesthetic, healing salve, a clean scalpel."

With those words I shivered. The other Soul brought the required surgical tools quickly. The Soul said, "This will only take a couple of minutes. Please lean over the desk. My assistant will make incisions in both our backs. He'll withdraw the Soul from my current body and insert it in yours. With the anesthetic, you should feel nothing more than a slight prick. You won't lose consciousness. You may feel something of a shock when I begin to integrate myself in your nervous system."

I protested, "But, you'll somehow ask me to show you what I want to?"

"Yes, I've done this a lot. I'll block everything except what you don't want blocked."

"How can you be sure?"

"Believe me, I've been in some resistant hosts. I know what is open and what they are trying to keep closed. I believe that the oath will work. I don't want to be rummaging around any more than you want me to."

I still wasn't satisfied. I hadn't felt anything, but in a short while I felt the shock that he talked about. It was like some unwanted lover caressing you while you were trying to resist. I heard his voice—not with my ears but in my head. He said, "OK. I'm ready. Go ahead."

I asked inside my head, "How do I do that?"

"Just call up to your memory what you want me to see. I'll see it."

It wasn't as easy as he thought. It was as though I were a Soul delving in a host's memories. Only, it was Wendt who was the host, and I was the Soul. Sometimes it was easy to find memories that I wanted. Sometimes it was quite hard. The Soul was gently prodding me. "Are you ever going to show them to me?"

I snarled inside my head. "This isn't as easy as you think. Give me a few minutes." I tried to think of a trigger that would bring the memory to mind. Then I had a thought. I tried to imagine the scene from the movie *Star Wars* when the planet Alderon was exploded by the Death Star. In that instant, I had it. I saw the inside of the ship in the Control Room. Wendt/I was sitting at the control panel of the weapons system.

I shouted in my head, "Can you see this?"

I heard the soft reply, "Yes."

The perception of time was different. I vaguely heard the voice asking me to choose the target. I was looking at the South Polar region of Mars. I seemed to be taking forever deciding. I moved the targeting reticle over the screen with a finger. I seemed to want to move it at random. I recognized that the pattern that Wendt was tracing was not random. It was actually him writing with my finger the name, Jennifer. Eventually, Wendt paused. The screen went white. When the optics recovered from the shock, I could see a vast hemisphere of expanding red-hot gas and magma. For a moment I was afraid that it would just keep expanding until it engulfed me. It didn't. I heard a gasp from somewhere. Maybe it was me. Maybe it was the Soul. I still don't know.

The cloud expanded horizontally, and parts of it had started looping down like the flow from a garden hose. I don't know if I actually cried, but I certainly did inside. The Soul said softly, "I've seen enough. Tell them that I've seen enough! Get me out of here."

I tried a couple of times opening my mouth. Once or twice I had experienced sleep paralysis. It was hideous and frightening. I wasn't able to move my body no matter how much I tried. This was like that only worse. I had to say something or this horror might continue forever. I think I heard a moan come out of my lips. I tried again. It seemed like I must be shouting, but nothing happened. Then I finally knew that I had said a single word, "Enough."

Shortly after that another shock convulsed my consciousness, and I felt some control of my body. It was like the experience of a limb falling asleep. There was little feeling in my body other than a tingling. I swallowed and formed a simple phrase, "He's had enough."

I heard Aurora say, "We know. We've removed him, and they've put him back in his own body. How are you doing?"

I nodded feebly and said, "OK. I guess. I want to stand up. I'm tired of my head lolling on this table."

Aurora said, "Sure." I felt hands under my armpits. My body felt light, but then my weight came down on my feet. I was still so weak that I had to use a hand to help me support my weight. I struggled around the table and sat in my original chair. Then I asked, "Convinced?"

The lead Soul seemed to have shrunk down into himself. He still seemed to be as disoriented as I felt. After a few minutes he sat up and said to his companions. "We've got to talk." He turned to us and said, "This may take more than a day. You should probably return to your ship."

I for one was happy to hear that. We agreed and returned to our ship. The trip up to the ship seemed almost nonchalant. We ended up spending three days waiting. The only person who was not progressively more nervous as time went on was the PAK leader. I asked him about that. His answer was, "I'm not really excited about the Souls getting off the hook. If my people arrive before they're finished with negotiations, and we obliterate them, it's as you folks say, 'no skin off my nose.'"

The summons came for us on the fourth day.

We were back in the original Conference Room but there were differences. There was only one Soul there—the lead Soul. He began the meeting with a peroration. "I am the only Soul here because I have no bargaining role. My only assignment is to agree to your terms and try to work out the details so that we actually can achieve them. So, go ahead and dictate terms."

The terms were much as we'd laid them out before. The Soul pressed us for details. What was the schedule for releasing colonies? Did we want a list of colonies and locations. He went on and on trying to coax details out. Finally, the PAK said, "I have no control of those details. As a matter of fact, I can't even guarantee that the PAK fleet commander will even be prepared to negotiate at all."

It was almost pathetic how willing the Soul was to meet any conceivable demand we might have. He began to make offers on schedules that seemed unbelievable to me. He offered to restore colonies to their natives one per week. I didn't see how that could be possible, but he said, "Is that not quick enough. We might be able to cut a few days off that, but it would be exceedingly difficult.

"We'd have to take chances with the retraining program so that the hos . . . that is natives could take over their own management."

I grimaced. He responded by saying, "Please. . . It's the best that we can do."

I shook my head. "Sorry, that's not my area."

He then made a personal request. "Could you please release me from that awful oath. I shall never forget the feeling of pressure and the terrible consequences of breaking the oath."

Aurora shook her head, "Sorry. There's no way. But there's good news. The only way you could get into danger would be if you were to re-insert yourself into Jaimie and try to overcome her resistance. Otherwise, you're as safe as though you had never taken the oath."

He didn't seem entirely convinced, but that was not my problem. He deserved to live in uncertainty like so many of his victims. I thought about it a moment and said, "Now you know what it is to be a slave—to live in fear."

He definitely didn't find that comforting. The PAK promised that he would contact the Souls as soon as a decision was made to negotiate with them or not. He finished by saying, "We've done all we can here. We will return to our ship and wait just as you will have to."

Those were the last words that were spoken on that planet by our party. We returned to our shuttle and flew up to our ship. Knowing that I did not have to return to that god-awful planet was unspeakably comforting. We approached our stolen ship. Airlocks linked and we stepped through to the interior.

We had only to wait. Well, we actually had more to do than that. I had to worry. A constant topic of speculation was how long it would be before the assumed PAK fleet would arrive. After a week or so the tension had grown to the point that even the ever imperturbable PAK decided that we needed to have a conference.

This time, we humans donned space suits and we met in a Conference Room in the PAK part of the ship. I've always had a hard time distinguishing PAKs one from another. Fortunately, there were only three PAKs present. One was the ship's engineer, recently promoted because of his superior's death. I suggested that we would call him Mr. Scott because his real name was too hard for humans to pronounce. I could usually identify him because he had a scar on the back of his right hand.

Going with the metaphor, I decided to call the PAK captain, Picard. He always was clearly deferred to by other PAK, so it was usually possible for me to identify him even though I couldn't find a clear physical distinguishing characteristic that he had. The third was the someone whose role I could never figure out. At least, he had a clear physical trait. He had larger ears than anyone else among the PAK on the ship. It was terribly tempting to call him Spock, but I resisted. I decided that I'd just call him XO because that seemed to be his role. When I proposed those nicknames, they accepted. On the fairly frequent occasions when I misspoke they corrected me.

All four of us humans were present. Picard started the meeting. He laid out the agenda. "We're here to discuss what will be happening when the fleet arrives."

I interrupted. "You're awfully sure that the fleet will arrive soon, aren't you?"

Picard smiled as he responded. "Yes, I am. We gamed this possible outcome in mission planning."

I was afraid to ask the obvious question. The B. G. anticipated me by asking with a bit of tremble in his voice, "You gamed having your mission foiled by humans?'"

Picard made that funny sound that I'd come to associate with laughter, "Of course, you foiled the previous mission. We would be fools not to prepare for the possibility." He quickly added, "But really, we gamed mission failure regardless the cause."

The B. G. gave a sigh of relief and then said, "Go on."

Picard did. "If our ship hadn't returned within the time it took to return to our home world plus a couple of days AND we had sent a message with the position of the Soul home world, a larger force would be sent to finish the job."

I was surprised that he expected the arrival of the fleet so quickly. Scott answered the question before I had a chance to ask it, "You're probably wondering at how quickly we expect the fleet. It took us several weeks to travel from Earth to the Soul's world. Shouldn't it have taken a similar time to travel from our world to the Soul's world?"

The B. G. nodded. I recognized that nod as one he uses when an idea's struck his fancy. Apparently, the XO noticed as well. He interrupted, "I think Mr. Brahms may have an idea about that."

The B. G. gave us a "who me?" look, but I agreed with the XO. I said, "Come on. The XO's right. Give."

The B. G. grumbled a bit about premature, half-cocked ideas but did give us his idea. "The thing is that when we traveled from Earth, maybe we weren't going as fast as we could have IF you'd known exactly where you were going. You only had a vague idea. You depended on our somatic memory of the travel to fine tune your course. That required you to go at the same, slower speed that the original mission was restrained to. So, you've substantially improved your ships since our first flight, right?"

Picard smiled again. "Yes, that's essentially it. There's a bit of uncertainty but I expect our fleet to arrive tomorrow or the day after. That brings us to the sticking point." He stopped

Dudley prodded him. "Which is what?"

Picard released a held breath and said, "Here's the thing. In our gaming, we hadn't anticipated that we'd survive but not be able to complete the mission, so the fleet is going to arrive intending to fire as quickly as possible. We've been transmitting a coded distress signal for the last couple of days.

"However, I have not a lot of hope that the fleet will receive it, believe it, and hesitate to demolish the star before we can stop them."

I asked, "Then we are doomed?"

Scott said, "Not necessarily. If we were to leave at the maximum acceleration that this ship can make right now, we might be outside the kill radius when the shock wave hits us. We don't know how strong the shock will be or how much impact this ship can take."

The B. G. asked, "If we do that, does that affect the probability that your fleet will get our distress signal?"

Scott just said, "It can't help."

Picard summed it up. "So, you see, we can maximize our chances of survival by abandoning the system right now. However, that minimizes the chances of stopping the fleet from destroying this star system. Thus we have a little moral question before us.

"I want your input on this decision. I don't guarantee that I'll follow it— just that I'll consider it."

The four of us looked at each other. Picard asked, "Do you want a little time and privacy to consider?"

My hope of returning to Sissy and Ed seemed to evaporate before my eyes. Picard prodded me. "So, do you want some time?" The rest of us were lost in our own thoughts about loved ones lost.

I said, "No. I think we should just each of us individually give our preference. As for me, I'm willing to trust your fleet to at least save us. I think we should stay and try to convince them to accept our negotiations."

Dudley almost too quickly agreed. "I'm with Jaimie on this. She's almost always right when it comes to moral issues." He colored a bit and added softly, "And just about everything else as well."

The B. G. shrugged, "I go along with them." Aurora nodded assent.

Picard said, "I'll make my decision shortly and let you know as soon as I do."

Scott said, "If the captain decides to run for it, we'll be undergoing some pretty wild acceleration. You should probably keep your suits on and take to your bunks. I doubt that the gravity generators will be able to compensate for the acceleration completely."

We went back to our section of the ships and took to our bunks. I wondered what Picard meant by soon. I didn't have much of a wait to find out. We were hardly in our bunks when the announcement came.

We received the anticlimactic announcement that we were going to stay put with disappointment. I think that the idea of doing something rather than waiting quietly for our fate appealed to all of us. Besides wanting to run from danger, I had the irrational desire to experience that tempestuous acceleration that Scott had promised. Instead we were going to be sitting.

So, we moped around the improvised meeting room/cafeteria in our section of the ship. We hadn't even bothered to take off our suits. I for one was half hoping that there would be a change in heart on the part of Picard and we'd need to prepare for emergency acceleration at any moment. It didn't happen.

What did happen was that we eventually had to take off our suits for a biology break. It was clear by then that we were in for the long wait. The next day during dinner an announcement came over the PA, "This is the captain speaking. The fleet has just arrived. They've located us and are about to rescue us. I've sent a message requesting that they hold off vaporizing this system until we've been rescued and have had a chance to present a request."

We'd barely finished dinner when the captain announced that everyone should collect their belongings and prepare for immediate evacuation to the main ship in the fleet. We suited up. Picard himself came down to our section to escort us onto the PAK ship.

It turned out to be a ship very similar to the one on which we'd come. We were ushered immediately to the bridge. It was much like the one that we'd been on before. Picard addressed the PAK who was apparently in charge of the fleet. He requested that the commodore enter into negotiations with the Souls rather than destroy them.

The commodore, whom I'd decided to call Kirk, was succinct. "Make your case and make it swiftly. My weapons officer is ready to fire on an instant's notice."

Picard said, "We've been dealing with the Souls for over a week. I think they are sincere in agreeing to stand down from all their colonies. They will return the planets to their native populations. If they renege, it will be easy for us to destroy the system. We can keep a small ship on station. Any attempt to approach it would trigger it to fire. Any turpitude on their part would result in the destruction of their system."

Kirk turned to me. "You did this, didn't you?"

I was surprised by the accusation—if it were accusation. I fumbled a bit before coming up with an answer. "It was not I alone. It was just right to prevent genocide where possible safely."

Kirk then said, "I can't make that decision on my own. I will consider the options and be back with you." He then turned to us and said, "I just don't know what to do with you humans." With that he turned and we were escorted off to the hangar where there were several ships of similar design to the one on which we'd traveled." We entered one via its airlock. Inside the air was pretty close to Earth normal.

The next day we were able to really relax for the first time since we'd started this crazy trip. I was pretty sure that the PAK would end up making a peace treaty with the Souls. We'd probably be sent home, and if we weren't, there was little we could do about it.

We had little warning when it happened. The ship's intercom came on and announced that we should prepare for guests. We all looked at each other, wondering whom they could possibly mean. They surely wouldn't refer to any PAK as a guest. There wasn't another human in a thousand light years. Whom did that leave?

The airlock cycled, and two figures in space suits came through. It was hard to tell who they were until they took off their helmets. When they did, Aurora exclaimed, "What are you doing here!"

The B. G. asked, "Frank and Jes isn't it?"

Frank replied, "Yes, you're right. We are here to return you to Earth."

The B. G. seemed to take it as something of an insult. He said, "We're perfectly capable of piloting this ship on our own."

Jes said, "Oh, we know that, but the commodore wants to be sure that you don't do something foolish like trying to follow the fleet to their home world."

Frank picked up the narrative. "He could have sent a PAK, but he thought that was a task too menial for a PAK. Our Soul leader thought of us when he was asked by the PAK for some Soul to accompany you—for your own safety, you understand. The commodore would hate to blow you out of the sky."

I said, "I'm glad to hear that."

Jes asked me, "Who are you and this other fellow?"

Dursley said, "This other fellow is Dudley Dursley. I was selected to go in place of Mrs. Wendt. She is Mrs. Jaimie Brewster. She was selected to go in place of Mr. Wendt, who was unavailable for the trip."

Jes shook his head in a clear sign of confusion, "Don't you mean the other way around? You replace Mr. Wendt and she replaces Mrs. Wendt?"

I smirked. I wondered how he'd answer that question. He did have an answer, "Mr. Wendt is irreplaceable, so I say I replace Mrs. Wendt. And . . . somehow Mrs. Brewster sort of channels Mr. Wendt. Of course, I sort of like having her on-board so . . ."

This had gone far enough. I broke in, "Well, for one, I'm anxious to get home. Can we get going?"

Frank answered, "Of course. If Mr. Brahms would care to take the pilot's seat, I'll take the co-pilot's and get in touch with launch control so we can get on our way." With that, the B. G. strode to the Control Room hatch and opened it. Frank followed. Shortly after they entered, the B. G. came on the intercom to announce that we were about to be cleared to exit the larger ship. It happened with a clang and hardly a shudder.

You Can Go Home Again . . .

The road home was not nearly so long as the road away from it. The flight took just over a fortnight. I had totally lost track of time. My watch was strictly a three hand analog watch with no other function. However, the B. G. had a really amazing totally mechanical watch that had day/date/ hour/ minute/second. It was pretty accurate as well. I sort of refused to know what date it was by the time that we arrived at the Soul home world. The cycle of day and night on the ship was synchronized with the PAK's home planet so by that time, my internal clock was pretty screwy anyway. On the way home, it didn't get any better.

The day before we arrived, I asked the B. G. what the date was. He said, "It's 6 September, a Monday. I suppose that Hogwarts is in its first week of the new term."

By this time, I'd completely forgotten that I was supposed to start teach- ing again. I'd already lost at least three teaching days. Besides that, it might take me a full day just to get lesson plans up to snuff for the next week or so. I was feeling a bit overwhelmed. The B. G. punched me on the shoulder and said, "Cheer up! We'll all be back to the people we care about tomorrow."

It was true. That raised a question. Where did I go first—home to Ed or to Hogwarts and Sissy? I'd probably have to waste some time if I went home first. Ed wouldn't be back home till supper time. But that was where I belonged first and where my heart drew me most.

The next morning at breakfast the two Souls were almost maudlin. Frank asked if this were the last time we'd see one another.

Dudley was the least involved emotionally with them. He gave the first answer. "From what I can tell, you guys keep popping up religiously. Why would anyone think that we won't run into each other again?"

321

The B. G. said, "No offense intended, but it seems like someone is always in big trouble when you show up. Frankly, I'd just as soon not meet up with you guys again soon."

Jes laughed. "None taken."

Aurora said, "Well, it doesn't matter. When it happens, it happens. I'm just glad to be back home to Hogwarts."

Frank turned to me. "What about you?"

Memories bubbled up from Wendt—the death of Minerva, the planets with hundreds of millions dead, a gun in his hands wreaking his vengeance on the two PAK pilots. It was as much as I could do to hold back the tears. I just shook my head. I don't know what the Souls made of that. I didn't care. I just wanted to be on solid ground again.

Of course, that didn't happen so quickly as I hoped. Shortly after breakfast, we watched the descent of our ship from upper orbit through the atmosphere. It was a little bumpy as we descended through a cloud level. Then the sea opened below us. At that moment I remembered that we would be returning via submarine. So, my rosy plans for the day with Ed evaporated before my eyes along with my hope of being on solid ground.

We shortly found ourselves standing on the deck of the USS Ohio. It was a cloudy day with gusting winds and chill temperatures. The hatch in the sail opened and we were ushered in and down to officer country. We entered the officer's Mess and were greeted by the XO, Mr. Wainwright. He stood and said, "Welcome home!" However, next to him was a civilian who was still seated. He was quickly introduced by Wainwright as Paul Rucker, an analyst with the CIA. We shook hands around. However, he never looked directly at any of us, even Wainwright.

He had a good bit to say, "I'm here for your debriefing. Mr. Wainwright will also be conducting it for the ONI. I hope this can be fairly quick. I understand your wanting to get home to hearth and family." His darting eyes that never settled on anyone made me wonder just how much he did understand that.

He asked all the standard questions. Where did we go? How much time did we spend at each location? What could we tell him about the technology that the Souls had? The PAK?

Eventually, he began to repeat questions. This seemed to be on its way to being like a police interrogation. He eventually stood up and began to rant. "You say that the PAK whom you call Picard went from being a fucking genocidal maniac to being a defender of the Souls. Do you think I'm an idiot?"

I almost stood myself. I said loudly, "You'd think we were PAK the way you're treating us."

Dursley seemed the least perturbed of all of us even though he was the youngest. He just smiled and said, "Mr. Rucker, do you think that you're going to pressure us into revealing some deep, dark secret. Maybe we have Souls inserted in our nervous systems? Maybe we are agents of the PAK? There's nothing more that we have to say. You've asked every possible question. I don't know about the rest of us, but I'm not answering any more questions. I'd rather go back to Little Whinging and eat my Aunt Marge's dog scraps than give you one more word."

That little speech, which was quietly delivered and without the least hint of rancor or fear seemed to galvanize the other three of us.

Aurora said, "I'd rather go back to Azkaban and eat prison food."

The B. G. said, "I'd rather go back to the SAS and eat Sally's cook's creations."

I said, "I'd rather go back to the Weasley's Wizard Wheezes and eat Puking Pastilles."

We all sat still and stony silent. Wainwright could hardly keep from laughing. He had been fully occupied making notes. Now he just leaned back and watched the show.

The show was brief but entertaining.

Rucker walked behind the B. G. and said, "You'll not enjoy Yemen as much as you enjoy the SAS bilge." No one budged an inch.

He walked behind Aurora and said, "You may not enjoy the federal penitentiary in Guantanamo as much as Azkaseltzer." She couldn't resist the temptation to say something. It was, "I'll tell you what. You go to Azkaban and I'll go to Guantanamo. The first one to cry 'uncle' sets the other free."

Rucker walked around the room turning ever more red. Then he walked behind me and said, "I think you'll find Guantanamo less appealing than Weaser's Weasel whatchamacallits. I actually giggled, but Dursley showed the first emotion since he'd made his statement. He squeezed the arms of his chair and showed signs of wanting to rise. He didn't.

Rucker said, "Ah, interested in the little lady, are you?"

Dursley immediately relaxed and said nothing. Wainwright could not restrain himself further. He began a series of wheezes that sounded an awful lot like laughing. Rucker whirled on him and shouted, "Call your captain down here!"

All humor fell from Wainwright's face like the ice-sickles from the roof on a cold sunny day. He said, "On the captain's ship no one tells him where to go." He paused and added, "I will call him and see if it is his pleasure to come down."

He picked up the phone and spoke into it softly for a moment. Then he came back to the table and said, "The captain will be here presently."

323

We all waited expectantly. It was about fifteen minutes. Rucker was clearly displeased but he managed to be under reasonable control. The captain entered the room. Wainwright snapped to attention and said, "Captain on the deck." We all followed suit including Rucker.

The captain asked, "Someone wanted to see me very much?"

Rucker said, "Sir, I'm not getting cooperation from these people."

The captain nodded and said, "You are the interrogation expert, aren't you?"

Rucker reluctantly said, "Yes." Perhaps he suspected a trick question.

Then the captain nodded and said, "So, you shouldn't need help, right?"

Rucker shook his head and said, "These are a bunch of tough cases. They refuse to talk."

The captain looked at us one at a time. Then he turned to Rucker and said, "Let's see, two women, a kid barely old enough to vote, and a geek. Those are the big bad terrorists who you can't get to talk to you." He then turned to Wainwright and asked, "What about you, Wain? Have you been getting what you need from these monsters?"

He shrugged and said, "Sure."

Rucker grumbled, "They're tougher than they look. I've got to take them with me for more interrogation."

The captain looked at Wainwright and said, "I promised you and your wizards the next shot. Go ahead."

I was surprised. We weren't done? Wainwright turned to the hatch and started to walk out. Rucker worked his way around in front of the captain. He shouted, "You can't do this. I'm not done."

The captain turned his head slightly to aim at Wainwright. He said, "Mr. Wainwright, on your way out, have the master at arms come to my mess."

Wainwright turned his head quickly and said, "Aye, sir." Then we left the mess. We went up to the deck level. Once up there, Wainwright opened the hatch and said, "Go out. I'll be there in a minute." He closed the door and true to his words, he appeared a minute later with a smile on his face. Then he said, "Disapparate to the Ministry of Magic. We're expected in the Minister's suite. Mrs. Brewster, please take me with you."

I nodded and took his outstretched hand. The Brahmses disapparated and then I did. I went to the beach which was our ordinary meeting point. Then I disapparated to Oxford. I prepared for the final jump and Wainwright asked, "Why Oxford?" He had barely said it when we took the final jump that landed us outside the Cauldron.

I answered, "I don't know. I guess it's always seemed pretty to me. I wanted somewhere familiar and nice after so much time in space." He still hadn't released my hand. I was about to ask why when I realized that I would have to have his hand so that he could enter the Cauldron. I led him to the door and let him open it for me. Inside, I waved at Tom. He waved back. I went over, but Wainwright anticipated me. He had a twenty galleon coin out which he thumped onto the bar.

He said, "A round for as far as this will go." Then he commented to me alone, "I always have a couple in my pocket, you know, just in case."

I looked up into his face and nodded. "Right-o, just in case." Then I took his hand and led him to the hearth. I led him in, threw down the floo powder, and said, "Ministry of Magic."

We arrived in one of the dozens of hearths just outside the atrium. There was a witch on duty at the Visitor's Desk. We signed in, listing the Minister of Magic as our destination. She handed us badges and commented to the XO, "I like your uniform." He said, "Me, too."

We took the elevator up. We got another visitor's badge in the reception area of the Minister of Magic's suite and sat waiting for others to show up.

We were quickly followed by the Brahmses and Dudley. We didn't have to wait long. The secretary ushered us into the Minister's Conference Room. We took seats for the wait.

Shortly, a couple of people from the Auror's Office showed up—the head and Ginny Weasley. We shook hands. Only Ginny spoke with me. She said, "It's good that you've kept yourself healthy. I so very long to see Wendt."

Wainwright started to ask me something, but the Minster came in at that point, and we all stood for her. All conversation ceased.

She looked around and said, "Good to see you all hale and healthy. Please be seated." Then she said, "So, your mission to the Souls' world was successful?"

The B. G. answered, "Yes, Minister Moertl, it was quite successful. We stopped the genocide that the PAK were going to commit against the Souls. We think they are on the way to a successful peace."

She nodded agreement. Then she asked us to describe our mission in detail. That was the last question that we heard for quite a long time. Both Wainwright and Ginny were taking notes. We had a lengthy discussion in which each of us took up the narrative at various points. Whenever there was a pause or a disagreement about details, we all spoke bringing resolution to the point.

After we reached the end of our narrative, Pamela shook her head and said, "I didn't realize that you were going into such immanent danger. Do you think that the earth is well out of this dispute?"

We went around the room. Each of us expressed his or her opinion. Wainwright was first, "It seems solid to me. On the one hand the Souls are scared to death of the PAK. On the other, it seems like the PAK will not abuse their position of power. Would you agree?"

The rest did. I produced the only dissenting voice. I said, "I think the peace is fragile. A misunderstanding could break it easily. However, the Souls certainly have plenty of reason not to break it, I'm not so sure of the PAK."

Moertl nodded. Then Ginny asked, "Do you think there is danger for us?"

The B. G. said, "You can't ever completely rule out danger, but I think that the main danger is past. We are off to the side in a little backwater."

My companions nodded. I agreed with them. By this time I'd lost all notion of time. I glanced over at the B. G. and mouthed the word, "Time?"

He glanced at his watch and said, "I see that it's already well past noon."

Moertl sighed, "I suppose I must let you go now, but please keep yourselves available for further discussions."

With that we all rose and left the room. The Brahms, Dursley, Wainwright, Ginny and the Auror head left by the main entrance to Moertl's offices. Moertl invited me to leave via her personal floo connection in her inner office.

I agreed. She asked me to stay a few minutes for a drink. I did. I asked for Black Label Johnny Walker. She nodded and conjured a glass. "Ice?" She asked. I agreed. She filled the shot glass. She sat in one of the guest chairs. I sat in another next to her.

She said, "I understand that you have a lot of insight into Professor Wendt."

I cautiously agreed.

"Then can you tell me where he is and when he'll return."

I took a deep sip, playing for time to formulate an answer. When I did, I said, "I won't tell you a lot. However, I can tell you this. He is on an extended sabbatical. I don't expect him back for . . . oh . . . up to two or three years from now."

Her face fell. Then she asked, "Truly that long?"

"I'm afraid so."

She grimaced and took a long pull on her drink. "Is there any way that you can communicate with him?"

I very truthfully answered, "He can communicate with me and occasionally does, but it doesn't work the other way."

"So, you can't ask any questions and hope to get an answer."

I shook my head.

"If you don't mind, what are the last couple of things he's connected with you about?"

I thought about that question for a long minute. "Well, he was reminiscing about his adventures in space with the Souls."

The Minister just frowned and said, "Useful for you on your mission. I suppose he did that before your mission. Just great!" She was obviously upset. Why?

To be honest I could only say, "Yes, it was very useful on our mission. That was all though."

She was clearly not satisfied and hoped to get something out of the conversation, but what? She cleared that up quickly when she said, "You are the only one that he communicates with that way, right?"

I answered, "Well, yes."

She leaped on that swiftly, "But why you? There's someone else, true?"

It was my turn to grimace. As I did, a smile crept slowly over her face as though she knew she had me in some sort of admission. I again answered truthfully but not fully, "Well, it just occurred to me that someone might have been listening."

She seemed to have found some sort of triumph as she asked, "Then he only communicates with you?"

I nodded. She finished her syllogism, "Then you two are in a relationship?"

"Well. . . "

She followed on. "A romantic relationship!"

I could, at least, answer that fully and truthfully, "I am not in any sort of romantic relationship with Wendt. I will just add that I am a married woman with a husband and daughter. I am anxious to get back to them, so I am going to leave." I rose and headed for her floo connection. My motion was so abrupt that the jerk loosened the bun at the back of my head. I'd hardly ever let it down through the entire trip. It looked like it might come down on its own before I got home.

She hurried to catch up with me, grabbing me by an arm and swinging me around, loosening more of my hair. She said, "Don't you hide behind your husband's . . . uh. . . uh . . . pants. You're in love with Wendt, aren't you?"

My eyes burned fiercely. "You, you, hag! I love my husband and none else. I'm going to him now." I started to reach in my purse for my wand and remembered that I'd brought more than my purse. I glanced around and found my handbag. I strode over to it. I picked it up, returned to the hearth, and picked up a handful of floo powder. Then I threw it down announcing triumphantly, "My hearth in my house."

Nothing happened. I looked around in confusion, searching for the source of my problem.

Pamela smiled wickedly. "You've forgotten, haven't you, that I have a password on my floo connection."

I snarled, "Use it or I'll walk and go straight to the *Prophet* with the story of being held against my will in the Minister of Magic's Office."

She flipped her head of loose hair and nodded grudgingly. She walked to the hearth and said, "Step back so you won't hear it."

I did. She said something indistinct and stepped back. I entered the hearth, threw some floo powder, and spoke my destination. I spun through hyperspace or wherever you go when you travel by floo and stepped out in my floo in my house. On the mantelpiece, the page-a-day calendar read Wednesday, September 7. The clock read 10:37 AM. That raised a question for me: Wait here for Ed to get back home or go to Hogwarts to see Sissy?

I decided to wait for Ed. After all, Sissy would be in classes. I'd probably have to pull her out of one. That might be OK for a normal mom, but I was a teacher. I couldn't pull her out of class.

After showering, shampooing my hair, doing it up, and changing into something nice for a change, I spent the afternoon reading the *Prophet*. I had not been on Earth in many weeks but the *Prophet* had virtually no real information about what was happening in the world. We normally kept a couple of back copies of the *Prophet* around the house. Ed had kind of let his housekeeping drop off. There were a week or two of *Prophet*s around. I looked at the headlines. Nothing much was going on.

The biggest headline concerned Gringotts making some sort of deal with the Prime Minister to mint gold coins.

As I read the article, something strange happened. Memories from Wendt welled up as each point of the article was proved wrong by those memories.

I had to laugh at that article by the time I'd finished reading it. Practically everything in the article was wrong. The only thing that was right was that Gringotts was going to mint more gold coins than they normally do. The list of wrong things were that there was no mention of where the gold came from. There was no mention of the Muggle Prime Minister and the Muggle government's loan to the Ministry of Magic to allow them to buy gold.

There were other articles that were not quite so filled with errors, of course. The reporting on the qualifying rounds of the upcoming World Quidditch Cup was correct—I guess. I'm not a sports fan. I couldn't tell you the difference between a Wronski Feint and Fainting Fancy.

I do like the crossword puzzle in the *Prophet*, though. I can nearly always solve them completely. I had at least ten days of puzzles with the answers in the next *Prophet* available. I started working on one when I heard someone appear in the floo connection. I ran to the Family Room where I found that Ed had just stepped out of the hearth. I ran to him. We embraced.

The first declaration on each of our lips was, "God, I love you." The first question on each of our lips was, "Have you been OK?"

After establishing that we were both well and safe Ed suggested that we go to the Cauldron for dinner to celebrate. I instantly agreed. We went through the floo hand in hand. At the Cauldron Tom greeted Ed and then saw me. He said, "Well, it's good to see that your little lady is joining you for once. Have you been out of town for a while?"

I didn't know whether to scream or throw my arms about him. I settled for saying, "I don't know whom you're talking about. Little Lady indeed! And, yes, I have been out of town for a while. Do you have a quiet table where we could have dinner?"

Somewhat chastened, Tom led us to a nice table in a corner. We both had eaten frequently enough at the Cauldron that we could give him our order without hesitation. After he left, Ed lifted my hand to his cheek. He said, "I can't begin to tell you how happy I am that you're back. Have you let Cecily know yet?"

"No." I was rather afraid that his response would be disappointment. He surprised me by saying, "Good! We can have the rest of the night to ourselves and maybe tomorrow too. Tomorrow night we can go to Hogsmeade, and on Saturday catch up with Cecily. In the meantime, I'd like to work on getting you pregnant."

My response was, "Wo! That's all awfully fast."

He shook his head. "You know that I've only had a few weeks with you since we married. Who knows how much longer we'll have—even though we seem to be guaranteed three years. I'm anxious for Cecily to have a sibling." He hesitated, and his eyes dropped, "And for you to be a mom."

I couldn't help smiling at that. "OK. OK. You've won the day or maybe it's the night." He smiled, too. He'd been smiling from the first moment that we were together, but his smile was so wonderful now that I just couldn't look away despite the embarrassing subject matter. He was making it even worse by playing footsie with me. Well, I was not very troubled by that.

After dinner we found our way back to our home somehow. You'd think it wouldn't be that hard going by the floo network, but we managed to make it seem a struggle. The main problem was that we were doing some snogging while setting our destination. The first miss sent us the wrong Brewster house—his parents rather than ours. His mum, of course, assumed that it was intentional. She tried to talk us into staying for dessert and coffee, "It's been so long since you've visited! It might have been a mistake, but I'll bet it was half intentional like those Muggles say—a Floydian slip."

Ed corrected her. "That's Freudian slip, and it wasn't even a Freudian slip. It was just a lip malfunction while we were kissing."

His dad said, "Distracted flooing. It's bad enough when teenagers do it, but adults and a teacher to boot! Tsch. Tsch. Tsch."

We couldn't get out without having a slice of her pineapple upside-down cake. I've never dared to let her know that I really don't like cooked pineapples or pineapple upside-down cake.

The next Freudian slip sent us to the Goblin Brewhouse. At least, we didn't have any trouble getting out of there and finally back to our home. Ed made sure the doors were locked with a couple of well-aimed spells and levitated me into his arm. He swept me up to our room.

When he was done with me, I was sure that if I weren't pregnant it was only because I was in the wrong point in my cycle.

◿

We had little time left by the time we were finished for sleep, but we were exhauted enough to make it effective.

The next morning we dragged ourselves out of bed—or at least Ed did. I was happy to pretend to get up and then fall back in bed after he'd left for work. After weeks and weeks of alternating boredom and terror I was exhausted. Finally back in my own bed WITH MY ED BESIDE ME, I could sleep in peace. I did. It wasn't until noon that I arose to dress for real. I leisurely packed my bag for a weekend trip. It was so very different from packing for space that it was a luxury. I put in a dressy dress. Then I decided that I'd want that for tonight. I replaced it with a nice serviceable skirt for day time. I threw in a pair of . . . ugh. . . jeans. Because you just didn't know what might come up. Of course, there were a couple of tops and undies and so on. It was just like going on a trip, a second honeymoon.

I was still packing when the familiar whoosh of someone using the floo connection sounded. I wasn't expecting Ed. I picked up my wand and entered the hall at the top of the stairs. I boomed out, "Who's there?"

Ed laughed. "It's just me honey. Don't petrificate me."

I tried to keep my sigh of relief inaudible and went downstairs to be wrapped in my hubby's gentle arms. After a little affectionate snogging I asked, "Why are you home so early?"

His smile lit the room. He said, "Can't a guy ever get the flu on Friday afternoon without being questioned relentlessly?"

I smiled so hard that my face burnt and crinkled, "Absolutely. I understand completely. What are we doing?"

"I thought we might register at the Three Broomsticks and have an early dinner there before going to Stratford-Upon-Avon to see a play. Then we could return to Hoggsmeade for some real play."

I agreed enthusiastically. Of course, I would have agreed enthusiastically to going skinny-dipping in the North Sea with Ed. This turned out to be much more enjoyable.

Just as we were leaving an owl showed up addressed to me. I opened the letter. A reply was not expected because the owl took off immediately without even an owl treat. The letter read:

"My dear Ms. Brewster, I've just heard of your return. Please take your time getting back to Hogwarts. You can take all of next week to prepare for classes. However, when you do get back, please drop by my office for a little chat.

"Best regards, Horace Slughorn, HMH."

Ed asked, "HMH? What does that stand for?"

I laughed. "You should know—Headmaster Hogwarts."

The dinner at the Broomsticks was not up to the best at Hogwarts, but it was wonderful to be back in familiar surroundings. Ms. Rosmerta tried to pamper us as best she could. She even brought out a linen tablecloth for our table.

Shakespeare was good. It was one of the less well-known plays, "Titus Andronicus." I could have wished for something lighter, but a depressing Shakespeare is better than a light Gilbert and Sullivan any day. We spent a totally heavy night in bed trying to get pregnant. Maybe I was in the wrong part of my cycle, but who cared?

The next morning we were up bright and early. We wanted to have breakfast with Sissy and hopefully surprise her. To maximize the surprise, we came in the floo in the Great Hall. We surprised more than Sissy. Everyone at the head table gave a gasp. Sissy was at our sides before we'd stepped out.

There were hugs and kisses all round. Sissy was paralyzed. She couldn't decide whether to ask me to tell about what had happened or monopolize the conversation herself about what had happened to her during the summer. I urged her to talk about herself. That won the day. She told us about going to Wizarding Summer Camp. They did things like camping out Muggle style one night—lighting a campfire with matches. Putting up a Muggle tent with only one "room", making smores on the campfire. She actually said that being a Muggle might be kind of fun—once in a while.

She also went to a tournament with her dad. It was a youth tournament. I asked her, "Was that boring? I think you must be better than the vast majority of players in that tournament."

She turned faintly red and said, "Well, it was a little like slumming. Once you've been to an adult tournament or two, the youth seem pretty tame."

Ed stared at her intently. She avoided his eyes. Finally she admitted, "Well, there was this one player that I lost to—in the final. BUT, really, he was really, really good."

I sighed. "I'm glad that you're not letting this setback discourage you."

She nodded. "Thanks, Mum."

I couldn't prevent a tear from forming in my right eye. I turned to Ed so that she couldn't see me. As soon as I could speak without a sob I said, "I hope you're not neglecting your studies."

She answered, "No, mum. I have the latest edition of *MCO* and I practice every night." She hesitated and added, "I know what you mean. I do my studies first. There's just one thing."

I shook my head. "What?"

"Well, I'm up for English lit this year. The head has been holding off having a sub. I think he was hoping that you'd be back soon. Here you are!"

I took up the thread. "And you were wondering what would happen with you if I were your professor?"

She nodded.

"Well, the Headmaster and I have to have a little discussion about that. I think it will happen Monday. I make no predictions as to what will happen, but I guarantee you this. If you are an ordinary student in my classroom, I will treat you that way—as an ordinary student. There will be no little preferences, no marks dropped from the grade-book, and especially no teacher's pet for you. Make sure you understand that from the beginning."

"Yes, Mum."

We whiled away the rest of the day and Sunday in various entertainments. We went to see a movie once. We went to Hyde Park for a picnic. We did a little clothes shopping at Harrad's. We even went to the British Museum. Sunday night we had fish and chips at a pub in the City.

After we dropped Sissy off at Hogwarts for the night, Ed and I went home and had a serious talk. I kicked it off with the discussion about where I'd stay during the school term.

Ed expressed his opinion clearly and forcefully, "I don't see any reason why you can't spend the nights here! It's only a few steps away to your office via floo in case you forgot something—like parchments to grade or incomplete lesson plans. You do a round trip in five minutes easy."

I said, "That sounds nice in theory. There is one or maybe it's a dozen problems with it.

"First, you're way too much of a distraction for me to do serious work like grading or lesson planning. Second, if I forget something, it's a major distraction to run off to find it. Third, Hogwarts is intended to be a residential school—not just for students—but for teachers as well.

"I don't have any problem spending the night here for special occasions or most weekends, but until I get my feet on the ground, I want to be able to be completely dedicated to my profession."

Ed snorted his disgust. "And what about your husband?"

"Oh, I don't think it will go on forever. Once I've got a handle on this school year and feel confident again, I'll spend a lot of evenings here—maybe even all evenings some weeks."

Ed grumbled, "Well, at least I should be able to spend some school nights with you in your suite."

It cost me a lot to say it, but I managed. "I don't think so at first. You are too bloody distracting for that at first." I took a deep breath and said, "And maybe I shouldn't come home the first weekend or two."

Ed threw his arms in the air. "Well, you might as well be at the center of the Galaxy for as much as I'll get to see you."

That released a well of tears that had been building throughout the argument. I quickly stopped them and declared, "You should have known that the life of teaching is not an easy one. After the first couple of weeks everything will ease up."

Ed turned his back and almost snarled, "That's what you say!"

"I do say it. And, I'm right. You'll see."

The nice thing about being newlyweds is that when you share a bed it's hard to stay angry all the time. We had a little make-up love making and got some sleep in.

That morning I was awake even before dawn. I couldn't sleep with the first day back at Hogwarts about to dawn. Ed was still asleep. I tried to get back to sleep but I was invincibly awake. I could lie there and imagine what school would be like or I could do something. I got up as quietly as I could, showered, did my hair, applied a little (very little) makeup and tried my best to dress without waking Ed.

It was a failure, of course. Ed was groaning as he rolled over in bed and said, "I guess we're all up. The sun is up a bit anyway."

I finished dressing and spent a half hour packing so that I could stay in my apartment in my office. Ed asked, "Aren't you going to have some breakfast before flooing away?"

I briskly said, "No time. I want to have breakfast at Hogwarts. If I leave right away, I can catch breakfast and maybe get a half hour with Slughorn before lunch."

He shrugged and asked, "How long before you leave?"

"Five minutes. I want to review what I've packed for completeness and leave right away."

He smiled. "Do you have one minute for a good-bye kiss?"

I smiled, too. "I think I can actually spare two minutes."

He claimed the two minutes right then. It was two minutes of the most intense kiss that I've ever had. Maybe it wasn't more so than any of Wendt's kisses, but I was not going to become a voyeur by rifling through his memories. When it was over, I picked up my handbag with my things and said good-bye. I hadn't checked things out, but it would be too dangerous to spend another minute there.

I walked into the hearth, turned to look back at Ed, threw some floo powder down, and said the fateful word's, "Professor Brewster's Office at Hogwarts."

I then stumbled out of my office hearth, tossed my handbag into my apartment, unpacked my bag, and ran down to the Great Hall. I discovered that most of the breakfasters were gone.

However, there was one lingerer that I was overjoyed to see—Sissy. She ran up to me before I'd walked half-way down to the dais where the teachers took meals. As she came close, I frowned and said, "We are now not Mother and daughter. We are professor and student. We will have no public displays of affection while we are in school."

Sissy gasped. It took my breath away too. She said, "Yes, ma'am. Sorry."

I relented a little. "That doesn't mean that we can't have some signs of affection when it's a Hogsmeade weekend away from Hogwarts."

She smirked. "Yes, ma'am."

"Now get along to your classes."

She turned and ran out of the Great Hall.

I proceeded to the office of the Headmaster. Sally was at her desk in the outer office as usual. She looked up and a variety of emotions played over her features. I think there was surprise, happiness, anger, and relief. Probably there were others. I couldn't define them. Finally, she asked, "You're here to see the Head?"

I nodded. She said, "I'm really glad you're back. . . but honestly. . ."

I thought I knew what she was going to say. I saved her the pain by saying it myself. "But you were hoping against hope that it would be Wendt who came through the door?"

Her mouth broke into the briefest smile as she said, "I'm afraid so. I'm sorry. . ."

I shook my head. "Don't be. I don't blame you. In your place that is precisely what I would have thought myself. As a matter of fact in the past couple of months there were times when I did wish that it were Wendt there rather than I."

She nodded and then suddenly said, "Oh! You know that Slughorn wants to see you. He's had me hold out an hour in his schedule morning and night for when you returned. Is eleven today too soon?"

"No. Believe me, meeting with him will be the easiest of the tasks I have today—I hope."

She was back to her usually efficient self. "You've got it.", she said brightly.

I returned to my office to try to make sense of the many memos and schedules that were stacked neatly on my desk. The two hours were past before I could have wished. I was then back to the Head's Office.

Sally greeted me with a smile and said, "Go right in. He's anxious to see you. I'll be bringing in something to drink and snacks if you are peckish."

I entered the inner office with the visages of all the old Hogwarts heads staring down at me. It's intimidating. I can see why the Heads like having all those portraits lining the walls from floor to ceiling.

Slughorn seemed to notice my gaze and said, "You know, it's probably more intimidating for me than you to have all those eyes looking over your shoulders." I laughed, and the nervous moment was broken. Sally brought in a tray with little water bottles, a steaming tea pot, cups, and a selection of biscuits.

I just said, "I'll have a cup o' if it's OK."

Sally just smiled and poured a cup. I refused sugar and cream. Slughorn said, "I refuse to use sugar substitutes or have them on any table in Hogwarts. Too many Muggle inventions already if you ask me."

He changed the subject. He asked, "I'm sure that you're not allowed to talk about your little adventures?" There was more of plea than question in the way he said it.

I had to agree. "Sorry. The story would be thrilling if I could tell it. . . as it should be."

Slughorn seemed genuinely sad, but went on to another topic. "There are really just two questions I have for you. First, how soon do you think that you can start up English literature classes?"

I answered, "I've not really had time to do a thorough assessment, but I believe that if I give it 24 x 7 as the Muggles say, I can be ready for classes next week."

He shook his head and clicked his tongue. "I'll not have any of my teachers running themselves into the ground before classes have started. . . Now afterwards is another story." We both chuckled at that, knowing how intense a profession teaching is.

I continued the smile, and said "Perhaps two weeks is not . . . too . . . much?"

"Oh, at least two weeks. If you need more time, just let me know. I doubt there are any English lit students that are pining away for it to start."

I said, "Well, perhaps there is just one."

He nodded. "Yes. That brings me to my second question. How do you think we should handle that one student who is pining for your class to start?"

I sank back into the red leather chair that I was sitting in and closed my eyes so that I could concentrate. "We had a discussion of that over a year ago."

"I remember. As a matter of fact, I've been thinking about that a good bit. It occurs to me that when we had that conversation I didn't know you very well. Now that I've had more experience with you, I'd like to propose something to you. If you agree."

"Go ahead and propose."

He leaned forward with a twinkle in his eye. "Here's what I have in mind. I know that you are a level-headed, intelligent young woman. I'm sure that you can handle the responsibility of teaching your own daughter and not giving her any preference. As a matter of fact, I suspect that you would lean over backwards rather than be perceived as giving Cecily any unfair advantage."

I nodded slowly. "OK. I think I agree. As a matter of . . ."

He quickly interrupted me. "Here's the thing. The real problem is with the other students who may think that you are showing her undue favor."

"I agree. So do you have any ideas?"

He chuckled, "As a matter of fact, I do." He leaned back. I suppose he wanted to increase the suspense. I just wanted him to get on with it. Then, he said, "I propose that you look for the first opportunity to discipline Cecily. Then instead of giving her lines or even an ordinary detention, send her to Filch for detention. I'll make sure that he doesn't do anything drastic, but it should be clear that you aren't making her the teacher's pet."

"I suppose that would work. It would probably be harder on me than her to give her such an extreme punishment for a mild offense."

Slughorn chuckled. "Oh, every student her age gets into trouble. She may even be more likely to do it in your class than in others."

I rolled my eyes. "I just gave her a lecture about how important it is that she tow the line in my class."

He clucked his tongue and said, "You've not had as much experience with fifth years as I have. She'll get into trouble, mark my words."

I closed my eyes and pursed my lips in hard thought. I decided that I'd like to try his offer. "Yes, I accept your proposal."

That was the meeting. He offered me lunch in his office, but I firmly refused saying that I really needed to work on my lesson plans. But as I was about to leave an idea occurred to me.

"Can I make a proposal to you?"

He was surprised, but agreed. I said, "You know that I teach English lit to alternate years—first, third, fifth, and seventh?"

"Sure. So?"

"Well, students lose a lot of what they learned one year when they have the next year off. We need to have some way to teach English the even number years."

Slughorn shrugged. "I think you've been doing a fine job as it is."

I hurried on to say, "But you don't have to teach the third and fifth years —like Cissy. We have to spend lots of time getting them back up to snuff."

Slughorn sighed, and his shoulders stooped. "I suppose you want me to try to find another English lit teacher."

I was gaining excitement as I went. "Not at all. I think there's a way that I can keep them up to snuff and not spend a lot of time."

Slughorn rolled his eyes but kept with me, "Go ahead."

"Well, I'd like to teach a one and a half hour course to the even number years. It would be strictly pass/fail. Parchments would be required monthly but I wouldn't grade them other than glance at them to be sure they were on topic. We'd just read and write reviews of what we read."

Slughorn snapped to when he heard my proposal. He started asking serious questions, "What about discipline?"

Thinking on my feet I said, "For small incidents, points would be deducted from their house. If it became habitual or for serious infractions, they'd be failed and would be ejected from class for the term. Failure to finish a term would result in having to re-take it the next year—with younger students."

Slughorn said, "Interesting idea. Would you try to do all three years this year?"

I shook my head violently, causing my fancy hairdo to simplify greatly, "No, I probably wouldn't even start next term except maybe with one year as an experiment. I admit that it might not . . ."

At this point Slughorn interrupted me to say, "We're into the noon hour. Please stay and have lunch with me while we discuss it further."

Since I didn't have anything else to do other than lesson planning, I agreed. Slughorn called Sally in and asked her to go down to the great hall to bring up a platter of sandwiches, fruit, and desserts.

I objected, "Sally doesn't even have magic to help her. I'm going down with to help her carry things." Slughorn grumbled but agreed.

Sally and I talked on the way down. She said, "I know you can't tell me anything about the mission you were on. Can you at least tell me if it was a success? Was it dangerous? Frightening?"

I answered, "You're right about everything. I can't tell you any details. It was a success. At least I think it was. It was dangerous. It was definitely frightening at times."

She then went deeply personal. "How are things with Mr. Brewster? I wouldn't like to lose my wife right after marrying her and then have her return just to leave again."

"Oh, when we're together just a slice of heaven, but you're right. We've not been together very much. As a matter of fact, I'm not seeing him until after I start classes up again."

Sally grimaced. She didn't have to say what she undoubtedly was thinking. I tried to explain how necessary it was to keep my concentration going until I started going. Sally wasn't buying it much. By that time, we were on our way up to Slughorn's office. I was levitating a platter of sandwiches and a bowl of fruit. Sally was carrying a plate with cookies and cakes.

We arrived at the office and set up on the small Conference Room table in Slughorn's inner office. We talked about details of my plans for the term and the future of the little classes that I called English survey courses.

The first week of planning went well. It was Sunday night of the second week. I had gotten to the point where all classes for the first term were laid out in rough. I was trying to decide whether to go back for a second round to smooth off the rough edges of the first month or so or to do a little noodling with the survey course idea I had. I was tired of planning, but I just couldn't leave it unfinished!

There was a whoosh in the floo. I looked up and found my husband emerging, covered with soot. I stood and started to say something, but he quickly rounded my desk and pulled me close enough to kiss. Then he kissed.

When we finished, he pulled back and said, "I thought you were kidding about spending the first couple of weeks without seeing me at all!"

I was suddenly struck with remorse about staying away from Ed so long. I could hardly meet his eyes. "Oh, you're right, but I have so much responsibility with this position here at Hogwarts. I just hate to stop before I'm finished."

Ed just shook his head slowly. "Don't you have at least a little sorrow about not meeting your responsibilities to me?"

I opened my mouth but didn't close it. It was partly because I didn't have a good answer. It was also partly because Ed's mouth had covered it and I found that I was totally happy about it. Shortly, I found myself being undressed in bed and then the real joy began.

That morning we parted very early. Ed didn't have any clothes in my apartment, so he left around 3 AM so that he could get in some sleep and then dress for work.

I dropped back to sleep but not until I'd reflected on the thought that it was the part of my cycle when I could get pregnant. I woke early convinced that I was pregnant. I went to the hospital wing to find Madame Pomfrey. She was not there, drat! I then went to the Great Hall hoping to find her at breakfast. No luck there! "Where could she be?" I wondered.

I finally decided that the best I could do was to go to the hospital wing to wait her out. She'd have to return sometime. When I arrived there, I found her in her office. I practically bit her head off when I saw her, "Where have you been! I could have been dying, and I couldn't find you!"

Pomfrey gazed at me unsympathetically. She said, "Well, I've been here all morning. And now you're keeping me from my breakfast, so this had better be good."

Full of indignation, I said haughtily, "Am I pregnant?"

She stared at me and asked, "Is that what's got your dander up? Why do you come to me? You could test that for yourself."

I was ashamed to admit that I'd not thought of that, so I meekly said, "Well, I just didn't trust myself to do the spell correctly."

That didn't mollify her, but she did say, "Well, come over here in front of me."

I was ashamed, but I stepped over to her and started to take my skirt off. She exclaimed, "What are you thinking of, girl? I don't need you to take your clothes off. Get dressed!"

I did. She pointed her wand at me but did her spell silently. After a moment she said, "Yes."

"Excuse me, what did you say?"

"Are you deaf, girl?"

I said "No."

Pomfrey announced calmly,"You are pregnant."

I jumped and whooped. She said, "Do you want to know the sex?"

"Oh, no. I mean, yes. I mean I have to talk with Ed about whether he wants to know."

"Well, you send him an owl and find out."

I practically skipped out of the hospital wing, almost forgetting to thank Madame Pomfrey profusely. I went to the Great Hall and caught the end of the breakfast. I was so excited that I could hardly force a couple of bites of scrambled eggs down my throat. I so wanted to tell someone that I started little conversations that I didn't know how to finish with the rest of the teachers on the dais. I said things like, "Isn't this a glorious day?"

Hagrid replied, "It's always a glorious day at Hogwarts. What's got you so excited?"

I could only open my mouth and say nothing. I tried to make up excuses for telling people, but I couldn't tell anyone before Ed. Then it occurred to me that there was one other person who had a right to know. right away. I ran up to the Head's Office and button-holed Sally. I asked her, "What class has Siss. . . that is, Cecily got right now?"

Her mouth dropped. I was afraid that she'd guessed what the news was, but I was wrong. She'd guessed the exact opposite. "Oh, Jaimie, something awful has happened, hasn't it?"

I laughed joyously. "Oh, No. NO. NOOO. It's just that. . ." Then I was stuck.

She shrugged and consulted a long print-out. "OK. She's in History of Magic class with Professor Binns. It's in room . . ."

I interrupted her rapidly, "I know where it is. Thanks! Thanks! A million times thanks! I'm going to pull her out of class this one day."

I sprinted all the way up two flights of stairs to Binns's classroom. I had to restrain myself from flinging the door open. Instead I just knocked on the door. A voice from inside called out, "Yes?"

I opened the door and said, "I'm sorry Professor, I'm pulling Ms. Brewster out of your class."

The ghost just nodded and waved his hand dismissively. She leaped up and said to me after we'd left the classroom, "Thank God!"

I did my best to remain calm and stern. I didn't want anyone to think I was giving Sissy any preferential treatment. I said, "To my office, young lady." That surprised Sissy and made her as solemn as I was trying to be. We walked, not ran, to my office even though every muscle in my body was straining to run and drag Sissy behind me. After going down a flight of stairs and walking the hall to my office, I opened the door, closed it behind me, and locked it. That was strictly against school rules, but I didn't care one whit.

I took her by an arm and turned her back to face me. Then I threw my arms around her and practically screamed, "I'm pregnant. You're going to have a little . . .uh . . . baby. . .uh . . . brother or sister."

She was stiff when I started to hug her but immediately squeezed me tighter than I squeezed her. "Oh, MUM, really?"

I laughed almost hysterically and shouted, "I'll take the unbreakable oath if you want!"

She didn't want. She asked a lot of question. Some pointless. Did I know the sex? Hadn't I already told her that I didn't? Some were very pointed. Had I told dad yet? No? Why in the world not?

I laughed again. "I don't want to seem like an emotional woman."

We both laughed at that. Then I brought up an important point. "You can't tell anyone until I've at least told your dad."

She nodded maturely and asked, "When are you going to?"

"Tonight. But even after that don't tell anyone. We may not want to say anything to other people until the baby has gone on for a month or so and is still OK."

She grumbled and promised that she wouldn't. "But you know it's going to be so very, very, very hard."

I agreed. I'd just done it for half an hour and practically couldn't stand it. I was going to send her back to Binns's class which wasn't over yet. Sissy just frowned at me and said, "You can't be that cruel can you?"

I relented. It was true. Binns's classes were hideous. It would be something that I just couldn't do. I told her to go back to her house until her next class and study.

Her last words to me were, "You've got to be kidding." I had to admit that she was right.

I then took to my desk and tried to get started with my homework. It was impossible—at least until after I'd told Ed, and we'd celebrated and slept together and who knew what else.

Then I realized that I really had to tell someone else soon—Professor Slughorn. I went to his office. Sally told me that he was at a meeting of the Board of Directors of Hogwarts but would be back after lunch.

"Sally, please get me into his one o'clock hour."

"Sorry, he's got meetings that he can't get out of this afternoon."

I sat staring at her. She pretended to look at papers on her desk and not see me. Eventually she looked up and said, "Oh. You're still here."

"Yes."

"Well, what is it that you want to see him about? If it were important enough, I might be able to squeeze you in somewhere this afternoon."

I was faced with a real quandary. How many people could I justify telling before Ed? I paced. Sally said, "If you don't come across with some-

341

thing in the next five minutes you're banned from the office for the rest of the week."

I stuttered and then said, "Well, I'm pregnant."

Sally jumped out of her chair and ran around her desk. She started to throw her arms around me and then thought better of it. She asked, "Is it all right if I hug the mother-to-be?"

"Completely all right."

She congratulated me and then said, "Of course, I'll get you into see Slughorn as soon as he arrives."

I was immensely relieved, but I had to ask for her silence. "Even Ed doesn't know yet. You have to swear to tell no one. I really mean NO ONE."

Sally readily agreed, but I added, "Do I need to make you make the unbreakable oath?"

Sally agreed immediately and held out her hand to take the oath. I said, "Oh, I trust you." Then we settled in to wait for Slughorn's return. Apparently he stopped for lunch in the Great Hall because it was well after noon when he arrived. Sally ushered the both of us into his office saying, "Mrs. Brewster has some important news for you—very important news."

He started to object. "But I've got a meeting with . . ."

Sally interrupted him. "This is very, very important. I'll keep your one o'clock entertained until you're done."

Slughorn threw his arms in the air and said, "I see I'm outvoted. Let's get this going. What's so important?"

I asked him to sit. After he did I said, "I'm pregnant."

He stared at me for a full minute. Then he said, "You aren't showing, so I suppose you can continue to work the first term if you wish to. I suppose that you'll want maternal leave for the second term?" With that he buried his face in his hands and mumbled, "Where will I ever find an English teacher for the second term?"

I said, "I just learned that I was pregnant this morning. I think the timing is very good. I can probably work until early June. And most first-time mothers usually deliver late. I might be able to work until the end of the term. At the very least I should be able to write final exams that can be graded by anyone. Then, I can give birth and by the beginning of the next term be off maternal leave."

He looked up from his desk and said, "Really? Would you be willing to do that?"

"Certainly. Of course, there will probably need to be some accommodations near the end of the term. And there's always the possibility of a premature birth, but I'm willing to do everything I can to make it work."

He scratched his chin. "Well, remember that if you ever change your mind, we'll work through whatever you need."

I was beaming when I left. As I reached the door, I turned and said, "Oh, one more thing. I'd appreciate it very much if no one found out about this pregnancy until Ed and I decide to announce it ourselves. Yes?"

Slughorn looked relieved as he said, "Of course. It will be hard to resist the temptation to reveal that we'll have our first pregnant teacher in over a century, but I will respect your privacy, of course."

"Thanks again."

Ginny's Story

The light was beginning to seep into my apartment. I was confused about the time—not just the time of day but the day of week. Then I began to find my memory. Was the polyjuice potion not finished? Was I not completely converted?

I struggled up off the bed. There was a note on the dresser mirror. Had the wizards discovered Post-It's? I staggered over to the dresser and saw that it was not a Post-It. It was an ordinary piece of paper taped onto the mirror with Spello-tape. I couldn't resist reflecting that there was nothing of a spell on Spello-tape. It was just that the wizards had not discovered truth in advertising. I pulled the note off the mirror and read, "Dear JW, the date is Wednesday, 4 July 2007. I have made sure you have appropriate clothes, etc. I am the mother of a beautiful daughter and a handsome son who will come to Hogwarts one day while we are teaching there. Love, JB"

I searched my face in the mirror for any signs of feminine adornment that I didn't want left on when I faced the world. There were no errant earrings, no necklaces, no pendants, no rings. It was then that I realized that there was a ring. It was an engagement ring. It was squeezing my left ring finger unmercifully. The finger was already a terrible red below the ring. I ran into the bathroom and lathered up my hand with warm soap and water. It made the ring a little looser so that I could slide it back and forth but there was no way that it was going to go over the knuckle.

I searched my mind. Who could I get to remove this damn ring which was now starting to turn my finger purple? Slughorn? Certainly? Dursley? Maybe? Any witch or wizard I ran into? Probably. I quickly took off my nightshirt and found underwear, jeans, and a shirt. I stuffed my purse into a pocket wondering if Jaimie had left her wand there. Then I ran to the door of my apartment and flung it open.

344

Standing just outside the doorway was Ginny Weasley! I shouted, "Thank God, Ginny. Can you get this bloody ring off my finger?"

She didn't take it with all the seriousness that I thought it deserved. She gazed at it for a minute and said, "Your finger is a nasty shade of purple verging on grey."

"Yes, get the damn ring off."

She was beginning to get the idea that this was not a funny practical joke and said, "How? I could cut it off, with a spell like difindo, but I'd be afraid of what it would do to your hand."

I was beginning to feel faint. I took a deep breath to steady myself and said, "*Engorgio*. Use *Engorgio*."

She stared at me as though I were a first year. "That would just make it tighter, wouldn't it?"

I shook my head wondering where she'd gone to primary school. "No, it's the perfect spell. It will expand everything, including the interior radius of the ring"

She stared at me. "Are you sure?"

"Damn it. Yes, I'm sure! It's simple physics. Just do it before I lose the finger."

She was still doubtful, but then she relented. She already had her wand out. She pointed it at the ring and said, "*Engorgio ring minima*." Nothing seemed to happen.

I shouted, "You can do better than that!"

She nodded, "Yes. Double *Engorgio* ring." With that the ring suddenly became twice as large and fell off my finger without any further urging. We threw our arms about each other. We kissed.

I said, "I am so happy to be back with you. I had no assurance that I would be back at all, let alone back and with you." I started to turn toward my apartment. As I started to pull her in that direction, she held back. She never looked away from me, but her face did change. It seemed that she was sad about something.

She said, "We've got a lot of talking to do." I felt the floor falling away from under me, as she went on, "Let's have a drink."

I nodded nervelessly and asked, "What do you want?"

"Do you have Johnny Walker Blue?"

I nodded. "I think so. Let me check." I looked in my desk drawer where I usually keep it. There was a bottle with not much left in it and a full bottle. I took it out, opened it, and poured some into two glasses.

She said, "Don't be stingy." I filled both glasses near the rim. I sat on the sofa next to her, took a sip, and placed my glass on the coffee table. She took a full swallow and kept the glass in her hand. Then she started her story. She looked me directly in the eyes and said:

345

It was about a year ago. I was at Flourish & Blotts to buy a copy of *Ringworld*. I wanted to develop a taste for that Science Fiction that you like so much. I couldn't find a copy, but as I was searching, I felt a tap on my shoulder. When I turned I discovered Harry Potter.

He said "Hello" and asked me what I was doing in F & B. I returned the favor asking him what he was doing there. His answer was, "I've decided to take up my boyhood ambition to become an Auror. I'm looking for study materials to prepare for the exam."

I replied that it was quite a coincidence that he should run into a working Auror as he was looking for books on the subject. He asked me if I could recommend any. Of course, now, it seems like a lot less of a coincidence than it did at the time. I led him through the bookstore picking out a couple of books that would be helpful. One, of course, was the standard, *So You Want to be an Auror*. However, there are a couple of others that don't seem like good material superficially, but that I find myself referring to every now and then. There's another standard, *Blackwood's Magical Law* and a couple of others that you've probably never heard of.

After we'd gone to checkout and bought our books we parted. Harry asked, "Maybe someday I might want some inside information from you on Aurors. What do you think?"

I agreed that I'd be willing to give him some help preparing for the exam. I didn't think much of it at the time.

I didn't think about it much for a couple of weeks. Then I received an owl from Harry. It read something like, "Dear Ginny, I wonder if we might have a working lunch or two so that I can prepare for the Auror exam? Any day would be fine. Thanks! Best, Harry"

I was happy to do that. It seemed a little strange that he'd need to practice for the exam. I arranged for us to meet later in the week for lunch at the Cauldron. We didn't actually do a lot of Auror prep. Instead, we talked about what had happened with him lately.

He said, "Well, after Riddle was defeated I did some traveling. I had a fair-sized inheritance from my parents. I thought it would be good to spend some time on the road. I went to the US. I saw a good bit of their amazing country. You know, I saw the Grand Canyon, the Mississippi river, Big Sur, and a lot of other places."

I asked him, "Did you see anything other than natural wonders?"

"I'll tell you that the most amazing thing I saw was the Lincoln Presidential Library. It was in a small town, but the way they educated the visitor about Lincoln's presidency was amazing. They had some exhibits that were almost magical. They had an animated map of the United States that showed the long terrible war between the North and the South in statistics and locations in only a few minutes. I almost think that if I could go only one place in that country, I'd chose Springfield, Illinois."

I was surprised. "Not even New York or Chicago?"

"Those would be hard to drop from the itinerary, but I still think so. What you see in those cities is not unique. You find comparable things—art museums, clubs, beautiful architecture in most large cities, but it would be hard to find the history the way it's presented in Springfield."

"Well, did you only visit the States?"

"Oh, no. I went to most of the large English speaking countries like Australia and Canada. I visited Brazil and Argentina. I went to Cairo. I saw pyramids and the Sphinx."

All I could say was "Amazing." I have to admit to being jealous of him. I asked him what he did after his world tour. He said, "Of course, the Souls invaded before I finished my tour. At that point I was in Asia, more specifically, Nepal. I sort of hunkered down there until things were over. Of course, if I'd had an opportunity to join one of the resistance movements I would have."

I said, "Right. If you'd been back here, you'd probably have been drafted into the Aurors, and you'd not have to take the exam and go through the training institute. So what happened after we kicked the Souls off the planet?"

"Well, I returned to my world tour. I had left off in Katmandhu, where by the way, it is really easy to hide. The Souls hadn't really completely infiltrated that society before they got booted. So, I continued through Asia."

It had been turning into a fascinating account, but there was an important question that I wanted answered, "OK. So that carries you to maybe three, four years ago when you finished your world tour. That still leaves a lot of dead space in your history. What happened then?"

Harry leaned back and smiled. "That does seem like a long time, doesn't it?"

He had really piqued my curiosity. "Yes, it does. Come on, give."

"Well, a strange thing happened as I was doing the tour. I didn't realize it at first, but there was a common thread to all the conversations that I ended up in—almost from the beginning—as I toured the world."

I was on the edge of my seat. He obviously relished that intensity on my part to know more. He drawled out what he said next. "People wanted to know about Riddle and what happened between me and him. There was amazing ignorance almost everywhere I went. Now, in the States, they seemed to be pretty well up on events. I'm not sure why."

I thought to myself that I might be able to give him some inside information on that but I held my piece for a while. It might make a good bargaining chip. In any case, he went on.

"I decided slowly over the course of my travels that I needed to do something to address that ignorance. It didn't come to me suddenly or early on. I eventually decided that I should write a book about Riddle. I initially decided to call it *The Fall of Riddle*.

"My plan was to have a few introductory chapters offering the history of Riddle before I went to Hogwarts and then take up the story at that point in detail."

I said, "That doesn't sound like a bad plan. But why in the world has it taken you so long?"

"That's a good question. If I'd stuck to that plan, even as a first-time author (with generous editing help from the publisher) I could have finished in a year or so."

I said cautiously, "But . . . "

"Yes, but things happened." At this point, he looked at his watch and said, "Wow, I've got to let you get back to work. And anyway, the rest of the story will require another lunch, I think."

I was disappointed, but I agreed. We decided to lunch the following Monday.

It was a long wait for that next Monday. When it finally came I was early for lunch. I was happy to see that Harry brought his study book with him. We started off with more stories of his new book.

He said, "We left off the last time talking about my original ideas for the book I'm writing. As I was writing it, I realized that I kept going back to the beginning of the book to add detail. After more than six months of working on it, I decided that I had to restructure the one book into several books. At the moment, I've divided it into the following books:

- *The Roots of Riddle*. This book covers Riddle's ancestors and especially his parents.
- *Riddle, the Early Years*. This book covers Riddle's birth and the years until Professor Dumbledore discovered him at an orphanage.
- *Riddle at Hogwarts*. This book covers Riddle's years at Hogwarts. Now this book I could refer to first person accounts from various Hogwarts professors, including Professor Haggrid. I so wish that Professor Dumbledore had been around to help with this entire series, but doesn't everyone?

- *The Youthful Riddle*. This book covers the years from graduation from Hogwarts until he met me.
- *Riddle in Exile*. This book is mostly about Riddle's Deatheaters while he was disappeared. I think that Peter Pettigrew is still around. He could be a valuable resource if I could convince him to talk to me.
- *The Fall of Riddle*. This book begins when I go to Hogwarts and goes through his overthrow."

I asked, "How did you support yourself all these years working on those books?"

Potter smiled shyly. "Well, I still had some inheritance left, and I had an advance from my publisher, too."

I said, "Well, it's hard to believe that a publisher gave you an advance on a single book and then agreed to expand it to six books."

Potter laughed. "Oh, yes. I actually have had two publishers. The first wanted a quick hit profit from a single book. I got into a lengthy argument with the first publisher. They were actually pretty nice about it. They let my second publisher buy them out at a small loss to them—provided that they got a cut of the profits on the final book, which would be the book that they wanted all along."

I was still skeptical. "Still, four years to write half a dozen books. Are you done yet?"

"I'm close on the first drafts. I want to have at least a first draft on all before publishing any. I'm working on the last."

Then it hit me. "I'm surprised that you haven't interviewed my family." That brought the inevitable thought, "Or me!"

Harry turned red. "Well, it's a little intimidating. Especially interviewing you would be . . . uh . . . scary."

I couldn't take him seriously. "How could I be scary?"

He stared at me a minute and said, "You should ask George sometime. You know that all the Weasley women are scary. Take your Mum."

I said, "Even so. Now, wait a minute. Did you ask me for help with the Auror exam just to get me to talk about Riddle?"

He tried to look offended. "No! No. . . Well, I really wanted the help with the exam. It's just that I could kill two birds with one stone."

"Let's move on to the other bird."

He looked relieved and said, "OK. Here's the main book." He put it on top of the table, shoving aside our plates.

I said, "The book is divided into four parts."

Potter said, "I figured out that much. There's the first section devoted to the basics of magical law that we have to enforce. Then there's the section on the theory of defensive magic. There's the actual defensive magic spells. Finally, there's the offensive spells and when you're allowed to use them."

"That's right." Then, I offered, "So, let's take one lunch for each of the sections."

That led us to the first section. We started it during that lunch. We went through the various aspects. The first was the Magical Secrecy Act based on the great treaty that all magical societies agreed to in the late 18th century. That fact brought me to a striking realization. Harry could see that I was distracted. He asked, "What's up? You look like you've seen a ghost."

"Maybe I have. This makes so much sense now. Do you know that Professor Wendt always maintained that wizard economics was stuck in the eighteenth century?"

"No. So what?"

"That's why! The Magical Secrecy Act divided the world into the Muggle and Magical."

He shrugged. "So what?"

"That's why the magical world is stuck in the economics of the 18th century. We haven't been talking with the Muggles! They developed economically while we developed magically."

Potter was skeptical. He asked, "Says who?"

I was a bit touchy myself. I said, "Says Professor Wendt!"

"Yeh. Wendt. You've been stepping out with him, haven't you?"

I began to see red a bit. "Yes, I am. Do you have a problem with that?"

Potter backed off a bit and said, "No. No. I've not seen you in a lot of years. Why should I?" He hesitated and added, "Still, just how did you and Wendt get together? After all, he's a lot older than you are."

I could have taken umbrage at that, but I chuckled to myself as I realized that the Professor U. had cornered the market on that. Potter said, "Well?"

I smiled. "Just a little private joke. On to your question. In the first place, he's only fifteen years older than I am. That's not unusual at all. His wife Minerva had even more years than that on him. Or if you look at all the people you know, that's not really unusual. Heck! Think about Mum and Dad. They have almost as many years between them." I did a little mental calculation. "At least nine or ten."

Harry held his hands up in surrender. "OK. OK. I'll give you the point."

"Anyway, I developed a crush on Professor Wendt when I was a Fourth year and took his class. He was everything that I thought I wanted in a man."

Harry interposed, "But the next year, you discovered that what you wanted in a boyfriend was me."

I nodded assent. "Yes, you had something that Wendt didn't. You were magical."

Harry agreed. "Right! What did Wendt ever do?"

He was beginning to vex me. "Harry Potter, you hear me out."

"OK. OK."

I went on. "You skipped out of your seventh year." Potter began to raise a hand in protest, but I beat him to it. "I know. You didn't have much choice, and you came back to save the school and so on. Something that you may not know is that the next year, Hogwarts gave all students the opportunity to repeat the year. Mum and Dad gave me the choice. I didn't repeat.

"That year, there was an incident with a different seventh year. She was kidnapped and would probably have been poisoned to death if it hadn't been for Wendt's quick thinking AND quick action. I knew her pretty well. I didn't like her, but I bloody well didn't want her to die!"

"After I graduated I applied to the Auror Office for a job. They gave me the test. I passed the first time." Harry interrupted to congratulate me. I went on, "The first year was easy. That was lucky, because the second year, as you've no doubt figured out on your own, was when the Souls showed up. Everyone had a hard year with that.

"Now, here's the thing. Professor Wendt worked with us to defeat the Souls." I hesitated as I thought back to those black years, which were really darker than even the Riddle years—first or the second time round. Harry thought I was done and started to speak, but I interrupted his interruption. "Sorry, I was just thinking back. As a matter of fact, I think he did an astounding job. The first days were critical. I learned later—much later—that he'd gone into the battle from the first. Did you get to read the *Prophet* at all during that year?"

Harry shook his head. "We barely heard anything. Even wizard radio was off the air. Everyone was scared to death to do anything. I think I saw one or two issues of the *Prophet* that year."

I nodded. "That's why you don't know about what Wendt did. For a change the *Prophet* reported things pretty straight up. Of course, there was hardly any mention of the fact that Wendt was a Muggle, but it was really pretty good reporting for the *Prophet*.

"During that year, Wendt and I worked on a couple of projects together. I began to appreciate that there was a lot more to Wendt than English professor."

Harry said, "So, you got another crush on the English professor."

I was beginning to take a perverse pleasure in denying his expectations. "No, I didn't. And, it wouldn't have done me much good if I had. He married Professor McGonagall shortly after the Souls had been defeated. If I felt anything, it was happiness for Minerva.

351

"But to get back to the story, the next year was quiet. I know that something happened because Minerva and Wendt left Hogwarts for almost the entire school year. Of what they did I haven't the slightest hint. My personal bet was that they were on another project for the Ministry, but no one among the Aurors knows what it was.

"However, I was asked to help with the wedding of a Muggle who works at Hogwarts."

Harry's jaw dropped. "You're kidding. Another Muggle?"

I shrugged. Sally had been around so long that I'd begun to take her for granted. "Yes, her name was Sally Harker. She was Wendt's . . . uh . . . I guess you'd call her a personal assistant during the year after Riddle took over the Ministry. She sort of stayed on with the Wendts as a secretary for Minerva when she became the Head of the school."

Harry threw his arms up and said, "Why does the Head need a secretary? Dumbledore never had one!"

I was really becoming disgusted by the way this conversation was going. "Yeh. Did it never occur to you how hard it was to find Dumbledore when someone really needed him?"

Harry grimaced. "Might have done."

"Might have done, indeed. I know it drove you crazy at times. Well, with Sally on the job, you could always get hold of Minerva if there were a real need. She took lots of the drudgery out of Minerva's life. Dumbledore was brilliant, but he was not always that organized."

Harry shuffled his feet and, looking down at them, said, "Well, there is a little truth to that. But he had Minerva to do all that stuff for him."

"Right!" I said, "While she had nothing else to do for herself except . . . oh . . . do lesson planning, conduct classes, grade parchments, be Head of Gryffindor, and on and on."

"All right. All right. Maybe the Head needs a secretary, but a Muggle?"

I shook my head. "I was skeptical myself, but she proved herself in the years following. When Minerva was gone for almost a year and Slughorn took over, she was the difference between chaos and an orderly school year."

Harry squinted at me and said, "She was gone for a whole year?"

"Well, that was later on in the story. Remember I was just telling you about helping with Sally's wedding. It would all have gone smoothly except that she wanted her Maid of Honor to be a Muggle. Sally drafted me to transport her around to wizard events concerning the wedding. She turned out to be very fainthearted about real magic, so I recruited James to help her. You know, give her confidence about working with so many witches."

Harry scoffed. "I'll bet that went well. Hey, who is James?"

"That is Professor Wendt. Anyway, we ended up spending a lot of time together. What happened is that the Maid of Honor, Haley, sort of fell for Wendt."

"Too bad for her what with Wendt already being married."

"Well, things got worse. She stole some of Dursley's really magic love potion."

At that, Harry stood, apparently in disgust. "Tell me you're kidding me. I know that Dursley after all has magic, but really! He makes potions too?"

At last, I had an answer that he found satisfactory, "It's not really his potion. Snape developed it. Dursley only uncovered it and decided with Slughorn not to publish it in their revised version of *Advanced Potions*. He did all the legwork of translating Snape's notes into legible form."

Harry sniffed but asked what happened. I went on with the story, "She gave BOTH Wendt and herself a dose of the love potion." I couldn't help gritting my teeth. I hated the idea of his falling in love with someone else.

"So, they were in love for a day or so. How did Minerva take that? Did Haley survive the experience?"

I sighed. "Yes. First, I want to make a couple of points. Dursley's love potion is permanent or pretty darn close to it. The two of them were disgusting. I don't know what a married man with integrity would do if he were still under the influence of that potion, but I have a guess. I think he would have loved her silently for the rest of his life."

Potter asked, "But something happened? He's no longer in love with her, is he?"

"You're right. I realized what had happened. I got Dursley and Slughorn to brew the antidote. I forced them both to take it. God, I almost couldn't stand the idea that Wendt was alive and was forced to be in love with someone. . ." I added under my breath, "other than me."

Harry caught that and asked, "I thought you weren't in love with him?"

"Oh, looking back, I see that I was in love with him. At the time I thought I was just defending Minerva from tragedy."

"So what happened?"

"Then, some really strange things started happening. Wendt completely disappeared, and his post at Hogwarts was replaced by another.

"I was called in to consult on a problem that had come up. I can't tell you what it was, but I can tell you that it was a developing trajedy. I had a suggestion or two.

"The really important thing was that some very influential . . . uh . . . people really wanted Wendt to be involved in the project that we were working on. It was at that point that I realized how much I wanted to be with Wendt. There were times when I wanted to volunteer to be on his team for this project. I lost a good bit of sleep thinking about crazy ways that I could get on the team. Of course, Wendt was nowhere to be found. It was so, so crazy to think that he would be back to lead this team that I doubted my sanity. Amazingly, somehow that . . . uh . . . uh . . . witch, Brewster, provided a connection to Wendt. He showed up and took over the project."

Harry said, "Of course, he took Minerva along wherever they went. I suppose you can't tell me where that was."

The irony of what I was about to say struck me. "You're right. I can't tell you that. Frankly, I don't even know that."

Harry had been putting two and two together and came up with the inevitable four. He said, "I know that Minerva died somewhere during that time period of your 'project', right?"

I nodded. "He came back practically catatonic. He was grieving and incapable of teaching or almost anything else. I knew that he'd have to recover from his grief before I could give him the love that I so very much wanted to."

Harry said, "So, you were stuck for a while."

I stopped for thought. I decided that I would confess at least the main thing I did to try to bring Wendt back from the brink. I said, "Not exactly. I'm not proud of it, but I went to the woman who had used a love potion on him. I convinced her that she might have another shot at him if she followed him to the States."

Harry leaned back and took a long sip from the drink that he had in his hand—almost without realizing he'd done it. He said, "So, did that work?"

I knew that my face must be as red as a beet, but I went on, "It was amazing, but it did. I think that the love potion must have left a mark on his affections even though he had the antidote. I don't know." I hesitated for thought. Harry gave me time for it. Then I went on. "He came back, and I used every trick that I knew of to keep him and Haley from getting back together. Again, the amazing thing was that it worked. In retrospect, it even seems easy.

"I met his airplane when it arrived. He had come back with Her, but I managed to separate the two of them. I disapparated him to Hogwarts and did everything I could to keep Haley away and encourage his love. It worked."

Harry looked downcast. He said, "Well, we've run out of time. Let's have lunch Thursday and keep going on tutoring me."

I agreed.

On Thursday, we met at the Cauldron and kept to the business that we were supposed to be doing. We went over the theory of defensive magic. It was a quick review. Harry had studied well. It was a quick, pleasant review. When we'd finished the review, Harry went back to where we'd finished a couple of days before. He said, "I've been thinking about what you've said before. I don't understand what happened. It sounded like you and Wendt were together like this." He held up his middle and forefinger twisted together.

I sighed in sadness. "Well, as far as you go, yes. Sadly, another Ministry of Magic project came up. It required Wendt to be gone for at least three years—maybe never to return."

Harry nodded. "So, you have been faithful."

I didn't think that I would have a hard time talking about it, but the tears were starting to leak from my eyes. I looked down so that it wouldn't be so obvious. Harry knew, of course. We just finished the meal with nothing more to say. He asked, "Can I do some practicing of defensive magic with you?"

I had myself under control by then. I said, "Yes, why don't you come by my parents' house on Saturday in the afternoon. We can go out in a field and do some practicing. You should do some practice on your own before then."

He agreed, and we separated.

I sent an owl to my parents, telling them to expect a visit from Harry Saturday afternoon. That evening shortly before I went to bed thinking about Wendt as I always did, an owl came from my Mum. It said,

"Ginny, having Harry visit would be wonderful. I hope you've asked him to stay for dinner. Please insist that he stay. Love, Mum and Dad."

The next day, I sent an owl to Harry relaying my parents' invitation. I didn't expect him to have time to reply before Saturday. I really wanted him to accept.

Saturday morning, I took my time. I usually waited for the evening to spiff myself up. This morning, I went through my luxurious pampering. Then I left for the folk's home. I arrived before lunch. It turned out that George was there too. He was in the kitchen talking with dad and mum.

When I entered the house, he looked up and pretended not to recognize me. "Well, young lady, I think you've wandered into the wrong house. Were you trying to take the floo to the Beasleys and mispronounced the name?"

I frowned at him and snapped, "You know perfectly well who I am George Arnold Weasley."

He pretended to shake in fear. "Oooh. The full name. I must be in big trouble." Then he said, "I just didn't recognize you because I've never seen you look this good before noon."

I grimaced and scoffed. He added under his breath, "Or after." I glared at him. He waved his hands in mock terror.

Then I said, "Dad, have you heard from Harry?"

He smiled as broadly as though he'd won the office pool of the Quidditch Cup. "Well, as a matter of fact, Mr. Potter did send an owl saying that he'd be happy to join us for dinner tonight."

George nodded approvingly. I could have cursed him silly, but I didn't want to give him the satisfaction of knowing that he'd hit home. Instead, I said huffily, "You obviously haven't been paying much attention lately."

We had a nice lunch all the same. Mum and Dad wanted to know what was going on with Harry. I told them briefly about how I was helping him prepare for the Auror exam. George insisted on being a right git. He asked, "Lots of late night sessions I imagine after a nice candlelight dinner, eh Sis?"

I knew better than to rise to that bait. I just shrugged, neither admitting or denying the idea. That is one way to really get George's goat. It didn't fail this time. He changed the subject and went on to talk about his latest supplier for his business. Mum and Dad were suitably impressed. I even congratulated him.

I wanted to know from George where his wife was. He replied that she was looking for a nicer apartment. He said practically nothing else. That was a subject that I would follow up later.

After lunch, George actually agreed to help clean up. He admitted that it was the least that we could do after sitting with our legs under the table for lunch.

Harry showed up around 1 PM. Dad and Mum greeted him enthusiastically. He was handing out hugs all around—even to George. I graciously hugged him. Was I mistaken that he squeezed a little tighter than absolutely necessary?

George offered to help with spell practice. Both Harry and I swiftly refused the help. Harry joked, "If I could use fainting fancies or puking pastilles, yes, your help would be useful. As it is, I trust Ginny more."

George just smiled and said, "You'll be sorry."

We went out in the field over a hill so we wouldn't be visible from the house. We started with some warm-up spells: *expelliamus*, stunning, *petrificus totalis* and so forth. I was the willing victim for those. Then we started dueling, no holds barred except that all spells must be defensive. The sparring was pretty one-sided at first. Harry had forgotten about disapparation as a defensive maneuver. After I had disapparated behind him a couple of times and stunned him gently, he started disapparating as well. He was out of practice and taking the short end of the stick. I teased him a little. "I've heard that guys can't walk and chew gum at the same time. I didn't used to believe it, but I think that you can't disapparate and stun at the same time."

That stung him, and I eventually paid for it. By the end of a good long session, he had regained most of his reflexes. We were both bushed, so we sat under a tree and talked for a while. I asked him for details about what he'd been doing romantically over the last couple of years, "Surely, you've stepped out with a few ladies?"

He shook his head regretfully. I asked, "Oh, when you were lying low in Nepal I'm not surprised that you didn't, but there were other years."

"Oh, I saw a few young ladies, but it's kind of hard to do anything steady when you're never anywhere for more than a couple of weeks. Also, most of the places where I was, the only place you could reliably find English-speaking women were sports bars. Also, most women in sports bars were accompanied."

I sniggered. "Come on."

He stood his ground. "I'm not kidding. I even learned about English football."

I laughed. "I suppose you're a fan now. What's your favorite team?"

"I don't have a favorite team. But I do know that almost everyone hates a team called Man U."

"You know, I got interested in football with Wendt. We watched some of the World Cup, and I have to admit that it was pretty exciting."

Harry sniggered, "Oh, you're just kidding me. The only World Cup is Quidditch."

"No. No. There's a football World Cup."

"Maybe, but it can't be exciting."

"Really. Now, I admit that regular season football is pretty boring, but the World Cup is different."

After a while we decided to go in and see if we could help with dinner. Mum had it pretty well in hand, but we got to set the table. Conversation at the dinner table turned to Harry and his plans for the future. Mum asked, "Is there a special girl somewhere?"

Harry sighed. "I'm afraid not. I've traveled the world around, but I've never found any young ladies to match the ones in England and none in England to match witches, and no witches to rival the ladies Weasley."

Mum sort of blushed, but I couldn't help wondering. He turned the conversation to his travels. It was interesting to hear about all the places he'd gone. I turned the conversation to his book deal. He talked at length about it,

357

and then we were finished for the night. As he left, again it was hugs all around. I could have sworn that his lips brushed my cheek, and then he was gone.

I was just entering the floo in the atrium at the Ministry of Magic when Harry leaped out of another hearth, looked around, and spied me. He ran over and said, "I'm glad I caught you. I need to celebrate, and you seemed like the best person to celebrate with!"

"What are we celebrating?"

"I passed the Auror exam! Have dinner with me?"

I was really happy for him. I nodded and said, "Sure. My treat."

He shook his head vigorously, "No! Mine! You deserve a reward for all the work you put in helping me."

I submitted and asked where we were going. His reply was, "I want it to be a little surprise. We'll disapparate directly there." With that he held out his hand for me to take. After a momentary hesitation, I took it.

We "spun through space and time" as Wendt would have said and arrived next to a beach. The sea breeze was invigorating. I looked out over the waves rolling down the beach. I felt a tug on my hand and suddenly realized that I'd not let go of Harry's hand. He was saying, "Come on this way. The restaurant is over here." I realized that I was holding his hand not the other way around, and I didn't let go.

We crossed the road that separated the beach from the town. The restaurant we were headed for was clearly a wizard establishment. All the Muggles were unconsciously avoiding it as they walked down the street window-shopping. We had no trouble entering, of course. We were shown to a table. The menu was full of fish entrees and appetizers. I commented, "I'll bet that none of the fish are caught locally, but none-the-less the restaurant prides itself on its fish."

We ordered. After our drinks were delivered we started celebrating Harry's success seriously. Harry asked what the Auror Academy would be like.

I smiled happily. "Oh, it will be pie for you. It's a lot like the D.A. practice back at Hogwarts. Of course, you won't be leading the practice. You'll be more like Luna Lovegood—talented but unpracticed. You should talk with George. He led the training at Camp Dumbledore during the war against Riddle. He and Fred. . . " I choked up at the mention of Fred. I'd learned that you're never free from grief. It can sneak up on you at the most unlikely moments, such as celebrating a good score on an Auror test. Harry

358

reached out and took my hand that had been resting on the table between us. As he took it, I realized that I'd left it there as an invitation, an invitation that he had just accepted.

I went on. "Yes, Fred." Harry gave my hand a very welcome squeeze. "They ran that training camp in the States to provide a larger more effective army than we were able to throw together in fourth year, that is, your fifth year." As I said that, I suddenly realized that the ghost of Wendt kept popping up. "You know, Wendt was the main reason that that camp existed."

Harry shook his head. "You know, I'd heard that he had something to do with Camp Dumbledore but I thought that was just a rumor. He really did?"

"After I joined the Aurors, I got to see some papers from that time. Yes, he and the Muggle Minister were behind it to a very large extent."

Then, we talked about what it would be like to work in the same office. That was an exciting discussion. I found myself hardly able to breathe with excitement about the possibility. Harry joked, "Well, there could be a difficulty if one of us had to work for the other."

I had to bite my lips to keep from saying something indecent like, "You mean under?"

By the end of the meal, I was anxious to find something else to extend our "date". I suggested that we walk along the beach. Harry agreed readily to the suggestion. There was a half moon that day, October 6. It was ideal. There was plenty of light to walk on the beach, but also the light was not bright enough to prevent the occasional misstep that caused one to lean into one's partner in the walk. We didn't really talk about anything until the moon was close to setting around 9:30. I stopped walking and pulled Harry close. I turned my face up to his and stood on tiptoe to kiss him.

The kiss turned into a deep, passionate kiss. When we broke, he said, "Do you fancy staying . . . "

I was way ahead of him. I said, "In an inn? Yes. Let's go. We're burning moonlight." Truthfully, there wasn't a lot of light left, but we ran back up the beach to find the row of restaurants, hotels, and pubs. In the failing light, we fell and bumped into each other several times, shrieking like banshees the whole way. I dragged Harry toward the first likely looking pub that we encountered. For the first time, he resisted.

He pulled me short and said, "But that's a Muggle place. I don't have any Muggle money with me."

I smiled triumphantly. "But I do."

He stared at me with incredulity. "Really? Since when do you carry Muggle money?" Then he answered his own question, "I suppose that you have been carrying Muggle money ever since you were dating Wendt?"

I smiled smugly. "No, I don't have any Muggle money with me. Come on in, and you'll see." We went in. I stepped up to the front desk and requested a room.

"One bed?"

I nodded. The clerk quoted a price in pounds sterling. I shrugged, "Sure, that's fine." Harry stood back a pace gazing incredulously.

The clerk asked, "Cash or credit?"

I reached in my purse and pulled out my Gringotts credit card. The clerk glanced at it as he took it and slid it through the machine. A little printing machine disgorged a receipt that he asked me to sign. Then he handed it back to me, asking, "Never heard of Gringotts. Is that one of those new fancy foreign banks?"

I just smiled and said, "Something like that." He gave us a couple of electronic keys. Because of traveling with Wendt, I'd seen them before and knew how they worked—basically. I was frankly thankful that Harry hadn't and let him ask how it worked.

The clerk gave him a bored explanation about how to slip the key into the slot in the door. He added, "Be sure you can see the arrow and that it is pointed toward the door."

Harry asked me if I'd known all that when the clerk had given me the key. I nodded absent-mindedly as I stared at the credit card that I was still holding in my hand. Until that moment I'd forgotten that it was Wendt's invention. This act was in a sense a betrayal of Wendt perpetrated with one of the tools he'd invented.

Harry had already started upstairs to our room. I followed slowly. When I arrived, he was standing in front of our door staring at the doorknob. When I arrived, he was scratching his head. I said, "Just use *Alohomora.*"

He answered, "No, I'm not going to admit that some Muggle salesman who could open this door in a second is smarter than I."

I laughed. "At least, you have better grammar."

He said, "Will you ever give up on Wendt?"

That surprised me. Sure, Wendt taught grammar. Was that why the comment came unbidden to my lips? I started to explain about the slot, which was not on the doorknob but usually above it when Harry slapped his forehead and said, "Of course." He then slipped the card into the slot. There was a satisfying click. Harry opened the door. He crossed the threshold and I walked up to it. I stopped at the doorframe.

Harry turned back to me and wondered, "Are you a closet vampire and need an invitation to enter? Or are you hoping that I'll carry you over the threshold?" I didn't answer other than to say, "It's the Rubicon." I remembered Wendt's frequent references to crossing the Rubicon. When I'd asked him what the obscure comment meant, he explained that the Rubicon was a river in Italy that marked the border of Rome.

Any military commander who crossed that river with his troops broke the law of the Roman republic. Julius Caesar crossed the Rubicon with his army to become the emperor of Rome. This was my Rubicon. If I crossed it, I would have forfeited any right to Wendt's love.

Harry asked, "Well?"

I took a deep breath and made my decision. I crossed the threshold.

Epilogue

During this story, we'd both managed to nearly finish off the bottle of Blue Label. She leaned back and finished her glass off in a single gulp. She then sat momentarily in thought. She laid her glass on the coffee table and said, "We stepped out together for several months. Then Harry asked me to marry him about two months ago."

I looked down at Ginny's left hand. She followed my gaze and said, "Oh, no. No engagement ring there. Harry wanted to give me his Mum's engagement ring. It was lost sometime around the time that Riddle took over. Knowing Mundungus Fletcher's proclivity for theft, including from the dead owners of homes, I wouldn't be surprised if he didn't somehow gain access to Harry's parent's house to steal everything of value that he could find. That would certainly include engagement rings.

"Anyway, Harry's been searching there and at his other house in Grimauld Place for the last month or so. If he doesn't find it soon, we'll buy one."

I was both disheartened and strangely freed by the account that I'd just heard. I had no idea when I gave up my body to Jaimie whether I would ever return from the dead or not, but I had not expected what I would find when I did revive. I sighed and said, "Well, it looks like I must thank you for having the courage to approach me with these events directly and immediately after my return. I know that it required a good bit. Of course, you have never lacked courage."

Ginny took the bottle of Blue Label and added some to her glass. She then drank it. As she spoke her vehemence grew steadily, "Well, of all the things that I expected, I never expected that you would just give up."

I was surprised. So it took me a moment to consider what she had just said. I actually closed my eyes and pursed my lips. Then I had my answer. I filled my glass, took a good swallow, and felt the fire in my throat. I would need that fire I realized as I began. "First, let me say that your decision was made months ago, and you've had lots of time to live with it. You would have either changed your mind or come here with a very different story if you were not determined to marry Potter.

"Second, you know the nature of love. You know that love wants the best outcome for the beloved even if the best is for the beloved to be with someone else. I love you and want you to be your best, happiest self. It seems that that is with Potter.

"Finally, I trust your judgment. You know that I love you and will always love you. There is nothing further that I can say that will change your decision."

We stayed seated on the sofa for some time. Finally, she took both my hands in hers and said, "Oh, Wendt, I am so sorry that it's come out this way. If I'd known what was going to happen, I'd probably not have tried interfering in your life." She rose and we embraced without thinking. She kissed me on the cheek and said, "I love you." I kissed her on the cheek and said with complete sincerity, "I love you." She transferred that kiss to our lips. Then she backed away into the hearth. She picked up some floo powder, laid it down, and turned back to me. She said, "Oh, one last thing. I have something for you as a sort of memento of me."

She reached into her purse and took what looked vaguely like a pound note out. She handed it to me and said, "Your idea of paper wizarding money came true. Take a careful look at it."

I did. I held it close. I easily saw that there was a picture of the main bank of Gringotts in Diagon Alley on that side. I turned it over and saw that there was a picture of Glorblazz on the other side. I couldn't help laughing. "I suppose that Glorblazz insisted on being on the note during negotiations."

Ginny laughed too. "You know it! But look closer. You may have to hold it up to the light to see the golden threads in the note. Your idea for making paper money impossible to counterfeit was inspired. It also inspired the art work outlined by the threads."

I did look more carefully. I still didn't see anything but the golden threads. Ginny scoffed. "Just defocus your eyes a little and you'll see."

Like one of those art works where the image is made up of a lot of smaller parts, the image in gold appeared to me. I gasped when I did see it. I asked, "Surely, that isn't a rough portrait of . . ."

Ginny laughed again. "Who else, but . . . "

I shook my head. "Me."

Ginny was still laughing, but I thought I detected a tear at the rim of an eye. She said, "I love you." She stepped into the hearth. Then she picked up another handful of floo powder, threw it down, and said, "My apartment." She disappeared in a cloud of ash and soot.

The End ?

About the Author

William Wilkin lived in a small Southern Ohio town until he began his college career. He has a Bachelor's degree in Physics from The Ohio State University and a Master's degree in Physics from The University of Chicago. He had a career in corporate Information Technology and currently lives in Nashville, Tennessee.

He enjoys music, both "serious" and "classic Rock". He reads classic Detective fiction and Science Fiction & Fantasy as well as trying to stay current in Physics.

He began writing seriously about 2005. He has a blog, in-midworld, where he writes about Science Fiction & Fantasy and remotely related topics.